KUSAC HAD TO FIND
HIS CREW MATES—

He didn't know how much exposure his companions had had to the Valtegans since their scout ship had crashed on this planet, but it was obvious to him that this was the species for whom his people had been searching. And now it was even more vital that he reach the rest of his team because he'd just found out that their computer crystal was in Valtegan hands.

The only thing he was certain of was that his fellow Sholans were heading for the life pod left by a survey ship years before for just such an emergency as they now found themselves in. And he knew that they'd tracked the pod as far as the large forested region which began not far from the settlement where he had found shelter with the Human called Carrie.

Though he had not been listening closely to the conversation between Carrie and the town doctor, his attention was abruptly pulled back to it as he realized Carrie was about to tell the doctor of the Telepathic bond between them. Icy fear washed through him, and, with no time for subtlety, he sent a negative command to her.

Carrie suddenly found herself unable to talk or move. Kusac's fear began to resonate along with hers and sheer terror gripped her. . . .

**DAW Books
is proud to present
LISANNE NORMAN'S
SHOLAN ALLIANCE Novels:**

TURNING POINT (#1)

FORTUNE'S WHEEL (#2)

FIRE MARGINS (#3)

RAZOR'S EDGE (#4)

TURNING POINT
LISANNE NORMAN

First Printing, February 1993

DAW BOOKS, INC.
DONALD A. WOLLHEIM, FOUNDER
375 Hudson Street, New York, NY 10014

ELIZABETH R. WOLLHEIM
SHEILA E. GILBERT
PUBLISHERS

First Printing, December 1993
2 3 4 5 6 7 8 9

DAW TRADEMARK REGISTERED
U.S. PAT. OFF. AND FOREIGN COUNTRIES
—MARCA REGISTRADA
HECHO EN U.S.A.

PRINTED IN THE U.S.A.

For Mum and Dad, who taught me to love words and paint pictures.

For the members of ASTRA, too numerous to mention, but still appreciated.

For the many friends who pushed and supported me into finishing this, including Andrew Stephenson, Ken Slater, Anne Page, and Marsha Jones.

Thank you all.

Prelude

Carrie slept lightly, on the edge of wakefulness as always when Elise was working at Geshader, the Alien Pleasure City. Despite the sleeping pill and her sister's mental block, vague images from Elise drifted through her sleeping mind, interweaving themselves with her dreams.

Once more dwarfed by the size of her parents, she tossed and turned in a sweat-soaked bed, moaning in agony as they and the doctor probed and pressed the livid bruises on her back and arm, looking for a more serious injury that didn't exist . . . for her. Then they thought to check her twin.

They found Elise sitting placidly with her right arm at an impossible angle and blood from the lacerations on her back slowly seeping through her clothes into the sofa. She had been the one who had fallen out of a tree.

Carrie had hardly felt the sting of the hypodermic amidst the fire in her back and arm.

"It's the damnedest thing. Her sister has no sense of pain," she'd heard the doctor's voice boom as she began to slip into unconsciousness.

"It hurts," she whimpered, stirring fretfully in her bed.

Monsters lurked in the fever dream, lizards of gray-green on two legs, lumbering slowly after her with a ponderous determination as, utterly terrified, she fled down echoing corridors.

"Stop!" The voice was low and sibilant, the English distorted by a tongue not made to form the words.

She hesitated, every muscle still poised for flight, staring back to where her pursuers waited for her.

"Tell us where they are hiding," one demanded.

An invisible hand closed viciously on Carrie's wrist, non-retractable claws pressing into her flesh. She jerked free, her other hand pressed to her mouth as the scene blurred.

"Valtegans," she moaned, drops of blood pearling on her wrist and dropping to the coverlet.

She dreamed again of standing shivering in her underwear as she stowed her clothes in the small locker beside the coffin-shaped sleep pod, the chill caused by more than the lack of heating in the cryo level. Then lying down on the form-shaped interior, waiting for the medic to come and attach her to the life-support and cryogenic systems.

Carrie glanced at her brother Richard before turning to grin nervously at Elise through the clear perspex sides as sensor pads were attached. Their parents hovered at the ends of their pods, anxiously waiting until all three children were safely asleep.

She jumped as a hand touched her.

"Don't worry. It's only a sedative to help you relax," smiled the crew woman, fixing the small adhesive patch to her arm. "Next thing you know, you'll be waking up in orbit around our new home.

"Just to remind you, the system is automatic so there is very little you have to do. If you turn your head to the right, you'll see it's printed on the plaque there.

"The main thing to remember when you wake up is to press that red button to release the pod cover, then take off the sensors. After that, you'll hear the instructions on the speakers."

Already she could barely make out the woman's voice.

"Sleep soundly, children. I love you," was the last thing she heard her mother say.

The cover slid into place over her and she began to drift gently, imagining herself surrounded by a soft, warm, gray mist.

Suddenly she was jolted to awareness by the sting of the hypo on her sister's arm.

The drug swept through Carrie's system, burning its way along her nerves, setting them on fire until her whole body was convulsed with spasms. She tried to fight it, to open her eyes, but all she could see were colors swirling around her until her stomach was heaving with vertigo. She felt herself slipping ... slipping. . . .

"Mother!" she had screamed, her mind and body trapped in the slow time cold hell of cryogenics, unable to do any-

thing as she felt at last her mother's blind terror at waking too soon.

She could sense her beating futilely at the walls of the cryo pod, trapped like a butterfly transfixed by a pin as she tried desperately to activate the release mechanisms that were locked in stasis.

Her mother's movements quickly grew sluggish, finally stopping as the limited air supply in the pod ran out.

"Mother! Don't leave me!" Carrie screamed, desperately fighting the effects of the drug that this time dragged her down into darkness.

Carrie felt herself pushed and pulled in every direction. Scaled faces loomed at her out of the dim light, clawed hands grasped at her, pawed at her, making her flesh recoil from their sharp, cool touch. She stumbled against bodies that thrust her away to fall to the ground, only to be dragged to her feet again. Noise surrounded her, loud, sibilant voices shouting. Like the images, the sounds faded in and out with her consciousness.

"We have to fight them, Carrie. I can't do it passively like Dad. I'm leaving to join the guerrillas. The Valtegans are soldiers, not civilians, and they're Alien. We can't appeal to their better nature because they haven't got one.

"I'm leaving now, tonight, for Geshader."

"Geshader? But . . ."

"Don't try to change my mind, Carrie," Elise warned quickly, "it's made up. As one of the women in their pleasure city, I can get close to the officers, a thing no man can do. And once I'm with them, I'm sure I can get access to all sorts of useful information."

"But to become one of the prostitutes . . . and with them! How could you?"

Elise gave her a wry grin. "Come off it, Carrie. It's the oldest profession going, and the women from Geshader that I've talked to say it isn't that bad.

"It isn't as if we can't keep in touch. There's our link after all."

"You just take care, for both our sakes!"

"Do you mind too much? You know the risks we face, don't you?"

"I know," Carrie nodded, "but you're the one taking the

real risks. I'll cope somehow. Jack Reynolds is used to us by now."

"At least you didn't pick up much when I was with that lad from Seaport this spring," her twin grinned, "so with any luck you'll be spared my 'working experiences.' "

Her voice faded, leaving only the impression of the grin behind.

"It's the only way I could fight them, Carrie."

Figures jostled her again, dark red light on pallid skins, rough claws digging into her arms, drawing blood. Again, every nerve flared with excruciating pain and she tried to arch her body away from it, but she only succeeded in cracking her head against the wall. Stunned, she heard her own scream as if from far away as her hands tried to grasp for something concrete—anything—to help her hold onto reality. She was aware of a sudden warmth running down her right arm. Blood.

Shock and fear brought her briefly out of her twin's world of pain. Blood. Dear God, there had never been blood before!

Footsteps pounded along the landing and her door burst open. Dimly she saw her father and brother standing there, their faces blanching when they saw the state she was in.

She lifted her head up from the floor and tried to disentangle herself from her bedding but only succeeded in slipping in her own blood.

"They've got Elise," she said, her voice made blurry by drugs and pain.

While the pain continued, she knew that Elise was still alive. When that stopped, her sister would probably be dead. Carrie began to whimper again, a low-pitched animal sound. Pain flickered through her body, but it no longer seemed to burn so fiercely. She lay there unthinking for the moment, thankful for the brief respite, while knowing the worst was not yet over.

Two days before, the Valtegans had seized Elise; two days and nights of torment for Carrie. Her one comfort had been the knowledge that nothing they could do would make her sister reveal anything about the Terrans' resistance movement on Keiss.

Elise was not particularly brave, it was more that she possessed no sense of pain. Born the stronger of the two, she had never had to suffer the hurts of childhood. Instead, in some strange way, it was Carrie who had suffered the agonies of her twin's broken arm, or the fever of some illness. As in the past, Carrie was the one suffering now.

She could feel Elise, a faint but unmistakable presence in the depths of her mind.

If I want to survive, I must remain detached, Carrie thought. *Blank. I must keep my mind blank.*

Slowly, she tried to edge out the consciousness that was Elise, pushing her sister down from the surface of her own thoughts. The response was immediate. Waves of fear began spreading upward, catching her unaware and pulling her back into that other life.

She cried out, flinging herself from side to side in an effort to escape the welter of pain that began to course through her fever-wracked body. Would they never stop questioning Elise?

Strong hands grasped her, pressing her down, but still she thrashed from side to side.

"My God, she's got some strength!"

"I'm afraid we might lose her, Peter. Even if she doesn't go catatonic as she did after the death of her mother, her system can't take much more."

The voice sounded faint and far away, receding farther until all the reality she knew was the awful shriek that echoed inside her head.

Abruptly, it stopped, and the terrible emptiness rushed in. That part of her mind where Elise lived was a void. There was no more pain or fear, just emptiness. Total panic overwhelmed her and she began to scream.

"She's dead! Elise is dead!"

All reason left her. She ignored the feelings of disintegration as mentally she stretched herself thinly in every direction, searching frantically for something to hold on to. Never since the moment of her birth had her mind been hers alone. Elise had always been there. Racing through every part of her mind, she checked over and over again, unable to believe her sister was gone, but there was nothing. Not a trace remained.

She opened her mouth to scream her disbelief—then stopped in astonishment. Like a faint glow from a dying candle, she could feel something in the corner of her mind. She reached for it, nursing it carefully, hardly daring to hope, but the thoughts were totally alien to her. Mentally she drew back, feeling the blind terror surging in once more, but the new personality clung to her, refusing to be ignored. Against her will, she felt herself being held and examined. In return, she could sense its surprise at the contact.

As if it understood her fears and terror, it began to reassure her, sending only thoughts of comfort and friendship.

Exhausted, Carrie began to relax, letting a sweet lassitude steal over her. Within moments she was asleep.

Chapter 1

A shaft of sunlight pierced the dirty broken window and crept along the rubble-strewn floor until it reached him.

In the sunbeam, motes of pollen and dust flickered and danced along its length. At first, from the depths of sleep, he was only aware of a vague discomfort around his face. This feeling grew until finally, brought to the threshold of wakefulness, he sneezed violently. Now fully aroused, he breathed deeply and began to stretch every muscle, trying to rid himself of the stiffness and tension caused by several days of living rough. He winced, almost crying out with pain as he tried to move his wounded leg.

Extending his fingers, he began to explore the injured flank. Several pieces of metal from the explosion had ploughed a deep furrow in his flesh, and the surrounding skin was angry and swollen. Gingerly he touched it, feeling the heat of the swelling. He knew the wound needed to be properly cleaned because despite his ministrations he could see bits of black fur sticking out of the congealed blood. He was also fairly certain that there was some metal still lodged within, but there was nothing he could do about it. Without anything to use as a bandage, he dare not even attempt to clean away the dried blood. At least it gave him some protection against any new infection.

Clenching his teeth, he sat up and began to work the leg gently, praying that the wound would not start to bleed again. Moving it loosened the stiff muscles and soon he was ready to try standing. He decided to play it safe and went down into a four-legged stance first, cautiously easing his hindquarters off the ground. The leg held, and he took a few tentative steps. Each one was agony, but after persevering for several minutes the pain became bearable. Light-headed and panting, he sank to the ground again. There was no way that he could travel upright, but perhaps that was all to the good.

There were several indigenous feline species on this planet and, moving four-legged like them, he was less likely to attract any undue attention. Normally he would make better speed that way, but with his wounded leg, speed was out of the question: it was endurance that counted now. He had to reach the girl before the fever took hold of him. Surely she would help him now that she had recovered.

His stomach began to rumble emptily, reminding him of more immediate problems. He needed to find food. For the past four days he had stayed in the ruined hut, hiding from the Aliens who had shot down his craft. Only five of them had survived the crash and subsequent explosion. Five out of a crew of eight!

He sighed and turned his mind back to the problem of food, trying to remember all that he had been taught about living off the land. A wise person, his father: he tried to see that his son was prepared for the worst contingencies of life.

By birthright you are a hunter, never forget that. Have pride in yourself and that fact. Only in extreme emergency, when you are too weak to hunt, should you beg or scavenge for food. No one should have to rely on charity or theft to keep alive. Either you survive on your own hunting, or you work for your food. Never use your Talent; it would be a misuse of a sacred gift.

Sound principles, but not very useful at the present time. Even if he had wanted to use his Talent, there had been no opportunity to do so. It was autumn here, a mild one so far, with plenty of berries and nuts for the wild creatures. Consequently they were taking no risks for stray tidbits. When he had been free of his vigil over the girl for any length of time the only food he had been able to find had been the occasional birds' eggs and edible berries that were readily available.

Squinting at the gleaming yellow orb in the sky, he determined it was not far past dawn. Slowly he got to his feet and limped carefully through the jumble of broken glass, earthenware, and bricks to the doorway of the cottage. Once outside, the air was chilly despite the bright sunshine. He shivered slightly, sweeping the surrounding area with his gaze, searching not only for any sign of the Aliens but also for the slightest movement of any animals suitable for breakfast.

Today the landscape looked even more dismal. The grass was low and sparse, growing in clumps among the springy heather. The moorland stretched for kilometers in every direction, offering him no cover at all. Overhead, the sky was a sharp blue, with the clarity that only a cold day can give. Clouds were gathering in the north, clouds dark with snow.

There was no real food in this area. What might live there in the warmer seasons had either burrowed deep into the ground for winter or moved down to the gentler lowlands. Kusac was faced with a choice. He needed food, water, and treatment. To get those, he had to reach a settlement in the foothills. If he left the comparative safety of the hut, he would have to run the risk of being caught in a blizzard. The alternative was to stay there and pray that he could cope with his septic leg and imminent fever. In his weakened condition, neither option offered a high rate of survival.

When none of the choices open to you offers more than extinction, choose the one that prolongs life the most. Always allow the unexpected time to intervene.

Well, nothing could happen here, so, trusting his telepathic link with the girl, he headed east. Perhaps he might come across some animal out for a short airing, or dig for some unappetizing but nourishing grubs.

He loped off across the moors, eyes and ears alert for any sign of danger or food, however unlikely the prospect. The heather was not an easy surface on which to walk; at one moment stiff, the next yielding, so that despite his cautious tread, he was often sent reeling as his feet caught in the hidden webs of branches. Every now and then he would glance at the sky, checking to see how much of it had been obscured by dark clouds.

Gradually the terrain began to change. Instead of being completely flat, the ground now had the remains of runnels cut into it, running in the opposite direction to the one Kusac was taking. The sharp branches of heather began claiming their toll; his legs were oozing small drops of blood from many minor cuts and scratches, and he had limped the last few hundred meters on only three legs.

Staggering to a halt, he squatted on his haunches and peered at the sky. It was now completely overcast and he could feel snow in the air. Things were not going well. At this rate, all his energy would be spent just trying to reach the settlement, and he could not be sure that he would make it.

Suddenly he heard a distant roaring coming rapidly in his direction. He flung himself into a ditch, crouching low until the groundcar had gone, its cushion of air buffeting him. Kusac crawled out, his breathing ragged as he sat panting for several moments before forcing himself to continue.

If you wish to remain free, be circumspect in all you do. Knowledge gives you power: let none have knowledge of you and what you can do, his father's voice reminded him.

We were circumspect, thought Kusac, *but our maneuverability and speed were just not enough. If we had been given a battleship instead of a light patrol craft, I would not be making this journey, and our people would now know we had found the Others.*

After your life, your freedom and pride are your most precious possessions, the voice continued, as Kusac wearily lifted one foot after the other. *What other wise tenets will he have to impart?* he wondered miserably as the first light flakes of snow began to fall.

I must keep on, he thought. *There is no shelter here. If I am caught in a snowstorm now, I shall die.*

This knowledge urged him on, making him force the injured leg to keep moving. Around him the snowflakes fluttered faster, landing on his nose and eyelashes. He darted his tongue out briefly to capture the moisture, but his mouth still felt thick and swollen with thirst.

"One snowflake won't do much good," he muttered to himself. "Soon there will be enough to drink."

The snow was heavier now, being puffed into his face as a wind sprang up. Within a few minutes he was in the midst of a blizzard, slipping and slithering on the mushy ground and blinded by the driving snow. His foot caught on a heather root, felling him with unexpected force and making him yowl with pain as he landed on his wounded side.

He lay there for several minutes, too weak to get up, until he realized that enough snow had collected for him to quench his thirst. Scrabbling frantically with his hands, he began to lap up clumps of snow from where he lay.

The warning voice spoke again. *Too much cold water when you are suffering from thirst, can kill as easily as the thirst itself.*

Kusac stopped and picked himself up. Though still thirsty, he knew he could take no more at present, and he had revived himself enough to press on. He lurched to his feet. Pain was a thing of the past, he was only aware of feeling curiously disembodied. Though he was thoroughly soaked by this time, his wet fur clinging sleekly to his skin, he was totally unaware of it and the fact that he was shivering violently.

Time and time again, the force of the wind flattened him to the ground. Each time it was that bit harder to get up.

Survival depends on the will to survive, he heard his father say.

"I've plenty of will, just not enough strength," growled Kusac, doggedly dragging one foot after the other through the deepening snow.

A shape loomed grayly up ahead of him, but his eyes were on the ground and he failed to see it. Blindly, he walked straight into the object, giving himself such a crack on the head that he was almost knocked unconscious. Lying there with his senses spinning, it was some time before he understood that it was a tree he had struck. Furthermore, that some recent storm had uprooted it, leaving a cavity deep enough for him to curl up in, sheltered from the snow. He squirmed and wriggled, forcing himself into the opening. It was cramped, but at least it was dry. Clawing and scratching, he deepened the hole slightly, using the loose earth to block up the opening until there was only enough space left for an adequate supply of air to enter. The exercise in the close confines of his lair had warmed him up sufficiently to stop the worst of his shivering. The pain in his leg had returned, but exhaustion was too great for that to keep him from a sleep which was nearer a coma.

He awoke many hours later, stiff, cold, and with a head pounded by a thousand angry demons. His limbs ached in every joint as he tried to pull himself toward the entrance. Through the tiny gap he had left, he could see that although it had stopped snowing, the sky remained an ominous slate color.

Shivering, he pushed back his blockade and crawled out into the snow. The light was fading and he judged it to be close to night. Tentatively he probed the depth of the icy white mass with his good leg: it was not going to be easy, the drifts were almost up to his knees. Sighing, he crouched carefully down onto the ground. Perhaps the snow would numb the wound's fire. He was reluctant to look at it for fear of what he might see.

Your Talent will be useful to you in many different ways, so start experimenting with it. No one knows the range of another's Talent, its limits may only be the ones set by you. Always keep testing your capabilities.

Father? thought Kusac incredulously. No. It can't be him, he's too far away to reach me. I'm just imagining things. "Still," he said aloud, "it isn't a bad idea. I have never tried using my Talent to control pain."

He shuffled his feet in the snow, trying to balance comfortably on all fours. Taking a few deep breaths and stilling his mind, he reached, trying to locate the pain centers in his brain. Several odd sensations coursed through him as he searched, but when all the myriad aches began to slowly fade, he knew he had found the right area. How blessed was that release! Until that moment, he had not realized how much he had been suffering. He opened his eyes and staggered slightly before regaining his balance.

"I might just make the settlement now," he murmured, starting to plod onward, his legs dragging furrows behind him.

Try to avoid extremes in all things. Extreme eating or drinking can kill you just as effectively as extreme weather. Snow will cling to your body, increasing its weight, making you sweat. Then you will lose body heat. Desiring to rest, your body will force you to continue. Either way, you will soon die unless someone aids you, his father's voice droned pedantically.

Great, thought Kusac wryly. *So what do I do about it? Why can't you give me some more sensible advice? I haven't got the time to chat!*

He was suddenly jarred back to reality as his feet scrabbled for a hold before sliding from under him. He was catapulted downhill, tumbling faster and faster, the sky and snow whizzing about him until he was brought to an abrupt and sickening halt by a large concrete slab projecting upright out of the snow.

Kusac groaned and lay slumped where he had come to rest. He was losing control; pain waves began to swamp him. Grimly, he reached out again, strengthening his hold until the pain receded once more. Something wet and sticky was running into his eyes. Putting his hand up, he brought it down covered with blood.

Ice will stop a wound from bleeding, came the cool reminder, and Kusac obediently laid his head on the freezing ground that was at once his enemy and his friend.

Despite the nausea that rippled through him, he had to rise eventually. Although he could not feel it, he knew that the snow was draining him of all warmth. The ground beside the concrete slab felt harder and firmer than that over which he had been traveling. His vision still blurred, he peered at it. There was writing.

Lifting his head, he saw that this flatter ground wove downhill to a cluster of faint lights in the valley below. He was on the road to the settlement.

Vartra be praised, he thought, lurching away from the stone and onto the roadway. Great was the danger of being seen, but greater still was a repetition of his fall.

Now the going was easier. Instead of having to pick his way across unseen and uneven ground, he knew that he had a continuous flat surface beneath him. The downhill slope, though fairly steep, was actually an advantage. He could intermix sliding cautiously with walking, thus making better headway.

Use the terrain to your advantage. Make it work for you, not against you. When walking on sand, your feet will not sink into the surface if you are on the damp area near the water's edge. Rocky ground? Then jump from rock to rock. Water? Then look for stones above the surface or just under it. Don't give yourself extra trouble. Accept the land's conditions.

"Yes, Father," said Kusac dryly. He knew all about these things, had since early childhood. Why did his father keep lecturing him on the obvious?

Behind him he heard the mechanical screeching and whining of another groundcar. Instantly he bunched his muscles and leapt for the cover of the bushes growing at the roadside, trying to stifle his cry of pain at the sudden movement. The car passed and he emerged again to continue his painful slithering walk.

The settlement was a collection of some twenty or so houses facing one another across a broad roadway. Behind each was a fairly large area of cultivated ground. As yet he had no idea which house he wanted: the girl's mind had

been in too much turmoil for him to find the information he
required. It had been difficult maintaining contact with her
at all throughout his journey. The link was strong enough for
him to trace her to the settlement, but not for him to pinpoint
her home. He had to call her to him.

Pushing his way into one of the gardens, he spotted a
small wooden hut far enough away from the house for him
to investigate without being seen. He limped over and, leaning against the door, pulled himself upright. With fingers so
numb he could hardly move them, he pulled at the restraining bolt. It slid back with a bang. Quickly he slipped inside,
pulling the door closed and securing the latch. It was a
toolshed, smelling of dried onions, rows of them hung from
hooks set into the wall. In the far corner he could see a pile
of rags and a large wooden box. Gratefully he limped across
and sat down. On closer inspection the rags turned out to be
sacks woven from thick vegetable fibers.

He could feel the pain beginning to steal back into his
body. Already his head was aching with the effort of trying
to maintain his control. Time was running out quickly now.

Rolling a couple of sacks into a wad, he placed it under
his injured leg, propping it up slightly. Pulling some more
free, he wrapped them round his shoulders to cushion his
back against the crate. He also figured out that the tantaliz-
ingly familiar odor he had been smelling for the last few
minutes originated from the box. Easing himself up slightly,
he thrust his hand inside, grasping hold of one of the round,
hard objects it contained. An apple! Ravenously he bit into
it, aware as he did so how dry his mouth had become.

His eyes refused to stay open any longer and reluctantly
he decided not to have a fourth apple. This was the part he
was dreading. To be sure of reaching the girl, he had to utilize all his Talent, relinquishing his control over the pain. He
was exhausted beyond endurance and knew he could not
have made it this far without the control. Whether or not he
could remain conscious long enough to make contact he had
no idea, but he had to try now. That he'd managed to make
it this far was a miracle. He'd come within a whisker of being found by those Alien soldiers. Why they hadn't seen
him, he'd never know.

Shutting his eyes, he lay down, making sure that he was
well covered. Cautiously, he allowed his mind to relax, trying not to shock himself into unconsciousness with the in-

flux of pain. He was pleasantly surprised: it was not as awful as he had imagined. Oh, there were aches in every limb and joint and he could hardly move his pounding head, but there was no pain at all from his leg. That was bad.

My leg must be worse than I thought. He pressed a hand to his face, feeling how hot he was. Almost immediately he started to shudder again.

The fever, he thought. *No wonder I was so thirsty! I must reach the girl.* Hurriedly he strengthened the link between them, making it narrower until he knew that he had penetrated her mind. Her thoughts were flooded with confused images slowly meandering through her subconscious and he had almost begun to panic when he realized she was deeply asleep. A drug induced sleep, if her slow alpha rhythms were anything to go by. There was no way of reaching her until she awoke. Too utterly spent to even curse fate, he withdrew, leaving her to sleep on in peace.

Chapter 2

A drink, she needed a drink. She reached out and began to grope along her bedside table for the glass, but before she could reach it her hand was taken and held.

"What is it, Carrie? What do you want, love?" Meg asked, her voice so quiet Carrie almost had to strain to hear it.

She tried to speak and found she couldn't. Confused, she attempted to pull her hand free. A small, faraway portion of her mind was trying to panic, but it was too much effort. With a struggle, she managed to open her eyes and Meg's familiar face swam into view, the image losing its blurred edges after a few seconds.

Antiseptic. Why did her room smell of antiseptic? Frowning slightly, she slowly turned her head to look around. Everything seemed the same, was in the same place, so what was different?

She looked back at Meg and wondered why the woman was holding someone's hand, a hand that was heavily bandaged.

"Wa . . ." was all she was able to croak as her thirst reasserted itself.

"Water? Of course, my dear," said Meg, reaching over to pick up the glass. "No, let me," she said, holding it up to Carrie's mouth as the hand in hers twitched slightly.

A mouthful and her thirst was quenched.

"Now you just lie down and go back to sleep again," said Meg soothingly. "There's nothing to worry about, you're absolutely safe."

Safe? thought Carrie. *Of course I'm safe. Why shouldn't I be?*

Meg leaned forward to replace the glass.

Carrie croaked a negative and reached out to stop her.

"More? Here you are," Meg said, holding it toward her again.

Carrie turned her face aside and reached for it herself. Her hand! It was *her* hand that was bandaged. She turned frightened eyes to Meg, knocking the glass aside as she jerked back in panic.

"Oh, Carrie," said Meg, reaching both hands forward to gently cradle her face, "it's all right, love. You're safe. The worst is over. Believe me, it's all right."

No, it's not, her mind said as she tried to push through the mist that was fogging her thoughts. *It's all wrong.*

"Jack Reynolds has given you a sedative; just rest, love. Sleep a little longer and when you wake again, everything will be fine."

"Elise? What happened?" she croaked, wincing at the pain in her hands as she clutched Meg's arm.

Meg hesitated.

"She was caught, Carrie. The Valtegans caught her trying to steal something for the guerrillas."

Fear and loss began surging in again, threatening to overpower her as she started to retreat from what Meg said. Then she felt her mind grasped firmly and held.

"The link between you and Elise was so strong this time, love, that you've suffered some of her hurts. Jack'll come and explain it to you when you've rested, but you're fine, you're in no danger, believe me. I'll stay here with you and watch while you sleep," said Meg, releasing her.

Despite the hold on her mind, terror still fluttered on harshly beating wings; the blackness again threatened to engulf her. Elise! She had to find her twin. She couldn't be dead. If only she looked. . . .

No. Stay here. You must live. If you die, you kill me, too.

The voice inside her head shocked her into immobility. Whose mind was touching hers? Who was *able* to talk to her?

Live for me. I need you, don't leave me. Sleep for now and regain your strength. It wasn't a suggestion, Carrie discovered as the same lassitude as before spread through her aching body and, against her will, her eyes began to close.

This time the room was empty. Carrie tried to lever herself into a sitting position, wincing anew at the agony in her hands. Once she'd sat up, she began to explore her body to find the sources of the pain.

Everything seemed to take an age, so muzzy was her brain.

Jack's sedative must still be working, she thought.

Without undoing the bandages—which was beyond her because of the state of her hands—she couldn't tell the extent of her injuries. She was, however, able to ascertain that she probably had a broken rib, plus multiple bruising and lacerations on her arms and around her face. Wryly, she decided not to bother checking in the mirror for the present. She knew from her past experiences what bruising of Elise's face looked like on hers.

Elise. Funny, thinking of her twin didn't trigger off the waves of panic like last time. In a detached way she searched inside her mind in that place where Elise had been, and found . . . something. What, she wasn't sure, but something, or someone, was there.

A noise from outside diverted her, and she turned her head toward the window.

She had to get up. There was something she had to do if only she could remember what it was: if only the drug wasn't clouding her thinking. The drug. She had to fight it and force herself to get up.

With an effort, she pushed back the bedclothes and struggled to swing her legs round and over the bed. Thank God she was wearing her pajamas! All she needed to do was pull on her coat, then she could go outside.

She struggled to her feet, forcing her mind to push back the woolly confusion caused by the remnants of the sedative still in her system.

Her slippers were under the bed. They weren't suitable for wearing outside, but at least they covered her bare feet. With each step she took, she found herself able to think more clearly and movement became a fraction easier. From her wardrobe she pulled out the first coat that came to hand and wrestled into it, the effort and pain causing her to swear profusely. Several times she thought of giving up and going back to bed, but the compulsion to go outside was getting stronger and her curiosity, if nothing else, would not let her give in.

Mercifully, the kitchen was empty. Meg must be in the taproom, she thought, picking her way carefully round the large rectangular wooden table. The smell of cooking filled the air and she heard her stomach rumble in appreciation. She was starving!

She hesitated, torn between the desire for a bowl of the broth she could smell cooking, and the knowledge she should go into the back garden. The compulsion intensified again, and she felt herself resolutely pulled toward the door.

As she opened it, the cold air hit her like a physical blow. The snow was at least a foot thick. Again she hesitated, realizing how silly it was in her condition to want to go outside in a foot of snow clad only in her pajamas and slippers. Then a patch of black, partially concealed by winter greens, drew her attention.

She stepped out, oblivious now to the cold and the snow, intent only on reaching what lay there. That was what she wanted!

"It's moving!" she said disbelievingly as she floundered toward it, her aches forgotten in her desperate need to reach the creature.

She knelt down in the snow beside it, stretching out a tentative hand.

As the amber eyes opened, she missed the brief flare of awareness in her mind.

"You're a cat," she said, disbelievingly. "A forest cat!" She touched him, her vision blurring momentarily. She shook her head to clear it.

"You're hurt," she said, leaning forward to touch his injured flank. The back leg was badly swollen, the wound covered with dried blood.

"Carrie, don't move," said her brother's quiet voice from behind her. "I've got the gun trained on him. Just get very slowly to your feet."

Carrie looked over her shoulder then flung herself across the cat's body.

"Leave him alone," she said, her voice still hoarse. "I want him. He's hurt and needs help."

"Carrie, he's a wild animal," said Richard. "He could attack you at any moment. Move aside."

"No. He's mine, I want him. Get Jack Reynolds. He's hurt, he needs our help."

"Carrie, for God's sake, be reasonable! He's a dangerous wild animal. Get out of the way!"

Carrie looked up at him, eyes glaring. "You're not killing him, Richard. Fetch Jack, or help me take him indoors unless you want me to spend the rest of the day out here in the snow."

Amber eyes flicked open again, a mute appeal visible in their depths.

Richard lowered his gun. "Carrie!"

"Carry him in for me, Richard," his sister pleaded, clinging more tightly to the animal's neck. "He hasn't made a move or a sound that could be seen as violent."

Richard slung the gun over his shoulder and moved closer, looking down at the creature.

"He's huge, Carrie, almost as large as me. We don't know anything about these creatures. Even the guerrillas, who see them fairly often in the forest, know very little."

"They've never said they're vicious, have they? Only that they avoid people. Please help me take him in. He'll die out here, and Jack has always wanted to study one of them. It's not as if he's even a real threat in this condition, is it?"

"I don't know, Carrie," her brother said, scratching his bearded chin thoughtfully. "Dad won't like it. The animal's large, powerful, and wild. These cats are predators and likely to be vicious. It isn't as if it was a kitten you could raise to be tame."

Carrie ignored the worried look on his face and pulled gently at his trouser leg.

"Come on, skinny," she urged. "I'll handle Dad. You just get my cat into the kitchen, then fetch Jack Reynolds. He'll know what to do."

Her brother sighed.

"Well, move over. I can't do anything with you wrapped around him like a blanket, can I?"

Carrie moved back and her brother hefted the injured animal into his arms and headed toward the kitchen door.

"And, Richard, please hurry," she added, steering him through the doorway and over to the table. She swept the various cutlery and dishes aside for him. "I'm sure he must be in a great deal of pain."

"We don't know these animals well enough to treat them with any success, Carrie," Richard warned, setting the cat down gently on the table. He hesitated. "I don't like leaving you alone with him. What happens if he goes for you?"

"He won't," said Carrie confidently as she ruffled the creature's ears.

Richard looked down at him for a moment. His sides

moved rapidly with shallow breathing, his ribs stood out against the tautly stretched fur. The eyes were closed now, and from between his teeth Richard could see the tip of a pale pink tongue. Unless he had help, very shortly, this cat would be dead.

"I'm going," he said, heading back outside.

Fetching hot water and disinfectant, Carrie busied herself with cleaning Kusac's wound, her own forgotten.

"Carrie! What on earth are you doing down here, and with your coat on? You shouldn't even be out of . . . oh, my God!"

"It's all right," said Carrie, turning round to look at Meg. "He's hurt, and he isn't dangerous. Richard's gone for Jack."

"I don't care! Get it out of my kitchen!" Meg said, her voice rising hysterically.

"No," Carrie said doggedly. "He stays. Don't worry, it'll be all right, you'll see." She turned her attention back to her inexpert swabbing.

"Get him out of my kitchen," repeated Meg, her voice rising a couple of octaves.

"It isn't your kitchen, Meg," Carrie replied quietly, a portion of her mind taken aback at her newfound determination.

A buzzer sounded, its insistent tone ignored by both women.

"What did you say?"

The silence lengthened till Carrie broke it. "I think that's the taproom. Hadn't you better see who it is?"

The door closed too quietly behind her as Meg left.

Carrie sluiced her cloth so energetically that water splashed everywhere. Damn! Why had she spoken to Meg like that? Since they'd landed on Keiss, Meg, also bereaved by the same malfunction which had killed their mother, had lived with them more as a loved aunt than a housekeeper. She hadn't deserved that comment.

I've got to save him, though, she thought. *I don't know why, but he's important.*

She went back to cleaning the wound, finding it soothing to do something that required no thought.

She had just about finished when her brother returned with the town's medical expert.

"Morning, Carrie," Jack said, stamping the snow off his boots. "I hear you've got an interesting patient for me." He gave her a calculating glance as he took off his parka and gloves, handing them to Richard before moving over to examine her.

Jack was a short man, almost on the tubby side, with a thatch of thick gray-brown hair crowning a face resembling that of a middle-aged faun.

"I must admit I didn't expect to find you awake yet, let alone running a rescue mission," he said, taking her by the wrist to check her pulse. "But then, what should I expect of someone with your recuperative powers? Trying to sedate you is like felling an elephant, and you still manage to come round far too soon! How do you feel?"

"Fine," she said absently, her attention obviously not on him.

"I'll check your hands before I leave, my dear. You've got the bandages soaking wet."

He turned to look at the form draped across the table.

"A forest cat, eh? I've never had the chance to examine one of these beasties before. Isn't he a darker color than usual?" His brown eyes twinkled briefly at her before he bent his head and began examining Kusac thoroughly.

"They come in all colors," replied Carrie, clumsily trying to move her bowls and cloths out of his way. "Sorry to bother you, Jack, but he needed help."

"No bother at all," he replied, "provided that you return to bed after I've finished. I suppose asking you to go now is out of the question?"

Carrie ignored his sarcasm. "Can you help him, Jack? I think he might have a fever, too. He's panting and he feels very warm."

"We should be able to do something for him," Jack said, probing the livid wound gently with his fingers. "I'll have to lance that gash though. The poisoning is certainly causing the fever. Pass me over some of that hot water and I'll get started."

Two hours later, Carrie sat looking down at Kusac, waiting for him to come round. Jack had not wanted to risk an anesthetic of any kind, but luckily their patient had solved the problem by drifting off into unconsciousness.

The injury had been quite deep and there had been a small piece of metal embedded in it. Jack had cleaned the wound thoroughly, but left it open to the air.

"If he's like Terrestrial cats, when he's feeling better, he'll want to lick the wound himself. Frankly, that's the best thing he could do," said Jack, preparing a syringe. "I'm giving him a hefty dose of antibiotics to help break the fever, but there's a risk that the drugs might react unfavorably with his metabolism. However, in his present weakened condition, we don't have a choice. If I don't try something, he'll die."

"He'll live," Carrie said confidently. "He's fought the poison this long, he won't give up now. He's too much of a fighter. I have a feeling he won't want to lick the wound, though."

"Another one of your intuitions?" Jack asked as he busied himself taking blood and tissue samples from his patient. "Now don't get upset," he added hurriedly, catching her frown. "I'm not doubting you. You've got a way with the animals on Keiss. You really are wasted here at the Inn, you know. You'd make a grand assistant for me when I go on one of my field trips. If you want, I'll have another try at asking your father to let you come with me when you're better."

Carrie sighed. "I think we'll be out of luck, Jack. Father seems to think women are more suited to the domestic role than anything intellectual."

"We can but try," he said, packing his samples away and going over to the sink to wash his hands.

"Ah, the luxury of hot running water," he sighed, letting the water course over his hands for a moment or two. "Half my problems in Valleytown would be solved if every house had an adequate supply of hot and cold water," he said, drying his hands and returning to the table. "I wonder if we'll ever have anything more than a subsistence level of existence."

"We will, if we can get rid of the Valtegans and if our second wave ship arrives safely," said Carrie angrily, tears springing to her eyes. "And if Father actually helped the guerrillas, rather than . . ."

"Hush, Carrie," said Jack, enveloping her in his arms and hugging her tightly. "Let's not open that old argument again. Your father does a good job leading the civil disobedience, and that's risky enough given the Aliens we're dealing with. Not everyone can pull up roots and hightail it out to the forest to be a rebel, you know. He's had you and your sister to think of. It's not so clear-cut when you've got a family."

"Oh, Jack," she said, tears running down her face, "why did it have to be Elise? Why did they have to catch her?"

"That's it, love," he said, patting her back awkwardly as she began to cry. "You let it out. Have a good cry, it'll help."

With Jack away tackling her father, and Richard out back trying to rig up something for Kusac to sleep in, Carrie was alone for the moment.

Exhaustion was beginning to creep up on her. Her ribs had begun to ache as had her hands, but the latter could be due to Jack's rebandaging them. From the glimpse she'd gotten of them before Jack had firmly blocked her view, it was clear that she'd lost most, if not all, of her fingernails and had a couple of broken fingers as well.

He'd also insisted on giving her another injection for the pain, despite the fact that she'd assured him she was able to block most of it out. He had never trusted her strange abilities. They weren't something he could study under his microscope, so he preferred to take no chances and had always treated both her and her sister with conventional medical remedies.

She flexed her hands, aware of a small amount of pain. Well, she'd certainly never play the violin, not that she had ever wanted to! Feeling cold, she pulled her coat more closely around herself and carefully put her hands in her pockets. She winced as something poked into her injured left hand.

With difficulty, she caught the object between her fingers and pulled it out. It was the piece of metal that Jack had taken out of the cat's leg.

A couple of centimeters long and irregular in shape, it was smooth on one side, dimpled on the other. Where had she seen its like before? Stranger still was how it had come to be in the cat's leg. They had hardly any refined metals yet on Keiss.

Their colony ship, the first wave, was mainly agricultural, with only minimal mining and blacksmithing personnel on board. The second wave would have a greater percentage of manufacturing skills among its personnel, the miners, smelters, and so on as well as a reasonable level of technology. The hope had been that their skills would be supported by their predecessors.

The only metals on the planet this sophisticated either came from the remains of the Terran Mothership which had landed at the site they called Seaport, or from something belonging to the Valtegans.

A moan from her patient drew her attention back to Kusac. Returning the sliver to her pocket, she leaned forward to stroke his head. He was making the most peculiar noises, almost as if he was trying to talk.

He became quiet and still, his eyelids flickering open. Carrie found herself staring again into the golden yellow eyes. Almost hypnotically, they held her gaze until voices in the hall broke the spell.

"It's exactly what she needs, Peter," Jack was saying. "Something to occupy her and take her mind off what's happened. Take my advice and go along with whatever scheme she suggests. If looking after a creature as ill as he is will keep her in her bed, I'd go for it."

Carrie grinned slightly. Trust him to find an angle that would appeal to her father. Jack was almost as bad as him, though, the way he always fussed over her—and Elise. Another wave of desperate loss swept through her and tears stung her eyes.

The door opened and her father came in, followed by Jack and Richard.

In appearance her father and Richard were alike, but on him the dark beard and mustache—longer and bushier—were beginning to turn brindle. Though the years may have lightened his hair, they had not thickened the lean frame that all his offspring seemed to have inherited.

"Well, my girl," he said, walking over to the table. "Let's have a look at this latest lame duck of yours.

"A forest cat? He's some size, isn't he? I haven't seen one as large before." Her father reached out gingerly to pat the animal. "He isn't likely to bite, is he?" he asked, his hand poised in midair.

"No," replied Carrie, putting a hand possessively on Kusac's head. "He's quite friendly."

Her father hesitated. "You know he's too old to tame, Carrie. A mature wild animal won't take kindly to captivity, nor can they ever be completely trusted."

"I know, Dad. I only want to give him a chance for his leg to heal, then I'll set him free."

"Very well. Get Richard to clear some space for him in the barn," he said, giving Kusac a friendly but cautious pat on the side.

As he did so, Kusac turned his head to look up at him, licking the man gently on the hand.

"Well, he seems very friendly," he said, mollified, before turning to look at his daughter. "What's wrong?" he asked, seeing her frown.

"If Kusac sleeps in the barn, the cold could kill him. There's no way to heat that place," she objected.

"You aren't seriously suggesting we bring a wild animal that size into the house!" her father exclaimed. "He could turn on you without warning. I'm sorry, but I'm not prepared to let you risk our lives. It's out of the question."

"Then I'll sleep in the barn, too."

"You'll do no such thing! You're far too badly injured to be anywhere but in bed now. There's no question of you sleeping in the barn."

"If it's too cold for me, then it's too cold for Kusac," Carrie interrupted calmly. "Kusac sleeps with me, either in the house or in the barn, I don't care which."

"For goodness sake, grow up, Carrie! We're talking about a wild animal, not some orphaned lamb!" Her father's angry voice filled the room.

Richard sighed and turned his back on them. He hated rows. Funny, but he'd always seen Elise as the argumentative one. It was unlike Carrie to cross their father like this.

"How much older do I have to be, Dad?" Carrie asked quietly. "I'm hardly a child now, and I do know what I'm doing."

"At twenty-three most girls are well and truly married," her father grumbled. "If you had a house to run, you wouldn't have time to bring in useless stray animals. I think it's high time I arranged a marriage for you since you don't seem capable of choosing a partner from among the young men in Valleytown."

"Stop ducking the issue, Dad. The barn or the house, which is it to be?" insisted Carrie.

"Jack? You'll back me up on this, won't you?"

"Me?" said the doctor, pausing as he put on his coat. "I don't want to be involved in a family argument, Peter. I will say this, though. The cat is too weak to be a danger to anyone at present, and living in a cold barn will certainly kill him."

Her father glanced from one to the other. "Oh, very well," he said, exasperated. "Have it your own way. You've obviously got it all organized between the two of you. But as soon as he's recovered enough to be moved, out to the barn he goes!

"Good day to you, Jack!"

With that he stamped out of the kitchen, back to work with his beloved wines.

"Thanks, Jack," said Carrie, trying to stand.

"It was nothing, but your Dad has a point, you know. Our friend could turn nasty at any time.

"Richard, you make some kind of cage to put Kusac in at night; and you, Carrie, you'll keep your promise to me by getting back up to bed before you collapse!" he said, accepting his gloves from Richard.

"By the way, how did you come by the name? Kusac, eh? Not bad, it rather suits him. Well, I must be off. I'll call back to see you both in a couple of days. If you need me, you know where I am.

"Just keep him warm and try to find something light that he'll eat. Soup or something like that. No meat for the time being, and the same for you, young lady," he said, waggling an admonishing finger in her direction as he followed her brother out through the taproom.

"Good-bye Jack, and thanks again," Carrie said.

Once they had gone, she ambled over to the stove and began to ladle some soup into a bowl for Kusac. It was a strange name, now she came to think of it. It sounded unfamiliar, yet it did suit him. She carried the bowl back over to him and set it down near his head.

The cat looked up at her, giving her hand a quick lick before raising himself on his front paws to lap the soup. Carrie smiled. His tongue tickled. There was an almost gentle roughness to it. She knew he wouldn't harm anyone, it wasn't in his nature.

As he ate, she pulled up a chair and watched him. His amber eyes never left hers until he lay down, his hunger satisfied for the first time in five days.

With a sigh, Kusac pillowed his head against her hands and closed his eyes. Though he could not yet understand the language of these people, he understood Carrie's thoughts completely. It was to his advantage that they thought he was a forest cat; no one could then betray him, and he would probably learn much more that would be denied to him as an Alien.

Besides, it had been a surprise for him to find two sentient species on this planet, so how much worse would it be for Carrie's people who had only known the repression of the Others? The Valtegans, he corrected himself, drifting off into a contented sleep.

Carrie felt her shoulder being shaken roughly. Looking blearily up at her brother, she pulled her hands carefully from underneath Kusac and rubbed the sleep from her eyes.

"What is it, Richard?" she mumbled.

"The Valtegans are searching all the houses. Dad wants you and the cat upstairs out of the way."

"All right," said Carrie, getting stiffly to her feet. "Have you finished Kusac's bed?"

"It's in your room," he replied, reaching out to help her as she staggered away from the table. "I don't know how you're going to manage to nurse our friend here when you're nowhere near fit yourself."

"I'm fine, Richard," she said, pulling away from him. "I'm tired, that's all."

"No, you're not, but I'm not going to argue with you about it. Let's get you and this character settled down before the Valtegans get here."

"What are they looking for this time?" asked Carrie as Richard lifted the sleepy Kusac.

"I'm not exactly sure," he said, following her upstairs. "But what is even stranger, I don't think the Valtegans know either.

"Five days ago there was a full-scale panic on. The sky was buzzing with aircars and scouters, all centered over the forest and hills behind us. Not long afterward, I saw something white falling toward the ridge. It could have been anything, a scouter in trouble, even a small spacecraft."

He fell silent, waiting for his sister to open the bedroom door. When she did, he went in and carefully laid Kusac down on the pile of rugs he'd arranged in a large wooden box on Elise's bed.

Carrie sat down on her own bed. "Well?" she prompted. "What do you think it was?"

Richard shook his head. "I don't know, but the Valtegans are doing a head count as well as searching every house. They want to know if we've seen any strangers."

"Could it have been a craft from Earth?" Carrie asked bleakly, staring at her clenched hands without seeing them.

"Earth doesn't know about our situation, Carrie. We haven't been able to get a message out to them. Even if we could, it would take years to reach them, and equally long for them to come to our aid," her brother replied, taking her hands in his and giving them a comforting pat. "And no one could have helped Elise."

"What does Dad think?" she asked, her voice still tense.

"He says it couldn't be anything to do with the second wave colonists. Their ship isn't due to reach midpoint for another two months yet. In fact, it can't be from Earth at all. That only leaves two realistic possibilities."

"A Valtegan in trouble, possibly a renegade from the hospital, or a satellite crashing," said Carrie, looking at him inquiringly, her interest fully caught.

"It wasn't a meteorite, that's for sure. The other possibility I had in mind was that the craft was Alien to both us and the Valtegans."

Carrie wrinkled her face in surprise, her eyebrows disappearing under her fringe.

"You have to be kidding, Richard. An Alien craft?"

"Why not?" he countered, letting go of her bandaged hands and beginning to pace the room. "No one believed in Aliens until the Valtegans arrived. If there are two species in the galaxy, why not three or even more? Who are the Valtegans fighting, if not other Aliens?" He paused by the window. "Dad thinks it's a viable possibility, and you can't escape the fact that the Valtegans are searching for several strangers," he said forcefully. "They'd hardly ask us if the strangers were their own people! They aren't from this colony, and they can't be from Earth. There is only one other alternative—more Aliens.

"Don't laugh," he said irritably, looking away from her. "It isn't that ridiculous an idea." He stared out of the window for almost a minute before it penetrated that he was watching a patrol of Valtegan soldiers making their way across the main street to the Inn.

"Carrie, they're almost here! I'd better get downstairs now," he said. "Get back into bed and stop giggling!" He strode over to the door. "Come on! We don't want to draw any attention to ourselves."

Still chuckling, Carrie took her coat off, threw it across the chair, and crawled back into bed. As she stretched out between the cool sheets, she realized how bone weary she was. She looked over to the other bed where Kusac lay supine among his blankets. The bed which up until a year ago had been her sister's.

"You aren't asleep," she murmured, "I can tell. Never mind, you play your little game, I don't mind. You're safer to trust no one." She reached out her hand and touched him gently on the head. "Sleep, you're safe now."

The door burst open, shocking her out of her nap.

"I've told you, she's ill! Leave her alone," came Meg's angry voice from outside.

"I decide," was the sibilant reply as two Valtegan soldiers forced their way into the room. Their energy guns focused instantly on Carrie and the cat as their cold gazes swept the room looking for signs of other occupants.

"What happen to she," hissed the leader, gesturing to the other soldier to enter and search the room.

"Accident," said Meg succinctly. "The oven exploded."

"So."

Carrie lay frozen with fear as the second soldier paced around the room, moving the curtains, opening the wardrobe doors, and finally lifting the end of her bed to look under it.

She was simultaneously aware of the presence in her mind growing stronger and a low, menacing, guttural sound that built in pitch till it filled the room.

Kusac raised his head and stared at the soldier at the end of her bed. The growl changed to a snarl as his lip pulled back to reveal a set of formidable canines.

The soldier dropped the bed and backed off hurriedly.

"Is no one else," he said to his superior as Carrie yelped in pain at the shock of the violent movement.

Both soldiers backed out, trying not to appear to hurry, their usually pallid complexions a shade or two paler.

"Next room," she heard the officer snap.

Kusac's snarl reduced to a low-pitched rumble as he continued to stare at the door. He kept it up until they heard the Inn door bang shut as the Valtegans departed.

"So they're afraid of you, are they?" she said slowly, reaching out to pat him. "Good boy. You keep it up."

Footsteps sounded in the passageway and Meg entered, carrying a tray.

"I thought it was time you both ate," she said, putting the tray down on Carrie's bedside table.

She helped Carrie sit up, plumping up her pillows behind

her, then setting the tray on her lap. Bending down, she reached under the bed and drew a second tray out from under it. This she cautiously put in front of Kusac's bed and shifted the second bowl of broth from Carrie's tray to his.

"There you are, my boy," she said. "Anything that can frighten those bastards is a friend of mine."

"Why, Meg," said Carrie, as the housekeeper sat down beside her, "you surprise me. I've never heard you talk about the Valtegans like that before."

"You should have seen the mess they made of the house after they left your room," she said heatedly. "It'll take me hours to put it to rights. Still, it was worth it. I've never seen them back off so fast in my life before!" She smiled at the memory. "Maybe your furry friend does have his uses after all."

"Meg," Carrie hesitated, spoon held in midair, "I'm sorry about . . ."

Meg smiled and patted Carrie's other hand where it lay on the coverlet. "Don't you worry, love, I understand. If your friend can behave like that when he thinks you're threatened, I reckon we've nothing to fear from him. If he'd meant us any harm, we'd have known it by now.

"Now come on, eat up your broth. There's plenty more in the pot where that came from."

Chapter 3

Valleytown Inn served a variety of functions. It was first and foremost the place where the adult members of the town—population some 300 souls plus assorted livestock and one forest cat—could relax. It was also where the Ladies' Sewing Circle met on Tuesday and Thursday afternoons, and the center for the informal exchange of information. The less charitable called it the Gossip Shop.

Its second most important function was as the central clearing house for information gleaned by the Passive Resistance movement run by Carrie's father, Peter Hamilton.

Unlike the guerrillas led by the Captain and what remained of the starship crew, the Passive Resistance did not use violence. They claimed that it only brought retaliatory action, resulting in more deaths of the already depleted colonists.

Though Carrie's talent lay in working with children, she was often called upon by her father to help out in the taproom during the evenings. She enjoyed the break from her routine and found it refreshing now and then to be able to talk to people who were over a meter tall. So for her first sortie back into the community life, the taproom was a natural place to start.

She had taken longer than she had expected to heal. It had been six weeks since . . . that night . . . and occasionally she still felt weak and drained from her ordeal. At least all the broken bones had mended and she could use her hands again. Even the faint scars from the lacerations on her arms were beginning to fade.

She looked round to where Kusac lay on the floor by her feet, nose on his front paws, tail curled round him. An ear cocked in her direction and his eyes opened slowly.

His recuperative powers had been something else. Of the

terrible wound in his flank all that now remained was a slight limp and a long patch of shorter fur.

He was like her shadow, never leaving her side for any length of time even on the couple of short walks they'd taken on the slopes out at the back of the fields.

This pleased Carrie. She enjoyed having him around, especially when the Valtegans did one of their sudden searches of the Inn. They showed Kusac a healthy respect that bordered on a pathological fear of him, although it hadn't stopped the soldiers from the local base outside the village from coming into the Inn when off duty.

Kusac lay quiescent, well aware of Carrie's surface thoughts. He desperately needed to know more about these Valtegans, but the girl's mind was strong—growing stronger since he had started teaching her—and now he doubted whether she would respond to a gentle nudge in that direction.

Carrie took another sip of her coffee, finding her thoughts slipping back to the past. Ten years ago when the Valtegans had descended on them like a plague of locusts, the colony had only just gotten itself established. Each interdependent unit was finally in its proper location: the fishing center remained at the landing site, calling itself Seaport; the mining community had set up its houses in the hilly country—Hillfort; and her own group had moved to the fertile plains they called Valleytown. Oceanview moved up the coast, taking advantage of the pure seawater to farm seaweeds and shellfish as well as the land.

They had only been on the planet two years, and what they had achieved in that time had been outstanding.

Keiss had been almost a new Eden. There was no intelligent dominant life-form on the planet, though given time it was argued by some that the felines could have filled that niche. The soil was rich and fertile, hardly even needing the manure they ploughed into it to help feed the Terran crops they had brought with them.

Most of the native grasses and grains were edible by livestock and humans alike, and the climate was temperate. It was all they could have wished for. Until the Alien ships landed.

Carrie's thoughts veered away from that back to the pres-

ent time and she grinned. At least the Valtegans hadn't found
the human population on Keiss a walkover. Despite delaying
tactics from the forced human labor groups, the two giant
domed cities of Geshader and Tashkerra had been built—
plus a major military base on the coast and local garrisons
at each of the four settlements, these last thanks to their
guerrilla activities.

The Valtegans' R & R planet—for such was the use they
had intended Keiss to fill—had ended up as armed camps
that their recuperating troops had to be virtually interned
within until they were fit to return to their spacecraft. It was
no holiday world.

Who and where the Valtegans were fighting was a puzzle
that no one could uncover. It seemed the Valtegans on Keiss
didn't even know. All the humans could discover was that
Keiss was well back from any combat zone, and this only
because over the years they had learned to judge the state of
the injuries of the hospitalized Aliens. The who and where
were recurrent topics of speculative gossip given their total
lack of any known facts.

Carrie pulled her wandering thoughts back to the here and
now, aware that she was supposed to be working.

Kusac lay quiet, piecing together what he'd learned. Apart
from having a good understanding of their language now,
he'd found out more in the last few minutes than in the last
six weeks.

The taproom was large and had a friendly atmosphere. Every effort had been made to create as pleasant surroundings
as possible. A solid screen stood in front of the doorway to
prevent the bitter winter winds from howling round the room
whenever the door was opened. Alcoves had been created
along the walls, the benches padded and covered with hand-
woven brightly colored cloth.

In the center of the room stood the open log fireplace, the
local resinous wood scenting the air with a smell reminiscent
of pine. Smaller round tables and chairs filled this middle
area.

The bar was opposite the door and this was where Carrie
was sitting. Reaching forward, she took the jug of coffee off
the hot plate and poured herself a second mug, adding
sweetener and milk. Out of the corner of her eye she saw

Kusac's head raise and his nostrils twitch appreciatively at the smell.

"Sorry, Kusac, coffee isn't for cats. You know where your bowl of water is."

She took a mouthful, then set the mug down.

"I'd better get started, I suppose," she said, letting herself slide off the high stool.

Taking the notepad and pencil out of her pocket, she went round behind the bar and began checking the bottles of wines and spirits off against her list.

They made all their own alcoholic drinks using a mixture of the grains and fruits they had brought with them as well as some of those indigenous to Keiss. Her father's passion was his vines, though, and he spent hours tending them in his greenhouses. He did brew lovely traditional wines, but Carrie preferred those made with the other fruits.

All their crops were either edible or tradable at the monthly markets held at Seaport, the only large gathering the Valtegans would allow them, and that only because it provided amusement as a tourist attraction for the Valtegans from Geshader and Tashkerra. The markets were sacrosanct, needed by the humans for their continued survival, so no anti-Valtegan activities were allowed for fear of losing the privilege of exchanging goods for foodstuffs.

As she checked out which bottles needed replacing, the outer door opened. Ever alert, Kusac turned his head, ears pricked forward, but it was only Annie arriving for work.

"Hello, Carrie. I didn't expect to see you in here so soon," she said, taking off her hat and coat and hanging them on the rack at the back of the screen.

Carrie glanced round. "Hello, Annie. Dad asked me to do a bar check on the spirits. He wants you to restock them from the cellar."

"Well, you go back to your stool and nurse your coffee. I'll read them out to you," she said, coming across the room toward Carrie.

"No, honestly . . ."

"Go on now," Annie smiled, squeezing past her and giving her a gentle shove. "You rest while you can. Your dad will have you worked off your feet again in no time."

"I've done nothing but rest," objected Carrie, returning to her perch by the coffeepot.

The door opened again, this time to admit the Merediths.

"Hello there, Annie," said Ted, coming up to the bar while his brothers settled themselves in the alcove nearest to the fire. "Three pints of bitter, love." He slapped a handful of assorted coins down on the bar and turned to Carrie.

"Hello, Miss," he said, nodding to her. "Nice to see you up and about again."

"Hello, Ted," she replied, aware of his increased uneasiness in her company. She saw his sidelong glance to where her hands lay folded on the counter. Anger flared inside her.

So everyone knew, did they? And it frightened them, did it? They knew that this time although the Valtegans hadn't laid a hand on her, she had suffered exactly the same injuries as those inflicted on her twin. She stretched her fingers along the bartop. Then let them see and be really afraid!

"Yes, they're healing nicely, thank you," she said, her smile brittle.

Ted took a step back.

"There you are, Ted," interrupted Annie, drawing his attention away from Carrie as she put the first of the pottery tankards of beer in front of him. "It's raw out tonight, isn't it? You wouldn't think spring was nearly due."

Ted turned back to her, relief evident on his face.

"Well, if it keeps those bloody lizards out of the Inn, all to the good," he said, picking up the first tankard and taking the second from her. "You can't go anywhere these days without tripping over a couple of them."

"Well, whatever it is they're looking for, they haven't found it yet," Annie said, pulling the last pint.

"One of my pigeons came in from Hillfort today. The message said as how the lizards turned them all out of their beds in the middle of the night last week. Kept them standing out there for two solid hours while they turned the houses over with their searching," he said over his shoulder as he carried the drinks to their table.

"I've heard it's only us and Hillfort they're searching," said Annie.

"I've heard that, too," said Bill, taking a hefty swig of his beer.

Ted ambled back over to the bar to collect his own drink.

"Don't let yourself get wound up so," said Annie quietly, touching Carrie lightly on the arm. "They're just curious, there's no harm in them."

Carrie let go of the anger the way she had been taught and managed a slight smile.

"That's better," said Annie. "Now let's get back to our list before we get any busier."

As she picked up her pencil again, Carrie could hear them on the edge of her mind.

I'm telling you, it was as if they were doing it to her, insisted Bill.

What, bruises and the like? asked Alan, leaning forward.

No, she always had the bruises. This was worse. This time she was found covered in blood.

Get on, said Bill, taking a sip of his beer.

You just look at her hands, then, said Ted. *How'd they get to be like that if it wasn't true? How'd they heal so fast, eh? And she's started answering you before you say anything.*

She was always, well, strange, said Alan. *Pity, she's a looker.*

You just leave her alone, snapped Ted. *I don't want the likes of her in our family, thank you!*

She tried to ignore it, but it was becoming less easy these days. She felt raw, hypersensitive to any mention of her name. She concentrated on listening to Annie, the other voices beginning to fade as they moved onto another topic.

They had just finished when the door banged open and a cold draft swept into the room.

"Is a search," said the Valtegan officer, sweeping his gun round the room in an arc as his two companions joined him.

"All in corner." He jerked the gun toward where the Merediths still sat. "Go."

As the score or so people in the Inn got to their feet and moved toward the corner, Carrie heard Kusac's growl start to build.

The smell, that musty odor they created, filled the room, bringing back memories of darkened corridors and rooms— the smell of fear and blood. She couldn't move.

Behind her was the door to the Inn's private quarters and from beyond it came raised voices. The door opened and her father and brother, followed by Meg, were pushed through. A fourth soldier accompanied them.

Kusac's growl became a snarl.

Carrie stood as if frozen as one of the soldiers advanced on her.

"Leave her alone," said Richard, trying to move back to her side.

The nearest Valtegan backhanded him in the chest, sending him reeling into the others.

Kusac stood in front of her, tail lashing from side to side, teeth bared.

The officer's gun pointed directly at his head.

"Move," he hissed at Carrie, "I kill it else."

Fear and anger in equal proportions exploded in Carrie's mind, none of it hers. The force made her reel and she stumbled against Kusac, breaking their deadly tableau. Able to move and think again, she grasped him by the collar he wore round his neck and, ignoring his strangled cough of protest, hauled him with her over to the others.

While the officer remained with his energy rifle trained on them, the other three soldiers began to search the room and its contents. Bottles were swiped from the shelves, tankards from the bar, and the pockets of any coats on the rack were gone through.

Carrie had gradually edged her way to the back of the group of people, taking Kusac with her. His growls had now subsided to a low rumble of discontent.

She was confused. For a moment she was sure she had felt her mental companion, but then he was gone. Why? Was he nearby, was that why she had felt his fear and anger? Could he see the Valtegans? She searched within her mind but, beyond the fact of his presence, she could not touch him.

The soldiers had turned their attention to the villagers now and had taken one of the men aside to search. They were not being gentle about it. Coming from a heavier world than Earth or Keiss, despite their apparent frailty, they were far stronger than the Terrans and were uncaring about compensating for it when dealing with them.

Carrie began to study the officer. If seen from behind, the Valtegans did appear Terran, although they were slightly taller and slimmer. The main differences were around the head and face, little things in themselves, but taken all together they made the Valtegans more grossly Alien. They seemed to have no foreheads. Instead, the line of their faces in profile curved smoothly down from the crown of the head, ending at the tip of the nose. Set on either side, their eyes were rounder, and of a universally dark green that contrasted badly with their pallid skins.

There were other differences, like the lack of eyebrows and the tiny, rounded ears, but it took longer to notice them.

As if aware of her gaze, the soldier turned to look at her. His eyes seemed to get rounder and larger as he, in his turn, momentarily studied her.

Fear gripped her stomach. It was never wise for Terran women to attract the personal attention of a Valtegan officer. Quickly she made her eyes seem lackluster and vacant, letting her facial muscles relax into a semblance of congenital idiocy, and began projecting the image toward the officer.

His round pupils narrowed, becoming vertical slits. After a moment, he looked away.

This search was different. They seemed to be looking for something specific this time. Perhaps she could touch their minds and find out what. Carefully she sent out a faint questing thought, only to feel it seized and returned to her.

Reeling back in shock, she leaned against the wall, gasping for air.

Your thought was too faint, said someone inside her mind. *Try to imagine it as a beam of light. It must be strong yet infinitely fine. Yours was too diverse and would have aroused the Valtegan's notice. Let me teach you how to read another mind unnoticed.*

"Who are you?" whispered Carrie, glancing around the room in panic. "Where are you? Show yourself!"

The man in front of her turned round, frowning.

"Hush," he said. "Don't cause any more trouble."

I have alarmed you, said the voice, its tone one of contrition. *I had forgotten that I had not yet spoken to you. Don't you know me?*

"Yes," she murmured, barely talking as she took a deep breath to steady herself. "But *who* are you?"

I had to stop you quickly, he said apologetically, *otherwise you would have given yourself away. Just "say" your words in your mind, I can hear them.*

Who are you? she asked.

Much better, he replied. *You can talk at normal speed, you know. Any time you want to speak to me, just reach out here,* he showed her, *and you'll find me.*

Let me show you how to reach for the Valtegans. I will

lead your mind, so relax your control. Relax, he urged, and Carrie felt a slight tug as he took over.

She could almost see their minds narrow down, sending a thin feeler toward the Valtegan officer. Matching brain waves, they looked for the surface thoughts, and finding the soldier's mind beginning to wander, tapped into the ongoing ramblings of his consciousness.

At once Carrie was aware of the differences in the Valtegan's mind. It was a cold, alien place, empty of emotions and filled only with the lust for fighting and hatred of his superiors for keeping him on Keiss. Vague impressions of winning glory and promotion by finding the Alien artifact began to creep in.

Again she felt the flash of a fear not her own. That was it. They had found what they were looking for. Before they withdrew, they felt the soldier change his mind, deciding that it was merely an exercise dreamed up for the hell of it to get them out of their barracks on a cold night. Since he had to suffer, everyone around him could suffer, too, not least these . . . beings!

Carrie felt the presence fade and tried to hold onto it.

No, don't go, she thought. *Who are you? Come back!* but he had gone, leaving only the echo of his presence.

"So Richard was right after all," Carrie said to herself.

Thoughts began to race through her head. Until six weeks ago, no one had touched her mind but Elise. It was rare, her father and others had told her, for there to be any mental link between people. Yet just as Elise had died, this new contact had been established. If Richard was right, it had happened the same day that the object, presumably some kind of spacecraft, had fallen to the ground.

Could her contact possibly be one of the Aliens? No, that was impossible! Yet it couldn't be one of the colonists or she would have recognized the feel of his mind. Besides, he seemed to know a lot about this extra sense, something which even Jack Reynolds knew only what little he'd learned from studying her.

Could he be a Valtegan? Every few months one of their ships came in with a load of injured, tired, and bored soldiers ready for a couple of months of high living at the pleasure cities of Geshader and Tashkerra. The turnover of personnel, except for those forming the permanent garrisons, was tremendous. Could it be one of them? She shuddered, feeling physically ill at the thought. It had to be another Alien: please God that it was.

Who are you? Where are you from? she asked. *Are you one of the Aliens?* There was no reply although she kept repeating the question.

Kusac trod firmly on her foot, drawing her attention back to her surroundings.

"Ouch!" she said as she pulled her foot from under his paw.

The Valtegans had searched a good half of the people in the room by now she realized as she looked around. Those who had been checked already were sitting or standing at the other end of the bar under the watchful gaze of a soldier.

"What's that Jim Healey up to?" she heard Ted Meredith ask his neighbor.

"No good, I'll be bound," John Innes muttered in reply. "Never could stand the man. Slimy little toad."

Curious, Carrie turned to follow their gaze. Jim was edging closer and closer to the officer—at least he was trying to. The unoccupied guard stepped forward and pushed him back.

"No move," he hissed.

"I need to speak to your officer," Jim said, stumbling against Ted and clutching at his arm for support.

Ted pushed him away.

"No talk."

Jim moved forward again.

The soldier waved the rifle threateningly. "Stay."

Jim glanced around like a frightened chicken. Everyone was looking at him.

"Look, I need to speak to your officer in private," he said, trying to keep his voice low. "I can help you."

"How help?" asked the guard.

Again Jim looked round frantically, as if hoping for a way to escape.

"I can help," he said. "I know what you're looking for."

"The bastard's a damned collaborator!" exclaimed Bill.

"Give!" demanded the soldier, holding out his hand.

"I want protection from this lot first," Jim said, his confidence coming back a little now that he had burned his bridges.

"Give," insisted the Valtegan.

Jim shook his head. "Oh, no, I want my . . ."

The rest of his sentence was strangled as the officer turned and reached out, grabbing him by the throat and lifting him half a meter into the air.

"So, you have all the time," hissed the officer, giving Jim a slight shake. "Waste our time. Give now!"

Jim, turning a distinct shade of blue, scrabbled at his right hand trouser pocket and drew out a small translucent cube.

Letting his gun swing free, the Valtegan took the object from him and examined it perfunctorily.

"Why we don't get sooner?"

"I'd gotten it back for you, I just hadn't had time to hand it over." His voice was hoarse and barely audible as he tried to hang onto the Valtegan's arm. "I'll be quicker next time!"

"No next time," hissed the Valtegan. "You no use now."

He tightened his grip, nonretractable claws pressing sharp tips into the man's throat.

Jim scrabbled frantically at the clawed hand, trying to prize it open, but inexorably it closed.

The claws punctured his throat, sending blood flowing down the Valtegan's hand and arm. The man twitched several times before his head lolled limply and he hung in midair like a broken doll.

"Messy," hissed the Valtegan with distaste before opening his hand and casting the body to one side. Blood splattered around the room.

With a sharp word in his own language, he turned and walked out of the Inn, the other three soldiers following him.

"Get the women out of here," said Carrie's father, breaking the horrified silence.

She could taste the metallic smell of blood in her mouth.

"Blood follows me around," she said dazedly to Richard as he took her by the arm and pulled her toward their private quarters. "Tell me it's only a nightmare and that soon I'll wake up," she pleaded, stumbling after him.

"God knows, I wish I could, love," he said, keeping the door open for Kusac to follow them. "I'm afraid it's all too real and there is no escape."

About an hour later Richard came up to her room. He found her lying hunched up on her bed.

"Come on, love," he said, putting an arm around her shoulders and helping her to sit up.

"Everyone's gone now. Dad wants us in his office."

Their father got up from his desk as they entered. His usually somber face was lit with something akin to excitement. He was a good man, but one rarely given to showing his emotions.

"One of our contacts from Seaport was at the Inn tonight. I managed to get some information from him regarding the object the Valtegans were looking for.

"Apparently they did shoot down an Alien craft. It was a light scouter, large enough to carry about eight people—given our morphology. When they reached the crash site, the Valtegans found the scouter on fire, but they suspect that several of the crew managed to escape."

"Do they know what the crew looked like?" asked Richard, escorting Carrie to a chair.

"No. The fire virtually gutted the craft. Any bodies were too charred to be of use, but they did find that crystal cube amongst the wreckage. I want to know what it's for."

Carrie began to come to life again as she felt a faint wave of relief from her friend.

"Did our contact have this information verified?" she asked.

"Not all of it," her father admitted, "but the guerrillas were able to piece it together from what they did find out, and they did have the cube for a few days."

"What exactly did they see?"

"Their precise words aren't important," said her father irritably. "What matters is that there are Aliens."

"Has anyone actually seen either the wreck or these Aliens?" insisted Carrie.

"Yes, they've seen the wreck!" snapped her father. "Really, Carrie, you're in a strange mood! I know that business in there was traumatic for you, but it's affected us all. What's got into you?"

"She's tired, Dad. That . . . business took a lot out of her," said Richard placatingly.

"In that case you had better go to bed and rest now. I want you at your best for tomorrow evening. I've invited someone over for dinner."

"What about the new Aliens?" asked Richard hastily, seeing that Carrie was about to speak again.

"Oh, yes. We must get to them first. If they came in a scouter, it couldn't have come far, so they must have a Mothership. I'm assuming the survivors will have some way of contacting their people, and if we help them, they might return the favor by sending a message to Earth.

"They may even help us against the Valtegans. Unless we can do something to rid the planet of them, we must stop that colony ship before it reaches midpoint. Can you imagine the catastrophic effect of our technology, scientists, engineers, and such falling into Valtegan hands?"

"What do you want us to do?" Richard inquired.

"Our agent is officially courting a girl here so he can't leave for a day or two. Get some pigeons sent with coded messages to the agents in the other towns. Tell them to contact the other members of our group and get them to keep their eyes and ears open for anything resembling another species of Aliens. Tell them to be careful. They're to report anything out of the ordinary to you or me. I also want a message about what's happened tonight sent to our contact in Seaport.

"You'd better get started now," he ordered.

"All right," said Richard. "I don't suppose you have the slightest idea of what these Aliens look like, do you?"

"None. But since the Valtegans are humanoid, I expect they're likely to be the same. The bodies were apparently bilateral."

When her brother had left, Carrie got to her feet. "Did you ask about Elise?"

A shadow crossed her father's face and he turned away from her. "Yes. They said they had already disposed of her body.

"Go and rest, Carrie. You shouldn't have been working in the taproom. It's my fault. I shouldn't have asked you. Next week when you're stronger, you can start teaching the children again. Until then, I want you to take things easy."

"But, Dad!" exclaimed Carrie, taking a step toward him. "I'm fine now, really I am."

"Carrie, for God's sake, go and rest!" her father said, turning angrily on her. "Will you do things my way for a change? First your mother, then Elise. I don't want to lose any more of my family. If I hadn't let myself be persuaded to allow Elise to do a Mata Hari act with the Valtegans, she would be with us now.

"You aren't a strong person, Carrie," he said, gripping her by the arms and speaking in a quieter voice. "Your health has never been good. Will you please me and go and lie down?"

Carrie sighed mentally. Now her father had a new form of moral blackmail to use against her. Reluctantly, she nodded her head and her father released her.

"Good. Off you go, then. I'll send Meg up with a hot drink for you."

She left the office and returned to her room. She felt sorry for her father, trying to run the Inn under these extreme circumstances, but even sorrier for herself. Life on Keiss was an impossible situation for an unmarried girl of her age who was dependent on her father. Add to that the fact that she was known to be "different," now that she was being seen as the next thing to the village witch, finding a suitable man prepared to have her would be difficult, to say the least.

Of the three or four young men interested in her, none had visited her or even inquired after her while she was still bedridden except for David and she wanted nothing to do with him. Who wanted to run the risk of what these good people considered "bad blood" in their family?

Not that she wanted to marry. Only the women strong enough to join the guerrillas were free from their duties of producing the colony's next generation. It was an option to consider, possibly her only one.

Chapter 4

Carrie lounged back in the chair, heaving a sigh of genuine relief as she pulled the cigarettes out of her pocket and lit one, inhaling deeply. Thank God, her first day was over. Her class had just left, homeward bound for their afternoon chores. Once more she was her own mistress. The job, her contribution to the Resistance movement, was no sinecure. Although the class numbered only twenty, they ranged in age from five to fifteen. After that, any further education was gained by being apprenticed to one of the trades within their settlement. Academic education was, for now, a luxury on Keiss. Survival in Valleytown depended on the more basic skills of farming and animal husbandry, although some technical skills were needed. Consequently, the children spent only a few hours every day with her.

The Valtegans opposed even this, with the result that the classes were conducted in secret. Carrie's extra sense had always told her when any Valtegans had been in the vicinity of the Community Hall, so as yet she had not been discovered.

She looked idly across the hall: there was no sign that it had recently been a classroom. Officially she was running a crèche, watching the younger children with the help of the older ones, while their parents were busy in the fields. Her glance strayed to where Kusac lay basking in a pool of sunlight. His eyes flickered open and regarded her lazily for a few moments before drooping closed again.

He had surprised everyone but her, she thought, smiling to herself. From the start he had been friendly and docile and except for the odd foray about the valley, he hardly left her side. Reluctantly, her father had given in and allowed him to continue living in the house.

She sat up abruptly, sensing someone approaching. She groaned, disturbing Kusac. It would have to be David Elliot!

She had tried to make it clear that she wasn't interested in him but her father would keep inviting him to call on them for dinner. Short of ordering her to accept David's advances, he had done everything in his power to encourage a match between them.

David owned the timber yards and bringing him into the family would be to their advantage. He was also wealthy enough to have several men working for him, so she would never be expected to do any of the hard manual work for which her father insisted she wasn't made.

"Racehorses aren't built like Clydesdales," he kept telling her.

The arrival of the Valtegans, plus the two pleasure centers which had mushroomed up near Seaport and Oceanview, had disrupted the lives of many of the Terran colonists, creating a small floating population comprised mainly of younger people filled with resentment. Colonists living near the sites of the centers had been dispossessed of their land and had drifted northward, unwilling to settle down permanently again. It was these people that David and some of the others in the valley employed. The more militant youths had joined bands in the forests under the command of the Captain and the remaining crew of the *Eureka*. They harried the enemy in any way they could, making guerrilla sorties on their outposts.

The door swung open and David poked his head into the hall.

"Hello, Carrie. Thought I'd come and see if you were finished."

"They've just left," she replied, getting to her feet and lifting her jacket from a nearby chair.

"I'll see you back to the house, then. There's a Valtegan patrol in the town today. It's not a good idea for you to walk back alone." He held the door open imperiously for her.

"It isn't very far, David. I can manage fine by myself," she said, walking past him and into the corridor.

David hurriedly caught up with her and frowned at Kusac as the cat padded silently between them.

"Can't you leave that animal at home? I don't like him; he unsettles me."

"Kusac is as free to come and go as you. If you want to see me back to the Inn, you'll have to put up with him, too," she replied shortly, pushing the outer door open.

"Isn't it time you got rid of him? He looks perfectly fit to me. You can't have him trailing after you for the rest of his life."

"I'm not going to get rid of Kusac to please you, David, so you had better get used to that," Carrie said, stopping to glower at him. "If you think we look ridiculous, why do you bother being seen with us?"

"Don't be silly, Carrie," chided David, moving round to her other side and taking her by the arm. "Besides, you're drawing attention to yourself." He nodded vaguely in the direction of a squad of Valtegans nearby. "I don't know how you'd manage without me around to keep you from getting into scrapes."

"I coped well enough before I met you," she muttered, allowing herself to be led past the interested Aliens. "Kusac gives me all the protection I need. The Valtegans don't like him either."

"That's as may be, but you know their attitude toward women, especially one as beautiful as you. Their very presence is a threat. You need to be accompanied when they are around. You are too independent at times for your own good."

Again Carrie stopped. She was seething. He really was too much!

"Don't get me wrong," he continued, unaware of her anger, "I value your independent streak, but sometimes you don't act in a completely rational fashion. I was going to mention it before now, but I was sure it was only a phase." He smiled at her. "With the right kind of guidance and responsibility you'll grow out of it."

"And you think you can do this?" she asked quietly.

"I could if you gave me a chance," he admitted. "You've got the makings of an ideal wife, once you've settled down."

Speechless, Carrie stared at him as if seeing him properly for the first time. His face reminded her of some animal, with its long, pointed chin and small dark eyes. A ferret, that was it! As for modesty, it was not one of his weaknesses. He was only too aware of his own worth as he saw it.

"Not for you, David," she said finally, shaking her arm free. "You don't want a wife, you only want a pliant female to mold in your own image."

"You're still young and want your freedom for a while longer. I appreciate that, and I'm prepared to wait for a few more months." He reached out for her again but found Kusac standing between them.

Carrie took advantage of the opportunity and moved quietly away from him.

"Good-bye, David. I'll manage the rest of the way on my own," she said over her shoulder.

"Damned animal," David swore, aiming a kick at Kusac and just missing him. He badly wanted this alliance with Carrie's family. Her father was respected by everyone in the town and her dowry would be generous, and useful, considering the expansion he planned for the paper mill. Besides, she was not an unattractive girl.

One way or another he'd get her. Since that business of her sister's death, all the other men—far too young for her anyway—had backed off, leaving him as her only suitor. Superstitious fools that they were! Still, their stupidity was his gain.

If he went to the Town Council and pressed his suit, they'd agree to it without question since she was a couple of years past marriageable age already. In fact, maybe just dropping a hint to her father that he was prepared to do that would be enough.

A slow grin spread across his face. Why not do it now, while the idea was fresh in his mind? Peter Hamilton would be alone in his greenhouses at this time of day. He crossed over the main street to the Inn, whistling a jaunty little tune, well pleased with his strategy.

Carrie stormed into the kitchen, coming to rest beside the table.

"That man!" she hissed at Meg, "he gets more arrogant and overbearing every day!"

Meg looked up from the list of foodstuffs she was compiling.

"Had another row with David, then?" she asked sympathetically.

"Row? You can't argue with a man who believes he's God's gift to women!" Carrie muttered, taking her coat off and flinging it in the general direction of the pegs by the door.

"He's not a bad man, Carrie. He's got many good qualities. You could do a lot worse, you know."

"Not you, too," exclaimed the thoroughly exasperated girl. "You're as bad as Father. He can't wait to get me married off either."

"No one is trying to force you to marry him. It's only that he can offer you a way of life that none of the younger men can. You aren't strong enough to work in the fields despite what you think," admonished the older woman.

"Your father only wants to make sure you're settled with someone who will look after you properly. You've got to marry, you know. You're past the age set by the Council. If you don't choose soon, they'll choose for you."

"There's far more to life than just marriage, and if that was what I wanted, I wouldn't choose David Elliot! I came all the way from Earth to Keiss for what? To lead a more restricted life here than I did there?" She shook her head. "No, Meg, I want more than that. If all of you don't stop going hysterical whenever I sneeze, and don't stop pushing me into a marriage I don't want, I'm going to leave here. There are other settlements, you know. I want to do something worthwhile with my life."

"Really, Carrie," chided Meg, getting up. "There's no need to be so melodramatic. You're beginning to sound like your sister! Marriage is a very worthwhile occupation for a woman, and you'll not find it any different in the other settlements. We lost too many people in the Crossing. We need a new generation of children now if we are to survive on Keiss."

"Survival isn't enough. I want something for me, Meg, and I don't mean marriage and children."

"What sort of thing did you have in mind?" Meg asked.

"I fancy working with Jack, studying the animal life. He's got some field trips planned which sound as though they might be quite interesting."

"I don't know about the field trips," replied Meg, going over to the stove to put on the kettle. "If I were you, I'd take one thing at a time. You were a very sickly child, always ill, and you seemed to take everything more severely than the other children."

"You're only going on hearsay!" exclaimed Carrie. "Didn't anyone think to tell you that half my illnesses were Elise's? They didn't, did they? They only told you what they wanted you to believe. I'm tired of being told I'm a chronic invalid. I'm as healthy as anyone else in this bloody valley!"

Beside herself with rage, Carrie rushed out of the kitchen and upstairs to her own room, Kusac bounding after her.

The door firmly shut behind her, she strode over to her clothes cupboard and began hauling out a couple of changes of clothing and footwear.

Kusac, crouching near the door, watched her with growing apprehension. Since he had begun teaching her how to use her Talent, he had found his mind linked permanently to hers in a light rapport. Because of this, he had been aware for some time of her growing anger with the restrictions her father and the community were putting on her life. He also knew she had been working herself up to a pitch where she would leave the valley, and it looked as if that time had arrived.

This fitted in with his long-term plans. He had been prepared to risk telling her that he was her teacher but only because he needed her help. He knew he could trust her. Her family, however, was another matter. They couldn't see beyond their own problems with the Valtegans and would only hold him back at this stage of his search. Once they were free of the settlement there would be time enough for her to meet her first Sholan. If only she would wait a little longer.

It's too soon, he thought, reaching for her. *Wait for a week, a few days even.*

I've waited too long already, came the tart rejoinder as he was thrust firmly out of her mind.

Reeling back on his haunches with the force of her rebuttal, he watched helplessly as she tucked the legs of her trousers into the tops of her boots.

Getting to her feet, Carrie went over to the door and opened it, peering cautiously into the corridor. It was empty.

"Wait here, Kusac," she whispered, stepping outside and closing the door behind her.

Kusac sat down again. "If only she would stay another couple of days," he muttered. He would rather have waited until his leg was completely healed before going in search of his fellow Sholans from the *Sirroki*. His limp wasn't painful, but he knew from his forays around the valley that apart from slowing him down, it would make him tire more quickly.

Carrie returned a couple of minutes later with her brother's rucksack tucked under her arm. Luckily, she'd seen it squashed into a closet in the hall a couple of days before. Dumping it onto the bed, she unbuckled it and began to check over its contents. It still contained much of the standard issue from one of Jack's field trips that Richard had been on. There was a stove and some of the small solar cell batteries that fueled it, a pan, eating utensils, a couple of lightweight insulated blankets, a basic medical kit, and some dehydrated packs of food.

"I hope you can hunt for both of us, Kusac," she said wryly as she shoved everything back into the rucksack and began ramming her clothes and spare boots in on top.

That done, she pulled a knife out of one of the side pockets and, loosening her belt, threaded the sheath onto it. Fastening the buckle, she settled the knife over her right hip.

From the wardrobe she brought out her thick winter parka and slipped it on. Taking a last look around the room to make sure she hadn't forgotten anything important, she picked up the rucksack and moved over to the door.

"Come on, Kusac," she said, checking the corridor once again, "we're leaving."

Stopping outside her brother's room, she gently probed it to see if he had returned, but it still felt empty. Unlike hers, his window looked onto the fields at the back of the house.

Not quite accustomed to trusting her Talent yet, she opened the door warily, taking a good look round before she stepped inside and went over to the window. Releasing the catch, she pushed it open and leaned out to see if there was anyone at the back of the house. When she was sure there was no one about, she lifted the rucksack up, balancing it on the sill. To the left, just below the window, lay a pile of sacks. That was ideal: it would break the rucksack's fall, and among sacks of the same color, it was unlikely to be noticed. Heaving it over the edge, she let it dangle at arm's length before swinging it toward the sacks. She let it go, and with a faint whump it landed right on target.

Shutting the window, she turned back to Kusac.

"Okay, old fellow," she said, "it's our turn."

Carrie made her way back downstairs to the now deserted kitchen. Taking advantage of the opportunity, she rummaged around in the pantry, emerging with a small package of food and coffee which she stowed in her pockets.

She had just moved toward the outer door when she heard Meg come into the room.

"Ah, Carrie, I'm glad I caught you before you left. Jack Reynolds is in the lounge waiting to see you."

Carrie hesitated, torn between a desire to go now while she had the courage to leave and the fear of drawing attention to herself by acting out of character.

"On you go," urged Meg, going over to the sink to fill the coffeepot. "I'll bring some coffee and biscuits in to you."

Balked, she went into the lounge, Kusac following.

Do not project your mood, came the gentle warning.

"Hello, Jack," she said, trying hard to tone down her frustration.

"Hello, my dear. Did I catch you as you were going out?" he asked, standing up as she entered the room. "Sorry about that, but I won't take up much of your time. I just wanted to check up on my two favorite patients."

"It's all right. Please, sit down," she said, taking off her jacket and sitting down on the settee opposite him.

"Let's start with Kusac," he said, moving over to where the cat sat at her side.

"Stand up, there's a good fellow," he said, stroking him between the ears.

Kusac obliged.

Jack felt down both his rear flanks, checking the hip and knee mobility, comparing the sound leg with the injured one.

"He's a bit stiff, but that should pass. I must admit I'm impressed at how fast he's healed, almost as if he's had some help," he said, giving her a sidelong look.

Carrie shrugged. "Don't look at me," she said. "I know nothing about healing."

"Hm," was all he said as turned to her. "Let's see your hands, then."

Carrie held them out for Jack to take and examine. Normally she disliked being touched by anyone except her immediate family, but Jack was different. His touch didn't make her uneasy, didn't feel like he was taking a personal liberty with her.

Jack studied her fingernails carefully. The new nails were already halfway up the fingers and were perfectly formed with none of the creases or bumps in them that he would have expected. He released her.

"How about the scars?"

Carrie pushed up her shirtsleeve. There was the faintest of

pink lines running upward from her elbow to disappear under the rolled up sweater.

"They're all like that," she said.

"There's not a lot I can say, is there? Obviously there is going to be little if any scarring, and your hands are perfect, my dear," he said, getting back to his feet and returning to his chair.

Carrie dug into her jacket pocket for her cigarettes and offered one to Jack.

"Thank you," he said, lighting up. "You know, I think last year's tobacco crop was the best so far."

There was a gentle knock on the door and Meg came in bearing a tray with a plate of biscuits and two mugs of coffee. She handed it to Carrie then left.

Now that she was calmer, Carrie could sense Jack's uneasiness. As she handed him his coffee and offered him a biscuit, she relaxed further, carefully letting her mind match his as she had been shown how to do with the Valtegan, and tuned in to his surface thoughts. He wanted to ask her some more questions about her link with Elise, that was why he was concerned about not upsetting her.

Her sense of humor reasserted itself.

"What do you want to ask me about Elise, Jack?"

Jack looked faintly startled.

"You've changed since your sister died," he said abruptly. "I must admit I expected your strange talents to disappear, but they haven't. In fact, they've increased.

"You'll have to take care, Carrie. They're talking about you in town. We may be civilized, but out here on this frontier world, superstition takes over, often overwhelming science and logic."

Carrie looked down at her hands.

"Sorry," she mumbled.

"Oh, it doesn't bother me. I know there is a rational explanation for what you do, and one day I intend to find it, with your help. Just, for God's sake, don't play your games with the townspeople. You frighten them, and frightened people can be dangerous."

"All right, Jack," she said, looking back up at him. "What is it you want to know?"

"We thought that this link with your sister was mainly telepathic, and only with her, so how come you now seem to be able to pick up other people's thoughts?"

"I could only sense Elise, but she was able to reach one of the guerrillas—a girl called Jo, I think—and send her the information she gathered in Geshader.

"No," she said, forestalling his question, "Jo isn't a telepath as far as I know, she only got vague images from my sister which she interpreted as hunches or intuition. Elise said Jo was never sure what came from her and what she had worked out for herself. If I remember rightly, Jo was the *Eureka*'s linguist.

"I don't know why I could only pick up my twin. Perhaps the link with Elise was so strong that it drowned out everyone else."

Kusac tuned out their conversation, focusing his attention on the fact that Carrie's sister had been in contact, albeit a very primitive contact, with one of the guerrillas. This could prove to be useful at a later date.

He had to find his crew mates. He knew that before they had left him they had said they were heading for the life pod that they'd tracked down to the forested region not far from Valleytown.

He didn't know how much exposure they'd had to the Valtegans, but it was obvious to him that this was the species for whom his people had been searching. It was even more vital that he reach the rest of his team now that he knew their computer crystal was in Valtegan hands.

His attention was abruptly pulled back to the girl as he felt her need to tell this man of her new link. Icy cold fear washed through him and, with no time for subtlety, he sent a negative command to her.

Carrie suddenly found herself unable to talk or move. His fear began to resonate along with hers and sheer terror gripped her.

Swiftly he took control, damping her emotions and searching for her short-term memory. He lifted the thought of telling Jack from her mind and backed out, gradually returning control to her.

Confused, Carrie suddenly found herself feeling light-headed and swayed a little in her seat.

"Are you all right?" Jack asked, reaching forward to steady her.

"Yes. Yes, I'm fine, honestly," she said, rubbing her eyes in an effort to clear her vision.

"I think I've overtaxed you," he said. "We'll leave it at that for today."

The door opened and her father came in. He looked angry and determined.

"Afternoon, Jack," he said, standing in the open doorway. "Carrie, I've just had a visit from David Elliot. Yes, well may you groan," he said tartly. "Unless you accept his proposal, he intends to go to the Town Council to have you allocated to him as his wife. I'll have no daughter of mine go through the indignity of a Council Marriage Hearing. I've assured him you will accept, so get used to the idea that you'll be married within the month." With that, he left.

Carrie sat stunned, unable to think of anything to say.

"David Elliot?" said Jack. "Surely you can find someone younger and better than him."

"Ah, well, you said it yourself, Jack. I frighten everyone else off. I don't exactly have any choice now," she said slowly, picking her coat up. "Will you excuse me? I think I need to go for a long walk."

"Yes, of course," said Jack. "Look, don't go doing anything foolish now."

Carrie flashed him a smile. "Who, me? No, I promise I won't do anything stupid, Jack. You have my word on it."

"Going out now?" Meg asked as Carrie walked through the kitchen to the door.

"Yes, I'm taking Kusac for a walk," said Carrie, reaching for the latch.

"There's no need to be on the defensive with me, Carrie," Meg replied mildly. "I'm not going to try to stop you. Don't go far from the settlement, though. There are a lot of Valtegans around today." Meg frowned briefly. "Are you sure that jacket's necessary, child? You're going to be boiled alive in this weather."

"Yes," said Carrie firmly, stepping into the yard and waiting for Kusac to follow her. "It may turn chilly later on."

Meg shrugged and turned away to get on with her work.

Carrie pulled the door closed behind her, leaning weakly against it for a moment, trying to control her jangling nerves. Now she had no option but to leave home. The knot in her stomach refused to relax and her throat felt tight with fear. Straightening up, she looked over to where Richard's rucksack lay a few meters distant.

She reached out for Kusac's mind, wishing as she did so that there was something beyond the normal animal thought patterns there. He was the only being, other than her tutor, on whom she dared to try out her increasing new abilities, and on him they did not exactly have a marked effect. Sometimes she could induce him to move in specified directions, but not very often. She hoped that now might be one of those times. If he would only move toward the sacks, she would have a legitimate reason for going over to them in case anyone was watching.

Come on, Kusac, she urged him mentally.

Stiffly, Kusac jerked to his feet, a slightly astonished look on his face. Carrie sighed with relief as he walked over to the rucksack, his movements seeming stilted to her because she knew him so well.

"Good boy!" she murmured, releasing him from her control before she ran over to grab the pack. Clutching it tightly against her chest, she urged Kusac on ahead of her.

As she made her way through the fields toward the river, she realized that she had not yet decided where she was going. There was only one reasonable option open to her; head for the forest and try to join one of the guerrilla bands that roamed there. Perhaps she could meet up with this linguist Jo.

Damn her father, damn David, and damn Meg! Why had they made it impossible for her to stay at home? Any one of them could have helped to make life bearable for her, but instead they treated her like some fragile semi-invalid, cosseting and protecting her from the harsh everyday world until she had almost come to believe they were right. And now she was to be sold off to the only bidder in the cattle market called marriage.

She stopped abruptly, seeing the bridge ahead of her. Once she crossed it, she was on her way out of the valley. To the west, across the slopes of the Plateau Hills, lay the nearest settlement, but another settlement wasn't what she wanted.

Defiantly, she stamped over the bridge and headed north to the forest. The guerrillas were another matter. Whereas her father's underground movement worked passively, cajoling and bribing information out of the Valtegans, the Terran

outlaws used aggression as their main tool. They existed in
a state of undeclared war with the Valtegans, harassing their
off duty troops and the permanent garrison alike, both in and
out of the main pleasure cities of Geshader and Tashkerra.
Being fighters, they weren't dedicated to perpetuating man-
kind, just to protecting it. They couldn't afford to be altruistic being so short on numbers. Every able-bodied person,
male or female, was expected to fight. Yes, it had to be the
guerrillas. Even her father couldn't request that they send
her back!

Kusac plodded gamely along beside her. He wasn't finding the going too difficult at the moment, but he suspected
it might become worse as time went on. His hip joint didn't
feel as flexible as it should, but that was probably just stiffness as the Terran medic had said. Anyway, he was trying
not to favor it.

Now that they were well on their way, he could afford to
relax his vigilance a little. He thanked Vartra again that the
girl had been too angry to notice his gentle molding of her
resolve. Had she not been so distracted, he had his doubts as
to whether or not he would have been able to influence her
at all. Her mind was becoming so much stronger these days.
When she "told" him to go over to the rucksack in the garden, he had instinctively tried to block the order. Against his
will, however, he had responded. Of course, she thought him
merely an animal not a sentient person and had been totally
unsubtle in her command, but it didn't change the fact that
it was the first time in his life that anyone had controlled his
thoughts or actions.

Could her Talent be greater than his? Only Vartra knew.
He sighed, dismissing the thought almost as it formed. That
was unimportant, but it did matter that Carrie soon learn the
code of ethics that went along with possessing a Talent.

Dusk was fast approaching when they reached the edge of
the forest. Carrie slowed to a stop as she looked at the mass
of trees ahead of her. In the half light, their tall dark boles
looked somber and menacing. Among them waited many
dangers, the least of which was the forest cats. The tales she
had heard of creatures in this part of the valley didn't bear
remembering. She groaned and, shutting her eyes briefly,
gave her head a little shake to dispel the phantoms that
seemed to lurch out at her from every dark shadow. She

opened her eyes again and found that everything had returned to normal. Kusac and she were alone amid the sea of dark towering trees. Determinedly, she suppressed even these thoughts. A vivid imagination was definitely not an advantage on a trip like this. At least she wasn't alone. With Kusac for company, she should be safe enough, especially from forest cats. Reaching out, she put her hand on his collar and began walking toward the nearest trees.

The ground underfoot was soft and spongy, a carpet of decaying leaves. Soon they would have to stop for the night. Carrie felt in her pockets for the torch she had brought with her. Dragging it out, she switched it on and swept the beam around her, looking for some dry ground on which to camp. The light picked out the trunk of a huge evergreen only a few meters away. Its massive spread of branches had protected the ground about its base from even the worst of the spring rains and when Carrie went over to it, she found the pile of needles surrounding it quite dry.

She shrugged her arms out of the straps of her rucksack and lowered it to the ground. With a sigh of relief, she stretched her shoulders, kneading the sore spots gently with her hands. Although the rucksack had seemed light enough when she left, for the last couple of hours it had felt as if she had been carrying a ton. She was not used to walking any distance either, she thought ruefully, giving her aching calves a good rub before calling Kusac over.

"Food, Kusac. Go and catch food," she said, taking his face between her hands. She tried to project into his mind the picture of one of the rabbitlike creatures that abounded on the planet.

"Hunt," she said, bringing the image of him chasing the creature into her scenario. "Fetch food." She released him, hoping that her earlier success would be repeated.

It was. Kusac had picked up the message loud and clear. Carrie was no longer a pupil; she had learned how to utilize her Talent, and was now beginning to exploit it—and him—to the full.

Kusac moved a few meters away and began to sniff the air near the ground. Picking up a scent easily, he loped off, quite enjoying the opportunity for a little night hunting.

His fears over his leg had proved to be unfounded. The slight stiffness he had experienced was probably due to lack of proper exercise. He was ready now to begin his search for

the rest of the scout ship's crew. At least he knew where
they would have been heading. The life pod, dropped by the
first survey team as a matter of course, had landed somewhere in the swamps ahead of them. That much they had all
learned before they had been attacked by the battle cruiser
orbiting the planet. His crew mates would definitely make
for there if they were still alive.

Aboard the pod was a transmitter capable of sending a
message directly to their Mothership. Within a few days, a
rescue mission would be on its way. But judging by the lack
of activity among the Valtegans, his crew mates had not yet
reached the pod and sent the message. This worried him. By
the same token, they had not been captured.

The Valtegans' discovery of their computer cube was a
bitter blow. Were they able to access its information, they
would have a map of not only their search area, but the
Sholans' home planet as well. He needed to get that information to Captain Garras as soon as possible.

Tomorrow would settle some of his worries. He would
have to tell Carrie who he was before they broke camp,
which would be no easy task, but he needed her help to
guide him through the swamp. Then, when they found the
rest of the crew, she could tell the Captain what message
she wanted sent to her home planet. They could do that for
the Terrans, if nothing else.

Kusac ducked quickly behind a low bush. In a small clearing ahead of him grazed several of the little rabbit creatures.
He tensed, then sprang. A split second later a scream of terror sent the animals rushing for cover. Kusac's mind seemed
to explode with the sound.

Help me, Kusac! The cry vibrated inside his skull, catching him in mid-leap and felling him like a stone.

He lay there, stunned for a moment by the force of her
call.

Coming, he replied briefly, trying to ignore the buzzing in
his head as he got to his feet and began making his way
swiftly back to the camp.

What kind of danger? he demanded, tightening his link
with her as he sensed her thoughts becoming incoherent with
terror.

Valtegans!

He tuned into her mind instantly, seeing her backed
against a tree, ringed by four Valtegans.

"How you live?" hissed their officer, taking her face roughly in his hand and turning it. "We kill you. I know."

"Kill again," said another, "but later."

"*You* killed her," whispered Carrie, her hand going up to catch his wrist. The physical contact let her feel his mind. "And you enjoyed doing it, you bastard!" Her other hand came up in a roundhouse, catching him on the side of the face.

The Valtegan reeled, stunned by the unexpectedness of her blow.

Moments later Kusac erupted into the clearing, his face a snarling mask of fury.

One hand, claws fully extended, lashed out at the nearest Valtegan, raking deep furrows across his chest and flinging him to the other side of the clearing. With a sickening thud, the body caromed off the trunk of a nearby tree to fall in an untidy heap at its base. The others released Carrie, who slid bonelessly to the ground, and began backing away, reaching for their guns.

With a deep-throated growl, Kusac rose to his feet and lunged at the first, hitting him a massive blow on the head. There was a sharp crack and the soldier collapsed.

Pain seared across Kusac's forearm as one of the energy weapons went off. A killing rage took hold of him and, leaping forward, he landed between them.

When reason returned, he stood alone in the center of a devastated clearing. At his feet lay two bodies. Carefully he nudged one with his foot but when he saw the head lolling at an impossible angle, he let it roll back into place.

Leaving Carrie where she had fallen, he checked the other three Valtegans. They were all dead. Good. When he had seen to her, he would drag them off into the forest and bury them somewhere.

His body began to tremble as reaction set in and he sat down hurriedly before his legs gave way beneath him. He had never killed a person before; animals, yes, but neither that nor his training had prepared him for the reality of taking a sentient's life. His anger had helped but, Vartra knew, it had been justified. They had killed Elise and dared to lay their filthy hands on his Leska!

He stopped, taken aback by his use of the term. It happened sometimes among his kind that a male and a female were linked through their Talent by an indissoluble bond, but that this bond could exist between two Alien races was just not possible! They were too different, surely. Yet there must be more similarities between them than he had guessed to make him even think that she was his Leska. No, it was just not possible.

The smell of hot coffee brought Carrie back to consciousness again. Remembering the Valtegans, she remained perfectly still. Hardly daring to breathe, she opened her eyes fractionally and, peering through her eyelashes, discovered she was lying beside a small camp fire. On the other side, not quite obscured by the flames, sat Kusac.

"Very sensible," he said, reaching for the mug and pouring some coffee into it. "But your caution is not necessary. I have dealt with the soldiers. Come, have some coffee. I've already drunk some and it doesn't taste too bad. It has a pleasantly euphoric effect, in fact."

Carrie sat up and reached for the mug that Kusac was holding out to her. Cupping her hands around it, she took a careful drink, keeping her gaze warily on him all the time.

"I should have guessed," she said quietly.

"I think you did on a subconscious level," he replied, raking in the fire with a long stick until he had pulled out two largish brown objects.

"I managed to catch some food as you suggested." His amber eyes narrowed slightly in amusement as he glanced up at her.

Carrie shifted uncomfortably, acutely aware of the amused overtones of Kusac's thoughts.

His mouth widened in his equivalent of a grin, and pulling the plate out of the rucksack beside him, he began to break open one of the objects before him. The outer casing of baked mud broke away easily, filling the air with the aroma of roast meat. Kusac dropped the meat onto the plate and began chipping away at the second rabbit's casing.

"You only brought one plate," he said, his tone slightly wistful, "so I am afraid we will have to share."

Images of Kusac tearing into the camp and laying into the Valtegans with massive and deadly paws drifted through Carrie's mind, to be firmly banished as she got to her feet and moved round the fire to sit beside him. A friend could not be rejected because of fears over the way he had protected your life.

Kusac felt an easing of the tension within him. She was not afraid! Their relationship must change, he was aware of that, but, thank Vartra, the girl did not fear him. He needed her help and cooperation, and for that she must also trust him.

"Be careful," he warned, seeing her about to reach for the meat. "It's hot, even for me."

Carrie nodded and lifted a piece of meat gingerly, blowing on it before popping it into her mouth. It tasted wonderful, the best she had ever eaten. With all the upsets and alarms she had been through today, she was ravenous. She reached for another piece, accidentally touching Kusac as she did so. Starting slightly, she stared at his paw, recognizing for the first time that it was a hand not unlike her own.

She looked at his face, realizing that it was not the cat's face she had always seen before, but one more nearly resembling her own people's.

Feeling her surprise, Kusac turned his hand over so she could see the palm and held it out to her.

"Fingers make life a lot easier, don't they?" he said, his voice almost purring with amusement.

Carrie looked down again and reached out to turn Kusac's hand back over. At the end of each finger, almost buried in the thick black fur, was a sharp, horny nail.

"We still use the natural weapons that Vartra gave us," he said, trying unsuccessfully to read the emotions which fluttered, half-formed, through her mind and across her face.

Her people appeared to be peaceful apart from the guerrillas, and the thought of allying themselves to a race with powerful natural weapons such as those of the Sholans might well be distasteful to them.

"Vartra?" she asked, letting go of his hand and smiling quizzically up at him.

"Our Creator and Protector," he replied, remembering his relief when he had discovered the Terrans were not a Godless race.

"Why have I never noticed your hands before?" she asked, picking up another piece of meat. "Or your face? Have you been disguising them with your Talent, the way I do when Valtegans are about?"

"It seems I have picked up a few ideas from you, but I have never needed to disguise myself much," replied Kusac. "Since I came to this planet, for one reason or another I have been restricted to moving about on all fours. I usually only travel that way when I need the extra speed. To do this, I have to retract my fingers like so," he demonstrated, and, like a cat sheathing its claws, his fingers disappeared within the thick fur. "That way I only run on the palms of my hands, which are fairly insensitive. Normally I walk upright like you.

"When my leg began to heal enough for me to move without too much pain, one of the first things I did was to hunt down one of the forest cats. I soon discovered why you thought I was one of them."

Carrie nodded thoughtfully, taking a drink from her mug of coffee.

"You looked similar to a forest cat, but your behavior, especially that first day, was more like that of a pet cat I once had on Earth. In fact, almost identical to his." She stared accusingly at him over the rim of the mug.

Kusac shrugged. "I have to admit that when you found me, I read your thoughts and quite shamelessly behaved according to what you expected of me. It wasn't until much later that I realized I was committed to playing the part of a domesticated pet!" He laughed, the sound a low almost crooning purr.

He reached behind him. "I thought you might like this back," he said, handing her the leather collar he had worn.

"Don't embarrass me," she said, flushing as she remembered how unconcerned she had been at his presence in her room. She threw it in the fire.

"Why didn't you tell me sooner who you were?" she demanded.

"For several reasons," he replied, shifting uncomfortably under her accusing glare. "At first I was too ill, then I had to learn your language."

"We've been communicating without words for several weeks."

"If I had told you before now, our relationship would have changed and others would have noticed."

Carrie shook her head. "Not good enough, Kusac. I know when you're holding out on me. I want the truth this time. And while we're at it, what brought you here in the first place? We weren't aware that Keiss had any neighbors, let alone two such different species."

Kusac's tail stopped moving as he looked back at her.

"My home planet, Shola, is not a neighbor of yours, but we did have three colonies in this sector, until the Valtegans attacked and destroyed two of them.

"We knew the nature of these Others from the few dead bodies we found. You call them Valtegans."

Kusac fell silent for a few moments before continuing.

"As soon as reports of the devastation came in from the Captains running the freighter lines, we sent a battleship and escort to investigate. Not one of our people was left alive on either of the two colonies attacked. They had slaughtered every man, woman, and child."

Carrie, her mind strangely open to every nuance of his, knew he was steeling himself as if to receive some rebuttal.

"We are primarily Traders," he continued, "and though we trade with several other species we have never come across the Valtegans before. Not only are they unknown to us, but to our allies also. You are lucky indeed that they did not see fit to exterminate your people as they did us. We desperately need to find out what we can about them as they are a threat to us all."

"You will have to organize some kind of planetary defense fleets for both Shola and your last colony," Carrie said. "So will the other people you trade with. That will take some doing. Meanwhile, you'll need an excellent intelligence service to know exactly where and when the Valtegans show up."

Kusac inclined his head toward her. "We have such a ser vice. I was part of it until our craft was shot down."

"What brought you to Keiss itself?" she asked, setting down her mug.

"Keiss was surveyed some twenty years ago, and when it proved to be capable of supporting our species, a life pod was automatically dropped on the surface. It was to conduct experiments on the biosphere over a period of several years, sending the information to an orbiting satellite which in turn would transmit it to Shola.

"When it suddenly stopped transmitting, nothing was done. We had no reason to suspect anything but a system failure. After the Valtegans struck, a possible relationship was noticed and we were dispatched to find out what had happened.

"Our Mothership, the *Khalossa*, dropped several light scouters in various sectors of space, each on a three-month reconnaissance mission. We had several planets to check in this area, Keiss being our last. Perhaps the boredom of finding nothing made us less observant. Whatever the cause, we failed to notice the presence of the Others until too late." He fell silent.

Carrie stirred slightly, pulling her knees up to her chin and wrapping her arms around them.

"How many of you are left on Keiss?"

"Five of us survived. I have no way of knowing where the others are, but we located the life pod before we crashed, so I presume they have made their way there."

He raised his head, looking her squarely in the face.

"I must go to the pod. Even without my colleagues I can send a message to the *Khalossa* about the Valtegans' presence here."

"I can see that you must," she replied, aware as she did so of a decrease in the stress she had been sensing emanating from him. They had obviously touched upon something Kusac feared, but since he was barricading the thought, and she was respecting his privacy, she had no idea what it was.

"Have you tried to locate your crew mentally?" she asked.

"Yes, but I can't touch their minds. Not all my people are Talented. It is mainly confined to the members of certain families, of which I am one. The rest of the crew were unTalented."

"What about that Valtegan? We read his mind. Perhaps together we could locate your friends."

"It's possible," Kusac replied slowly. "Though with my people the problem is different. The unTalented seem to have a strong natural barrier which prevents contact unless both parties are willing. With the Valtegan, there was no such barrier."

"We could try," she persisted, warming to her theme. "Aren't barriers weakest when one is sleeping? What if we look for the barrier rather than for them? If we tried now, we might succeed."

"It might be possible. With our combined strength we may be able to pick up some faint echo from them."

"So what do we do?"

"Sit comfortably and relax," he said, twisting himself round until he was facing her. He flinched as he moved his left forearm onto his knee.

"What is it?"

"Nothing," he said. "Just a graze. One of the Valtegan energy weapons clipped my arm."

"Let me see," she said, leaning forward to look. The effects of culture shock hit her briefly, scrambling her thoughts for a moment as she saw first an animal's foreleg then an arm almost the same as hers except for the fur.

She gave a short laugh. "We see what we expect, don't we?" she said. "I don't know how I ever thought you were a feline."

"But I am," he said gently. "I'm a feline person."

"You know what I mean," she said. The wound was reasonably deep, but it had been cauterized by the beam of energy from the weapon. It had already begun to scab over.

"It really should have a dressing over it to protect it," she said.

"Later."

Carrie released his arm and moved into a cross-legged posture, letting her hands lie slackly along her thighs.

"Link with me," he said.

Carrie's view of Kusac started to mist, and gradually her field of vision shrank until all she could see were his eyes. She felt light-headed as she sank deeper and deeper into those amber depths. Almost against her will, she felt herself being pulled into a warm, dark whirlpool.

Fear was beyond her, and for what could have been an aeon, she watched the faint flickers of light that pulsed around her.

Carrie? The thought surrounded her. *I cannot reach you.*

She hesitated, momentarily unwilling to venture farther.

Carrie. His tone was gentle, urging.

She reached out for him, letting the final barriers snick open. A tide of Kusac's thoughts and memories flowed over her, threatening to sweep her away. Panicking, she reached out for something to hold on to, but all she touched were images of Kusac's past—his pain and terror when his Talent first manifested itself, the gradual growth of understanding as his father started to train him in its use.

Her terror began to grow as she swirled among these scenes, feeling her control of her own identity begin to slip. She tried to retreat, to retain her individuality, but she had already gone too far. Inexorably she was swept toward him, propelled by instincts and emotions she had not known she possessed.

Carrie.

It was as if a hand had clamped onto her arm, preventing her from being swept to destruction. Now they joined, each experiencing the other in a meshing deeper and more intimate than anything either of them had experienced before. She felt him draw her closer, enfolding and protecting her. His smell, mingled with that of slightly damp fur, enveloped her. He felt warm and soft against her skin. Between them there was a total understanding, a total commitment that nothing, save death, could dissolve.

Leska, now we must find my companions. Strangely, his tone sounded unsteady.

Kusac gathered their thoughts and channeled them, sending a narrow beam of consciousness throughout the surrounding area, searching for the missing Sholans. At one point there was a faint presence. They stopped, increasing the strength of their probing.

Carrie noticed the barrier first. She led them to the wall, searching for an opening.

There is no way in, Leska, but you are right. That is the barrier of my people. They are west of here.

In a cave, added Carrie. *We can find them.*

We can. Let us return.

The beam shrank, bringing them back to the clearing and their own bodies.

Carrie groaned. Her head hurt. There had been too many headaches of late. She lay still, hoping it would go away if she ignored it. Besides, she was comfortable. A hand touched her forehead gently and she opened her eyes, smiling weakly up at Kusac.

"Your head aches? I had these pains when my Talent was developing. Perhaps I can ease it and then you can sleep."

Carrie, unable to think or speak, lifted her head fractionally. That slight movement sent waves of pain jarring through her head, and even Kusac's soft voice was almost unbearable.

She felt his mind touch the agony inside her skull and gradually all pain ceased, leaving her limp and exhausted.

Kusac leaned back, reaching for the rucksack. Fumbling one-handedly inside it, he pulled out two emergency blankets. Trying not to disturb her, he spread first one then the other around them.

He looked down at where she lay against his chest. So different from his own women. Her face smooth skin, her hair blonde and long, cut shorter above her eyes. The eyes, a brown darker than he had ever seen, the whites almost startlingly blue. Eyes that right now he was drowning in.

A thought drifted up to him from her.

What is a Leska?

It has to do with our merging, replied Kusac, trying to steady his thoughts. Their joining had been so complete that their rapport needed no strengthening for mind talk.

We are as one—Leskas to each other. Now sleep. I have overtaxed both of us. I had no idea our search would take this course. He faltered, trying to suppress some of the half-formed thoughts that demanded attention.

Carrie closed her eyes obediently.

"Good night, Leska," she murmured. "In some matters events happen as they will."

Kusac sat for some time looking down at the sleeping Terran girl. What in Vartra's name had he done to them? His was the responsibility, the blame, as the girl's tutor. This bonding with her was irreversible for them both. He knew with every atom of his being that she was his true Leska, his life-mate.

No other relationships could ever have the depth of meaning or sharing that this held. Among Talented Sholans this was accepted, but where did that leave the two of them?

It wasn't as if they could hide their relationship; they would betray themselves in many little ways every moment of their lives, whether waking or sleeping. There were bound to be reprisals, from her people if not his own.

The Terrans would claim he had controlled her, used her mind until it belonged to him. This was the greatest sin a Talented person could commit. His people—so like the Terrans after all!—were quite likely to accuse him of the same crime and destroy that area of the brain where Talent was located.

He shivered, chilled by the very thought. To be cut off from this world, the full pleasures of which he had only just begun to taste! It did not bear thinking about, and firmly, he pushed these worries to the back of his mind, unconsciously holding Carrie closer.

Besides, he tried to comfort himself, he had been linked to Carrie before. No one knew what triggered a Leska bond. That this linking should have gone so much farther had not

been his doing. He had been swept along on the same tide
as she, and for a time control had been taken out of his
hands. Vartra alone knew why it had happened, for it was
certain he did not. But if it was Vartra's will, then He would
protect them. Whatever the future held, at least they would
face it together.

Tonight had been inevitable from the moment their minds,
both stretched beyond endurance, had met for the first time.

With this thought, he lay back, carefully clasping the
sleeping girl. He could feel her presence nestling in his mind
like a small, warm cub.

Chapter 5

Kusac dozed for an hour or two, then woke while it was still dark. The fire glowed warmly beside them, giving him enough light to see by. Carrie still lay curled up across his chest, one arm tucked around his waist. He moved his hand, putting it up to stroke her cheek with his fingertips. Her skin was so soft, unlike anything he had ever felt.

For seven weeks he had lived with her under conditions that, had he not been considered an animal, would have been called intimate. There was little about her that he did not know and, whether he looked at her from the inside or the outside, he found her beautiful.

He'd been attracted to her from the first, which was strange. He wasn't one to seek out female company, in fact, usually the opposite. It would be interesting to see what the other Sholan men's reactions to her would be.

His hands clenched briefly as he thought of Guynor. He'd played the role of pacifist long enough. Now he had someone to fight for.

Once again, he pulled himself up short. As a telepath he was unable to fight at all because he would feel the pain he inflicted, yet he had just killed four sentients and was contemplating fighting Guynor if the need arose. Why? He didn't remember feeling anything but rage with the Valtegans, none of their pain.

It had to come from Carrie. She had no such problem with fighting. Her anger blocked out her sensitivity. Was there an overlap of their Talents? Had he acquired some of her abilities when their minds had merged? What else had he retained?

He let his hand relax, cupping it across her cheek. He could still feel its softness even through the tough skin on his palm. Heightened sensitivity when they touched; he should have expected that. With that came the knowledge that he loved her and wanted her—badly. Where they touched, flesh to flesh, his body felt alive, tingling. She began to stir in her sleep.

Panic swamped him, and desperately, he tried to damp down his emotions and desire. He wanted her, yes, but when she was ready, too, not now.

The effort left him trembling with fatigue. Vartra, but he'd never felt like this about any woman, not even his first. This had to be the Leska bonding. At the Telepaths' Guild they'd all heard of its intensity and sniggered over it, but he had had no idea, how could he?

Carefully, he moved the sleeping girl until she lay on the ground. He tucked one of the blankets around her, then, taking the other, moved a few feet away. Until she was ready for him, it would be better if he had no prolonged physical contact with her. Wrapping the other blanket around himself, he tried to relax. He needed to work now while she was asleep.

He wanted to go over the link she and Elise had shared. Ever since he had known Carrie that link had disturbed him, but until now there was no way he could investigate it.

He began by remembering the flashes from her early life and was immediately grateful that the memories no longer carried the reality they had earlier that evening.

At first the twins had developed parallel to each other, but by the age of three, Elise had begun to outstrip her sister. She had figured out that no matter what she did to herself, it didn't hurt and she'd become more domineering and aggressive as a result. It had toned down as she got older, but some of her cavalier attitude had remained. She hadn't tried to get hurt, but going out of her way to avoid it as others did was not in her makeup.

So Carrie had grown up as the dominated twin, quiet and reserved, and worshiping her more adventurous sister. She was the really Talented one, the strength of her Talent boosting her sister's lesser one through their link. And down that link had come only her sister's pain and fear, nothing else.

It had become automatic. Carrie sensed it when her sister got hurt and she took the pain from her. Elise, knowing Carrie would take the hurt away, pushed it to her twin. It was a vicious, self-perpetuating circle.

To Kusac, it was horrendous, an absolute abomination of

what a telepathic link should be. Such a link should let you share pleasures and joys, feel compassion for your partner, be aware of her moods, and enable you to mutually support each other. Yes, sharing pain and hurts came into it, but by halving them, not by one of you taking on all of the burden.

He would have to try to explain what had gone wrong before or else *their* joining would suffer. So far he had not been aware of her taking on any of his pain. He would have to watch for that and show her how to block out this feedback.

As yet she had not shown any fear of their minor link. He'd had to forge it or let her follow her twin into death. There had been no choice. At the time, she had grasped his mind like the lifeline it was, and had calmly continued to accept it since then. But if the Leska link heightened all their senses when with each other, how would she respond to it? Could she cope, would he be able to make her see how good it could be for both of them, or would she only anticipate more pain?

Fatigue began to pull at him and he lay down beside the fire. There was nothing much he could do at the moment except worry. Sleep was definitely preferable if he could relax enough for it.

It was daylight when Carrie woke. The canopy of interlaced branches allowed a gentle green light to filter groundward but prevented her from catching sight of even the smallest patch of sky. She had no idea what time of day it was.

Lazily, she straightened her limbs, stretching them as far as they would go before sitting up. Her mind beginning to function again, she remembered Kusac. He lay sprawled asleep, tangled in one of the blankets. He seemed close to waking; there was no need to disturb him.

As she got to her feet and began folding her blanket, faint wisps of memories began to stir in the recesses of her mind. What had happened the night before? Apart from the mind link. She frowned, trying to concentrate, but the train of thought was elusive and refused to be pinned down. Shrugging it aside for the time being, she went over to her rucksack and began rummaging among its contents for something suitable for breakfast.

She'd just finished making the coffee when she heard Kusac stirring.

"You timed it well," she said, looking over at him as he stretched sinuously from head to tail before ambling over to her.

"It's only bread and cheese, but at least it's better than the emergency rations we'll be having tomorrow." She looked up at him and for the first time noticed how tall he really was. He would top her by nearly a foot if she were standing.

Kusac squatted down on his haunches beside her and made a low growling noise, laying his ears flat along his skull.

"If they're anything like our emergency food, starvation is almost preferable."

Carrie grimaced in agreement. From Kusac she could sense the sickly concentrated taste of their protein packs.

"So the Valtegans are not at war with you?"

Kusac's question was purely hypothetical. There was no reason for them to use verbal speech now, but in an unspoken agreement they knew that neither of them was ready to rely totally on their mental channel.

"No," replied Carrie, passing the mug of coffee to him. "I think they have a rough idea of where Earth is, but they seem totally disinterested in it. Do you know who they are at war with?"

"No idea," Kusac mumbled through a mouthful of cheese. "None of the Allied Worlds knows anything about them. If the Valtegans have chosen Keiss as an R & R planet, then the chances are it's close to their battle zone, yet far enough away to be safe. That puts our two razed colonies near enough to the possible fighting zone to be a threat."

"And that, coupled with their lack of interest in both Shola and Earth," Carrie continued slowly, accepting the coffee back from Kusac, "could lead one to surmise that they have more than enough to contend with, without looking for new adversaries. I presume your colonies weren't heavily populated."

"They'd been established for four to five generations, but were still nowhere near as densely peopled as our home world," agreed Kusac, helping himself to more cheese. "If we knew who the Valtegans were fighting, we could try to weight the odds in favor of those on the receiving end."

"What are our present priorities?" Carrie asked. "We have to find the rest of your people first, I know that.

"We have to, Kusac," she insisted, catching his new reluctance. "Are there any telepaths on the team other than yourself?"

"None."

"Then they can't know anything yet. Even if there were, what could they do to us?" she asked, gulping a mouthful of coffee before handing him the mug again.

Carrie returned Kusac's amber gaze, caught by its intensity though it was directed not at her but beyond her.

His eyes began to focus normally again and he shook his head slightly.

"How did you know what I was thinking about?" he asked. "I thought I'd managed to conceal it from you. However, you may be right," he admitted grudgingly, getting to his feet. "Let's hope we don't have to put it to the test."

He kicked a shower of earth over the camp fire then stamped on it to make sure it was out.

"It's time we left. My injured leg has cost me enough of a delay already. As you reminded me, we must find my colleagues."

Picking up the rucksack, he stuffed the empty mug and Carrie's blanket into it. Moving over to where they had slept the night before, he retrieved his blanket, stowing it away, too.

"Aren't you coming?" he asked, grinning down at her. "If you are, you'd better empty that pan and give it to me."

Carrie scrambled to her feet and handed him the pan.

"You're our finder," he said, starting to hustle her along a small path that wound its way through the trees. "I can't trace the rest of my crew without you."

A trifle bemused by his sudden surge of activity, Carrie allowed herself to be propelled forward.

"Which way?" Kusac demanded as they came to a fork in the path.

"I don't know!" she exclaimed, rounding on him in mock anger. "I'm not really a finder, I'm just me!"

There was a flicker of anger in her. If she could feel it, then so could Kusac. Hurriedly, she pushed it to one side of her mind and blocked it off from him. She was grateful this facility still existed, but how long she could maintain it was another matter.

Kusac's head tilted to one side as he regarded her calmly.

"Carrie," he said quietly, taking her by the arm. "Don't try so hard, just feel it out. If you attempt to reason things like this, you lose them. This time you're the finder because you, quite simply, found my crew mates. I meant nothing more than that.

"Now, which way do we go?" he asked, giving her a little shake.

"Left," she replied, not fully convinced either that this aspect of her Talent could be wholly trusted or that Kusac wasn't keeping something back.

They continued on for some time with Kusac leading and Carrie shouting out half-hearted instructions every now and then.

The path began to fade into invisibility and Kusac had to borrow the knife and try to hack a way through the thickening tangle of undergrowth. Overhead, the trees had choked off the daylight and they were left in a green half-light that only served to heighten their senses. For the last hour an unnatural silence had grown between them, so palpable they could almost touch it, yet neither one felt able to break it.

"Would your people be willing to join mine against the Valtegans?" asked Kusac at last.

"Of course, but I doubt that we would be of much help," replied Carrie. "Terran ships don't have anything like the speed you need, nor the armaments."

"You made it out here, didn't you?" he asked, trying to chop through the stem of yet another ironwood vine.

"Yes, in a sleep ship," she puffed, lifting an armload of loose greenery and sticks from the path and thrusting it behind her out of the way.

"By the time we meet the other Sholans, we're going to be incredibly fit!"

Kusac gave a throaty chuckle.

"You could well be right. If we helped you with the ships, would your people be able to provide the crews?"

Carrie straightened up, looking at him incredulously.

"You're asking me? You know as well as I do that you couldn't make enough ships to hold the volunteers once Earth learns what has happened to us on Keiss!"

"Good," nodded Kusac, turning back to his chopping. "We shall see if we can persuade Sholan High Command that you would be useful allies.

"That message you are thinking about," he continued, "how long have you got before the next colony ship reaches midpoint?"

"Um!" she exclaimed, taken aback by his question. "About two weeks," she said, doing some rapid calculations. "But how did you know? I'd hardly begun to think about it."

Kusac chuckled again, a sound halfway between a growl and a purr.

"Your mind is quite open to me. I can see many of your thoughts and with this one, I could see where it was leading."

"Oh," she said, as her mind returned to the night before. She remembered falling, falling into a whirlpool of brightly colored lights, watching them, fascinated. . . .

"Carrie!" Kusac said sharply, feeling himself being jerked puppetlike toward her.

Had someone called her? The sound was so faint she was probably imagining it.

"Carrie!" This time the call was both verbal and mental. Someone was shaking her.

"Kusac? What's wrong?" she asked, bewildered to find herself looking up into Kusac's face.

His grip on her arms changed, becoming gentler as he moved his hands to her shoulders.

"You were reexperiencing last night. You must be more careful, Carrie," he said, his voice harsh with fear. "You were setting in motion a chain of events neither of us can control."

"I don't understand you," she said, putting her hand up to push her hair away from her face. "What did I do wrong? I was only trying to remember last night. What did happen then?" she asked, raising her eyes questioningly to his. "Apart from our Leska link, I mean."

Kusac flattened his ears against his skull. He could feel the girl searching his mind: there was no avoiding the issue now. He lowered his mental barriers, not even trying to conceal his fears and worries from her.

"Does it really matter what happened? Do we have to know?" he asked softly, his fingers tightening slightly on her shoulders.

Carrie could feel the cool, gentle pressure that was his presence touch her thoughts.

She searched his face, not knowing what she was looking for, especially in a person so different from her own kind.

With his ears flattened almost out of sight, he looked more human somehow. The fur covering his face was short, unlike his body hair. This close to him she could tell that it was not the black she had supposed, but a rich, dark brown. His cheekbones were high and the nose—not quite a muzzle—short. It was his eyes that clinched it: round, liquid amber, holding a look of friendship, love and . . . worry. She knew the soul that lay behind them, she didn't need to probe any further.

"No," she said. "I don't need to know any more."

"I'm glad," he sighed, feeling the tension flow out of him. He pulled her face close to his, resting his cheek against hers.

She felt the gentle touch of his tongue against her neck before he released her.

"We had better continue," he said, turning back to pick up the knife he had dropped when he had been pulled toward her.

Nothing he knew of the Leska bond suggested anything like the degree of personality interchange or the flow of power through and around them that they were experiencing. And Carrie had done it at will! They had something unknown and wild here that would require careful control. He shook his head slightly. The situation worried him.

Perhaps it's because we are of different species, came her thought. *Nothing about our relationship can be compared to any other. We seem to lose ourselves and become a third being—a gestalt—when we are linked in that way.*

There are limitations, though, returned Kusac. *I have a feeling that we will find ourselves unable to use our physical bodies during such a merging. They will be vulnerable and easily attacked.*

Perhaps, but we should be able to keep some kind of a watch on them, if we have need of that depth of merging.

Turning their attention back to the task at hand, they continued to cut their way through the forest until they came across another path.

"I can't go any farther without food, Kusac!" Carrie exclaimed, sitting down heavily on the remains of a tree trunk. "I don't know about you, but I'm starving."

"Fair enough," said Kusac, setting the rucksack down beside her. "I'll get some firewood rounded up. You can begin getting some food and coffee ready. I refilled the flask at our last campsite."

"We've got the stove," said Carrie, delving into her pack. "There's no need for a wood fire." She pulled a sealed foil pack out. "I don't much fancy emergency rations, do you?" she asked, pulling a face as she waved them in Kusac's direction.

"No, but there's no point in trying to hunt just now. The noise we've been making will have scared away the game for miles around."

Carrie grunted in reluctant agreement.

"Oh!" she exclaimed, taking out the first aid pack. "Your arm. I meant to put a dressing on it this morning. Let me see it."

Kusac held out his left arm, trying to remember if he had been aware of it hurting. They both examined it to find that in a couple of places the scab had fallen off to reveal the brighter pink flesh of a newly healed wound.

"Um, I don't think you need a bandage after all," said Carrie, putting the pack away again.

She busied herself lighting the stove.

Kusac sat back, totally nonplussed. He flexed the arm, not even a twinge. There was no doubt about it, one of them was a healer—but which one? He filled the kettle and gave it to Carrie to put on the stove.

Carrie began to unpack her rucksack, refolding every item as she took it out. He knew she was just making work for herself. He leaned forward and caught her hands in his, stilling them.

"I need to explain to you about Telepath links," he said.

"I suspect that if you know about it, then so do I," she said.

"Probably, but knowing and understanding are not necessarily the same."

"True," she conceded, her hands finally relaxing in his.

"Our people have only the one mental Talent compared to the several I have already discovered you possess. That's the ability to transmit and receive thoughts.

"We understand this Talent well, and those with a greater degree of it would train to become interpreters for Alien trade, to help in the law courts as truthsayers or even as judges, to work with the mentally ill—all manner of professions are open to us with our Talent. Each profession involves working with others by means of a greater or lesser mind link."

"That makes sense."

"Obviously we cannot be totally at the mercy of the criminal or insane mind, so we build in our own protections to keep out those thoughts we do not want.

"I will need to teach you how to do this. We are lucky, we start training at the Telepaths' Guild in early childhood. You are rare among your people so there was no such training for you.

"Now is neither the time nor place, but I promise I will teach you as soon as I have the opportunity."

He released her hand and leaned forward to brush her cheek with his fingertips. Her eyes took on an extra depth, becoming heavy lidded. Abruptly, he pulled back, leaving her dazed as if she were coming out of a trance. He'd been about to take her in his arms before he realized what was happening to them.

Taking advantage of her confusion, he swiftly created a mental barrier behind which, for the moment at least, he could think. Thank Vartra that she hadn't yet figured out that their Leska link involved a sexual compulsion. That was all he needed. At least she appeared to be less affected by it than he.

Anger flared briefly inside him. He needed to know that what they felt for each other was real, not the product of their link. It might not even be that, it could be the attraction of two different species for each other, but that was equally biological.

"What is it?" she demanded, shaking his arm. "What happened?"

"Nothing, I just felt dizzy for a moment. Look, the kettle's boiling. Let's make the coffee while I explain some more."

"Are you sure you're all right?" she asked, concern written on her face and in her mind.

"I'm fine," he assured her, giving his equivalent of a smile.

She nodded. "I'll do the coffee, you do the talking."

"This is the hard bit, Carrie," he said, handing her the mug and settling down on the ground beside her. "Like all the other students, I took a tour of experience with the Medics as well as the other departments. I'm telling you this so you understand that I do know what I'm talking about."

She glanced up at him as she stirred the coffee. "You sound as if it's serious."

"I'm afraid it is. I was worried about your link with Elise, so I took a long look at your memories of it. Because your people don't recognize Talent, as your link with your twin developed it got twisted out of true. What should have been a bond of shared joys as well as pain, became a nightmare of pain for you."

"Let me get this straight," she said quietly, passing him the mug first. "You're telling me that the link Elise and I shared was twisted."

"That's right. You were only experiencing the negative side of what a link should bring."

"And just how do you think this happened?"

Kusac took a drink and handed her the mug. "Elise was the dominant twin. She led, you followed, essentially. At a very young age when morals don't exist, she discovered that she could do what she liked without it hurting her, so she did. As she got older she realized this was wrong and did try to modify her behavior, but the pattern was set by then.

"Without knowing it, you had created a feedback loop so that when your twin got hurt, you automatically took the pain away from her, and she, understanding that you did this, was happy to send it to you."

Carrie was silent for a moment. "Elise would never do that!" she said angrily. "You're saying she used me! She wouldn't. What do you know about it anyway? You're picking apart secondhand memories—I was there, I lived with it!"

She threw the rest of the coffee out and stuffed the mug back in her rucksack.

Kusac let her fumble with the stove and kettle, only too aware of the blazing anger directed at him. Damn! Why hadn't he left it to one of the Counselors on the *Khalossa* to deal with? He couldn't just leave it, he had to say something.

"Carrie, I'm not trying to apportion blame. I just wanted you to appreciate that a link can be positive, too."

"Look, I don't want to talk about it. Leave it alone."

"I know you're afraid, I can feel it . . ."

"Kusac, drop it," she said, picking up the rucksack and stomping off along the path.

Carrie continued to guide them, despite her misgivings and even though the atmosphere between them remained chilly for several hours, by dusk, she was prepared to talk to him in more than monosyllables. They stopped for the night only when the light filtering down through the dense canopy was insufficient for Carrie's human sight.

While Kusac went to track down some supper, Carrie began to search for the exact location of his crew mates. Her mind reached out through the forest looking for the natural barrier of the Sholans. Once she found it, it was an easy matter for her to penetrate it without alarming any of them.

Her view of the location was poor due to the darkness, so she touched the nearest mind lightly, discovering what she needed to know. She withdrew, but before she did she felt the mind she had touched leap toward her.

Kusac? Is that you?

She returned to her own body slightly surprised by the faint contact with the stranger's mind. Hadn't Kusac said he was the only telepath on the ship? Filing the thought away for the future, she got to her feet and began to search for firewood.

The next morning, Carrie gave Kusac a mental picture of the cave in the cliff face where the Sholans were living.

"It isn't far, Kusac," she said as he led the way.

"Good. The sooner we get the initial meeting over with, the better," he growled. "Just remember to be careful. I want to avoid giving them the slightest inkling that we are Leskas."

"All right," she agreed. "By the way, I forgot to mention that someone noticed my presence last night and thought I was you."

"Are you sure? None of the others have any Talent, of that I am positive."

"Someone reacted to my touch," she insisted.

"Let me know when you recognize who it is and I'll check it out. The last thing we need is a partial or wild Talent around us. They go around broadcasting at random without realizing it. I can block it out once I know who is responsible."

Carrie let the matter drop, but she was still slightly perplexed by the whole incident. Despite the mistake in identity, the mind that had touched hers was obviously used to
Kusac's mental touch. It bothered her and she resented that.
However, there were more important things to concern her at
the moment.

Within a couple of hours they were approaching the cliff
face. At the edge of the trees, Kusac halted.

"You wait here. I'll meet them alone first. My reappear-
ance will be enough of a shock for them."

"No," said Carrie firmly, taking her knife back. "We go
there together. It would be better if they meet both of us
now. It will be only one shock instead of two."

"Very well," he said, "but stay behind me. They'll be
armed and may shoot at you instinctively."

Carrie's eyebrows disappeared under her fringe. "You do
make them sound friendly."

"You're an Alien, remember? They may not yet have seen
any Terrans, or they may have been hunted by them. There
are many reasons why they could feel threatened by your
presence.

"Do you still want to come with me?" he asked, his head
cocked to one side in amusement.

"Just lead the way and stop the delaying tactics," she answered acidly, poking him in the side with the knife pommel
before she returned it to its sheath.

Kusac advanced into the clearing with Carrie behind him.
The cliff face was steep but rugged, with many outcroppings
of jagged rocks. Stunted trees and small bushes perched here
and there among the lichens and ivy.

"I can't see a cave," he murmured after a few minutes.
"Are you sure this is the right spot?"

Carrie turned a withering look on him. "You know
damned well it is. You sensed the direction through me. The
cave is behind those bushes," she said, pointing above them
and slightly to the left. "You'd better call to them. They
know we're here."

Kusac called.

She had never heard him talking in his own tongue before.
The words had a slightly guttural sound but were delivered
in a singsong tone. Aware of his speech only peripherally,
she listened with her mind, hearing not only him but the
Captain's answering call. Part of her noted with an academic

interest that when she and Kusac had merged, along with all
his experiences, she had acquired a knowledge of his language.

"Kusac! What in Vartra's name are you doing bringing a
native with you?" The Sholan who stepped from behind the
bushes was as forbidding as his voice.

Ignoring the gun pointing in her direction, Carrie moved
forward a few paces.

"I brought him here, Captain," she said, stumbling a little
as her tongue tried to form sounds that were truly Alien to
her. "Perhaps you would have preferred him to remain
among my people masquerading as a forest cat—like you."

The muzzle of the Captain's gun wavered slightly.

"She speaks our language!" His voice was almost a whisper.

"Of course," Carrie replied, her intonation a little surer
now. "May I suggest that we join you? There are guerrilla
bands of my people roaming these woods, plus the odd detachment of Valtegans. We have no wish to meet either of
them, even if you have."

The Captain's tail began to switch violently from side to
side as he peremptorily motioned them forward.

They clambered up the incline, Carrie edging her way into
the cave first.

Kusac was held back briefly.

"You had no business allowing her to accompany you,"
said the Captain, ramming his gun back into the holster he
wore strapped to the belt of his sleeveless jacket.

Kusac shrugged the restraining hand away.

"You did not need to let her enter the cave," he replied
amiably.

Just beyond the entrance the tunnel turned at right angles
and widened out, forming a natural cavern of adequate proportions to house a dozen Sholans.

At regular intervals around the three walls were placed
jury-rigged lighting systems. The glow they gave off, though
soft, was bright enough to see by. The floor had been covered with dried grasses and bracken which crackled slightly
underfoot as Carrie walked farther into the den.

A sibilant hiss from behind sent her reaching instinctively
for her knife. Before she could draw it, her hand was
clamped to her side by an iron grip and she was swung
round to face a powerfully built Sholan.

"An Alien!" he growled. "By what right does Kusac bring one of these carrion here?" His grip tightened, the nails digging into her flesh as he yanked her hand away from her belt knife.

Helpless, Carrie looked up into a face contorted with hate. She sensed his inner fear of strangers and knew that he was capable of crushing the life out of her with as little compunction as she would have in destroying a cockroach.

"Look at it!" he mocked, forcing her round to face the other Sholans, "Hairless as the insects that crawl in the dirt on this Godforsaken planet."

"Guynor, let her go." Kusac's voice was deceptively quiet.

Contemptuously, Guynor raked Kusac with his gaze.

"I see you've gone native, too. Don't you believe in clothing any more? As for this creature," he shook Carrie, making her lose her balance and stumble, "what use is it to you or anyone?"

Seconds later, Guynor was lying sprawled on the floor nursing his head.

Kusac took Carrie's hand and looked briefly at the blood coursing down it. He glanced toward a small Sholan standing nearby.

"Vanna, do you have a medikit? Carrie's wrist needs attention."

As he led her over to the roughly made table and benches, the rest of the crew relaxed visibly.

Vanna went over to the far corner of the cavern to rummage through some boxes, returning with a small case.

"What is your name?" she asked kindly, indicating that the girl should sit, then taking her arm and examining the puncture wounds around the wrist.

"She's called Carrie," interrupted Kusac. "The cuts look deep. Will you be able to close them?"

"You know I have coped with far worse, Kusac. Just go and get me some warm water. I need to wash this blood away so I can see the extent of the damage. Do you know if her system can cope with our drugs?"

"I suffered no ill effects when they treated my wounds. I suspect our systems are not very different.

"Will scars show? She has no fur to cover them."

"Kusac, fetch the water," Vanna said sternly. "She could bleed to death while you stand and chatter."

Carrie looked at her wrist in fascination. Vanna was holding it just above the wounds and the slow flow of blood had almost stopped.

Kusac hesitated, then moved off to where one of the others was calling him.

"Our males are all the same," smiled Vanna. "Not very practical when it comes to the aftermath of a fight.

"Are your males just as bad?"

"Most of them," said Carrie wryly, thinking of her brother's panic over a nosebleed he'd collected in a fight with one of the other youths.

Kusac returned with a bowl of water.

"Thank you," said Vanna, taking the bowl from him with her free hand. "Now go and do something useful instead of hovering around me. I'm sure the Captain will want a report on your activities these past few weeks. You might as well do it now, before mealtime."

Kusac shifted his weight from one foot to the other.

"Are you sure there is nothing I can do?"

"Nothing except report to the Captain," said Vanna briskly as she began to clean Carrie's wounds with some dampened gauze. "Go and do it now before you ruffle his fur any more." She nodded to where the Captain stood at the entrance to the den, hackles raised, glowering over at them.

"You've caused quite a stir, you know. We haven't had so much excitement for days. Not only do you return as if from the dead, but you bring an Alien with you." Her eyes, a deep green, glanced up humorously at Carrie. "Not content with that, you round it off by besting Guynor—for the moment."

Her tone became serious. "I don't need to warn you to be careful of him, do I? Both of you," she emphasized, stopping for a moment. "No one beats Guynor, least of all you, Kusac, since your caste of Telepaths forbids personal combat."

"I take your meaning," nodded Kusac.

"Then scat, and don't antagonize our Captain any longer," she ordered, reaching into her box for a canister from which she liberally sprayed a clear liquid over Carrie's wrist and hand.

"It's easier treating you than it is one of us," Vanna said. conversationally to the girl. "I don't have to cut back any fur before I can start treating the wounds. You only have vestigial hairs and not enough of them to cause any concern, except on your head."

"Our ancestors were once covered in body hair," murmured Carrie, watching the wounds as Vanna released her grip. The bleeding had stopped and so had the pain. "We are descended from primates. Was that a coagulant spray?"

"Yes, and an analgesic. I'm afraid I will have to close the wounds. You seem to know something of medicine. Have you had any training?"

"No, but I've picked up bits and pieces. My job was to teach the children."

"You're the first of the natives we've seen up close," Vanna said. "I thought no sentient life was found when we did our first survey twenty years ago. How did you manage to avoid being seen by our scout craft?" she asked curiously, placing an object resembling a staple gun over one of the punctures. A slight click and she moved to the next wound, leaving the previous one neatly tacked closed.

"We're not indigenous here," Carrie corrected her absently, almost mesmerized by the efficiency of the little gadget. "We're colonists."

"That explains many things that have puzzled us, and settles an argument," laughed Vanna. "Guynor loses again! Mito and he were convinced your people came from this world. It isn't his day today, is it?

"Now, I'm going to give you something to ensure the cuts don't become infected, then I'll bandage your wrist. If you feel any strange effects—dizziness, sickness, anything—let me know immediately. I have an antidote for the drug. As for the stitches, they will dissolve in a week. At least they do with our body chemistry," she amended, taking out a hypodermic gun.

"It should be all right," said Carrie, as the female placed the tip against her flesh. A slight sting and it was over. "Kusac didn't react adversely to our antibiotics."

Vanna put the hypo away and picking up a slim packet tore it open and took out a sterile dressing.

"Hold out your arm," she said, placing the pad over the wounded area.

"Do take my warning about Guynor seriously," she continued, fastening the bandage. "He has several reasons for disliking Kusac, and today's incident has only made the situation worse. No one has ever struck him before, and for it to be Kusac . . ." She shrugged expressively.

"Apart from our Captain, Guynor is the strongest member of the crew. If things don't go his way, he lashes out, but never when Garras can see it. To hit Guynor back means a worse beating.

"He used to take a delight in baiting Kusac, knowing that as a Telepath, he wouldn't even consider defending himself. But Kusac has changed." Her eyes narrowed slightly as she stared at the girl. "He is not the same person we left in the woods the day we crashed. He is older, and stronger, and has a sense of purpose, unless I'm mistaken."

Carrie remained silent, gently probing Vanna. The Sholan's last sentence had said more than the words alone.

Drawing some energy from Kusac, she was able to read the surface of Vanna's mind, but beyond that was the natural barrier that took their combined strength to break through unless Vanna willingly removed it. She was certainly no Telepath. This was not the mind she had touched before. She sensed her concern for Kusac over a female that Guynor had claimed, and her curiosity about Carrie and her place in Kusac's life—obviously an important one—but nothing more. She withdrew and returned her attention to what Vanna was saying.

"So keep out of Guynor's way. You cannot stand up to him yourself: you don't have our natural weapons. Never go anywhere alone, that would give him the opportunity to Challenge you when none of us were there to prevent him."

"Why should he Challenge me?"

Vanna looked puzzled. "To be able to claim superiority over you, of course. Don't your people fight for superiority?"

"Not physically on a personal level. Superiority in strength doesn't mean superiority of intellect among Terrans. Surely that applies to you, too?"

"You can only be Challenged by someone of your own grade," Vanna said, her tone slightly stiff.

Carrie felt something brushing against her leg and glancing down, she saw the Sholan's tail twitching slightly back and forth.

"Would your people follow a leader who was not the strongest member of the crew? Ours would not."

"We follow those thought to be wisest. We believe wisdom comes with age," replied Carrie.

"So do we, but in certain fields such as our armed forces, the old ways still linger. Yet our senior leaders tend to be older, like Garras," Vanna conceded, beginning to gather her medical equipment together. "Many of us dislike the personal combat procedure, but obviously the stronger ones among us wish to continue it. Besides, it is the best way to choose the Junior Officers, and if you allow that to be the deciding factor among them, then it must be allowed throughout the lesser members of the crew. It is only fair." She closed her case and picked it up. "You stay here while I fetch you a hot drink, then you can tell me how you met Kusac."

Carrie watched Vanna's retreating figure, really looking at the Sholan woman for the first time. Like the Captain, she wore a multipurpose sleeveless jacket covered with various sized external pockets. From the utility belt at her waist hung a side arm. What the pouches contained, Carrie had no idea, but presumably they held various medical and personal items. Over her right shoulder was a wide band of blue—probably a mark of her status or profession.

Vanna's fur was also differently colored from that of Kusac and the Captain. They were dark; she was light beige with darker marks banding her tail.

Looking over the rest of the company, she saw that of the other three members of the crew, only one was similarly colored. The banding of darker fur was echoed on the face around the eyes and ears. A gentle surface probe revealed a lesser barrier than she had encountered from the other Sholans, and she identified the feel of the mind that had mistaken her for Kusac.

The shock of her experience with Guynor had left her too drained to probe any further even had she wished to, so she withdrew, turning her attention to where Kusac was still talking to the Captain.

"Right," said Vanna, setting two mugs of steaming brown liquid down in front of her, "now I want to hear how you found Kusac."

Carrie picked up the crude pottery mug and sipped the drink cautiously. It tasted vaguely like coffee but was insipid by comparison.

"First, tell me why you left Kusac behind. If we hadn't found each other he would have died."

"It wasn't my decision, it was the Captain's."

"When we crashed here, we had very little time to make our escape. We knew the planet had produced a feline form not unlike our own and the Captain reasoned that with any luck we could be mistaken for them if the need arose, but only if the bodies of our dead were destroyed. We took anything useful we could lay our hands on, then we set the craft alight and were moving into the forest just as a small group of the Others . . ."

"Valtegans," interrupted Carrie.

". . . Valtegans landed near us. There was a fight during which another of the crew was killed and Kusac was wounded. There was barely time to throw the body into our blazing scout craft before we had to leave.

"It was important that as many of us as possible escaped to find the life pod that had been dropped here by the first survey. There's a transmitter in it, and with it we could contact Shola and report that we had found the Others and were stranded on the planet.

"Kusac was too badly wounded to keep up with us, so the Captain ordered him to follow our trail as best he could, when he could."

Carrie kept her expression impassive as Vanna ground to a halt.

"I wasn't even allowed the time to put a dressing on his wound," the Sholan continued after a moment or two. "We had to ensure that we escaped to warn our people. Millions of lives still depend on our sending that message."

"I can appreciate your point," said Carrie, "but I'm afraid I would have at least treated his wound."

"None of us had time to think!" exclaimed Vanna. "We had just crashed on the planet, gotten out of the scouter, and been attacked again on the ground. We reacted purely by instinct, otherwise we'd all have perished in the Valtegans' second attack."

Carrie shrugged noncommittally, knowing that Vanna was upset—and probably right. "Possibly I would have acted the same way, I don't really know."

Vanna nodded. "Perhaps you would. Now will you tell me how you met Kusac, and came to speak our language so well—for an Alien."

Carrie told Vanna an abridged version of her meeting with Kusac, leaving out anything that had to do with their telepathic bond, except for the language transfer. By the time she had finished, Kusac had returned.

"Everything should be fine now," he told her, sitting down at the table. "I have told him about our computer cube and spoken to him about sending the message direct to your colony ship and he says he will consider it, although he sees no reason to refuse."

"Good. Have they found the life pod yet?" Carrie asked.

"No, but they know where it is," Kusac replied. "It's in the swamp just north of here."

"Oh, dear," sighed Carrie. "That creates a problem."

"I know."

"We've been trying to find a way through that swamp for months," interrupted Vanna, "but the place is full of treacherous bogs and quicksands, not to mention the local animal population, which appears to be composed mainly of teeth," she said wryly. "I seem to have done nothing but treat animal bites."

"I don't know the swamps," said Carrie. "The person you want is Jack Reynolds, our doctor and xenobiologist, though even he hasn't ventured far into that region. I'm afraid no one in our settlement can be of any real help."

"Then we are stranded until the *Khalossa* finally realizes we're missing. With the current situation, that's not going to be for quite a while yet as we were running behind schedule—unless you know the location of a deep space transmitter."

"If we knew of one that didn't require a large army to reach it, I assure you we'd have used it ourselves long before now! Vanna, we have a colony ship due to reach midpoint in about two weeks. If we don't contact it, another fifteen hundred of our people will be landing here, totally unprepared for life under the Valtegans," Carrie replied.

"It occurred to both Garras and me that if the *Khalossa* is bound for Keiss, there is no need to stop your colony ship. By the time it arrived, Keiss would be completely free of any Valtegan presence."

"That's an option I hadn't considered," said Carrie thoughtfully.

"Yes, the *Khalossa*'s a fully armed warship, well able to

cope with fighting on a planetary scale," Kusac continued. "It's well worth thinking about.

"Meanwhile, there must be someone who knows the swamps. What about these guerrillas of yours? They live in the forests, they must have traveled through that area at some time."

"They're certainly more likely to have done so than anyone else," Carrie admitted.

"How do we contact them?" interrupted a voice from behind Carrie.

She turned to find the Captain standing there. He moved round the table, seating himself opposite them.

"I've no idea. How do you suggest we find small bands of people who roam around a forest the size of this one?"

"How do you contact them when you need them?" he asked, his ears twitching in irritation.

"We don't," she replied shortly. "They contact us."

"Carrie," said Kusac, his hand reaching out to cover hers where it lay on the table. "They need provisions—food, weapons, things like that. Where would they go to get them?"

Don't antagonize him, Leska. He is better as a friend than an enemy.

"They would probably go to Seaport," she said, moderating her tone while mentally sending Kusac a series of rude noises. "People from all over go there to market the various goods that are their speciality. Hillfort mines for metals. They produce tools and jewelery. Seaport itself produces seafoods. It's also the site of our original landing, and sections of the *Eureka* are still there, incorporated into the town. The computer is housed there, also the beacon to guide the second ship down."

"The Valtegans have allowed you to keep the beacon then?"

"In a way. We aren't allowed access to it in case we might try to prevent it from sending out the homing signal."

"I'd have thought that the Valtegans would have tried to keep any more of your people from landing here," said Kusac, "considering the damage your guerrillas already do. Surely they are creating a potentially explosive situation for themselves?"

"They know that our second wave contains many scientists as well as their equipment. Plus they hope to recruit

more of our women for their pleasure centers." Her voice
sounded bitter as she said this.

"Some of your women are in their pleasure centers?" said
the Captain, his face creasing with concern. "Is there no way
you can rescue them? Surely your guerrillas? . . ."

"They went voluntarily," Carrie interrupted. "When the
Valtegans arrived, they took over the site of one of our settlements. There was opposition, of course, and many of the
men were killed. Most of the survivors left and joined other
settlements but some remained, going to stay in Geshader
with the Valtegans.

"The women used to visit Seaport occasionally, but when
they started trying to persuade some of the younger girls to
join them in the center, the settlers drove them out.

"We aren't all like that," she said defensively, "but no
matter how carefully you screen people, you can't test for
every situation."

"What are the chances of contacting the guerrillas if we
go to Seaport?" asked Kusac, breaking the silence that followed her outburst.

"I've no idea, but we can hardly traipse round the forest
hoping to bump into them. There's only one problem with
your idea. I'd be recognized in Seaport, and my father will
be looking for me."

"That is unimportant for now," said the Captain. "Do you
know the places these people are likely to frequent?"

"I know where to look," she admitted reluctantly.

"Then you can prepare for your journey tonight and be
ready to leave first thing in the morning."

"No," said Kusac quietly.

The Captain swiveled round to face him.

"I said no," Kusac repeated, ignoring the fact that
Guynor's ears had flicked sideward and back.

"Carrie has been injured by your First Officer. She needs
at least a day or two to recover. Traveling through the forest
is not child's play, it's hard manual work. Once her wrist has
healed, we will leave.

"There is also the question of her being recognized. That
problem has to be resolved before it is safe for her to enter
Seaport."

Vanna sat rigid with shock, unable to believe what she
was hearing. This was so unlike the Kusac she knew.

"Kusac, I'm fine. I'll be all right . . ." started Carrie.

"If we have to hack our way back through the trees, then there is no way you could possibly cope," Kusac said flatly. "Vanna, as the medic, do you agree with me?"

Vanna kept her eyes on the Captain as she answered.

"She is not a Sholan so I have no way of gauging her recuperative powers, but even if she were, I would advise at least one day's rest if she has to use her hand for any heavy work. The journey to Seaport will take much longer—and may even have to be canceled—if she collapses from shock or exhaustion."

"Very well," snapped Garras. "If you consider that it would jeopardize the mission, then I will delay it for a day or two. Time is of the essence. The Valtegans will be trying to use our memory cube and if they can access that ... I leave it to your imagination.

"Let me know when she has recovered sufficiently to travel." With that, he stalked off to the other end of the cavern and disappeared through one of the tunnel openings.

Vanna released her breath in a long sigh.

"What, in all the shades of the Underworld, has come over you, Kusac? Are you going out of your way to antagonize everyone?"

"Me, Vanna? You know I'm a pacifist."

"Don't turn those innocent eyes on me!" she rejoined tartly. "I don't know what you're playing at, but I hope you're prepared for the trouble you're creating for yourself and Carrie."

"Believe me, Vanna, I'm not trying to cause trouble, but I'm not having anyone trampling over Carrie. She isn't one of us and no one has any right to order her about. Our ways are not hers. I want everyone to understand that they don't Challenge her but me."

"Hey, wait a minute!" Carrie protested. "I'm not exactly a weakling, you know."

Kusac and Vanna turned to look at her, a shared amusement on their faces.

"I have heard you described by other Terrans as a diminutive slip of a girl," said Kusac, grinning. "You're just tall enough to reach above my shoulder. Do you really think you could defend yourself against one of us? Even against Vanna, who is the smallest of our crew?" He shook his head. "You don't have our muscular build, let alone our claws, and in a Challenge, claws are not sheathed."

Carrie mumbled a few choice words under her breath.

Kusac laughed before turning back to Vanna.

"When we left the scouter, we all grabbed the nearest things worth salvaging. I don't suppose there was any clothing among what was carried off, was there?"

"As a matter of fact, there was. If you remember, Mito was in . . . her cabin." She hesitated, trying not to glance at Kusac. "Predictably, she grabbed some clothing and personal possessions, bundling them in a couple of blankets. Not the type of things that aid survival on an Alien planet—except for the blankets."

"On the contrary, it is exactly what I need. Where did she put them?"

"I don't know. You'll have to ask Mito. I expect in the sleeping quarters she shares with Guynor."

"Then I'd better go and ask her to show me what she brought," he said, looking around for Mito. "I have an idea that might prevent Carrie from being recognized.

"Will you wait here till I return? As you said, I don't want to leave Carrie on her own." Saying this, he got to his feet and made his way across the cavern to where Mito sat beside the cooking area.

After a brief conversation, she reluctantly led him out of the main cavern and down another smaller tunnel.

He was back in five minutes, carrying an armload of various materials which he deposited on the table. As he did so, Carrie noticed he was wearing one of the jackets with a purple band over the shoulder. He also had the utility belt, but there was no weapon hanging at his side.

"We have to make her look like a male Terran, Vanna. You can help me."

"A male! What for?"

"Her father is one of the leaders of the Underground and he will have all their people watching for a female answering her description. They will not be looking for a male."

"But her color," objected Vanna. "How can we change her color? And how will Mito's robes help?"

"Unlike us, the Terrans are all the same color. It is their shape that is different," he explained, casting a cautious look in Carrie's direction.

"Her shape?" echoed Vanna, her professional interest aroused. "In what way?" She looked from Kusac to Carrie and back again.

"Ask Carrie sometime," he said evasively, his tail beginning to flick with embarrassment.

"It seems I won't need much disguising," Carrie replied dryly.

"You won't, but not for the reasons you think. Remember I've lived with you for several weeks. If we can make you a loose tunic and a cloak of some kind to conceal your face with your hair bound back out of sight you should be unrecognizable."

"Fair enough," agreed Carrie, "but I can only guarantee to lead you to Seaport. From then on we'll need all the good luck we can muster."

"In that case, we can start now. I have the necessary sewing things in my medical kit," said Vanna.

"The rest are organizing a hunting party. Why don't you go with them, Kusac? Guynor will be going, so Carrie will be safe with me."

Kusac hesitated.

Go with them, Kusac. They are your people, you have to take your place among them again, Carrie advised mentally.

"Very well," he replied. "I'll see if I can catch something more interesting than those rabbits we've been living on for the last couple of days."

Chapter 6

The next few hours passed quietly for Carrie. While the two women sorted through the tabard style robes that Mito had donated, they chatted, each curious about the other's culture.

"What's your home world like?" asked Carrie.

"It's just home," Vanna said.

"Yes, but what makes it home? Why did you leave it for space?"

"Our Clan lives on the outskirts of . . ."

"Clans? You live in Clans?"

"Of course. Don't you?"

"No. We live in smaller family units."

"Oh. Well, our Clan owns land on the outskirts of one of the major cities on Shola. It's good crop growing land, with a small reservation of wooded roughland for hunting. You'd like it."

"Is the Clan large? How many of you live there?"

"The Clan land is like a village with many small houses as well as communal ones and the main house of the Clan Lord. There's always room for the main Clan members to live or stay there, and even enough to accommodate several of the wives and families who marry into the Clan should their husbands meet with some disaster."

"So who lives in the cities?" asked Carrie, taking up the scissors to snip the ends of the thread she was using.

"As well as the Clans we have the Guilds. They are craft oriented . . . but you must know all this," said Vanna.

"Yes, it's familiar when I hear it, but I don't understand it," Carrie said. "Go on, please."

"The Guilds are craft based, except for one which is also a Clan. That's the Telepaths' Guild. Telepathy is mainly hereditary, so the Guild and the Clan are virtually the same. Kusac, for instance, could have a position of importance in the Clan as well as at the Guild house."

"What about you?"

"I'm a member of the Guild of Medics. I showed a talent for biology at school and won a place for myself at the Guild, where I trained. The Guild is my second home, as are all the Guilds for their members."

"What do they provide apart from an education?"

"Protection, legal advice, a roof over your head in every city you visit—everything you could ask for. We all pay Guild dues, of course, to fund this."

"Mm." Carrie sewed in silence for a moment. "Is there a difference in the way the sexes are treated?" she asked at length.

"Well, yes, of course there is," she grinned. "Don't you make sure your young men are kept out of trouble during adolescence?"

"Pardon?" Carrie looked up at her, startled.

"You mean you don't?" Vanna looked intrigued. "How do you cope with their need to prove themselves physically, and their willingness to fight anyone—they aren't fussy who—over anything?"

"Ours don't really do that. At least, only for a year or two," she amended.

"Until our youngsters are at least thirty, you can forget getting anything useful out of them unless they are in the military!" said Vanna, putting down her work and resting her chin on her palm. Her ears flicked forward as she fixed Carrie with her chartreuse eyes, the vertical slits narrowing slightly in concentration.

"In the military, with the Challenge system, their aggression is channeled at an age when they cannot control it themselves. Once they have reached their thirties, most of them choose to return to Shola and take up the Guild training appropriate to their abilities.

"Despite taking longer to mature, they do make as worthwhile contributions to society as we do."

"What about women, then?"

"We mainly stay on Shola though those, like me, who want to go into space can do so. I wanted to study Alien species as well as practice medicine, and the best way for me to do that was through the military.

"We form the basis of society and from there on it is skill and ability that decides how far you go in your chosen Guild.

"What about you Terrans? What are the differences between your men and women?"

"Men are mainly the doers, with women at home having the children and providing their backup. We can have careers, but not here on Keiss," she said, a note of bitterness in her voice. "We lost one hundred and sixty-three people in the Crossing and they were mainly women. It diminished our gene pool, creating a need for children if the colony is to survive."

"So you ran away," nodded Vanna, reaching out to clasp her arm in sympathy. "I can understand why. We have no such problem. When our young men have left the military, there is time enough to start a family. In that the Clan supports you with its crèche. You are free to pursue a career yet still have your children.

"What is it you would like to do with your life?" she asked, taking up her work again.

"Much the same as you," said Carrie with a grin. "Study Aliens!"

They laughed, each finding in the other something of herself and liking it.

By the end of the afternoon, they had managed to construct a short tunic and an all encompassing hooded overrobe out of a darker color.

"I'm afraid there's nothing much left of Mito's clothing," Carrie sighed as she folded up the remaining bits and pieces.

"They serve a more useful purpose camouflaging you than decorating her," said Vanna. She cocked her head to one side. "That sounds like one of the hunting parties returning. I had better start building up the fire. Those who don't take part in the hunt are in charge of the cooking," she explained. "I hope you know something about cooking because I could do with some new ideas."

"I know a little," said Carrie, following her over to the fire. "It depends on what they bring back. Between us we should be able to concoct something edible."

Mito and Guynor entered the cavern as Vanna began feeding wood onto the fire.

"We found nothing but small game," Guynor said with disgust, throwing several furry creatures onto the ground by the fire. "Is there any c'shar? My mouth is as dry as the plains of Navaan."

"In a moment, Guynor," Vanna answered, pulling a couple

of mugs toward her. From a pot on the side at the fire, she lifted a ladle and spooned the steaming drink into mugs.

"Would you take these over to Guynor and Mito?" she asked Carrie.

"Of course."

"I refuse to allow that creature to touch our food or drink," snarled Guynor.

"Then you're going to be very hungry and thirsty, aren't you?" Carrie replied tartly, banging the mugs down on the table in front of the two Sholans, "because I'm helping Vanna with the cooking."

"Oh, leave her alone, Guynor," sighed Mito. "Her touch won't contaminate the food."

Guynor growled deep in his throat. "She is an abomination, a hairless abomination—a nonperson!"

"Your insults mean nothing to her, Guynor," said Vanna. "You won't provoke her into Challenging you. Her people have no rite of Challenge."

"Then she is hardly worth my notice," he said, turning his back on them.

There was a slight commotion from the entrance as Kusac, followed by Garras, came in.

"You got back before us, I see," said Kusac, nodding to the other two as he made his way over to Carrie. "How did your hunt go? Only those? Ours was more profitable, then." He threw the carcass of a large long-legged animal down beside her, thankfully taking the hot drink she offered him.

"A good kill, Garras," said Guynor, walking over to inspect the beast. "A fine rhakla. We'll eat well for several days. But why do you let Kusac throw it at the feet of this creature?"

"It was Kusac's kill," Garras replied, accepting the mug that Carrie held out to him. "He picked up the trail. When it scented us we gave chase, but it was Kusac who caught and felled it with one blow. A good, clean kill as you say. It's been a long time since I enjoyed a hunt so much."

Guynor grunted. "Still, he should not have given it to the hairless one."

Garras' ears twitched angrily. "The kill was his to award where he wished. Be thankful he gave it to the Terran and not to Mito!" The Captain stalked over to the other table, effectively ending the conversation. Guynor spun on his heel and rejoined Mito.

"I hope one of you two knows how to skin this deer, because I haven't the faintest idea where to even begin," Carrie said, her voice sounding small in the sudden silence.

"When I've finished my drink, I'll show you," said Kusac, mentally cursing himself for being a fool over the rhakla.

It was dark by the time they had finished eating. The other Sholans were sitting in pairs around the fire—Mito with Guynor, and Vanna with Garras. Carrie lounged on the bench, while Kusac sat on the floor by her feet. They were listening to Vanna tell a story set in the dawn of Sholan history. As they listened, Guynor began to groom Mito. Without thinking, Carrie reached into her rucksack for her own brush and began to do the same for Kusac. She had groomed him every night at the Inn, long sweeps of the brush until all the loose hair was removed from his coat and it gleamed like polished ebony. Lost in the story and her task, she failed to notice the reactions of the other Sholans until Guynor's hiss drowned out Vanna. The female Sholan's voice faltered, then was silent.

"Captain, he has let this . . . female go too far! First he encouraged her by giving her the kill, and now this! She treats him as if he were her mate, and he lets her. Even if she were not an Alien, she is not of our Grade. An ungraded kitten will fight, yet not her! At every moment in his dealings with her, he breaks tradition. It cannot be allowed to continue."

Carrie sat motionless as fear swamped her. Kusac had warned her they must be careful, and by her unthinking, foolish act she had placed them in danger.

Kusac reached up to where Carrie's hand still held the brush against his fur. He moved her hand and the brush forward, indicating that she should continue.

"As you said, Guynor, she is an Alien, so she cannot be judged by our customs and traditions. If she was a Sholan, her Grade would be the same as mine because of her abilities among the Terrans—and the Sholans. As for fighting, Terrans fight, and so does Carrie, but her unwillingness to take you on when she—as you rightly point out—has no protective fur or claws, is caution not cowardice," Kusac said mildly. "Concerning her grooming me, she did this for me when I was too ill to tend myself."

"Then why does she continue? You are no longer ill. I say that . . ."

"Enough, Guynor!" snapped Garras. "You have altogether too much to say! You see threats where none exist. It is as Kusac says. She is Terran and we should not judge her by Sholan standards. If you cannot listen to Vanna peacefully, then retire!"

Guynor glowered at the Captain for several seconds, ears down and hands flexing at his sides, before he was forced to lower his gaze.

"Mito, are you coming?" he demanded, pulling his protesting crew mate to her feet.

"There's no need for this, Guynor. I want to hear the story."

"You've heard it before. Come."

Vanna watched their retreating figures.

"Shall I continue with the story?" she asked at length.

Garras sighed. "No. Guynor has broken this evening up yet again." He got to his feet, moving away from the fire. "Every day I expect him to issue a Challenge to me. He is a by-the-book man, with no flexibility. Everything must be black or white for him.

"There is another chamber that one of you can use. I believe there's enough spare bracken to make it reasonably comfortable."

When Garras and Vanna had gone, Kusac moved up to sit beside Carrie, taking the brush from her now limp grasp.

"Don't worry," he said quietly, beginning to brush her hair. "Garras sees you as a non-Sholan and makes allowances. Guynor feels threatened by us and so hits out at you verbally when I am there. He won't dare to actually harm you because he knows that without you, we face a long exile on Keiss. This is an old personal conflict between him and me."

"I'm not so sure."

"I am," he said, handing the brush back to her and drawing her to her feet as he stood up. He hesitated, then making up his mind reached out to put his hands on her shoulders, gently drawing her closer—all the time watching for fear or resistance but there was none.

Their disagreement over her link with her sister had gone unmentioned, but it still lay between them. He knew she cared about him, he could feel it through the link, but he needed to know if it went deeper than that for her. Dangerous though it undoubtably was, he had to know now while their link was still new. Nothing was being resolved between them at the moment, nor would it be unless he made the first move.

He laid his cheek against hers, feeling her hands on his arms, her fingers pushing through his fur to the skin underneath.

She could feel his tongue like rough velvet against her cheek then, as she relaxed into his embrace and tilted her face up to his, he moved to explore the space behind her ear. A small noise, almost like a purr escaped her and he laughed, his voice unsteady as he released her. This was real, this was no compulsion acting on either of them.

"Go, or you'll get no sleep tonight," he said, capturing her hand briefly and touching it to his mouth. "You go into the chamber. I'll stay here."

He let her hand go and gave her a little push when she demurred. "I'll keep watch on the entrance from here. No one will bother you tonight."

Carrie hesitated. She could still feel the gentle pressure of his teeth against her fingertips, the texture of his fur.

"I found out who it was that responded to my telepathic probe. It was Mito."

"Mito?" repeated Kusac, wrinkling his nose. "She's no telepath. Still, I suppose it makes a kind of sense."

"Were you close before?" she asked hesitantly.

Kusac's eyes narrowed to pinpoints. "We had a brief ... relationship," he said. "There was no more to it than that. She is too ambitious for anything more than personal advancement, with a little light entertainment thrown in now and then. For a few days I was that light entertainment."

His face relaxed, and when he looked down at her again, his eyes were heavy lidded with fatigue.

"Go and sleep now. You will be safe, I give you my word," he urged gently.

Carrie nodded, feeling as if a weight she hadn't known existed was suddenly lifted from her. Surprised, she felt it echoed in Kusac.

"Till the morning," she said, moving off toward the sleeping chamber.

From the moment the forest had started to thin out, they had been able to see the remains of the Terran colony ship.

Only a fraction of its former height, it still dwarfed every building in Seaport. Its main function was to house the computer library and the communications system that prior to the arrival of the Valtegans had linked all the townships and was the colony's only source of contact with the second wave ship.

It had been early morning when they arrived, sneaking through the fields to the dockside, searching for their present hiding place—an upturned boat, storm damaged beyond easy repair. They had watched the small fishing fleet return and unload its catch amid a flurry of noise; seen housewives and tavern keepers bargaining over the boxes of fish and crustaceans and heard the sullen, hate-laden silence as a detachment of Valtegans arrived for their daily quota of fish. Overhead, the seabirds wheeled and screeched their litany of complaint.

The market session over, the fishermen and the settlers began to drift away. Before long, the dockside was virtually deserted.

Carrie stretched her cramped muscles, sighing with relief.

"Now we can do something, instead of skulking under this boat like a couple of rats! If there are any of the guerrillas in town, they'll be in the tavern with the fishermen. You wait here for me."

"No," said Kusac, uncurling his damp tail and pushing himself into a more upright position. "I'm coming with you. I want to be near in case of trouble. Don't worry," he added, forestalling her. "I'll stay out of sight."

"I don't see how you can," Carrie objected, checking her surroundings mentally before scrambling out from under the boat. "A cat your size isn't exactly an everyday sight here."

"I'll manage," he said with finality, joining her on the quayside.

They made their way quickly across the open market area to the houses on the other side, ducking around and behind lobster creels, wicker baskets, and drying nets. Keeping close to the walls, they hugged what shadows there were and prayed that the townspeople would be too busy eating their midday meal to look out onto the main street.

They reached the tavern without incident. To one side of the building, a narrow lane led to the ubiquitous vegetable plot. Kusac padded silently down there and, keeping his belly low to the ground, wormed his way deep among the rows of peas and beans.

Keep your mind open to me, he thought to her. *I want to know everything that happens.*

You're too cautious, she replied, tying her hair back before pulling the hood over her head. *They are my own kind. I should have nothing to fear from them, provided they don't discover who I am.*

Kusac snorted. *I trust no one—bar you. Take care.*

As Carrie approached the door, she heard the sound of raucous laughter. She hesitated briefly then, taking a deep breath, pushed the door open and stepped inside.

The air was hot and reeked of ale, tobacco, and fish. She pushed her way past several burly fishermen, making her way to the bar where the landlord's harassed daughter was serving.

Catching the girl's attention, she ordered a mug of cider and some bread and cheese, the best the few meager coins she had brought would allow. Clutching her lunch, she headed for the only darkened corner of the room, settling herself in a spot that gave her a modicum of invisibility yet still enabled her to see everyone in the room.

She munched her bread as she scanned the faces around her. How could she possibly tell who was likely to be a guerrilla?

Check the room for exits first, came Kusac's thought. *You may need to leave in a hurry.*

Obediently, Carrie looked around the tavern. It wasn't too different from her father's. To the far side of the bar, stairs led up to the bedrooms. On the other side was the doorway to the kitchens and the private quarters belonging to the landlord and his family. Through there would be the door out to the garden and the fields beyond.

Too many places you could be stopped. Let's have another look at the windows.

They were large, glass covered, and closed.

Not much better, Kusac muttered. *Still, if you need to leave in a hurry . . .*

Now may I look for our guerrilla?

By all means, came the polite rejoinder.

Still munching bread and cheese, Carrie resumed her study of the tavern's customers.

Most of them looked like seamen—stockily built and

wearing waterproof boots and trousers. The rest looked like farmers, which was reasonable enough considering that in every community there were farmers, even in Seaport. What made her think she could spot a guerrilla? They couldn't exactly walk about proclaiming their profession, could they? Not with the Valtegans searching for them. Maybe there weren't any here today. She sighed, taking a drink of her cider.

Alert for any trouble, she began to sense the people nearest to her looking for a kind of independence, a freedom of spirit, something that would tell her its owner was not just another colonist.

At last she found what she was looking for, a man over by the bar talking to the barmaid. There was a rebelliousness of spirit that marked him apart from the others.

So, she'd found him. Now what?

Get him to look your way, to notice you, suggested Kusac.

A nudge here, a suggestion there and . . .

No! exclaimed Kusac. *That is manipulation! You mustn't do that.*

It's effective, and it's easy, replied Carrie briefly.

"You looking for someone, lad?"

Managing to look surprised, Carrie twisted round, mug ready to fling at the stranger.

"Don't waste your drink on me, I mean no harm," he continued, slipping onto the seat opposite her. "What brings you off the land at this time of day?" he asked, helping himself to a small lump of cheese from her plate.

"Be my guest," Carrie murmured dryly.

"I will," he grinned, helping himself to another piece. "So what brings you here?"

Carrie shoveled the last of her meal into her mouth and studied him closely.

A shock of dark wavy hair framed his face, almost obscuring his brown eyes. The features were regular and pleasing, but with a brooding quality about them. He was well built and would probably stand about one and a half meters tall.

"Well?" he prompted.

"It's my rest period," Carrie replied.

"You're not from here, are you?" he asked abruptly. "I know most of the people here, but you're new."

Carrie shrugged, taking a mouthful of cider. "I wanted to visit the big town. We've nothing like this inland."

"Which settlement are you from?"

"Back inland," she replied, "toward the south. Boring there, it is. Nothing to do all day but work."

"Have to work, lad, or we don't eat," he smiled slightly. "My name's Skai. What they call you?"

"Richard," she replied, picking the first name that came to mind. "What do you do, then?"

"Oh, this and that," he replied. "What's needed and where it's needed. I like to travel. I'm one of life's itinerants."

"Yeah? Sounds better than working the land. I wasn't cut out to be a farmer. Never did like digging and planting things."

"What would you rather do, then?" Skai asked, leaning back and taking a long drink of his beer.

"Dunno. There must be something more interesting than digging sods and hoeing up weeds, though. Maybe something like you do," she said craftily, "though I have never heard of casual laborers that did well. Most of them just manage to stay this side of starvation, and you don't look as if you go short of anything."

"I do well enough. But you, now, you interest me," he said, looking at her appraisingly. "It's not usual for people to travel from the settlements to here for pleasure. For business, yes, but not just for pleasure. Even then they do it in a day or stop overnight at another settlement. But you look as if you've spent at least a couple of nights roughing it."

Carrie began to panic slightly. Skai was just a little too observant, and he had the relaxed look of a dangerous man. She was pretty certain he was one of the guerrillas, but had he penetrated her disguise?

"Yes, I have a feeling you are more than you seem, Richard," he said.

"Me? That's good, that is. Here's me looking for adventure and you think I've already found it!" Even to herself, her laugh sounded forced.

"Which settlement are you from?" she asked, trying to fill in the silence which followed her last remark.

"Hillfort."

"What made you leave?"

"The same as you."

"I doubt it," she muttered unguardedly.

"I thought you were a runaway."

Carrie feigned confusion, and while Skai basked momentarily in his own conclusions, she probed quickly and efficiently at the edges of his mind.

Suspecting her of being a runaway, he had seen in her a likely recruit for the guerrilla bands.

There was a surge of pleasure from Kusac. *Good, you have found our guide! Now bring him outside.*

I've found a guerrilla, she corrected.

"Never said I was a runaway," Carrie muttered sullenly.

"Didn't have to," he said. "It was pretty obvious. I'm not going to persuade you to go back," he added hurriedly, as Carrie shifted in her seat. "I'm going to offer you work."

"Work for you?" she said incredulously. "You travel about yourself!"

"My present employer would offer you work."

"Don't want to be a farm laborer."

"Not farm laboring, that I promise you," Skai grinned.

Carrie hesitated.

"Why not come with me and see what you think once you've met the other men. You might like it."

"I might. If I was a runaway," said Carrie, getting to her feet.

"If you were," agreed Skai.

Skai pushed his way out of the tavern into the street, grabbing hold of Carrie just as she was about to walk into a squad of Valtegan guards.

"Watch it," he said. "Don't you know that the guerrillas have been hitting the Valtegans badly these past two months?"

"What caused all this activity?" asked Carrie as she followed Skai past the houses, angling for the forest. They were virtually retracing the route Carrie and Kusac had used entering Seaport.

Skai shot her a look. "You really have been out of it, haven't you? It's midpoint for the *Erasmus* in nine days' time. They're trying to find some way of getting a message to the ship to make it turn around."

Carrie made a grunt of assent and gently began probing his mind to find out where he was heading. Looming at the forefront of his thoughts was concern that his gun would still be where he'd concealed it in the undergrowth. Minutes later, from behind her Kusac silently thrust the weapon into her waiting hand before he merged into the bushes again.

When they reached the spot, Carrie let Skai hunt futilely for a couple of minutes before stopping him.

"I'm afraid you won't find it there, Skai," she said apologetically. "I've already got it."

As he turned round, she raised the gun to point squarely at his chest.

"How did you get hold of it? Give it back to me," he said angrily, taking a step forward.

"Get back," she said harshly. "I'm prepared to use it if I have to."

Skai retreated as she fingered the trigger action.

"Careful, those things don't need a lot of pressure. Look, I don't know what you're playing at, or who you think I am, but I'm nobody," he said, trying to be conciliatory. "I'm just a simple . . ."

"Don't insult me. A farm laborer you are not," said Carrie. "They don't go around carrying Valtegan energy weapons.

"I came to Seaport to find a guide. Do you know your way through the forest and the swamp? Don't lie to me," she warned, bringing her other hand up to support the gun. "I'll know if you do."

Skai hesitated, then gestured helplessly. "Look, lad, I don't know what your problem is, but this is no way to solve it," he began.

Carrie lunged to one side as Skai suddenly launched himself at her. Turning quickly, she pointed the gun down and fired into the undergrowth by his foot.

"Don't fool with me, mister. I meant what I said." She relaxed her stance slightly. "Now, my time is short. Do you or don't you know your way around the forest and the swamp?"

"Yes, I do," replied Skai. "Just what the hell is it you want?"

"Later," said Carrie, throwing back her hood. "Put your hands behind your back, please."

Carrie watched various emotions flicker across his face with amused detachment as it struck him that he'd been outmaneuvered, not by a lad, but by a girl. Then his face went chalk white.

"Elise," he whispered. "But . . ."

Carrie had no difficulty picking up his thoughts. Skai had been the lad her sister had left to go to Geshader.

"No, Skai," she said, her voice gentler, "my sister is dead. I'm Carrie."

He took a deep breath. "You're so like her, even down to the way she wore her hair." His color was gradually returning.

"We were identical twins."

"But what are you doing out in the forest?" He took a step toward her. "Come on, give me my gun back. A joke's a joke."

"Get back, Skai. I'm deadly serious." Her voice took on the hard tone he remembered from her sister. "Hands behind your back."

"What the hell do you want to go through the swamp for? What crazy scheme have you got cooked up?"

"Just get your hands behind your back and stop asking so many questions."

Angrily, Skai complied and as Carrie moved nearer, felt his hands being roughly tied from behind. He tried to peer over his shoulder, but a movement from Carrie stopped him.

"Don't," she said. "You'll meet him later." She took off her scarf and, moving nearer, threw it past him. "Blindfold him, Kusac."

"Now just a minute," exclaimed Skai, beginning to move, but a hand with an iron grip held him still.

"I said later. If you make any more protests, I may gag you, too," she said, a hint of laughter in her voice. "You lead him, Kusac."

By the time dusk fell, Kusac had taken them deep into the forest, heading in the general direction of the swamp. He seemed to be able to sense the body of stagnant water.

Skai muttered angrily as he was hauled to his feet for the umpteenth time after pitching headfirst over a log.

"This is a fine way for a guide to travel—blindfolded and bound. I don't know why you brought me, lady, but you sure don't need a guide."

"This is a good place to camp," said Kusac, holding Skai steady by the arm. "We can't travel much farther tonight."

Carrie nodded. "All right. You tie him to a tree, then we'll get a fire going. Our rations should do for three of us, shouldn't they?"

"I'll hunt tomorrow," Kusac agreed.

Once the fire was going and a pot of water was boiling, Carrie turned her attention to Skai.

"Take off his blindfold, Kusac," she said, sitting opposite the man.

Skai blinked and shook his head. He'd been deprived of sight for so many hours that his vision was blurred.

"I think you owe me an explanation, you and your friend." He looked round for Kusac. "Where's he gone?"

"You'll meet him soon enough.

"As for our explanation, it couldn't be simpler. In the swamp is a space-going life pod. On it is a transmitter capable of reaching *Erasmus*. Kusac and I need to reach that pod so we can signal our ship."

"Wait a minute. We don't have life pods with transmitters. The only one on the planet belongs to the Valtegans."

"No. Kusac's people have one."

Kusac emerged from the shadows and squatted beside Carrie in the full glare of the camp fire.

Skai took a deep breath. "Ah. You're that Carrie, Peter Hamilton's missing daughter. I should have remembered immediately. I guess I was just thrown by how much you look like Elise. And your cat . . . isn't, is he?"

Kusac showed his teeth in a grin. "I'm Sholan. Our scout craft was shot down on this planet several weeks ago. The life pod is ours and was dropped here years ago when we first surveyed the planet.

"If we can get to the pod, we can signal my people for help, and they can contact *Erasmus*. But we need to negotiate the swamp. Will you help?"

Skai pulled against his bonds, trying to get his anger to override his fear.

"You expect me to trust you when you treat me like this? How do I know you're any better than the Valtegans? We could be just changing one set of overlords for another," he exclaimed. *God, look at the size of him!* Skai shuddered and tried to suppress the thought.

"You're the only human apart from me who knows Kusac is an Alien. Do you think I'm fool enough to give you that information near Seaport where anyone could overhear us, or you could run to your superiors? We need someone who's man enough to act on his own without a committee decision. As you said, we have only nine days before *Erasmus* reaches midpoint, and we've still got to find the pod. Are you going to help us or not?" demanded Carrie.

The silence lengthened as Skai tried to come to terms with the dual problems of a second race of Aliens—possibly friendly ones—and sitting opposite his dead lover's twin.

"We're the only chance you have," said Kusac finally.

"I know, damn it! It doesn't make you the right one, though."

"He's cautious," said Carrie. "He's afraid for his own skin."

"And you aren't, I suppose," said Skai bitingly. "You're willing to throw your lot in with these Aliens and risk all the people on Keiss, not to mention the millions on Earth, just on your say so? How can you be so Goddamn sure? Elise was sure she knew what she was doing, and look where that got her!

"If you knew he was an Alien, how come you didn't tell us earlier, when there was time to come to a reasoned decision?" Skai pulled angrily at the ropes again.

Carrie sighed. "Release him, Kusac. He isn't going anywhere.

"Until a few days ago, I didn't know he was anything more than a forest cat," she said as Kusac leaned forward.

Extending his claws fully, he slashed through the ropes binding the man to the tree.

Skai rubbed the circulation back into his chafed wrists, keeping a wary eye on the Sholan. He didn't want to get too near those claws.

"I'm a psychic. I know these people, I know how they feel. They share many of the same hopes and goals that we have. They won't betray us."

"God! That's all I need. An hysterical female who thinks she's a psychic as the first human contact these folks have!"

"Show him, Carrie," said Kusac. "Give him the proof he wants."

Carrie reached mentally for Skai, finding the rhythm of his thoughts and tuning in to them.

Skai stiffened slightly, a look of utter shock coming over his face.

Send him the images of your two colony planets, Kusac. Show him what the Valtegans did to your people.

Kusac complied, and for several minutes Skai remained

rigid while he "saw" the devastation that was all that remained of the Sholan planets murdered by the Valtegans.

When Kusac released his contact, Skai slumped forward, breathing heavily.

As he opened his mouth to speak, Carrie forestalled him.

"No, it isn't a trick. That's what you were going to say, wasn't it? Kusac's people have psychics, too, but to them it's a respectable profession, bound by its own rules."

"Do you believe us now?" she asked.

"I have no choice," said Skai, his voice ragged from the shock of the contact and the mental images Kusac had sent him. "As you said, they're our only chance. Yes, I'll help you."

"Good," said Carrie. "Now let's eat. You look like you need a good hot drink.

"Do you really know your way through the swamp?" she asked as she pulled out their only mug and the remains of the coffee.

"Lady, you don't know how lucky you are," said Skai, gratefully holding out a shaking hand for the hot drink. "We all do a tour of duty in the swamp, watching the Valtegan base on the other side. I just came off duty last week. Yes, I know the dry paths through there, but it's a dangerous place. There are flesh eaters of every shape and size, not to mention the quicksand. It's a tidal swamp, and if you don't pick the right time, the safe route can kill you.

"The swamp goes right up to the coastline where the base is. It's a dangerous trek even for those who know the way. We had to lead the next detail through the path to show them the changes in the land. What's safe one week isn't necessarily safe the next."

Kusac threw him a trail bar and a strip of dried meat.

"We should reach the swamp by this time tomorrow," he said. "I'll hunt for a midday meal, then we can contact the rest of the crew. They can meet us there tomorrow night with provisions. When the tide is right, you can lead us to the pod. By then I'll be able to 'show' you where it is mentally."

Skai nodded.

"How many of you are there on Keiss?" he asked.

"Only four others. We lost three in the crash."

"Let's eat and sleep," said Carrie. "Questions can wait till tomorrow. We'll have to be up at dawn. Time is short for us."

She settled down beside Kusac, taking the emergency blankets out of her backpack and handing one to Kusac. Wrapping hers around herself, she lay back and leaned her head on the now thin bag while she munched on her meat and biscuit.

Kusac threw more wood on the fire, then, putting his blanket over them both, stretched out beside her, his tail curling protectively over her. He luxuriated in the warmth from the fire for a few moments, then closed his eyes.

Skai regarded them, part of his mind wondering if he could manage to escape once they were asleep, or at least get his gun back from the girl. The other part saw Carrie lying there, so like Elise—and there was an Alien beside her.

What was it with those Hamilton girls? Weren't their own men good enough? Could he have done more to stop her? Elise had known how he felt, but it hadn't stopped her, she'd still left him. Perhaps he was getting a second chance with Carrie.

"Don't. Like your cats, I sleep with one eye open," said Kusac, his voice slurred to a velvet purr. "I know you're not fully convinced, but stay around. You will be. Meanwhile, leave Carrie alone. She's not her sister."

Just what did he mean by that? Skai wondered. Faced with the inevitable, he gave up and settled down to sleep.

Skai wakened before the others. He lay staring at Carrie, wondering about her. He only knew what all the guerrillas knew—that she was the sister of Elise and the daughter of Peter Hamilton, head of the Passive Resistance, and that she and her cat were missing. Except the cat was an intelligent Alien, one of a race with more than two well established colony planets, and probably faster than light spacecraft. God alone knew how wide the technical gap was between them!

Wait till Captain Skinner heard about the Aliens. What did she say they were called? Sholans, that was it. Shame the girl had to be their first contact. He would have driven a hard bargain for their help. He'd have demanded access to some of their higher technology, but she'd just offered it for free. Just like a woman. No sense of the value of things.

He was drawn to her. It wasn't surprising considering his unfinished affair with Elise. She had long hair like her sister and he liked women with long hair, they looked more feminine. Most of them on Keiss kept their hair short, said it was more practical. He'd have to try and get her away from the Alien.

He frowned as Kusac stirred in his sleep and curled more protectively round Carrie. What was the Sholan after anyway? He was a bit too familiar with the girl. Surely they couldn't be lovers.

Never mind. He was something the Alien could never be, human like her and that was what would count in the end. He could charm a country girl like her, no problem. That's the way it had started with Elise, but then she'd gotten under his skin.

He fingered his wrist communicator thoughtfully. By rights, he ought to contact the Captain at their base. He could play this his way and maybe come out looking pretty good. And there was Carrie. He wouldn't be missed for a day or two, so he had the time to play with. It could be an interesting few days.

Carrie stirred and began to stretch against Kusac, waking him, too.

I see our guide is still with us, came Kusac's thought.

Of course. Had he tried to leave, he would have found it impossible, like walking through a solid wall. I planted that thought last night before you let him "see" your two colony planets.

But that's mental manipulation! sent Kusac.

So? It was necessary. We can't trust him.

That's a crime among my people, Carrie. You can't do that.

Kusac, it isn't a crime for me. We have no code of ethics for telepaths.

You mustn't do it, Carrie. You will have to adopt a code if your people have many more like you. Telepaths mustn't take advantage of others by using their Talent. It infringes on the rights of the individual. Can't you see?

Yes, but we're at war at the moment, and that changes the rules. We cannot afford to lose him.

It doesn't matter. Please do not use your Talent like that again.

His tone was so worried and concerned that she relented a little.

I'll try to stick to your code, but I can't promise. Now come on, we have to get moving.

Carrie stretched again and smiled across at their guide, who was beginning to show signs of life.

"Good morning. I'm afraid we didn't introduce ourselves officially last night. This is Kusac," she indicated the Sholan, who was rekindling the small fire. "As you surmised, I'm Carrie Hamilton."

"Skai," he responded, smiling and holding out a friendly hand.

Hesitantly, Carrie took it. His touch was firm yet gentle, almost a caress. She was glad when he released her.

"What made you leave your settlement?" he asked.

"I wanted to join the guerrilla forces," she replied shortly, handing the kettle to Kusac. "We need some water," she said. "Can you smell any nearby?"

"There's some not too far away," he replied. "I'll not be long." He melted silently into the bushes at the edge of their campsite.

Carrie handed Skai a piece of dried meat and began chewing one herself.

"How far is the beginning of the swamp from here?"

"Thanks to you, I can only guess where 'here' is." said Skai, moving round to sit beside her. "I take it we're traveling by dead reckoning?"

Carrie nodded, chewing hard on her food.

"Kusac can sense where the swamp is, but we have no idea of the distance involved."

"Judging from the amount of walking we did yesterday, I'd say we'd reach it by nightfall. We can't attempt to cross the swamp in the dark, so we'll have to camp again tonight."

Skai reached out to touch a stray lock of her hair.

"You have lovely hair," he said, fingering it gently.

Carrie brushed it back out of the way.

"Don't," she said sharply.

"Don't you like to be admired?" he asked softly.

"No. I've had enough of the Valtegans leering at me and—Elise," she said bitterly, moving away from him.

"I'm not a Valtegan, though."

"Just let's leave it, Skai. I don't want to talk," she said, while sending a short reassuring thought to Kusac, who was clamoring to know what had angered her.

"I didn't mean to bring back bad memories," Skai apologized.

"Look, I'm not in the market for a man, so you don't need to impress me with your concern," she said coldly.

Skai sighed. He wouldn't have thought her such a cold fish. Pity. Still, there was plenty of time. Perhaps when she got used to his company she would thaw a little.

"Tell us more about the swamp," said Carrie, falling back to let Kusac take his turn using Skai's machete to cut through the dense underbrush.

Daylight did little to break the perpetual gloom that pervaded the heart of the forest through which they now worked their way.

"I told you. It's a tidal delta, thickly overgrown with swamp grasses and a rambling network of trees. Every high tide changes the dry areas slightly, and by the end of a fortnight, the safe route you took in no longer exists. Parts of it do, but our scouts have to adapt to the ever changing geography."

"Boats?" asked Kusac, hacking through the trunk of a particularly resilient bush.

"Too overgrown. The whole thing resembles a lake covered with strips of shifting sand and vegetation."

"So how do you manage?" asked Carrie, hitching her backpack into a more comfortable position.

"We rotate every two weeks while there are still some identifiable swamp marks, and we leave markers that only we would notice."

"What about the shift coming off duty? You said they guide the next shift in."

"One man takes them in, showing them the new markers."

Carrie nodded. "Makes sense. You've just come off duty, haven't you? Think you can guide us through safely?"

"From one side to the other, yes, but you want to reach some object . . ."

"The life pod."

". . . buried in there," continued Skai. "I can't guarantee we can reach it safely."

"How deep is it? Can we wade or swim through it?" Kusac called back.

"No way. That water is alive with creatures you wouldn't want to meet. Leeches like small eels, with teeth to match, crocodiles, carnivorous fish—you name it, if it's nasty and has teeth, it lives there. You wouldn't survive more than a minute in the water.

"Then there're the insects."

"Great," groaned Carrie, catching a branch that threatened to lash her in the face, "I don't think I want to know any more for now. What do we do if we can't reach it?"

"Worry about that when the time comes," growled Kusac. "Let's just get there and find it first."

The passage of time was difficult to gauge in the flickering gloom, but eventually there came a point when muscles ached and bodies were too tired to stand any longer.

To call it a clearing was a misnomer, but at least the undergrowth was less dense. A small area large enough for the stove was cleared and a larger one was trampled down for sitting.

Skai activated the stove and put the water they'd carried with them on to boil while Carrie kneaded the worst of the cramps out of Kusac's shoulders.

"I don't know why you're bothering with hot water," she said. "We used the last of the coffee this morning."

Skai smiled, taking a packet out of his jacket. With a flourish, he produced some muslin tea bags and a small quantity of sugar.

"We guerrillas carry a few emergency rations of our own," he said, grinning.

"Tea!" exclaimed Carrie. "I haven't tasted any since the Valtegans took over the tea plantations up by Geshader. And in bags, too."

"We have our sources," said Skai. "Unfortunately, I haven't any milk.

"Now, how about giving my shoulders a rub when you've finished with your friendly Alien's?"

Carrie stiffened, but a flick of Kusac's ears relaxed her.

He stretched, rising to his feet. "I must hunt now, before I stiffen up. I will not be long, Leska," he said. Reverting to a four-legged stance, he loped off.

Skai gave an involuntary shudder. "It's uncanny how he does that. Inhuman."

Carrie grinned mirthlessly as she moved behind him. "He isn't human, he's an Alien."

"I know. Perhaps it's because he resembles a cat that he

doesn't seem ... Ouch! Do you have to be so rough?" he complained as Carrie kneaded his shoulder and neck muscles vigorously. "... quite so Alien," he continued, still wincing a little.

"If you want to get rid of the stiffness, then it's going to hurt," she said, trying not to smirk.

Skai grunted. "What are the rest of the crew like?" he asked.

She thought for a moment before answering.

"Different from Kusac. The Captain seems a fair man, but Guynor, the First Officer, he's suspicious and belligerent. The two women seem friendly—at least one of them does," she amended.

"Their hierarchy is different from ours. Age and maturity don't matter as much as the ability to win a Challenge if you're an enlisted man or a Junior Officer.

"There, that should be better now," she said, sliding her hands off Skai's shoulders.

He caught hold of her before she could move away.

"Let me do your shoulders," he said persuasively. "You've been doing as much trailblazing as Kusac and me."

Carrie hesitated, then shrugged. She twisted her hair out of the way and turned her back to Skai. It was a risk, but she ought to be able to sense in advance if he planned to make a sudden move against her.

Despite herself, she relaxed under his gentle massage.

"What's Challenge?" he asked.

"When they feel they have the ability to move up a grade in their own field, they Challenge their immediate superior. It's a fight to submission."

"A bit barbaric, isn't it? Not to say stupid. How do they make sure that intelligence and brawn go together?"

"I've no idea. I do know they have a family caste system. Some are born to their professions. For instance, Kusac's family are all telepaths."

"Seems very haphazard to me. What about people from one family who have a talent for another craft? What do they do?"

"No idea. I haven't studied their sociology. I've only been really aware of them as Aliens for a couple of days, but their infrastructure seems based on more of a pack system. We don't have an analogy because we evolved on a different planet," she said dryly. "Thanks for the massage. My muscles don't feel quite so rigid now.

"Just remember that on Shola, Kusac's people are the dominant predators, probably more efficient ones than we are on Earth," she said.

Carrie began to move, but Skai stopped her.

"I haven't finished yet. Your neck is still very tense. Now, doesn't that feel better?" he asked, his tone as gentle and caressing as the fingers that moved lightly up and down her neck.

Caught unawares, Carrie found her body responding to the massage as faint thrills of pleasure coursed through her.

Having finished his hunting, Kusac paused in the bushes at the edge of their clearing. Silently, he observed their interchange, sharing through the link her reactions to Skai's touch. This was how it should be. She needed a close relationship with a male of her own species, a mate of her own kind. This bond of theirs—Vartra alone knew how it had happened!—was not right, not natural. What would happen to her when he had to leave the planet? The only way the Leska bond was broken was by death.

He tried to remember what his father had said about it. He'd only mentioned it once. It didn't happen to every telepath, he'd said, only to a few, but when it did it was like lightning, it struck where it would.

Not much help, but then no one, least of all himself, had imagined he would find a Leska from another species, millions of miles from home. Maybe the fact that she wasn't Sholan would make a difference to the bond. Maybe they would be able to part when the problem on Keiss was over. . . .

His thoughts were interrupted by Carrie pushing Skai away.

"Thanks, I'm fine now," she said brusquely, getting to her feet.

Kusac tried unsuccessfully to repress his delight. She didn't like their guide either. If Skai continued to bother his Leska, he'd be forced to Challenge him. Shocked, he tried to stop that chain of thought. Telepaths couldn't Challenge, and he was reacting as if Carrie were a true Sholan Leska. What was he to think and do? What was really at stake here, them or two different worlds?

The politics of the situation he couldn't begin to gauge:

whichever way he looked at it, everything seemed disastrous. A new species is contacted and they are fellow Telepaths of potentially amazing abilities. They've been brutalized for years by these Valtegans, and when first contact is made, what happens? He bonds Telepathically for life to one of them.

Suddenly his spirits lightened and he grinned. Well, he'd run away to find adventure, hadn't he? Not even he could say his life was boring now.

His mind was made up. *They* were what mattered, not all the Allied World Councils nor the Terran equivalents. He'd speak to the girl, find out what she felt, and explain what a Leska bonding really entailed. It was their problem; only between them could it be solved.

Kusac pushed through the bushes and handed Carrie two small deerlike creatures.

"This should give us more than enough for tonight as well," he said, the Sholan equivalent of a pleased grin on his face, "just in case the rest of the crew are late reaching the rendezvous."

"Wonderful," said Carrie. "Real food again."

"I'll help you skin them," Kusac said, getting his knife out of Carrie's backpack.

Soon the carcasses had been skinned and gutted, and were set to cook above the small fire. Skai made up a little of his tea, all of them preferring to save their resources and drink a weak brew now with the prospect of more later.

Carrie leaned back against a tree trunk, feeling replete at last. Giving her fingers a final lick, she sighed.

"We haven't left much for later," she said wistfully, "but it was so nice to eat properly. I'd almost rather starve than eat another piece of dried meat or a trail bar, no matter how well your crew mates make them."

Kusac grinned, displaying a row of white, even canines that made Skai wince.

"They should be at the meeting place well before us, and they won't come without meat, believe me."

"I hope not," she said. "I suppose we'd better contact them before we start off again."

"You contact Vanna. You spent quite a lot of time with her yesterday, and if I know you, you were tuning in to her every now and then. I'll give you the extra power you'll need."

His thought followed immediately. *We cannot risk merging for this contact, Leska. It would leave us unprotected with Skai, and I don't trust that one.*

Are you sure I can contact her on my own?

I'll be with you. You won't be alone.

"All right," said Carrie, making herself comfortable as Kusac took her by the hand.

Crossing her legs, she rested their clasped hands on one thigh, letting the other fall limply in her lap. Eyes closed, she called to mind Vanna's face, trying to sense her presence. As the image sharpened, she saw the Sholan woman's eyes widen as she became aware of them. The picture began to fade slightly, and, hurriedly, Carrie drew on Kusac's strength. Vanna's face became clearer. Quickly, she passed on an image of the swamp and their meeting that evening. Feeling Vanna's acceptance, she let the link dissolve, breathing deeply before opening her eyes.

"Vanna got the message," she said tiredly, releasing Kusac's hand and rubbing her eyes.

"Well done," he said. "No one could have done it better. You progress well." He touched her cheek with his hand before starting to pack away their things.

"You rest for a moment while we clear up. I'm afraid we can't afford the time to let you rest properly." He reached for her rucksack and pulled out a slightly fluffy trail bar. "Eat this. It'll help," he said, trying to pick off the fluff before handing it to her.

"By my reckoning, we have about seven days till midpoint," said Skai, breaking his silence. "A reasonable safety margin."

"It's too close for comfort," she said. "I have a bad feeling about this whole pod business. How long has it been on the planet, Kusac?"

"About twenty years, I think."

"That's a long time in the type of swamp that Skai has described." She shook her head as she got to her feet. "We know the pod's been partly disabled. How do we know there's anything at all working in it? The whole thing could be a mess of rusty wiring and metal by now."

"No," said Kusac firmly. "It was designed to survive all reasonable types of climates and animal life. Even if the exterior sensors and transmitters have been damaged, there are still the manual units inside. As well as being a remote biosphere laboratory, it does have emergency life-support facilities on board. There's a manual transmitter, food rations, a medical kit—anything that could be of use to an investigatory team in difficulty."

"Let's hope you're right, because if we aren't in difficulty, I don't know who is," said Skai dryly, gathering his bits and pieces together.

Getting to her feet, Carrie kicked dirt over the fire, stamping it down well. "Time to leave," she said, picking up her backpack. "Who's blazing the trail this time?"

"I will," said Skai, taking the machete from her.

It was fully dark by the time they reached the fringe of the forest where the Sholans had set up their temporary camp. They were well back from the water's edge, under the cover of the trees so that their small camp fire could not be seen.

"Captain," said Kusac, stepping into the firelight, followed by Carrie and Skai.

There was a collective rustle as four guns were replaced in their weapons' belts.

"We've been listening to your approach for quite a while," said the Captain.

"I expect you have," replied Kusac, hunkering down by the fire. "Terran feet are not as quiet as ours, and we've had to hack our way through the bushes."

The Captain nodded. "This is our guide?" he asked, pointing at Skai, who was still standing on the edge of the circle of firelight.

Kusac turned round and gestured to the man to join them.

"Yes. Be careful with him. He is an opportunist and I sense there are several things he is concealing from us, but my oath forbids me finding out under the present circumstances."

"Your oath can be damned convenient at times," growled Guynor.

"Also beware of the fact that this Terran, in common with all the others on Keiss, is not used to dealing with Aliens other than the Valtegans," continued Kusac, ignoring Guynor's interruption. "He does not trust us, and it will take some time before he does."

"I will note your warning," replied Garras. "Before this state of war, I was involved in escorting Trade missions to the Chemer on the planet Terney. I have some experience of early, if not first contact.

"Now introduce us. Vanna, give them some food. We'll talk while you eat."

Vanna handed Carrie a chunk of roasted meat. "It's good to see you again," she said. "I was surprised to get your message."

"After Kusac, I know you best," she said. "For now, I'm just grateful to sit down," she continued, settling herself next to Kusac. "If I never see another bush or tree, it will be too soon!"

Skai's pallor was beginning to fade as he concentrated on breathing evenly. Somehow the Sholans, though about the same average size, seemed to mass larger and he felt dwarfed by their presence. He tried to concentrate as Kusac introduced them one by one, but he was only aware of the Alienness of them. Gratefully, he accepted the meat offered to him and bit into it hungrily. Life had ceased to be clear cut for him; it was full of gray areas of which he was unsure. Common sense took hold as he began to feel less ravenous and by the time he was offered a hot drink, he was able to look around at the assembled Sholans with a bit more equanimity.

Laboriously, Kusac asked him questions in English, then translated his replies to the Captain in a language that was lyrical in tone, yet had many guttural sounds.

He doesn't lose much of the accent when talking English, Skai thought.

After some time, Carrie interrupted Kusac.

"Why don't you give Skai the knowledge of your language telepathically? We can't pronounce yours very well, but what's to stop us understanding it?"

Kusac looked at Garras. The Captain's ears dropped and his eyes narrowed. "No," he said. "I don't want him understanding all we say. He knows enough about us for the present if your reading of his character is correct."

"This exchange of information is taking too long. If we need to know something in a hurry, the delay could be fatal," said Kusac. "I can give you the ability to speak their language. You could then understand and talk to him, but our language would remain Alien to him."

"That makes sense, but give all of us this knowledge. If the swamp is as dangerous as he says, we will need to heed his warnings immediately. Yes, go ahead and do that," nodded Garras.

"It will be less of a drain on me if Carrie helps."

"As you wish. This is your field, not mine."

"Carrie, you deal with Vanna, please. Hold her hand. It makes the transfer easier," said Kusac, reaching for the Captain's hand.

"What do I do?" asked Carrie. "I've never done this before!"

"Tune in to her brain pattern and project a concept of your language to her. It's similar to what you did earlier today. You'll know how to do it when the moment comes. Use your intuition," he said.

It took several long minutes for Carrie to find the right level from which to work, but once found, the rest was easy. She could feel Vanna's initial resistance fade, to be replaced with a sense of wonder.

So that's where the main differences lie! Carrie heard her think. *Look, this is us.*

Almost immediately, Carrie received a flood of information about the Sholans' schema of their world. She broke contact when it was done and sat there stunned while her subconscious mind tried to assimilate what she had learned.

"It must be marvelous to work directly with the mind itself," said Vanna, in a tone that Carrie now recognized as one of awe.

"I don't know," she replied, pulling her scattered thoughts together. "I'm new to this myself." She gave a shy laugh as Vanna squeezed her hand. Carrie withdrew it hurriedly when Vanna's claws pricked her flesh.

"Oh, sorry," said Vanna contritely. "I keep forgetting you haven't got fur to cushion our touch."

"It's all right," said Carrie, surreptitiously rubbing her hand against her trouser leg.

Kusac had finished with the Captain and, like her, was recouping his energy.

"That's some Talent you have," said Garras, his ears twitching rapidly as he blinked to clear his head. "Skai, can you understand me?" he asked, his tongue stumbling over the unfamiliar sounds.

"Ah, yes," said their guide. "How come you've learned English so fast?"

"Kusac has given me your tongue. We will all be given it so we can talk more easily, yes?"

"Yes," said Skai hesitantly, unsure of himself again in this new world of rapid changes.

"Kusac, teach Guynor and Mito."

"No," said Guynor unequivocally.

"You will not disobey my orders," warned Garras.

"I will not let his thoughts pollute my mind, nor will I let the language of such hairless beasts pollute my mouth!" he growled, rising to his feet.

"You will do as you are ordered," repeated Garras, his voice a low snarl as his ears flattened and flicked out to the side.

"Why do you order me to submit to these ... animals? Are we not superior? I say again, I will not!"

"Are you Challenging me?" Garras' eyes had narrowed to vertical slits as he prepared to leap to his feet. "If I can learn from these people, then so can you. Submit!"

"It is your fault! You caused this corruption!" Guynor lunged toward Carrie.

"You cannot Challenge the girl," said Vanna urgently, rising to her feet and blocking him with her body. "She is not of our kind. It would only bring you shame."

"Kusac, then!" Balked of his prey, he wheeled round on Kusac. "He is the one who sank so low as to pair with this creature. I Challenge him!"

"Nor Kusac!" shouted Vanna, grabbing at his upraised arm. "He's not your Grade. You cannot in honor Challenge him!"

Gods, thought Kusac, his mind spinning as he leapt to his feet. *It's happened.* The confrontation he had feared, and it had come too soon. He wasn't ready for it. Neither was the girl.

He glanced at Carrie. She was ashen, her face a mask of shock. He thrust her behind him as he felt the adrenaline surge into his system. His head began to swim and his stomach turned over.

"Honor?" growled the enraged Sholan, crouching lower. "Where was his honor when he entered her mind and used her? Or when they paired? I claim the Blood-rite Challenge, to purge the crime!"

"Denied!" snapped Garras, leaping to his feet. "We're at

war. I can't afford to lose any more people. If there is a crime to answer, he will face a court-martial, not you."

With a snarl of rage, Guynor launched himself at Kusac, talons ripping across his exposed flesh, knocking him to the ground.

From far away, Kusac heard Carrie start to scream, but he was too busy fighting for both their lives.

Chapter 7

Kusac hit the ground hard, barely noticing the chest wounds as Guynor landed astride him. Automatically, he raised his hands to protect himself. Guynor's face was a snarling mask of fury inches from his throat and it was taking all of his strength to keep him from getting closer.

The First Officer had chosen his time well, a detached part of Kusac's mind observed. Utterly exhausted after their journey through the forest, he had virtually no energy left for this, even if he didn't have a Telepath's inhibitions.

He felt Guynor's legs move and knew the vicious hind claws were going to rake his stomach. He relaxed briefly and as the claws caught on his belly, managed to twist just enough to throw his enemy off balance. The claws slashed shallowly across him, but the injury was slight compared to what could have happened. Pain exploded in his shoulder as Guynor sank his teeth into it and with a yowl of pure rage Kusac retaliated, catching him by the ear with his teeth.

Shock at Kusac's attack made Guynor release his shoulder enough to pull his teeth free and jerk back out of range. Blood from the torn ear was pouring down his face, blocking his vision. He shook his head, sending droplets splattering over everyone.

The fresh agony of the teeth ripping free made Kusac cry out again. Frantically, he pushed the pain to one side—he couldn't let it distract him, too much was at stake.

The mist of pain cleared and Kusac was able to take advantage of Guynor's surprise to pull his leg back and kick him squarely in the chest, sending him flying backward. He pushed himself up and dived at the Sholan, landing on him with his full weight and knocking the breath out of him. Propping himself up on his hands, he pressed down on Guynor's shoulders trying to reach the other's throat.

Guynor's arms were in his way and as he snapped at

them, catching the left forearm in his teeth, Guynor grasped his injured shoulder and dug his talons deep into the already torn and bleeding flesh.

A wave of fire screamed through Kusac's body almost making him black out. Kusac released Guynor, giving an involuntary low yowl of pain. His arm, unable to support him, buckled and he fell against Guynor's chest.

Feeling Kusac weakening, with a growl of triumph, Guynor moved his free hand to reach for his throat.

Desperation made Kusac faster. He knew his strength was spent and he could take no more. The risk was worth it. As soon as the arm moved, he stretched upward for the now exposed throat and clamped his jaws firmly round it.

Guynor stiffened, knowing he was in a death grip. He loosened his hold on Kusac's shoulder and began desperately trying to break free, hands scrabbling at Kusac's mouth.

Kusac tightened his jaws, his canines breaking the skin. He tasted blood and loosened his hold slightly. He had no wish to kill Guynor. Bringing a hand up to the Sholan's throat he encircled it at the base of the neck and pressed. Guynor began to gasp for air.

"Submit!" he heard Garras shout above the sound of his own panting. "Enough of this madness, Guynor! Submit. You have lost!"

A gargling sound came from Guynor. With difficulty, Kusac opened his hand. Drying blood was sticking their fur together. He felt sick.

Still Guynor could not speak.

Kusac opened his jaws a fraction. He dare not loose his grip any further.

"I submit," Guynor finally managed to gasp.

Kusac was aware of people taking hold of the Sholan under him.

"It's all right, Kusac. You can release him now. We have him," said Mito, touching his uninjured shoulder.

Kusac released Guynor. Hands grasped his arms and helped him to his feet. Staggering, he almost fell, but Vanna was there to steady him. He wiped his face across his forearm, but the smell of blood seemed worse. He held onto her for support while he tried to steady his breathing, to ease the burning ache in his lungs. His stomach began to spasm and he bent over, starting to retch.

"No," said Vanna, pulling him upright by the fur between his ears. "You won't throw up. Take deep breaths, fill your lungs. That's it," she said as his breathing became less erratic and he began to straighten up.

"You've done fine," she said quietly. "Your woman is safe and you fought well. Now let me see to your wounds."

Kusac shrugged free. "I'm fine; see to him."

"Kusac, I need to stop the bleeding," she said.

"I'll see to Kusac," said Mito firmly from behind him. "You see to Guynor. Don't worry, Kusac," she said as he turned round. "He's in no state to do anything. The Captain is dealing with him." Her ears dipped slightly as she put her head to one side.

All this was lost on Kusac for he was looking over to where Carrie sat huddled against a tree with Skai. When the fighting had started, he'd had the presence of mind to grab her and haul her clear of the combat.

"Kusac," Mito said softly, putting out her hand to touch him, but Kusac brushed her aside and walked over to the Terran girl.

He held out his hand to her. "Come," he said.

"Just a minute . . ." began Skai.

"Carrie, come," he ordered, reinforcing the words with a mental command.

Carrie looked up, her eyes no less glazed with pain than his. She shivered convulsively and got to her feet.

Blood glistened darkly on his shoulder, running sluggishly down his left arm.

Kusac took her hand, holding it tightly despite her feeble effort to release it.

Ignoring the five pairs of eyes watching them, Kusac drew her with him away from the camp into the forest. He led her unresistingly back along the path they had cut only a few hours before—now an eternity—until they were far enough away not to be overheard. He stopped and turned to face her.

"We have to talk," he said.

"Yes," she said dully, refusing to look at him.

Kusac cupped her face in a hand now gentle, talons retracted.

"Look at me. Please."

"Why?" she asked tonelessly.

"I need to see your face," he said simply.

She looked up. He watched her eyes move across his face,

taking in his Alienness, the aftermath of that bloody fight. Each second was like a death for him. He daren't listen to their Link for fear of what he would find.

"What do you have to say?" she asked at length.

"I wanted to talk to you, to get to know you as a person, to tell you about our Link, but we haven't had the time. We've been so busy for everyone else, both our races—No, by Vartra! Call it what it is, our species!—that we've had no time for ourselves. I have to tell you . . . Oh, damnit!" he swore, turning away and pounding his fist against a tree. "Why is it suddenly so hard to talk to you?"

The silence lengthened until he thought she had left. He felt a light touch and turned round.

Ignoring the throbbing pain, he put his hands on her shoulders, looking at her closely. She seemed less distant. He still dared not touch her mind, dared not hope.

"Carrie, because of what I did when your sister died, the link we formed the other day, it . . . it isn't an ordinary link."

"I know," she said quietly.

"Among our people, this Link makes the two people Leskas to each other. This I have told you."

She nodded.

"I haven't told you the full truth because I didn't think it could apply to us, because we are . . . different." He took a deep breath and tightened his grip, making his talons extend slightly.

"I've been afraid for several days now that this isn't so. We are true Leskas."

"I know."

"No, you don't know! Leskas are life-mates, bound by something stronger than either of them. You and I, we're bound together . . . for life. We. Cannot. Dissolve. The bond." He punctuated the words by shaking her slightly. "Do you understand me?" he asked.

"Yes," she said, tears beginning to course down her face.

"Only death can separate us—the deaths of both of us, not just one. We cannot part from each other for long because it causes mental suffering." He stopped, taking a deep breath.

"The bond is also sexual. It gives us a need for each other, flesh to flesh, mind to mind. The Gods alone know why, but they have made us one. Now do you *fully* understand?" He took a shuddering breath and waited for an answer.

"What do you want to do?" she whispered, the tears still falling.

"Want? I have no say in the matter," he said, his voice ragged. "I cannot see you as other than my true Leska, my life-mate. May Vartra and the other Gods have pity on me, because I would have no other than you!"

Carrie looked down at the ground, aware of the weight of his gaze and of his hands on her shoulders. She knew he was telling the truth, not only because she could feel it, but because she'd worked most of it out for herself.

From the first she'd felt drawn to him in a strange fascinating way. Then she'd felt it change to something more. Was this truly what she wanted? Could she again have no say in the matter? It seemed not. She knew that two worlds not two people stood beside the tree. Could they, would they . . . dare . . . make that bridge?

When she spoke, her voice was a barely audible whisper. "Then may your Gods pity me, too, because I seem to have no choice either."

Kusac froze. "What are you saying?"

"That we aren't very different. That I find myself as drawn and bound to you as you are to me."

"Then we will face the future together?" he asked, hardly daring to breathe.

"Together," she replied, looking up at him and seeing again the person that he was as well as the Alien form he wore.

Kusac pulled her close, wincing at the pain lancing through him from his bitten shoulder. He lowered his face to hers and began to run the tip of his tongue across her cheek, finally able to admit to and express the emotions that had grown in him over the weeks he had known her.

Carrie buried her face in the fur on his chest, deeply breathing in his musky scent. She clutched at his back, running her hands through the soft pelt, aware of the strength of the muscles underneath.

Their link had reasserted itself and they were surrounded by the joy they took in each other's differences. Carrie turned her face to him, capturing his mouth in a kiss that was a first for both of them. She felt his start of surprise, then he relaxed, letting her take the lead.

"I never thought I'd find a mate so far from home," he said at length, wiping the last of her tears away.

"I love you, Kusac," Carrie said, rubbing her cheek against his good shoulder.

Kusac laughed, a low rumble that seemed to vibrate through his whole body. "I never hoped I would hear you say that, Leska. I still can't make up my mind if the Gods are blessing us or playing some cruel elaborate joke.

"I love you, too," he said, laying his head against hers for a moment. "We must get back to the camp. You and I, we have work to do tomorrow, finding that life pod."

Carrie sighed and reluctantly disengaged herself. She rubbed her hands together. They were sticky. Blood. Always blood.

"I know," said Kusac, his ears flattening briefly against his skull as he took hold of her hands. "I'm sorry, but I couldn't let him touch you." He gave a little bark of a laugh. "Look at me," he said, "fresh from a Challenge and covered in blood. Hardly looking my best to win my mate, am I?"

She smiled, her whole face lighting up, and reached out to touch his cheek. "Don't," she said. "I know."

He kept her other hand in his as they began to walk back down the path.

"We will have plenty of time for us, I will see to that, don't worry," he promised her.

"Your wounds!" she exclaimed guiltily, suddenly remembering them. She stopped and tried to examine his injured shoulder, but Kusac held her firmly away.

"I am fine. There is nothing that Vanna can't treat easily. I'll let her tend them as soon as we get back."

"You promise?"

Kusac gave a deep, throaty purr. "I promise!"

Guynor was lying with his back to the fire when they returned, his bandages visible against his tan fur. His pelt looked dull and lackluster even from a distance.

"I don't think we'll have any more trouble from him," murmured Kusac as they joined the others round the fire. He was vaguely surprised that he felt neither remorse for fighting Guynor, nor even an echo of his evident pain. Perhaps it was because his own was so great.

Vanna rose as they sat.

"Will you let me see to you now the important business is out of the way," she said archly, with an openmouthed grin.

Kusac sat patiently while she clipped the fur around the wounds and examined them.

"I'm afraid this will take quite a time to heal," she said, as she carefully swabbed the dirt out of the deep gouges and puncture wounds. "You shouldn't use your shoulder at all for several days: in fact I want your arm in a sling. I can't tack the tears together, they'll have to heal naturally.

"The ones on your chest and stomach aren't deep, thankfully. They'll heal fairly quickly."

She finished off by spraying sealant over all the wounds and breaking open a sterile dressing pack.

Kusac's world was limiting itself to pain and tiredness. He was so exhausted it was all he could do to sit upright. He finally succumbed to Carrie's mental suggestion that he lean against her.

"Give me a hand with the bandage please," Vanna said to Carrie, getting her to hold it in place.

"There, that should hold if you don't do anything too energetic in the next day or two." She grinned again and sat down beside Carrie to dig in her first aid kit.

Kusac rose stiffly and went over to where Carrie had dropped her backpack.

Vanna gave the girl a sidelong look as she took out a hypoderm gun.

"So, all is now well with you and Kusac?"

"Er . . . Um . . ."

The Medic made a purring noise Carrie now recognized as a chuckle.

"I'm so glad that our barbaric Challenge ritual didn't cause trouble between you. Normally it isn't that vicious, but Guynor called the Blood-rite and that is to the death."

"I know. Remember, you gave me the equivalent of your racial history when I linked with you."

"At least you know that particular Challenge is extremely rare. Guynor had no right to Challenge Kusac at all. Telepaths can't be Challenged because of their Talent. There are too few of them, and the mental pain of combat is too great. How Kusac coped, and is coping, I don't know."

"It's probably because of me," said Carrie. "I have more—Talents Kusac calls them—than your people, and one of them is to be able to fight without sensing the pain my opponent feels."

Vanna looked round and saw Kusac returning. "Just remember," she said hurriedly, "despite what you saw in the fight, Kusac's a very gentle person."

"I know."

Kusac returned carrying Carrie's hairbrush. "I want to brush your hair," he said, sitting down behind her.

"Kusac, you should rest," warned Vanna. "We've all got a heavy day tomorrow."

"I will, but I have to do this first," he said, beginning to brush Carrie's hair with long but gentle strokes, giving it his total attention.

"I'm going to give you an analgesic and an antibiotic," Vanna said, putting the hypo gun to his thigh. "The skin around your nose and eyes is too pale. You need to eat and then rest to replace the lost blood."

He shook his head. "I couldn't eat, Vanna." The brush was still.

Carrie turned around and took it from his unresisting hand. "What if I brush you and Vanna cuts some small pieces of meat . . ."

Gratefully, he looked up at her, amber eyes dull with pain. "Please, it would be the next best thing to a shower."

Carrie began to brush carefully, teasing the knots of blood and dirt out of the silky fur.

She felt his pain almost as strongly as he could and was working hard to try and block it, remembering what he had said about her sister. Not that she believed him, but . . . He was trying to stop it from reaching her too but he was as weak as a kitten. Perhaps she could lessen it for him without actually experiencing it. She could try.

Gradually it began to diminish and she felt a sense of satisfaction.

"Do you think you could speak to Skai and explain things to him?" she said to Vanna. "I don't want him going xenophobic on us."

"Already done," said Vanna cheerfully, handing her a plate of small slices of meat. "He's talking to Mito at the moment. Oh, by the way, you put her nose nicely out of joint, Kusac. She really expected you to want her now you've bested Guynor. Serves her right, opportunistic little . . ." The rest was lost as she moved away from the fireside.

"Kusac," said Garras, leaning toward him. "I know you'd rather it were otherwise, but Guynor will face a court-martial for Challenging you. However, the charge he laid against you of Misuse of Talent is just as serious and will have to be answered."

"I know, Captain. We'll answer it."

"Good. I'll speak for you, of course. There are mitigating circumstances. Without your . . ." he hesitated briefly, one ear flicking questioningly, ". . . Leska, we would not be able to locate the pod."

Kusac's eyes darted to the Captain's face. Carrie felt his fear.

"I have come across a Leska pair before, lad. I know something more than the layman about their needs. As I said, I'll speak for you."

He hesitated. "You're going to need all the help you can get, Kusac, you realize that, don't you? Oh, not because of anything you did or didn't do, but because it happened at all." Garras inclined his head toward Carrie. "Her family is prominent on this planet and I'd be surprised if they didn't make a great deal of noise about your link. Then there's your family, or maybe that won't be a problem?"

"There will be trouble," said Kusac heavily.

"I'm mentioning it now to both of you not to be alarmist but so you are prepared for it when it happens. As I said, I'll do what I can."

Kusac relaxed. "Thank you, Captain. Don't place too much hope on finding the pod yet, this is a Talent new to me and I have still to see if it works," he said, halfheartedly chewing on a piece of meat.

"With the two of you, and our guide, I think it's a foregone conclusion. I just hope you are up to traveling tomorrow."

"I won't hold you back."

Garras nodded. "There's something about you, lad, that doesn't quite add up. I don't expect you to tell me, but I'll work it out. Why you ever joined the military I'll never know, you're not the type, and with a Telepath's upbringing to boot. The only person you might have needed to prove yourself to was you, unlike the Guynors of this world.

"Well, I'm turning in for the night. You do the same. Nothing heals like sleep. Good night."

"Good night, Captain."

Carrie sneezed and was abruptly awake. She was aware of the unfamiliar pressure of arms wrapped closely around her and strained against them, trying to free herself. She touched fur and relaxed just as Kusac released her and pushed himself up on his good elbow.

"Good morning," he said as she turned to face him. "The sunlight woke me, too." Wincing, he brought his injured arm round so he could touch her face with his hand. His fingertips were gentle as they caressed her cheek.

"Even compared to Sholan women, you are beautiful," he purred softly, bending down to run his tongue across her ear.

Carrie shuddered with pleasure as she reached up to stroke his face. "Isn't it a bit public for this?" she whispered.

Kusac nuzzled her shoulder. "Only if anyone is looking," he murmured, working his way across her neck.

"Be serious," she admonished, wriggling in his grasp. "What if someone should look?"

"We're only indulging in little intimacies," he said, moving round to lie partly across her. "We have nothing to hide, have we?" he asked, his mind touching hers.

Carrie shook her head, smiling. "I know," she said. "If we can accept each other, they can accept us."

"The sooner the better. Life on board the *Khalossa* lacks much in the way of privacy unless you are in your quarters, and we can't stay there forever." He felt her stiffen slightly.

"We will have to leave the planet for at least a few weeks," he said. "There is Guynor's court-martial, and I have to face charges concerning our bond. It may only be a board of inquiry, but I will need you with me." His tone sounded concerned.

"I'll come," she replied. "How could you doubt it? I just haven't had time to think ahead. What will we do when this is all over?"

Kusac brushed her hair back from her face. "Let's leave that till later. We have enough to occupy us for now," he said, returning to his exploration of the space behind her ears.

A loud throaty noise came from nearby. "If you two want breakfast, you'd better get it now while there's still time. Skai says we move off in fifteen minutes," said Vanna.

Kusac sighed. "We're coming." He rubbed noses with Carrie before pushing himself to his knees and helping her to rise.

As they walked over to the fire, Kusac's good arm negligently draped around her shoulders, Carrie was aware that his open display of affection was not only for themselves, but also for the benefit of his crew mates. He was publicly laying claim to her and forcing them to acknowledge it, if only to themselves. She was also amused to detect an element of jealousy, not closely enough guarded from her, of Skai because he was Terran like her.

They sat beside Vanna and the Captain, who nodded in greeting.

"Before we leave, Kusac, I want you to imprint English on Guynor and Mito if you are up to it."

Kusac flexed his shoulder slightly. "There's some pain and stiffness, but not as much as I'd expected," he said. "I cannot do an imprint if Guynor will not cooperate."

"He will. I have his word on that. What preparation will you need to do for locating the pod?"

Kusac poured himself and Carrie a hot drink. "We'll need several minutes to Link and Search for it. Once we've eaten and dealt with Guynor and Mito, we'll make a start. Carrie, you can cope with Mito, can't you?" He took the piece of cold meat that she offered him and began to eat.

"No problem," reassured Carrie. "I'll do it now." She gestured to Mito to join them. When the Sholan was seated, Carrie held out her hands and instructed Mito to grasp them. Reluctantly she did so. A look of concentration came over both their faces for a few minutes, then Carrie released her.

"That wasn't too bad, was it?" she asked the other woman.

"No," Mito said, surprised. "There was no sense of you invading my mind at all, there was just a sharing. And you don't seem cold and Alien!" She shot an angry look at Guynor. "I'll let you finish your breakfast now," she said, rising and moving quietly to sit beside Garras.

Kusac touched Carrie's shoulder, drawing her attention back to him. "It's too noisy to Search for the pod here. We'll have to go back into the forest, I'm afraid."

She nodded and rose. "I'll collect my things first," she said, stuffing a piece of meat into her mouth and going back to where their blankets lay.

"Hello," said a voice from behind her.

"Good morning, Skai. What can I do for you?" she asked, pulling out her brush and running it briefly through her hair before packing it and the blankets into her backpack.

"I was thinking about last night. I don't know how far we can trust these Sholans. They aren't as peaceful as you seem to think, are they? Your pussy cat really knows how to use his teeth and claws."

"Last night you witnessed rampant xenophobia," she said, rounding on him, "not the rational behavior of the rest of the crew. And what about us?" she demanded. "We aren't exactly tame pussy cats either! Seen from an Alien viewpoint, I'm sure we look just as bloodthirsty at times."

She softened her tone and continued. "Look, Skai, you have to learn to see the people; their similarities to us, not their differences. We're all too used to seeing Aliens as the Valtegans, creatures to hate and fear. The Sholans aren't Valtegans. You must learn to take them on their own merit. Don't try to put Human values on what they do, they aren't Human, they're Sholan."

"Like you do?" he asked sarcastically. "No wonder you weren't in the market for a man. You were after something more exotic, just like your sister."

Carrie fetched him a stinging blow across the face. "Don't you dare talk to me like that again! I don't have to justify my actions to you or anyone. If we're going to work together, you'll keep your opinions to yourself. Do I make myself clear?" She stalked off, leaving Skai cursing himself for alienating the one person to whom he could relate.

Kusac was sitting opposite a sullen Guynor when she returned to the camp fire. She could feel him stilling his mind and trying to match Guynor's: she was also aware of Kusac recoiling from the undisguised hatred that Guynor was projecting.

"It isn't easy without your cooperation," sighed Kusac. "It might even be painful."

"I've been ordered to submit to your teaching, but no one can make me like it," snarled Guynor.

There was no option but to force the initial contact if he had the power. He could get Carrie to help, but with Guynor's mind in its present state there was no knowing how he'd react. He'd have to do it alone if he could.

Slowing his breathing, he stilled his mind, gently searching through the wide band of interference that the First Officer was transmitting until he located its source. He had the key, now to put it in the lock. There was no point in gentle probing, it would only be repulsed by Guynor's barrier of hate. Kusac gathered his energy and sent a sharp, incisive probe deep into the other mind, grasping control firmly and subduing all irrelevant activity. He experienced the gasp of pain and terror that Guynor could not vocalize, but was able to subdue it instantly. Quickly, he located the relevant area of memory and implanted the necessary information.

Now that he had control of Guynor's mind, he could withdraw more gently and not cause any further pain. Within moments Guynor was sitting nursing a splitting headache, and Kusac was wondering over the new dimensions to his Talent. An exercise like that should have left him feeling drained for several hours, yet he had used hardly any energy at all. Just as well, considering the pain he was in and that he and Carrie still had work to do.

Guynor's gaze followed him as he rose to his feet, and this time there was an element of fear along with the hate.

Kusac made his way to where Carrie was talking to Vanna. "Let's go and find this pod," he said.

"Do we know what we're looking for?" Carrie asked.

"Ah . . . No."

"Wouldn't it be a good idea to find out first?" she suggested.

"Captain?" called Kusac. "What does the pod look like?"

"I'm afraid I have no idea. I suspect that it was probably cone shaped to reduce friction on entry. By now it should have some exterior manipulatory protrusions—grabs and such—to take soil samples," he replied. "If it's any help, just look for a large body of metal."

"Great," muttered Kusac, taking Carrie by the elbow and leading her through the trees.

"Why do we need to come here to work? If you could handle Guynor in the camp, why can't we locate the pod?"

"We need the privacy to work," he said shortly.

"Kusac, what are you hiding from me?" she asked, coming to a halt.

"Nothing that I know, believe me," he replied, trying to draw her on.

"We are too close for that. What are you hiding that you don't know?" she asked, refusing to move.

Kusac sighed and ran his hands across his ears in exasperation. "Look, I don't know anything, remember that. I just recall that newly bonded Leskas work in privacy until they can control the . . . the intimacy of their linking."

"Oh," said Carrie in a small voice, allowing herself to be led forward. "Could this have happened to us that first night in the woods?"

"Maybe," he replied, squeezing her arm reassuringly. "I don't know. I don't remember. Do you?" he asked, looking at her.

"No," she said hesitantly, then chuckled.

Catching her thought, Kusac grinned. "I know, if it had, you'd like to have remembered it. Me, too," he said, stopping to caress her cheek. "I think we're safe enough here. Let's get comfortable," he said, moving over to sit with his back against a tree. "You sit in front of me, like that. Now lean back. That's right." He put his arms around her. "Now relax, make your mind still. When we link, I want you to let me guide you in the search, so listen for my instructions. We're going to imagine we're drifting above the trees, then across the swamp, looking down on the land below till we find this pod."

His voice was getting softer and softer, and Carrie felt herself begin to link with him. The whirlpool of sensations drew them slowly together until she felt her own identity begin to dissolve into Kusac's.

Now we rise above the trees, Leska, came Kusac's/her thought.

It was slightly unnerving to look down and see themselves still sitting at the base of the tree as they moved leisurely toward the swamp.

Let's go higher to start with, so we can see the extent of the swamp. Good. We don't know exactly what it looks like, so try to tune into any electrical activity in case the pod is still transmitting.

I sense activity from the Valtegan coastal base, but nowhere else in the vicinity, she replied.

Then try for metal objects.

The base swamps my senses again.

We'll have to quarter it, then. Tune your range down to a few feet in any direction.

For what seemed hours, they searched up and down the length of the swamp until Carrie finally sensed something. They homed in on it and found a mound of what looked like vegetation sitting near the center of one of the multi-trunked trees.

That's it, thought Kusac, *and it appears the Gods are with us. The ground feels solid. Can you remember the location?*

Now that I can visualize it exactly, there will be no problem, she replied.

Let's return. Our job is done for the moment.

Swiftly they returned to where their bodies lay undisturbed on the ground.

It seems we have found how to control our Link, thought Carrie.

This task was easier than I anticipated, responded Kusac. *Time-consuming, but not difficult. Remember, our bond is unique. We have no one else's experiences to learn from. We will continue to work in privacy for now. Besides,* he continued, his tone of thought humorous, *at the moment it's the only time we get alone, and we both enjoy it.* He let his feelings come to the surface, and for a precious few moments they relaxed in a glow of mutual pleasure.

Wistfully, they parted and returned once more to their own identities, still sharing the moment but on a less enhanced level.

Kusac's arms tightened round her, and his rough tongue found just the right spot behind her ear. He sighed. "We must return to the camp, Leska."

When they got back, everyone was packed and ready to leave except for Vanna, who met them with steaming mugs of c'shar and some emergency rations.

"I've worked with the Talented before, Kusac, so I knew that you would need the food and drink to rebuild your energy levels. We're ready to leave when you've finished."

"Thanks, Vanna. I should have thought to ask you before we left," said Kusac gratefully.

Garras came striding over to them. Mito followed him, carrying Kusac's waistcoat which he had left behind when they went to Seaport.

"Did you find the pod?" asked Garras.

"Yes, Carrie can lead us there. It's northeast." He took the jacket and belt that Mito held out, slipping it on and getting Carrie to buckle it up. Mito got a brief flick of his ears by way of acknowledgment.

Vanna descended on him with a sling for his injured arm and spirited away the mugs.

"Skai, how does that correspond to your route through the swamp?" asked Garras, turning to where the Terran stood.

"We can start out on it, but when we get level with the pod it's all new territory," he replied, putting his heavy jacket on against the chill morning air.

"You lead, then, with Carrie and Kusac behind," said Garras, picking up his pack.

Skai looked round at his following of Sholans. They looked very agile, virtually all solid muscle honed for action. Like a pack of guerrilla jungle cats walking upright. He sighed inwardly, feeling very much in the minority.

"Can I give you a piece of advice?" he asked. "Your feet are bare, watch where you stand and keep your tails up unless you want the fish or the crocs to think they're food."

Four tails flicked in irritation. The owner of the fifth grinned and squeezed Carrie's arm.

"Naturally," muttered Mito, falling in behind Vanna as they followed Skai into the clearing and across to the edge of the swamp.

"Step where I step," Skai's voice floated back to them as they jumped from tussock to tussock.

Every now and then they stopped while Skai checked the solidity of the next part of the route.

The piece of ground on which Carrie and Kusac were standing was quite large, supporting several small bushes and plants. Over one of them hovered a large butterfly, its wings glowing with pearly iridescence.

"Oh, what a lovely butterfly!" exclaimed Carrie, bending toward it.

"Stop her!" yelled Skai, dropping his stick. He swung round and leapt back to their island.

Kusac hauled frantically at the girl, pulling her back from where the creature was hovering.

Skai landed beside them and swatted at it with the pack he was carrying. "There aren't any butterflies on this planet. It's a flying leech, and poisonous."

The "butterfly" backed off, hovering over the swampy ground at about chest height.

"Let me," said Garras, stepping forward and pulling out a small pistol. A faint beam of energy hit the creature, incinerating it in a burst of flame.

"Handy toy," said Skai, eyeing the smoking remains thoughtfully. "You don't happen to have any spares, do you?

We could do with a few ourselves." He reached into his pack, fumbling about for a moment or two, then drew out what appeared to be a broad metal bracelet with a raised circular device set in the center.

"It might be arranged," replied the Captain, watching Skai curiously as he returned the gun to his weapons' belt. "What does the leech do?"

"Burrows into your skin. It has to be cut out, not a pleasant experience for anyone. Stay clear of the water and anything that moves on the dry areas, and we might just make it to this pod of yours in one piece.

"I've still got my sonic bug screen with me, but there isn't much charge left in it, only a few hours. It's good for up to a ten-meter radius, so stay close.

"Let's get moving. It isn't even safe to stay in one place for long."

"Are you all right?" Kusac asked Carrie.

She shuddered. "I'm fine," she replied, forcing herself to jump over the gap of water to the next dry islet.

The next couple of hours passed uneventfully until Carrie called a halt.

"We have to go west from here," she said. "Would it be safe to stop for a few minutes?" she asked Skai. "I think we could all do with a rest and a drink."

"Make it quick," he replied. "I could do with one myself, but our presence in one spot for any length of time tends to attract the carnivores, not to mention Valtegan air patrols."

They were strung out over three patches of ground, about as safe as they could be given the circumstances.

Vanna and Mito were carrying homemade water packs, which they passed out down the line.

"Leave some for later," warned Vanna. "We can't be sure there is a working water purifier in the pod."

"I'll test the swamp ahead and tell you when to follow," said Skai, probing the ground in front of him with his stick.

"I wondered what that was for," murmured Carrie, taking a long swig of water.

The air in the swamp was warm and humid. She had been feeling hot and sticky since they'd left. On top of that, she had the Mother and Father of all headaches. Squinting her eyes against the sunlight, she handed the water back.

"Let's go," said Skai.

Ahead of them grew several of the multi-trunked trees

that were specific to the wetter swampy areas of Keiss. They grew fairly tall, with broad branching limbs that dipped toward the water, sending down myriads of rootlets from which sprang new trees. It created a network of spreading branches, almost a pathway, above the treacherous waters of the swamp. Unfortunately, the trees were fairly well spaced out, making it impossible to rely on them alone for a safe passage to the area they wanted.

Skai took two or three moves before he signaled the others to follow. The strain of this section of the journey was intense. Twice Mito slipped into the water and had to be pulled out quickly.

Garras stopped on a piece of sandy ground for a breather. The Captain was the oldest of the Sholans, and the trip was beginning to tell on him. He tried to move and found his feet stuck in the wet sand. He pulled harder but found himself sinking even lower. Yowling in protest, he drew the others' attention to him.

Kusac leapt back to where Garras was sinking deeper and deeper into the quicksand. Grabbing him by the arm, he tried to haul him free.

"Leave him for me!" shouted Skai, racing back to where the two males were struggling. "That isn't the way to free him!" He shouldered Kusac out of the way and took hold of both of the Captain's arms, pulling him slowly toward the dry ground. Garras was now up to his knees in the treacherous ground.

Skai transferred his grip to the Sholan's back and forced him to lie flat on his stomach.

"Not you, you're injured," he said to Kusac. "Guynor, over here." The two of them moved round to where Garras' legs had begun to emerge from the sand. "Pull," ordered Skai, hauling sideways on one limb. Guynor grabbed the other leg and began to haul, wincing a little at the pain in his forearm. Slowly they pulled him forward until, with a last sucking sound, he was free. Garras lay shaking convulsively for several minutes while they all recovered from the shock of his sudden brush with death.

Skai looked around to make sure the others were safe and noticed the water beginning to swirl beside them.

"Come on, let's get out of here. The vultures are gathering," he said, getting to his feet. "We'll stop when we get to the tree. At least we'll be safe there."

"What is it?" asked Mito, fascinated by the turbulence. She picked up a stone and tossed it into the middle.

"I wouldn't," Skai called back.

Mito took a step back just as a small mud-colored reptile surged up out of the water at her. She screeched, jumping back farther so it landed at her feet.

A brief flare and it died. Guynor put his pistol away.

"Frogs with teeth," said Skai. "Cute, aren't they?"

He moved back to his lead position while the others followed as quickly as the terrain and their tired bodies would allow. Before long, the last one had been hauled up to safety on one of the lower branches of the tree.

"We'll have a meal stop now," said Vanna, checking Kusac's reopened wound despite his protests. She took a pressure hypoderm and an ampoule out of her bag and proceeded to administer another analgesic.

"Kusac won't be able to travel again until this takes effect." She looked up as she put her instruments away. "Besides, we're all done in."

"It's not as bad as she makes out," Kusac muttered to Carrie, but she noticed he cradled his right arm in his lap. Gratefully, they accepted the food and water as it was passed down to them.

"At least it isn't dried meat," said Carrie, leaning back against the main trunk. "I've had more than enough to last a lifetime." She closed her eyes and tried to concentrate on reducing the pounding in her head to a bearable level.

"Well, your wounds are beginning to heal nicely," Vanna said tartly, giving Guynor's ear a cursory glance. "Luckily, the wound on your arm is minor. Kusac had the decency to only bite, not tear like you did. You'll live." With that, she clambered back to her place beside Carrie.

Garras pulled a blanket from his pack and began trying to clean some of the mud off his fur, an almost impossible task without water. He was leaning forward to dip the end of the blanket in the water below when the peace of exhaustion was broken by an agonized yowl from Guynor.

Food went flying as he almost overbalanced and fell off the branch. He scrabbled frantically for a hold, finally managing to sink all four sets of claws into the bark and pull himself back up.

Frozen with shock, the others watched as his tail whipped up to thump against the branch with a wet thwack.

"In the Gods' names, get it off!" he yowled, his voice high and penetrating. "Get it off!"

Mito lunged for the afflicted tail, but the pain was so intense that Guynor was unable to keep it still and it whipped about as if it was independently alive.

Snatching up Skai's stick, Carrie leaned forward. "Grab his tail at the base," she ordered Mito. As soon as the Sholan had it pinned down, Carrie pounced on the middle section and gave the fish several hard thumps with the stick.

Guynor's face was still contorted with pain, but his tail was only twitching faintly now. Mito grabbed it by the end and examined the dead creature cautiously as Vanna clambered over to them.

Handling his tail as gently as possible, Vanna turned it this way and that before speaking.

"I'll have to cut the fish off, Guynor. Even dead, those jaws are locked solid," she said.

"Do it," he hissed between gritted teeth, keeping his face turned away from Skai.

Vanna pulled her hunting knife and hesitated. "Do you want an analgesic first?" she asked.

"Just do it," he moaned, trying to control the involuntary flicking of his injured tail.

Vanna inserted her knife as far as possible into the fish's mouth and sawed away at the heavy jawbone. It was a slippery and unpleasant job and several times the knife slipped, narrowly missing both her and Guynor. At last she was able to pry apart the jaws. She handed the fish to Carrie, who looked at the massive array of teeth with a shudder before giving it to Kusac.

Now that Guynor's tail was free, Vanna could see that there was no permanent damage. She got out her antiseptic and analgesic spray and coated the whole wound with the sealant.

"That should stop hurting in a few minutes," she said, checking his face for the telltale signs of shock. "You'll do, just take care."

She returned to her place on the branch to finish her meal, noticing with a faint grin that all the Sholans, herself included, had curled their tails up beside them. No one was going to be caught like that again. One of their oldest instincts, forgotten in exhaustion. They would all have to be far more careful. Still, it was a nice irony that it had been Guynor who had been caught.

For the rest of their stop Guynor sat with his back to everyone, his tail resting safely in his lap, and sulked.

All too soon it was time to gather their packs again and inch their way along the branch behind Skai. They were able to cover a couple of hundred meters in this fashion before they ran out of branches sturdy enough to support their weight.

While the others waited by the central bole of the last tree, Skai sat astride the lowest limb and wriggled slowly along its length. Every so often he stopped to probe the swamp below for solid ground.

"It's solid here," he shouted at last, sitting up. "Garras, you join me. Don't worry, the branch is strong enough," he said, noticing the anxious flick of the Captain's tail. "You haven't got a rope in one of those bags, have you?"

"No rope," Garras said.

"Bring a couple of blankets, then. We'll tie them together and you can help lower me to the ground."

Garras unslung his pack and pulled the blanket free once more.

"Here," said Mito, handing him hers.

Garras flicked his ears in acknowledgment and began to twist both blankets securely around his body. Cautiously he edged forward to Skai. Once he had reached him and handed the items over, Garras moved back slightly to allow Skai room to tie them together into a makeshift rope.

"You hold this end," instructed Skai, tying the other around his waist. "I suggest you lie down to get a better grip on the branch, because you'll have to support my weight as I climb down. I'd hate to end up in the swamp," he said, with a smile.

Garras' ears flattened at the thought, and he stretched out beside Skai, digging his rear claws firmly into the underside of the branch.

Skai handed him the excess length. "Just play it out slowly," he said, dropping his stick down before he began to lower his legs over the edge. "I'm letting go now."

Garras braced himself and managed to absorb the shock of the extra weight of the Terran. Muscles already aching, he slowly fed out the blanket until it suddenly went slack.

"I'm down," Skai called. "I'm going to check out the next

couple of dry patches before anyone else comes. Just wait
there."

"It's like stepping stones," said Carrie quietly to Kusac.
"Did you ever play that game when you were young?"

"What are stepping stones?" he asked, leaning back
against the trunk.

His shoulder was giving him more trouble than he would
admit, but he wasn't about to let Vanna know. She'd have to
increase the drug to a level where he'd be a liability to them
all, and he didn't have the necessary peace and quiet to try
to deal with it his own way—the way he had learned at such
a high cost when he had first landed on this planet. At least
he was blocking it from Carrie.

"Stepping stones are stones you stand on to keep your feet
out of shallow water when there isn't a bridge. It's also a
children's game back on Earth."

"No, we don't have such a game. With bare feet, it
doesn't matter so much if they get wet."

Garras' call caught their attention. "Carrie, you next, then
Kusac. One at a time, please."

"Here we go," muttered Carrie, taking Kusac's hand for
support as she tried to get astride the branch.

When Carrie reached Garras, he handed her the blanket
rope and instructed her to tie it round her waist. Gamely but
clumsily, she lowered her hands to the branch, holding on
tightly as she slid first one leg and then the other off. Her
grip slipped and with a shriek of surprise, she found herself
hanging suspended in midair.

Garras' arms were nearly wrenched from their sockets,
and Kusac hurtled along the branch to join him, nearly falling off himself in his urgency.

The weight lessened, and Garras was able to move his
chest and breathe again.

"I've got her," yelled Skai. "Let down the rope before she
swings over the swamp!"

Garras fed the rope out hand over hand as fast as he dared
until he felt Skai take all her weight.

"She's down," he said, keeping her in his arms. "You're
safe now," he said. "I wouldn't let you fall."

"Then let me go," she said.

Reluctantly, he released her. "I'd like to talk to you later,"
he said.

"We've nothing to talk about," she replied shortly, moving one cautious step backward.

"Carrie," shouted Kusac, "are you hurt?"

"No," she said, looking up at him, "I'm fine. I just slipped and got a fright, that's all." She could sense his fear receding. She staggered slightly, putting her hand to her head. The heat and humidity were really making her feel ill. She'd be glad when they reached the pod and she could rest properly.

"I'll take her to the next dry spot. This bit is only large enough for two. Come on," Skai said, businesslike again.

She followed carefully in his footsteps to the next dry patch, which luckily was a good bit larger.

"Stay in the middle," warned Skai, "and you'll be quite safe." He moved off toward the tree. "Remember, I want to talk later," he said, turning back to her for an instant.

"Damn!" Carrie swore under her breath. She glowered at his retreating figure but couldn't shout a reply without looking foolish. As if her life wasn't complicated enough without having him to contend with. He seemed to have gotten the idea that he and Kusac were in competition over her. She'd have to deal with him once and for all, before Kusac did.

"You're next, Kusac," said Skai.

"Garras, you go now. I'll wait and get Guynor to lower me down."

Garras pushed himself up on his elbow. He stared hard at Kusac, wrinkling his nose in thought. "I didn't have you figured as stupid, lad, but I may have to revise that opinion."

Kusac's ears flattened in distress, and he tried to control the involuntary flicking of his tail.

"You know as well as I do that Guynor is unlikely to lower you anywhere but into the swamp, and I don't intend to lose another good crewman, especially to his psychoses. Now tie that blanket round yourself and let's get you down. I'll get Guynor to lower me next. His injuries won't prevent him from taking his share of the heavy work. You tend to the business of helping your Leska locate the pod."

Kusac's mind was spinning as he fastened the rope. He knew that Garras had said he would speak for him when they returned to the *Khalossa,* but he hadn't realized that the Captain had accepted his personal involvement with Carrie. Now he thought about it, it was completely in character with Garras' past experience as an escort to Trading missions with other Alien races. He obviously didn't share Guynor's species prejudice. He shook his head to clear his thoughts, and gingerly favoring his injured shoulder, swung himself off the branch.

Once the Captain was down, Skai left him to supervise the descent of the other Sholans and returned to where he'd left Carrie.

She was deep in conversation with Kusac and broke off as he approached.

"We need to head north, Skai, toward that clump of greenery there," she said, pointing into the distance.

"How much farther is it?" he asked, shading his eyes as he checked the position of the sun.

"Two or three kilometers, maybe four," answered Kusac.

"You'd better hope it's nearer two," muttered Skai, "or we might not make it before dark. We have to be under some sort of cover by then or we won't survive the night."

"We'll make it," Carrie reassured him. "It's difficult to judge distances from ground level when I've only seen it from above."

Skai gave her a disbelieving glance before he turned to start probing the swamp again.

The sky was shot with red and purple streaks by the time they reached the next tree complex. It was larger than the last one, comprising several main trees plus dozens of offshoot trunks. Skai had to utilize their blanket rope again so they could climb up to the lowest branch capable of sustaining their weight.

"It's just over there," said Carrie, too weary to have any enthusiasm at reaching the end of their journey. She was cold and all she wanted to do was sleep. She indicated a large overgrown area between the central trunks. "The ground there is solid."

Skai snorted doubtfully and clambered from branch to branch until he reached the clearing. He probed the ground with his stick, then lowered himself until he could jump down.

While he checked the area, Carrie slumped down where she sat, head between her arms.

Vanna leaned forward. "We'll soon have the pod open and be able to rest and eat," she said quietly. "You've done well to guide us here. I know what a strain it has been for both of you."

Kusac laid his hand on her arm. "Our part is done. From now on, the rest of the crew take over."

"She's right," Skai's voice floated over to them. "We've a large area of solid ground here with what looks like your pod on the edge of it. You're damned lucky it didn't fall in the open swamp. Better get down here now before dusk falls. I just hope your craft is large enough for seven, because if not, we've really got problems when the night life starts moving."

Wearily, they got to their feet and dragged themselves the last few meters. Once down, the Captain and Guynor joined Skai by the large mound of vegetation.

"Don't touch it with your hands," warned Skai, reaching out to stop Garras. "We don't know what's made its home in there."

Using the machete, he began to hack away at the base of the growth. Clouds of tiny insects swarmed upward accompanied by several large iridescent green beetles. The beetles hovered for a moment, then headed straight for Skai.

Before Skai had time to react, several flares went off simultaneously.

"Shit! Looks like the bug deflector has died. Thanks, fellas." He poked his stick through the greenery and pulled it aside. Underneath was the dull gleam of metal.

"That's it," said Garras exultantly.

Something pale flitted past them through the lengthening gloom.

Skai glanced up again. "Keep your guns out, all of you. I want two people on guard to shoot anything that moves," he ordered crisply. "We'll have to get the hatch uncovered now, the rest can wait till morning."

"We could use the guns to sear the growth at the base," said Guynor. "There shouldn't be anything vital down there."

"It's a risk we'll have to take," replied Skai as he stood back to allow the two males room to work.

As they burned their way around the pod, Skai followed them, pulling the matted fronds down with his stick until he found the entrance.

"Stop," he yelled over the sound of sizzling greenery. "Found it!"

Garras rushed round to where he stood and began to examine the panel at the side of the hatch. A series of indentations and symbols suggested a coded numeric or alphabet system.

Skai shifted his weight impatiently. "Well, open it," he said.

Garras used a claw tip to poke a sequence of buttons and waited expectantly. Nothing happened.

"There's a lot of splashing from the water over here," Mito hissed from the edges of their little islet. "I think we ought to hurry. It's heading this way."

Garras tried again, a worried frown on his face. When nothing happened again, he began rapidly punching out a short series of keys.

"The door lock's malfunctioning and I can't get the manual override on!"

"By all the Gods, what is that?" demanded Guynor, watching in terrified fascination as a leathery green head emerged from the turbulence. The barrel chest and splayed legs were visible as it crawled out of the water, its body twisting first to one side then the other to match its leg movements.

Skai glanced round, peering across the gloom to where Mito stood. "A swamp dragon! Try and keep the bloody thing at bay, herd it away from us. Their bite's poisonous, and they move fast."

The reptile gaped its mouth and roared, showing rows of banked sharp incisors. Its long, thick tail flicked, ripping out a small bush that was in the way.

Garras was still frantically punching buttons when there was a sudden deep metallic thunk and the panel on the outside was illuminated. Reaching around his neck, he pulled out a necklace bearing a narrow metal strip and hauled it over his head.

There was another deep roaring noise followed by a high-pitched squeal, then the sounds of pursuit through vegetation.

Fumbling, Garras threaded the strip into the slot at the bottom of the panel. There was a loud clunk, then the doorway slid open with a faint hiss of compressed air.

With a faint moan, Carrie slid bonelessly to the ground. As Skai and Kusac rushed to catch her, Garras jumped into the black opening. Within moments they were blinded by the glare of the interior lights.

Guynor and Mito came crashing into the clearing.

"We couldn't contain it," said Guynor, gasping for breath. "It's headed this way."

"In!" urged Skai, virtually pushing Guynor through the opening. "We can't stay out any longer." He grabbed Mito and gave her a shove in the right direction.

He bent down to where Vanna and Kusac were leaning over Carrie.

"You get in. I'll carry her. You can't manage her with your shoulder," he said as Kusac tried to take his arm out of its sling. "Get in, damn you! We haven't time to argue," he insisted while Kusac still hesitated.

The roaring was getting nearer.

He hoisted Carrie into his arms as the other two tumbled in, then passed her to the waiting Garras. Several arms grabbed him and hauled him inside.

As the door hissed shut behind him, the swamp dragon hurled itself against the side, making the pod reverberate hollowly. Teeth grated on metal, and even from inside they could hear the angry roars.

"You'd better pray to your Gods that this pod is whole, otherwise it could be our coffin," said Skai, untangling himself from the Sholans.

He looked round for Carrie. She had been handed shoulder high to the back of the craft and was now lying on a pull-down bunk with Vanna bending over her.

"God, but that was too close," Skai said, wiping his sweating face on his sleeve. "What's wrong with Carrie?" he asked.

"That's what I want to find out," replied Kusac, trying to edge his way over to her. "I know she's utterly exhausted."

"I want a medical opinion," frowned Skai, also moving forward.

Vanna looked up. "Kusac gave you the medical opinion," she replied sharply. "You forget that what she experiences, he experiences. She needs to be left to sleep now. Go and do something useful with the others," she ordered, then watched to see he went.

"Kusac, you sit with her while I look at your shoulder again. Most of Carrie's exhaustion is due to your suffering," she continued reprovingly.

"Guynor, you and Skai locate the galley area and find us something to eat and drink," ordered Garras, squatting on the floor. "Mito, you check out the pod's life support, engineering, and communications. See what's still operational—and open an external air sphincter if the filters are still functioning. No point in depleting the internal air supply when we don't need it," he said, lowering his head to rest it tiredly on his forearms.

"Aye, sir," replied Mito, moving over to a glowing bank of lights on one of the walls.

Displeased, Skai followed Guynor. He was able to get a better view of the interior of the craft now—his first look at Sholan culture. It surprised him. Although cramped, it was roomier than he had thought from outside. There was a central pillar with what appeared to be various computer or control modules set into it. Surrounding the column was a narrow circular bench seat. Round the outside walls were several more of the pull-down bunks, plus more of the display panels, their dials and lights winking urgently now that Mito was punching in commands at a terminal near the hatch.

Guynor abruptly reclaimed Skai's attention by shaking him. "We aren't sightseeing! Check these hatches over there. See if you can find anything that looks like food," he said brusquely, pointing to the section of hull behind him. "I'll check the central column."

"Sure," murmured Skai, squeezing past the Captain.

Meanwhile, Vanna was concerned about Kusac. His inner eyelids were nearly closed now that the danger was past and he was able to rest. She touched his arm gently.

"Just how much pain are you in? Truly, now. You'll do nobody any good in your present state," she admonished. "I need to know so I can assess Carrie's condition."

He sighed. "Quite a lot," he admitted, shifting his arm slightly in his lap to give it more support. "I have been doing my best to block it from Carrie, but some must have got through. I couldn't say anything . . ."

"I know," interrupted Vanna soothingly, "but we're safe now for at least a day or two. Let me see your shoulder." She moved round behind him and began loosening the blood-soaked bandage.

The wound had reopened. Though it was clean, there was some swelling.

"Have you come across the medical supplies yet?" she called out to Guynor.

"Yes," he said, passing them to her.

She opened the case, quickly going through the contents. "Wonderful!" she said. "At last I've got a reasonable selection of drugs and instruments. We'll have you both right in no time," she said with satisfaction.

She wiped Kusac's arm with an antiseptic pad before placing a freshly loaded hypoderm against it. "This might sting a little," she warned as she depressed the trigger.

Kusac winced.

"Just one more, then I'll dress the wound," Vanna said, taking out another ampoule. "You should have a fever because of a minor infection in the wound. You haven't, but Carrie has."

After injecting his arm, she sprayed more of the antibiotic sealant over the wound and rebandaged it securely.

"I didn't get a chance to tell you, but Carrie pulls the pain from those she cares about without knowing she's doing it," mumbled Kusac.

"Tell me about it tomorrow. You should feel a lot better by then," she said.

Kusac rose to his feet, then staggered, nearly falling over.

"Careful now," warned Vanna, catching hold of him.

"What have you given me?" he groaned, trying to focus on the medic.

"A hefty dose of antibiotic and analgesic, plus a mild sedative. I want you to sleep properly tonight."

She gestured to Skai to pull down the bunk beside Carrie's and helped Kusac weave his way over to it. As he sat down heavily, she swung his legs up for him.

"Now sleep," she ordered, pulling the blanket over him.

Kusac grabbed her arm urgently as she was about to move away.

"Watch Carrie for me," he whispered.

Vanna frowned, glancing over at Skai. "Don't worry," she whispered. "I'll keep an eye on you both."

"Preliminary checks finished, Captain," Mito said, turning away from the console. "Do you wish a status report?"

Garras looked up. "Carry on."

"The interior of the pod and the life-support systems are stable, therefore the inner hull has not been breached. I've opened the sphincter valve and we are now on an external air supply. Air filters are sound, so no indigenous life can enter."

"What about the state of the transmitter?"

"The automatic transmitter linked to the scientific programs is not functioning. Without the benefit of an external examination, I presume that the outermost hull, containing the experimental packages, has suffered damage sufficient to shut down the experiments. As for the transmitter, I have no information at present. We cannot gauge the extent of any damage until morning, but we seem to be in no immediate danger of being overrun by anything from outside."

Garras rose stiffly to his feet, supporting himself against the hull. "Well, we knew that the pod had ceased transmitting, now we know why. I assume that the Valtegans have destroyed our satellite, which leaves us with only the manual emergency transmitter. Have you located that yet, Mito?"

"No, sir, but I have located an inventory and procedure check for anyone having to use the pod. It should be listed there," she said, returning to the screen.

"Have you found the galley area?" continued Garras, peering round the column to where Vanna was dressing Guynor's tail while he continued to check the panels.

"I've located the food heating unit," Guynor replied, "but no food."

"Is this what we're after?" asked Skai, holding up several packages. "I've also found what looks like the water purifier, and it's full."

"In that case, I suggest we all eat and sleep before doing anything more," said Garras, rubbing a hand across his scalp and scratching his ears. "It's been a long day. Is there an electronic alarm system, Mito, or do we have to post a watch?"

"The alarm is already set and functioning, Captain."

"Stand down from duty," said Garras tiredly, moving over to one of the bunks, but Vanna was there before him and had it pulled down and waiting.

"Will you be able to sleep tonight, or do you want a sedative?" she asked, concern showing in the angle of her ears and the flicking of her tail.

Garras shook his head. "I'm so tired that I don't know if I can stay awake to eat," he confided. "It will be tomorrow when I'll really need those pills and potions of yours, especially one for that most tenacious of all diseases, age." He groaned as he swung his legs up and lay down.

Vanna laughed. "I haven't got anything for that, I'm afraid, but I should be able to do something for the minor aches and pains."

"What about Kusac and the girl? How are they?"

"He's got a minor infection in his shoulder and all the signs that he should have a fever," said Vanna, "but it's Carrie who has it, not him." She hesitated. "I've treated them both for the fever symptoms, but this link of theirs worries me. It's so unlike anything we know. I've never heard of a crossover of physical problems to this degree. Their link seems so much more intense." She shrugged. "Perhaps I'm wrong, after all, between us we know next to nothing about Leska Links, and Kusac seems to be plucking what he knows from thin air. It's almost as if the Link is telling him."

Garras took hold of her hand. "You've really taken to these two, haven't you?"

"Yes," she said. "Before we crashed here there was a . . ." she searched for the appropriate word, ". . . vulnerability about Kusac. He didn't seem to have much experience of life. Now, well, you can see for yourself. It's as if he's a new, stronger person now he has the responsibility of Carrie."

"As a Telepath he should have been incapable of fighting Guynor," said Garras, "but since he returned, there is little that is typical about him. The things he's doing now with Carrie make me sure that he's a much higher Grade than his official military listing says. I wouldn't be surprised to discover he's well placed in one of the Telepath Clans. That young man is used to giving orders as well as obeying them.

"What about Carrie? What do you make of our young Terran?"

"She's good for him. I like her. As a species, I think we're not too dissimilar in outlook. As a Telepath, in my humble opinion as a non-Guild member, I would say she's as powerful if not more so than Kusac, and I agree with you about his rating. He's certainly not a Fifth Grade, judging by what he's been doing lately."

Garras' eyes were closing with tiredness. "You should have spoken to Kusac sooner, Vanna. You are always underestimating your own worth." He gave her fingers a gentle squeeze before releasing them.

"I have a feeling all hell will break loose over these two once the *Khalossa* arrives. They'll need all the friends they can get. How would you like me to insist you are seconded from me to the Ship's Medical section as the only Medic with a working knowledge of Terran physiology? I know you want to work in xenobiology. This could be your only chance."

Vanna was stunned, unable to think of anything to say. What Garras was suggesting was not only a chance for the career she'd always wanted but an advancement in rank as well.

"I take it that means yes," said Garras, yawning. "Now go and get some food and rest, that's an order."

Chapter 8

It was dark in the pod when Carrie woke. She felt for Kusac, sensing him nearby, but he was still deeply asleep. There was a brief moment of panic until she remembered that she had passed out as the pod hatch opened.

Her head still throbbed as she tried to move it to look around her. She ached all over. She began to shiver, finding it difficult to breath. Pain flared agonizingly in her shoulder, making her whimper.

Almost instantly, Vanna was at her side, rubbing the sleep from her own eyes as she switched on the personal light above the bunk.

She took one look at Carrie, then glanced over to where Kusac slept on the next bunk. He was beginning to move restlessly. She turned back to the Terran girl, briefly touching her damp forehead and then feeling for her pulse. It was weak and rapid as was her breathing. Her color was odd, too. Instead of her usual pinkish brown, she was almost gray.

"I'm cold, Vanna, and it hurts," whimpered Carrie, looking up at her with eyes made huge by fear.

I don't know enough about her, Vanna thought, beginning to panic. Then common sense took over. *Wait a minute, there's nothing wrong with Carrie, it's Kusac! What did he say about her? She takes the pain from those she cares for? And she was suffering his fever earlier? Then right now she's in shock because of his shoulder wound!*

"It's all right, little cub," she said, touching her fingertips to the girl's cold cheek, "I'm here, I'll see to it." She pulled Carrie's blanket back and began to loosen her clothing. Several of the fastenings were unfamiliar, but she managed.

Then she added her own blanket to the one Carrie already had and wrapped them both loosely around her. As she folded the girl's jacket to place under her legs, she reviewed the drugs she would use for a Sholan. There was nothing she dared use on the Terran for fear it would cause more harm than good. With any luck she wouldn't have to if she could treat Kusac independently.

She checked her again, taking her pulse and feeling her skin temperature. At least the shivering was diminishing.

"I'll be back in a minute," she said. "Don't worry, you'll be fine."

Moving carefully around the sleeping bodies, she went over to Mito's bunk and began to shake the Sholan awake.

"Vanna? What's up?" Mito asked, blinking as she sat up.

"I need your help," said Vanna. "Carrie's gone into shock because of Kusac's wound, and I daren't treat her. I need you to help me monitor them."

"I don't understand. Why should she go into shock?" whispered Mito as she got up.

"She's using their Link to take his symptoms away from him. It's apparently not something she can control. I want you to watch Kusac for the moment and let me know if his condition changes," she said, leading the way back over to where the Leskas lay.

Vanna squatted down beside Carrie, reaching under the blankets to take her hand. She felt a little warmer, but her pulse was still erratic.

"Carrie," she said, "I need your help. Kusac's the one who's ill, not you. I can't help him because you're stopping his symptoms. You aren't helping him, cub, you're making it worse for him—and yourself. There's no need for you to suffer like this."

Carrie turned to look at her. "I don't understand you. How am I making him worse?"

"You are using your Link to take his pain, Carrie. You mustn't do that, it stops me from treating him."

"I'm not!" she said fretfully, trying to pull her hand away.

"Yes, you are," Vanna insisted gently, preventing her from breaking their contact. "There is nothing wrong with you, Carrie. The pain you feel is Kusac's, not yours. You have to break the Link, cub, or I can't treat him."

"But I'm not doing anything."

"Carrie, you are. Trust me. You have to block your Link to Kusac so that I can treat him. I don't have any psychic suppressants, so I can't help you. You'll have to do it on your own. Block that Link, Carrie," she urged, giving the human's hand a squeeze.

"My head hurts so," she moaned.

"I know, cub," said Vanna soothingly. "Just block the Link and it will stop, I promise."

Pain flared through her shoulder again. "I'll try," she whispered, shutting her eyes.

"Vanna, what's . . ." began Garras, pushing himself up on one elbow.

"Hush!"

"Kusac's beginning to pant," said Mito, "and his breathing is getting shallower."

"Good girl!" said Vanna, her free hand caressing Carrie's cheek. The color was rapidly returning to the girl's face now and her breathing was becoming deeper and more regular. "In a minute, Mito will sit with you while I see to Kusac."

Carrie nodded, eyes still closed, as Vanna let go of her hand.

"Mito, get me an IV pack and catheter," she ordered, picking up her Medic's kit as she moved over to Kusac's bed.

Quickly, she checked him over, finding him now exhibiting all the classic signs of shock.

"Kusac's gone into shock," she said, glancing briefly up at the Captain.

She swabbed Kusac's right forearm down, inserting the catheter when Mito handed it to her. Securing it round his arm, she then unsealed the IV drip nozzle and connected them. Above the pull-down bed there were several hooks set into the hull and one of them was placed at an appropriate level. She hooked the pack onto that.

Carrie was peering past Mito, watching as Vanna loaded the hypo gun and gave him two shots.

There was no pain now, even her headache had cleared. Did blocking the Link make all that difference? If Kusac was right, then it meant she had wasted some twenty years of her life suffering the full quota of Elise's pain for no reason. He couldn't be right; it didn't bear thinking about if he was.

She felt along the Link, trying to work out what she had just done and why it had been necessary, but she could find nothing to explain it. She lowered the block slightly, feeling again the pain Kusac was experiencing. Immediately, she pulled back. She couldn't cope with any more pain, especially not through another link.

Vanna was perched on the end of Kusac's bed, holding his wrist. Sensing Carrie's gaze on her, she looked up and smiled encouragingly.

"He'll be fine," she said. "He's beginning to respond to the treatment."

"Can I help? He's in so much pain, Vanna, I don't know how he can stand it."

"Not for much longer. I've given him the strongest analgesic I have. He'll sleep, which is exactly what I want him to do. You can help by keeping that block up and by resting. I need to be sure I'm picking up all his symptoms. Garras will give me a break in an hour or two. You try and get some sleep."

Carrie began to sit up, but Mito pushed her back.

"You heard Vanna," she said, not unkindly. "Stay in bed and rest."

"I need to be with him," she said. Though the Link was blocked so she couldn't feel his pain, she was still aware of him mentally and of his anxiety and his need to feel her touch.

"Rest, cub," said Vanna, letting go of Kusac's wrist to run some other checks on him.

For the next hour Kusac was semi-delirious with the fever. He called constantly for Carrie and eventually Vanna had to give in and let the girl bring her bedding over to the floor beside his bunk.

Carrie sat near his head, holding onto his hand. Keeping the Link blocked was taking a lot of concentration and energy. She hoped she could keep it up.

He quieted then, drifting off into a natural sleep, but every time she tried to let go of him he began to toss fretfully.

Mito turned in, taking back one of Carrie's blankets. Then Garras relieved Vanna, letting her sleep till dawn.

Carrie napped as best she could, leaning against a piece of equipment that Garras had brought over and padded with his blanket.

She had the time to think her own thoughts now, time apart from Kusac. Why did Links have to bring her pain? She had just been freed from one such bond, and now this.

She put her head back against the support and closed her eyes. Granted that without Kusac she would probably have died when Elise had, but was a future similar to her past one to be wished for?

. . . a bond of shared joys as well as pain, echoed in her mind. Kusac. He was the difference, literally a world of difference. A faint smile crossed her lips as she remembered some of the shared pleasures of the last few days. His hand stirred in hers, briefly tightening its grasp and then relaxing, as did she.

The noise of the last changeover roused her. Kusac was still sleeping. She knew the fever had broken and his pain was under control. She tried again to ease her hand from his and this time he didn't stir. Her stomach growled faintly, but she was too tired to want to move and the hunger pangs were not very insistent.

As she curled up where she was, a faint glow from the central column's two VDU screens drew her attention. She raised herself slightly on one elbow to get a better view.

One was obviously a computer control screen. The other seemed to be a view of the swamp outside the pod. Day was breaking and the sky was tinged with light. She settled down and began to drift into sleep.

This time, she woke with a jolt. Sunlight was streaming in through the open hatch and strange bumps and bangs reverberated throughout the pod.

"Here, drink this," said Vanna, thrusting a steaming mug into her field of vision. "Kusac's fine, he's still sleeping soundly."

"I know," Carrie mumbled, taking the mug from her. "What's this?"

"A protein drink," Vanna said soothingly. "It boosts up the energy levels fast. Did you manage to get enough sleep?"

Carrie sat up and blinked, clearing the last of the sleep from her senses.

"Some," she said, taking a cautious sip of the drink, then a large mouthful. "Not bad," she said. "What's been happening?"

"Mito and Guynor have located the manual transmitter and are checking to see if the satellite is still in orbit. Garras and Skai, as you can hear, are checking the outer hull for damage."

"Don't let them clear the vines off the pod or we'll be too visible from the air," she warned.

"Don't worry, they know what they're doing," Vanna assured her.

"How long will Kusac be on the drip?"

"That's finished now," said the Medic, squatting down beside her. "He's just utterly exhausted, and the analgesics will keep him tired. He'll probably sleep for another few hours yet."

Carrie finished the drink before getting up. "What are we supposed to do today?"

"Fetch and carry for the others because we can't help them."

Carrie looked round at Kusac. Because of their Link, she was able to read his expressions and body language. Just now he lay partially curled with his back to the hull. His shoulder was beginning to hurt again. She reached down to gently touch his face.

"He's in pain again," she said.

"I'll see to it when he wakes," said Vanna.

"Captain," called Mito from outside where she and Guynor were working on the portable transmitter. "It's no use. If the satellite is still in orbit, it isn't receiving us. Without a hyperspace relay, we have no chance of reaching the *Khalossa*." Mito's ears were laid flat against her skull and her tail was flicking jerkily, showing her deep distress.

Garras stuck his head inside the hatch, looking for Carrie. "Have your people any deep-space transmitters in orbit?" he asked.

"No," she said, walking over to the opening. "We never developed . . . what did you call it? Hyperspace relay?"

"Carrie," Skai called insistently, guessing that something was seriously wrong. "What are you talking about? What's happened?" He moved quickly to the hatch and leaned forward, grasping her by the arm. "Stop talking in that outlandish language and speak sense, for God's sake!"

"Their satellite's not functioning," she replied distractedly.

"In English, Carrie," he said, shaking her. "As the only military representative here, I outrank you and expect to be kept informed."

A sudden sharp pain made him yelp and look down as Carrie repeated herself in English. He saw a dark-furred

Sholan hand on his wrist and attempted to shake it off. Five sharp claws held him in a rigid grip. Droplets of blood were beginning to well from under the claw tips.

"Don't," said Kusac, his teeth bared in cold anger. "She is not yours to touch."

Skai flinched. "She isn't yours either," he retorted.

"Both of you stop it," said Carrie, batting Kusac's hand away from Skai. "I don't belong to either of you! I'm not a piece of property to be argued over like this."

"Of course you have free choice," murmured Kusac. "I did not mean to imply you hadn't."

"Just so you both remember it," she said, somewhat mollified. "And, Kusac, just what are you doing up?" she asked, turning round to him.

"I woke and needed to stretch," he said urbanely.

Carrie made a small noise of disbelief.

Vanna came up behind them.

"Kusac, before you move around too much, I want to change that dressing," she said, handing him a protein drink.

He hesitated.

I'm fine, sent Carrie. *You worry too much.*

I care, he replied, touching her face lightly with his fingertips before following Vanna.

Carrie turned back to Skai. "Have the Valtegans any communication satellites in orbit?" she asked Skai.

"No," he replied, thrusting his anger aside for later as he rubbed the back of his wrist. "Their deep-space transmitter is in the base at the other side of the swamp, which is why we stake it out. We're hoping for a chance to get in and use it. You wouldn't believe how tight their security is."

"Could we gain entry to their transmitter from here through their local communications?" asked Garras.

"If we knew their access codes," replied Guynor.

"We have a panoramic receiver, so it should be possible to work out the radio frequencies given enough time, but the access codes will take longer," said Mito.

"How long?" asked Carrie.

Mito shrugged. "Depends how frequently they communicate with the base and how predictable their codes are."

"Couldn't you link into a Valtegan at the base and get the necessary information?" Garras asked Carrie. "We've got to get our message out as quickly as possible before the Valtegans manage to read our computer memory crystal."

"The Valtegans are too far away for us to do that," replied Carrie. "Is it likely that they can read it?"

"With a lack of any knowledge of their tech level I have to assume the worst," said Garras. "Go ahead," he said to Mito. "Monitoring the base seems the most viable course of action."

"I'll need help, though," she said. "I don't speak Valtegan."

"Then we have got a problem," said Skai, "because none of us know more than a few words, certainly none of their technical language. Unless, Carrie?. . ."

She shook her head. "I probably know less than you, and as I said before, there aren't any Valtegans near enough for me to contact."

Her remarks were met with silence.

"It looks like we're going to have to get into that base," said Garras at last.

"How? We've been sitting there watching them for about eight years! If we can't get in, how the hell can you?" exclaimed Skai.

"I could get in easily," said Carrie.

"What did you say?" demanded Skai, rounding angrily on her.

"I said I could get in easily, and I can."

"What're you going to do? Just walk in the front gate?" he asked sarcastically.

"Of course. Getting me in isn't the problem, it's what to do next," she said.

"Explain," said Garras, his ears pricked hard in her direction.

"Elise told me that occasionally the base officials will send for one of the women from Geshader. I just convince them that I've been sent for, which is easy."

"You're not going in alone," growled Kusac from within the pod.

"Too right," echoed Skai. "I'm going in, too."

"I couldn't take a Terran male with me," she replied. "There's no way they'd let you in, and having seen you, they would probably keep you for questioning."

"You're not going alone," repeated Kusac, coming back to the hatch despite Vanna's protests.

She followed him, getting him to squat down while she replaced the dressing on his shoulder.

"We need Mito or Guynor to go in, not you, Carrie," said Garras. "You don't have the knowledge to help us."

"No, but once inside, I'm close enough to the Valtegans to read them and get their knowledge, which Mito and Guynor can't do."

"Do these women from Geshader arrive alone?" asked Kusac.

"No, they are usually taken there by groundcar," replied Carrie, looking puzzled.

"I have an idea," he said slowly. "I wonder if between us we could make the Valtegans think they are looking at one of their own soldiers escorting a woman. That way you have some protection, and there would be two of us to handle anything Mito says we need to do."

"But how?. . ."

Carrie was cut short by Mito.

"If you can do that, then, yes! Telepathically, we can give you the information you need to access the transmitter and send our signal."

"It could work," admitted Guynor grudgingly, "but we need to interface into the Valtegan computers. They're probably incompatible with ours."

"What do you mean by interface?" asked Skai.

"Basically, our computers will probably run at a different speed than the Valtegans'. Also the computer language we use won't be understood by their machine so I need to build a translator to allow our computer to talk to theirs, and vice versa," explained Guynor.

"So this translator is your interface?" questioned Skai.

"Exactly, but the next problem is to get hold of some Valtegan electronic equipment so that our interface can be connected to it without damage to either system."

"What kind of Valtegan hardware do you need?" continued Skai. "Maybe we have something that would do."

"We need some communications device. Not a personal communicator, but one from a building or a vehicle," said Mito.

"We have a groundcar. Would that be any use?"

Mito's ears pricked up. "That would be ideal! What state is it in?"

"Pretty good. Last time I saw it, about a fortnight ago, they had repaired most of the damage caused by our attack. I know the radio is all right because they were using it to monitor Valtegan transmissions, trying to work out more of the language."

"Where is it? When can I get it? It sounds ideal for our purposes!"

"At our base just south of here, near the foot of the hills."

"It might as well be at Hillfort!" said Carrie bitterly. "How are we going to get word to them in time?"

"Actually, that is the least of our problems," said Skai smugly. "I never told you, but I have a wrist communicator and can get in touch with the base anytime."

Carrie favored him with a look of dislike. "I knew we couldn't completely trust you," she said.

"Oh, come on now! You kidnap me in the middle of the forest, introduce me to a new species of Aliens, and you expect me to give away my one ace? Be realistic, girl. Anyway, it's going to be our biggest asset now."

"Certainly an asset," interrupted Garras smoothly, "but perhaps not our biggest. We still have to ascertain if Carrie and Kusac can work their disguise. Without them, we cannot reach the transmitter inside the base."

"Have you got any communications operators and technicians among your people?" interrupted Mito.

"Sure. We've got most of the crew of the *Eureka* left."

"Captain, we must contact them. There are things I need, tools this pod doesn't provide. I must talk to them now," said Mito urgently.

"No!" exclaimed Guynor angrily, stepping forward. "Captain . . ."

"Enough," said Garras, his voice deceptively mild. "Now we have no option but to trust the Terrans. Unless you are suggesting that the seven of us mount an armed raid on the base with nothing more than these few side arms?"

"There are explosives and rifles in the pod," replied Guynor stiffly.

"We are a reconnaissance unit, not a combat group. We are also vastly outnumbered and outclassed. Our strength lies in stealth, not force. I am glad to hear we have extra munitions at our disposal. They will be useful to the Terrans as a backup in the event of trouble—if they will aid us. They have the military and strategic knowledge, we, the technical.

"Skai, contact your base and let me talk to your Commanding Officer," ordered Garras.

"I think it would be better if . . ." began Skai, stumbling

to a halt as he saw the Sholan Captain's ears flatten and his eyes narrow.

"Yes, sir," he said hurriedly, cursing inwardly at fate for robbing him of his chance to appear in charge of the situation.

Carrie looked at him curiously as he keyed his call signal into his wrist communicator.

"I don't know why you are worrying," she said. "You did the job we asked you to do excellently. You're bound to get praise for that. Why do you need more?"

Skai gave Carrie a shocked glance before the tiny voice on his comm unit claimed his attention.

"Davies, is that you?" he asked.

"Identify," the voice repeated.

"Don't be stupid, you know it's Skai!"

"Password," it insisted pedantically. "And where the hell have you been the past four days? Screwing your way round Seaport, I've no doubt!"

Skai flushed. "Come on, Davies," he muttered, "I've got company."

"I'll just bet you have! Password."

"Bramble, you son of a bitch, and I hope you've stepped on some eggs this week!"

"Identity verified," replied Davies smugly. "Captain Skinner will enjoy hearing where you've been. I hope the excuse is a good one this time."

Skai began to grin. "Oh, it is. Believe me, it is. Put me through, will you? I'll need a secure line."

"Just for an excuse? Come on, what are you up to?"

"Patch me through, Davies," ordered Skai, feeling the situation come back under his control again. "Once Skinner hears what I have to say, he won't thank you for delaying me."

"I'll make it my business to find out what you're playing at, Skai," warned Davies.

"Skinner here," interrupted a crisp voice. "When you've quite finished your banter, I'll have that secure line, Davies."

"Yes, sir."

"What have you got to report that requires security status?" asked the Captain.

"I've located the Aliens who crashed two months ago," replied Skai.

There was a short silence. "Repeat what you just said," ordered Skinner.

"I found the Aliens."

"You found?" murmured Carrie.

"Who else is with you?" demanded the Captain.

"Carrie Hamilton," replied Skai, giving the girl a sidelong glance. "Actually, she found them."

"I thought she'd end up with us. Too much spirit in that one to be a farmer's wife."

"Captain," urged Skai, "the Aliens. I've got them here with us. They want to talk to you. They can help us."

"Ah, the Aliens."

"Here, give the damned thing to me," said Carrie, grabbing hold of his wrist. "Captain, I know it's difficult to accept, but believe me, we have here the five surviving members of the craft that the Valtegans shot down. They are called Sholans, and they have a battle cruiser out in deep space. They will help us, but their transmitter is out of action and they need our assistance to get a message through."

"What assistance can we give them?" asked the Captain, recovering his equilibrium again.

"Skai says you have a Valtegan groundcar. They need it to make some kind of interface into the Valtegan communications system."

"We have a groundcar, and it's working after a fashion," admitted Skinner, "but the only practical way to get it to you is to fly it, and it's not capable of doing that at present."

"Give me the wrist comm," ordered Garras, pushing forward and holding out his hand. "I'll talk to him and find out what the delay is."

Mito murmured briefly to him in Sholan as Skai took off the device and handed it over.

He nodded.

"Who's that?" asked Skinner sharply.

"Captain Garras of the Sholan scout craft *Sirroki,* Captain Skinner," he answered. "We need that Valtegan craft to be able to contact our Mothership. Once we have alerted the *Khalossa* to our mutual predicament, it will be in orbit around Keiss within days.

"It has the firepower, and the incentive to rid this planet of the Valtegans. We have also suffered at their hands.

"As for your ship, with the Valtegans gone there will be no need to stop it from landing on Keiss.

"We don't have time for the diplomatic niceties, I'm afraid. Let's leave that to our politicians. You and I are men of action, and action is what is needed right now. Can we cooperate?"

There was a slight hesitation. "Certainly. We'll get that craft flying somehow. Meanwhile, how else can we help you?"

"Mito, tell the Captain your requirements," ordered Garras, handing the comm to her.

"I need trained tech personnel and their equipment. Have you got the following items or equivalents?" she asked, reeling off a list of some half a dozen tools.

"I'll get my people on it right away. Stay in communication and I'll put you through to our expert in that field. I've got a fix on your location so we'll have no difficulty reaching you. Is there anything else?"

Garras leaned over and spoke. "Put as many heavily armed men in the craft as you can. Two of your people will have to break into the base here to patch our device into the Valtegan transmitter, and I want the means to rescue them if necessary."

"Break into the base?" Skinner echoed in disbelief, briefly forgetting diplomacy. "Are you mad? Have you any idea what you're up against?"

"Yes, Captain Skinner, I have," said Garras. "We don't intend to break in by force. I presume you will be coming with your men; I will brief you when we have made our final plans."

There was a short silence. "All our personnel are trained fighters," said Skinner. "By the way, I must compliment you on your grasp of our language."

"We have the benefit of an excellent team of Telepaths. The credit is theirs, they imprinted us with your language."

There was another pause. "That's a useful technique. I wish we had those methods at our disposal. We must talk about it sometime."

"Certainly. As for your people not having those skills, the girl Carrie is half of our team. Along with Kusac, our Telepath, they make the most gifted pair I've come across in many years. Don't you make use of this Talent?"

"I'm afraid that as far as we humans are concerned, it's regarded as a fringe phenomenon and highly unreliable."

"I see there are a few differences in our outlook," said

Garras. "Still, it would be surprising if there were not. Telepaths are a valuable resource to any civilization. This is a matter that our diplomats will doubtless discuss at length later." Garras' eyes flicked briefly over to Carrie and Kusac.

"Doubtless," replied Skinner. "Tell Carrie that her brother arrived here today. He intends to join us. Has she any messages for him or her father?"

"Tell them I'm safe and well, but I won't return," she said, leaning over the comm.

"There's no reason for you to go back, my dear. Richard has given us some idea of your problems. It looks like you could have an interesting future ahead of you with us."

"No, I mean I'm not returning ..." she started, breaking off as Garras caught her by the arm. He shook his head slowly, warning her to silence.

"We'll sort something out, never fear," reassured Skinner.

"Captain, I'm afraid we cannot accommodate any more personnel in our life pod. It's intended as emergency accommodation only for a normal reconnaissance crew of six. We number seven. Also our food supplies are limited. I am sorry to be so inhospitable ..."

"That won't be a problem, Captain Garras. We can sleep in the groundcar and I'll make sure we bring plenty of food."

"Thank you. My First Officer may be able to help your mechanics get the groundcar flying."

"Any help would certainly be most welcome," replied Skinner. "I'll hand over to my senior technician for the moment."

Carrie felt a tap on her shoulder and turned round to find Vanna beckoning Kusac and her aside. She moved away from the hatch and back toward the central pillar.

"I think they are going to talk what you call 'shop' for the moment. Why don't we go and organize the food situation? If you're like me all this technical jargon is another language, one I don't understand," she said once they were out of earshot.

"Too true," murmured Kusac, gently trying out his shoulder and wincing immediately.

"They can't make me stay on Keiss, can they?" asked Carrie, obviously distressed as she clutched at Kusac's good arm.

Vanna caught his expression. "No, they can't," she replied

soothingly, putting an arm around the girl. "Once we have the *Khalossa* here, I can use the transmitter to tie into the medical banks for all the documented information on Leska bondings. When it's known that to separate you would be a hazard to both your lives, then a solution will have to be worked out. Frankly, I'm positive our people won't leave you both on Keiss in such a backward culture."

"Excuse me speaking so plainly, but compared to us, you are backward. We have had several hundred years of experience in trading with Alien races, and our space-based personnel have very little trouble with xenophobia, Guynor being an exception.

"There is also your people's lack of understanding of Telepaths. We couldn't leave Kusac in that kind of environment for the rest of his life. I'm afraid you'll probably not have a choice about remaining on this planet," she said, drawing Carrie farther into the pod, with Kusac following because she was still holding on to him.

"Are you sure?"

"I'm sure. You are of more use to us than Kusac is to your people. Now come on, if we're going to play host to a group of Terrans, we'll have to check over the galley again. I hope they bring some interesting food with them."

"I'm glad that they can manage to sleep in that groundcar they're bringing," said Kusac, moving Carrie's hand from his arm into his hand. "We're already short of space inside the pod at night."

"I forgot to ask how you were coping with the cramped and unshielded conditions," said Vanna.

"It's bearable so far," Kusac replied. "After all, I've been unconscious most of the time! What tonight will be like, I have no idea."

"If you need drugs to help you sleep, don't hesitate to ask. We have plenty. I'm afraid I have no psychic suppressants, though. A normal recon unit doesn't include Telepaths.

"Let me give you another shot for the pain," she said, picking up her case. "I want you spending today resting," she said, looking at him fiercely.

Kusac sat down on his bunk. "Don't worry, I will," he reassured her. "We'll cope. I'm finding that things I thought impossible before are now achievable. My personal Talent is developing in new directions, to say nothing of our bond." He smiled up at Carrie.

The drug dispensed and the case closed again, Vanna crossed over to the water purifier and pulled out a small package which she threw to the girl.

"Can you fill this from the swamp, please? We're getting low on water."

"Certainly," replied Carrie, turning to go.

"Get Skai to choose a safe area," warned Kusac. He waited until she had left.

"What worries you?" he asked, leaning back against the hull.

"You do," she answered. "I've been thinking about what you'll both have to go through once our ship arrives."

"You think I haven't? Believe me, I have."

She dipped her head to one side in negation. "Leaving aside the board of inquiry, the Guild of Medics will want to give both of you a thorough going over to find out why you bonded, and the extent of your abilities. They'll really give Carrie a good working over. Just think of it, the first ever other Telepathic species; a new Alien physiology to categorize and label. They'll be in their element, and they won't necessarily care that she's a Telepath."

"I am thinking," said Kusac grimly.

"Can you both cope with it? Should you ask her to go through all the psych profiles and medical tests?"

"What can I do? As you said, we can't survive here. Our only possible future is on the *Khalossa*."

"Can't your Guild adopt her and protect her from the worst of the investigations?"

"They could, but they'll be just as anxious to study her."

"Aren't there any other Leska pairs on the ship that could help?"

"I believe there is one," he said thoughtfully. "They might be persuaded to help on a personal level if I can reach them early enough.

"I'm already concerned about how Carrie will react to being the only Terran on the ship. Up till now she's never been in wholly Sholan company for more than a day. She could find the species isolation too much to cope with. It could drive her insane."

His ears were twitching spasmodically with the effort of keeping them erect despite his distress. He shook himself and stood upright. "Carrie is questioning my mood. We cannot continue this discussion any longer or she will become aware of our fears."

"Is the bond that close, then?" asked Vanna. "I was led to believe Telepaths can only pick up the surface thoughts."

"Normally, yes, but what is normal in our relationship? Leskas are acutely aware of their partners, but we are more deeply linked. Her strength is such that I can barely control her, and I have to because she has none of the moral codes or inhibitions we are taught.

"Many of the traits of her Telepathy Talent are similar to ours, but she has them to a greater degree. As to her other Talents, there appears to be a degree of crossover to me. I am finding I can do things that have nothing to do with Telepathy."

"What's she like as a person?" asked Vanna abruptly, putting her head to one side.

Kusac looked slightly startled at the question. "Partly what you see, Vanna. Young, scared, and ready to fight because of it. The gentler side only I know. I love her—and she's returning," he added, moving forward to meet Carrie.

The next few hours were long ones indeed. There were now two distinct camps of people. Those outside who knew something about electronics, and those inside who knew nothing. For the latter, there was little to keep them occupied. Skai moved between the two groups, trying to offer advice and keep abreast of any progress that Mito, Guynor, and Garras were making.

Vanna tried to keep herself busy by checking and redressing Guynor's and Kusac's wounds. The brief scrutiny which was all that Guynor would allow was enough for her to tell that he was well on the mend. Kusac was another matter.

"Pity those Talents of yours don't include Healing," she grumbled, swabbing the wound with an antiseptic pad.

"What, and put you Medics out of business?" teased Kusac.

"There'll always be plenty of work for us, never fear," she said, taking a fresh dressing and bandage from Carrie.

"Don't you have Healers?"

"Very seldom. It's an erratic Talent," replied Kusac.

"There were all sorts of Healers amongst our people on Earth, our home world, but they weren't always successful."

"Then why don't you try?" suggested Kusac. "The limits to your Talent may only be those set by you."

"Are you still in as much pain?" inquired Vanna, rummaging in her medical kit as Carrie ran her hands lightly over the site of Kusac's wound.

Kusac and Vanna's voices began to recede as Carrie found her world narrowed to encompass only the wound. She perceived it as an angry dull red glow surrounded by a faint ambient green. She could sense the shattered nerve endings and their electrical messages of pain.

Placing her hand on his shoulder, she looked for the damaged nerves and slowly dimmed their power, noticing as she did that the redness began to recede. Slowly, very slowly, the green glow took its place. She let her intuition guide her and as the last flicker of red died, she turned her attention to the damaged tissue.

What she wanted here was to increase the speed of re-growing tissue. Again she let intuition take over and allowed the energy to flow from her into the wound. She knew when the time was right to remove her hand.

Abruptly, she returned to the world of the pod.

She was aware of Kusac's strong grip catching her as she stumbled.

"What did you do?" he asked, concern and confusion flowing from him on every level. He guided her down onto the bunk beside him.

"I don't know," she replied, rubbing her hands together. "I just did what seemed right. My hands feel hot and itchy," she complained, holding them out to Kusac.

He massaged them gently for a moment. "I'm not surprised," he said. "The amount of energy that's coming from them is unbelievable. I've never come across this before, but I know you'll have to control it or you'll drain yourself completely."

"How?" she wailed, rubbing her palms against her trousers in obvious discomfort.

"I think if you shielded yourself that would work. I'll show you how later. For now, just hold my hands."

She did as he asked and gradually the discomfort passed.

"I don't know how you did it, cub," he said, pulling her closer, "but the pain in my shoulder has stopped."

"By Vartra, Carrie, you have some Talent there," swore Vanna. "I take it you won't need an analgesic," she said to

Kusac, fumbling a little as she loaded her hypoderm, "but I'm going to give you some Fastheal. I don't like using it unless I have to, but I'm unhappy with the way the wound is not responding fully to my drugs. At least with that in you, I can be sure you're on the mend."

"Somehow, I don't think I'll need it," said Kusac, resting his chin on Carrie's head.

Vanna grunted and pressed the hypoderm against his shoulder. "I'm giving it to you anyway," she said.

Skai came over and Carrie was aware of a flash of disapproval as he caught sight of them together, but it vanished almost immediately in his desire to tell them his news.

He squatted down beside them as Vanna got to her feet and retreated to the food area.

"Garras has just finished coding the message for the *Khalossa*, and guess what Skinner's authorized him to do?"

"No idea," replied Kusac with a lazy purr.

"He's given your people the access codes to wake the crew on *Erasmus*. Apparently, once they've dealt with the Valtegans on Keiss, they're going to send out some FTL tugs to bring the *Erasmus* here."

"Makes sense," said Carrie.

"Ah, but that's not all," he said triumphantly. "You know that the second wave contains mostly trained mechanics and technicians and such like? Well, Garras is going to try and persuade his people that it would make sense to give us the technology necessary to defend our area of space from further attacks by the Valtegans. They can show us how to build anything from scout ships to star ships! Now we've got a real stake in space."

"Weren't you satisfied with the colony?" asked Carrie.

Skai gave her a disgusted look. "I was never cut out to be a sod turner. I don't know what I'd have done if the Valtegans hadn't turned up," he said frankly.

"It's certainly more romantic being a fighter pilot than a farmer," Carrie observed.

Skai frowned. "Aren't you surprised at my news?" he demanded.

She shook her head. "No. We discussed this possibility several days ago, when I first met the rest of the crew."

"Bloody women!" he muttered, stamping back to the hatch. "Think they know it all. If that's your attitude, then I won't bother to keep you informed."

"No chance of that," murmured Kusac. "That one enjoys bringing news if he feels it gives him an advantage."

"Mm," said Carrie, beginning to doze off in the warmth of Kusac's arms.

Two trail bars landed unceremoniously in her lap, bringing her back to wakefulness with a jolt.

"I'd just fallen asleep!" she complained, sitting up and brushing her hair back from her face.

"Just?" said Vanna, pointing through the hatch at the sky. "See where the sun is? Feel the chill in the air?" she asked, watching Carrie shiver. "That was over an hour ago. Mito and Guynor are bringing their equipment inside now. It's too near nightfall for them to continue working outside."

Kusac let her go, stood up, and stretched, each muscle group rippling sinuously in turn from his head to his tail. Carrie picked up his surprise as he began to touch his shoulder, at first gently, then more firmly.

"It's itchy," he exclaimed, "and I've got most of the movement back again." He grabbed both Vanna and Carrie and hugged them tight, swinging them off the ground before he put them down.

"You two make wonderful Healers. I can't believe how much better I feel."

"Let me see!" demanded Vanna, reaching for his bandage, but Kusac danced away.

"Tomorrow, tomorrow," he promised, heading round the other side of the central column.

"What's up with him?" Carrie asked, bemused. "He looks like the cat that's got at the cream."

"Uh?" said Vanna, trying to puzzle out the analogy.

Carrie picked up the two fruit bars and rose to her feet.

"Here," she said, "you may as well have one. It doesn't look as if Kusac needs any extra energy."

Munching their bars, the two women followed him. He was busily punching buttons on the keyboard of the pod's computer.

"Don't disturb me for the moment," he said. "This is important."

Hurt, Carrie reached for him mentally and found his mind closed to her for the first time. Confused, she let Vanna draw her away to the galley area.

"Once again when the technical staff have work to do, it falls to us to do the cooking. Not that the others don't take their turns," she continued, "they do. Now Garras, he's a good cook," she prattled on. "He's been around long enough to know the restorative qualities of a really well cooked meal rather than ship's rations served as they are packed.

"I've been preparing a stew for us tonight. I packed a few of the local roots and plants that we found growing near the cave, and they really taste quite palatable in a stew—if you like vegetables," she added, her jaw dropping in a grin.

A few minutes later, Kusac joined them. "I found the answer to that small problem we were discussing earlier, Vanna," he said, draping his arm around Carrie's shoulders and dipping a cautious finger in the stew. He wrinkled his nose in dislike.

"I hate to say it, but it doesn't taste very good."

"It isn't cooked yet, give us a chance. So what's your solution?"

"Can't tell you yet. You don't know how to set up an automatic transmission from here to the *Khalossa* when it gets within range, do you? I've got a personal message I want forwarded without delay."

"I think so," she replied. "Have you coded it ready for transmission?"

"Yes, I just need the transmit codes put in."

"It shouldn't be any different from sending a status report from the scout vehicle," she said. "I take it you haven't cleared it with the Captain?"

"No, but I'll tell him when we leave the Valtegan base."

"I'd better do it now then, before anyone else returns," she said. "Just a slight detail, but have you checked that our main transmitter is working?"

"Mito checked it out. As far as she can tell, it's still functional. There isn't any obvious sign of damage. Once the *Khalossa* is within range, it will pulse out all the recorded data it hasn't been able to transmit, my message included."

Vanna moved over to the main console by the hatch.

"Thanks," said Kusac.

Guynor, Mito, and the Captain came in festooned with various bits of electronics. Mito laid hers on the floor and pulled down one of the sleeping benches, sweeping the bedding onto the floor. They then proceeded to set up their workshop. Mito picked up several of her tools, and, going over to the tower, pulled open one of the cupboards and set them into their slots to recharge. She looked round to where Kusac, Vanna, and Carrie stood.

"I'm afraid we'll have to work into the night," she said. "Guynor managed to solve the groundcar problem, so Skinner and his men will be here sometime tomorrow."

"Wouldn't they be better off traveling at night?" asked Kusac.

"They'd have to use lights. As it is, they will have to travel above tree level because of the dense undergrowth. At least there is a form of radar on board so they will have some warning of any Valtegan air activity. Apart from that, we have to trust to the Gods.

"Is that food?" she asked, her nose twitching as she sniffed the air.

"Yes. It'll be ready in a few minutes," replied Vanna.

"Good, I'm starving!"

"What are you doing with the transmitter?" asked Carrie.

"Hey! Doesn't anyone around here speak English?" demanded Skai, sealing the door. "You can all understand me, but I can't make head nor tail of your damned purrs and growls."

"We were talking about food," said Vanna in English. "It will be ready shortly."

"Good. Anything to drink apart from water?"

Carrie threw him a mug.

"Careful," he said, just managing to catch it.

"There is c'shar in the packs over here, and water in the purifier," she said. "Help yourself. You can have the heater when we've finished cooking."

Skai ambled over to the purifier.

"Come over to the bench and I will tell you what we are doing," said Mito.

Carrie turned to Vanna.

"Off you go. There really isn't anything to do but wait for it to cook."

Carrie and Kusac followed Mito back to the bench where Guynor and Garras were working with various circuits.

"We're redesigning certain areas of the computer so it will be able to link up to the Valtegan equipment that Captain Skinner is bringing tomorrow. We don't know exactly what fittings we'll need until they arrive, but we can do the groundwork now."

"Then what?" asked Kusac.

"I design a program that will interrogate the Valtegan computer in such a way that it won't be noticed until too late. Once we have their access codes, we can patch into the transmitter itself, masquerading as their computer."

"Then you order it to transmit the signal?"

Mito gave a negative head movement. "No, we can't do that until the transmitter is pointing to the correct quadrant of the sky. To move the antenna we have to put it into a Search mode. Considering the amount of traffic they deal with, they will probably have frequent Search routines. We are just starting our own one."

"And hoping the Valtegans don't notice," murmured Carrie.

"You noticed the flaw, eh?" said Mito. "If we do it in the dead of night, the chances are there will be a bored operator on duty and he will assume it's routine. I've done enough night shift duties to know that he'll probably be too tired to question it.

"We stop the Search when the antenna is pointing toward the *Khalossa,* then our program will override the transmitter and send the message in a high speed burst. With luck, it won't even register on their monitors. That's the plan. However we have a problem."

"What's wrong?"

"The software. Given long enough, our computer could break into the Valtegan system, but there are so many options to contend with that by the time we succeeded, our presence would have been noticed. What I really need is some Valtegan software to work from."

"Food is ready," called Vanna as the appetizing smell filled the small room.

With obvious relief, the group around the makeshift workbench broke up and headed to the galley area.

"I guess that none of us will get much sleep tonight," sighed Carrie, helping herself to a ladle full of stew from the dish.

"It will give us time to talk," said Kusac. "We need time to be by ourselves."

"As well as time to plan and practice our part in this raid," said Carrie wryly.

Kusac growled. "I forbid you to mention work until tomorrow!"

"I don't think I heard that," sniffed Carrie, pulling down the nearest sleeping bench to sit on.

After they'd eaten, Kusac spread Carrie's blanket more comfortably on the floor by his bunk and turned off the personal light. Then he fetched her hairbrush and looked hopefully at her.

Carrie laughed. "You're incorrigible," she said, taking the brush from him and sliding off the bunk to sit behind him.

He unbuckled his belt, taking off the jacket and putting it to one side.

"I itch all over," he complained as she began to brush him.

"It's because you've been ill, I expect," said Carrie. "Your fur has gone dull and you're shedding."

"Mm," said Kusac, his back arching slightly to meet her brush strokes.

She watched the muscles move, fascinated. Through their Link, she could experience for herself the pleasure that Kusac felt.

As a species, we're more sensually oriented than you, he sent, turning round to face her. He leaned forward, tipping his head down so she could reach it.

Your fur's longer there.

It can grow as long as yours when it isn't cut. His mental tone was amused.

"Well, how was I to know?" she asked.

It is as I said, we need the time to get to know each other, he replied, moving his head to one side so she was brushing his ear, too.

Carrie concentrated on his ears for a moment, then stopped.

Do you want to do the rest yourself?

"It's much nicer when you do it," he purred, his voice like liquid velvet.

She gave him a long look. "I'll tell you what, you used a bloody good glamour back at Valleytown to make me believe you were a forest cat!"

He put his head to one side, flicking his ear.

What is different now?

"You know," she changed to mind speech, *damned well! You're not an animal, you're a person.*

He reached for her hand and brought it and the brush against his good shoulder.

Is that a problem? he sent, one eye ridge moving questioningly, amber eyes looking calmly back at her.

Yes. I mean . . . Oh, I don't know. She began to brush him again.

He moved to sit up on his heels, edging closer to her so her arm was less extended.

Your fur is longer at the front, too. She could feel the vibration of his purr through the brush as she drew it carefully down his chest to his belly. His eyes were half closed in pleasure.

It is with most furred species, even your forest cats.

He held out his arms for her and she switched her attention, keeping clear of the bandaged shoulder.

"Thank you," he said, teeth flashing whitely as he smiled, Sholan style. He took the brush from her and cleaned it, putting the loose fur on the floor beside him.

"Now you," he said, reaching forward to take a lock of hair in his hands. *Your hair is so soft, Leska. I have never felt anything like it before. And the color . . .* He ran it through his fingertips before beginning to brush it.

Turn round, then I can reach it all.

Carrie turned round, sitting with her back to his knees. Across the room she could see Skai frowning over at her. He rose and began to move toward them, but Vanna called him over. The others were busy with their electronics.

This is our time, Leska, sent Kusac, putting the brush aside. *Vanna will keep him busy for a while.*

She felt his hands touch her shoulders and start to feel along them for the muscle groups.

You are tense. Let me relax you. He began to gently knead the muscles there and at the back of her neck.

She started to relax, enjoying the massage.

Now you're purring like a Sholan, sent Kusac, surprised and pleased.

A part of me is forever Sholan now, she replied.

His fingers moved gently just under her ear. "Do you regret it?" he whispered.

Not when your hands are as magical as this.

Kusac laughed, shifting his hands to her waist and moving his legs to pull her back against him.

Perhaps there is less of a sensual difference between us than I thought!

Carrie rested her head against his shoulder—it was becoming a familiar place—and closed her eyes. Like this, there were no problems.

Kusac wrapped his arms around her.

We need to be serious now, he sent. *Vanna told me what happened last night, how you were linking in to my pain and drawing it all to you.*

Carrie stirred, feeling defensive.

Hush, I know you didn't realize it was happening, that was my fault. I should have noticed sooner that the pain was diminishing faster than Vanna's drugs could act. The point is, we have to do something to stop that happening again.

What do you suggest? she asked.

I thought perhaps a system similar to that we use when working with the Courts or with the mentally ill, a kind of filter to keep the unwanted thoughts away.

You're not classifying me among the mentally ill, are you? was her tart response.

Kusac gave her a little shake. *You know very well I am not*, he sent, his tone chiding. *It is impossible to lie to each other because of our Link. Thoughts and emotions are too closely entwined and too quickly felt. Trust the Link, Leska, and use it.*

I do, Kusac. This time her tone was gentle.

Kusac was silent as wisps of memories and fears came to him from her. Then the bits fell into place.

Leska, we Sholan males are not like your men. The concept of owning a person is not one we have, it is Human. How can they think that another individual is their property? She could feel his disapproval.

Quite easily, from my experience, she replied.

Our lives are firmly bound to each other because of our Link, but I assure you that you will find you are free to make your own choices within those parameters. You may do what you want, and be with whom you want. I do not own you, nor you me.

I can choose?

You can choose.

She was silent for a moment. *Could we do that filter now?*

Of course. Let me place it for you, then you can examine it and duplicate it later. Sit up and face me, he sent, moving his arms so that she could.

When they'd finished, Carrie curled up on the blanket, yawning. She still held one of his hands.

He was large compared to her, she noted once again, her hand almost hidden by his dark-furred one. Her head was tilted back so she could see him.

She *was* small, he thought, looking down at her: childlike, barely reaching the height of an adult. Long eyelashes cast shadows on her cheeks and her throat turned to him.

She felt relaxed, with a warm, comfortable glow that made her disinclined to move. Her eyes opened slightly and she tugged gently on his hand.

Come down with me.

He stretched out beside her, lying on his good side.

Tell me about yourself, she sent, her other hand idly stroking the fur on his chest. Its texture was so soft and silky.

What do you want to know?

Have you any brothers or sisters?

I have two . . . he started, but trailed off as he found himself unable to concentrate on what he was saying.

The temperature in the pod was warm, warm enough for her to have taken off her sweater and opened her shirt at the neck. And she had a beautiful neck, long and slender—and exposed to him. Even the way she lay stretched out on her side made her look like a Sholan woman. Her hair, the color of sunlight even in the dim lighting, cascaded over one shoulder and down onto the blanket.

He looked better without his uniform on, she thought, his fur almost glowing in the half light. She let her hand stray lazily through the silky tide until it crept around his waist. She urged him closer.

As he moved nearer, she noticed how well he matched the curves of her body. The smell of his fur, warm and clean with a sharply musky tang to it, surrounded her. She could feel his heart beating—so fast!

For the first time, he was intensely aware of her scent— warm, musky, and very female. Despite her smallness, her body accommodated his perfectly. He could feel the softness of breast and thigh touching him. All the signals were there, Sholan and Terran overlaid.

Through half closed eyes she saw his face come down toward her, his mouth closing on her throat. His jaws tightened gently and they could feel her blood racing against them. The pressure increased and she tilted her head back further. A low growl of pleasure from him and she was released.

Little bites coupled with tiny flicks of a rough tongue rained across her face. It was unlike anything she had experienced before. She began to shiver with pleasure.

Her skin was so soft, tasted and smelled so good—an accompanying shiver ran through him. Amber and brown eyes, both barely open, locked briefly. He found her ear. So tiny, almost pointed like his.

A wave of panic flooded through her and she brought her free hand between them, pushing him firmly back.

At the same moment, Kusac realized what was happening to them. He pulled back from her, rolling up into a sitting position, radiating alarm.

He fought the compulsion, trying desperately to push it back. Any pairing would happen when *they* were ready, not because of their Link!

It took several minutes, but at last he had himself under control. He turned to look at her.

Carrie had been fighting her own battle, one with fear. One which Kusac, otherwise involved, knew nothing about. The intensity not only of what she was experiencing, but what he felt for her, had been terrifying. She'd recognized the compulsion and for her it had been easier to break free. Fear had been the trigger.

Now she lay with her back turned to him.

Kusac sat there, miserably aware that most of the good their earlier talk had done was now wiped out because of what had just happened.

There is a sexual compulsion because of our Link, he admitted, unwilling to vocalize lest anyone else hear them.

She said nothing.

It only starts if we touch for too long, and not always then.

He waited a few minutes but there was no reply. Even through their Link he could sense nothing but quiet.

Carrie, I don't like this any more than you do, but I couldn't help it. I responded to you.

I know.

If we're careful and keep touching to a minimum, it shouldn't happen again.

Silence.

He leaned forward to touch her and she pulled sharply away.

Don't.

Suppressing a flash of anger, he got to his feet and

stepped over her. Squatting down, he lifted her bodily and sat her up facing him, then released her.

Stop this now, he sent, his tone firm. *You're a grown woman, Carrie, don't behave like a terrified youngling. Surely you trust me by now?* He took her face in his hand, forcing eye contact between them.

Look at me. Remember the night in the cave, before we went to Seaport?

She nodded, unable to move her eyes from his.

I felt the compulsion briefly then. Had I not been honorable, we would not be having this conversation as this problem would be solved.

You have to decide sooner or later, Carrie, but it's your choice, not mine. Like you, I want you to want me for myself, not because of the Link compulsion. He let her go.

"Go and get some sleep now," he said. "If we need to talk, we can do it tomorrow."

"Kusac, I'm sorry," she whispered. "I know it was my fault, but everything all together . . . I panicked."

"It was no one's fault, cub," he said, briefly touching her cheek. "This is all as confusing for me, too. Let's just take things as they come." He switched to mind talk.

Tonight, neither the place nor the time is right. It is as well we came to our senses when we did. If we're careful, we shouldn't trigger the compulsion again.

She nodded, catching at his hand. "I do love you," she murmured, rubbing her cheek against him.

"I know," he said, gently squeezing her hand before helping her stand. He gathered up the blanket. "Get some sleep now though."

He waited for her to get onto the bunk then spread the blanket over her. Leaning forward, he gently licked her ear before leaving her.

Carrie closed her eyes. Sleep would not come easily, she knew that. She couldn't forget his touch. Echoes of it still flickered across her face and neck and she had to block the memories before he sensed them. When she finally fell asleep, amber eyes like twin suns glowed compellingly in the dark before her.

Chapter 9

Kusac picked up the hairbrush and, throwing his jacket and belt on his bed, finished grooming himself. Carrie had been right. He was shedding, though not excessively.

Not wishing to disturb her, he stowed the brush in the recessed locker by his bed and went over to the galley to use the garbage disposal unit. Vanna was there.

"Protein drink or c'shar?" she asked, her hand hovering beside the dispenser.

"Protein, though I could do with one of their coffees!" he said ruefully.

"Coffee?"

"It tastes like c'shar but stronger."

She handed him his mug. "One day I must get the chance to try it. You had your talk then."

He hesitated.

"No need to tell me if you don't want to," she said, taking a mouthful of her drink.

"For every step forward I take with her, Vanna, I seem to take three backward," he said, his tail flicking. "There are so many similarities to us, it would almost be easier if she were totally different."

Vanna glanced over the makeshift tech lab.

"Mito's coming over. Let's talk back there where we can't be overheard—and you can still watch Carrie," she said, leading the way to her bunk area.

The bunk was raised so as not to reduce the already cramped quarters further.

"Hold my drink a moment, please," she said, handing him the mug.

She pulled the bed out far enough to grab her blanket. Folding it up, she laid it on the floor.

"I hate sitting on bare metal," she said, rescuing her drink and squatting down comfortably.

Kusac joined her.

"Surely your Link helps you to understand each other bet ter?" she asked.

"That's a knife with two edges, Vanna," he said heavily "I'm sure our Leska Link is unlike any other."

"There may have been other anomalous Links before . . ." she began.

"No, none. If there had been, I would have known abou them. My education as a Telepath was thorough."

Vanna's eyes narrowed thoughtfully as she stored thi piece of information away for the future.

"Garras is having me seconded to the ship's medical sec tion when the *Khalossa* arrives," she said abruptly. "He wants me there as the expert on Terran physiology. If you're finding sleep difficult, how about giving me some back ground information on Terrans?"

Kusac looked round at her, eye ridges arching up in sur prise.

"So you'll be involved in the tests on the *Khalossa?*"

"That's the general idea," she said. "However, I nee some information to justify a position on that team."

Carrie was the last to wake. When she sat up, she foun the pod deserted. The knowledge that Kusac was outside came to her automatically as did the fact that the day wa pleasant. She waited for a minute or two, but he did not ap pear. She did, however, receive a brief greeting.

Feeling a little hurt, she nevertheless took advantage o the solitude to put on fresh clothes from her backpack. Col lecting herself a protein drink for breakfast, she went to th hatch and peered outside.

Kusac immediately looked round, acknowledging he presence with a flick of his ears before he returned to help ing Garras. Everything appeared as it had the day before, al most as if nothing had been moved for the night.

As she stepped out, the sensible portion of her mind re minded her that Kusac was a member of the crew and woul have had to return to his duties at some point, and that poin was obviously now. She had no need to feel put out, but sh did.

Finding a piece of log to sit on, she sat watching the oth ers, for the first time feeling somewhat superfluous. As sh sipped her drink, she began to notice how constantly she was aware of Kusac through their Link.

It was the first opportunity she'd had to look at their situation dispassionately and she took advantage of it. Suddenly, it occurred to her that this was partially why Kusac was otherwise occupied and hard on the heels of that came his approbation that she had figured it out.

Moods, emotions, and the surface thoughts of either one was experienced by both. If mentally she went down a level or two that took a little effort, not much but she would have to concentrate rather than have the knowledge at her fingertips.

She explored the Link further, finding in him his feelings for her. Though he instantly laid them open to her she shied away from them, still not ready to face what he felt.

There was a barrier, an area walled off from her, and she backed off. This was fair because she, too, had such a barrier. With so much they could not hide from each other, they both needed somewhere they could have a semblance of privacy.

A shadow fell across her, pulling her back to the more mundane world.

"Good morning, Skai," she said, draining her mug.

"Good morning. I thought we could have a chat," he said, sitting down beside her. "I gather that you and your brother are both joining us."

"It would appear so," she said, remembering Garras' warning.

"It'll be nice having you around," he said, smiling at her. "I expect that once their ship arrives, this crew will be recalled and we'll be working with another group."

"Probably," she said. Then, pinning down what was bothering her, she asked, "Why are there no insects around, Skai?"

"Uh? Oh, Guynor tinkered with my bug screen, hooking it up to a power source and so on, but that was yesterday." He frowned. "Look, I want to give you some good advice. It might be wiser if you spent a little less time with the Sholans when our mob arrives," he said. "They don't know you and they could get the wrong idea."

"Wrong idea about what?"

"You spending so much time with the cats."

"With them, Skai?"

"Okay. With their Telepath, then."

"Kusac?"

"Yes, with Kusac," he said sharply. "I've seen you two together, Carrie, seen the way he looks at you and touches you. It isn't right. You shouldn't encourage him. It's not as if he's even human!"

"Who are you to say what's human and what's not?" she asked angrily, getting up. "How dare you talk like that about us!"

As she turned to go into the pod, Skai caught at her arm. She pulled away and stepped through the hatch acutely aware of Kusac's anger on her behalf but also of his resolution that this was something she must deal with herself.

Skai followed her and this time he did manage to catch her.

"Look, Carrie, Elise threw herself away on the Valtegans. I can't stand back and let it happen to you, too," he said, trying to sound reasonable.

"Kusac isn't a Valtegan."

"He's an Alien, damnit! He's not human! He's not one of us!"

"Let go of me, Skai, or, so help me, I'll hit you," she said, her anger now coldly dangerous. "I'll make up my own mind who I'll have as a partner. What Kusac and I share is beyond the understanding of you and your grubby little mind.

"What Elise did was get vital information for sanctimonious bastards like you. She didn't enjoy it, or maybe you didn't realize that! I wonder how many men would have volunteered to work in the cities to get information if the Valtegans had been female. You sure as hell wouldn't have. You're not man enough to do the really dirty work!"

"Now, let me go," she said, pulling away from him again.

Anger suffused Skai's face and as he drew his arm back, he found himself grabbed from behind. He swung round to face not Kusac, but Garras.

"I think not," said the Captain, restraining him. He turned to where an enraged Kusac stood waiting by the hatch.

"Take your Leska outside while I have a word with our young Terran," Garras said.

With a filthy look at Skai, Carrie walked past him to Kusac. He stood aside to let her pass, then followed her.

"Are you . . ." he began.

". . . all right?" She smiled briefly. "You know I am. Angry like you, but all right."

"Will many of your people think like him?" he asked, tail and ears flicking.

"Probably. We Terrans have a lot of hate in us. Hatred for those with a different skin color, with a different religion— you name it, some of us will find a reason to hate it.

"Never mind, let's talk about something else. Are you still busy?"

"No, we're ready for your guerrillas."

"That's good," she said, reclaiming her perch on the log. "Can you stay with me now?" she asked, looking steadily up at him.

"Yes," he said, returning the gaze and knowing that she had finally crossed at least half of the gap between them.

It was not long after noon when they heard the faint sound of an approaching groundcar. Though they were well under cover, camouflaged blankets were draped over any equipment outside the pod to prevent the slightest glint of sunlight on metal and everyone huddled together under the overhanging branches of the tree.

"I hope it's ours," muttered Skai, still subdued after his talk with Garras.

"It better be," growled Guynor. "We're running out of time ourselves. We need to send that signal before the Valtegans access our crystal."

"Kusac, check and see whether there are Valtegans or Terrans on board," Garras ordered.

Kusac moved away from the others and squatted down, closing his eyes. After a few moments, he turned back to them.

"Terrans," he replied. "Eight of them."

They stepped into the open, beckoning to the vehicle as it sped above the surface of the swamp.

Carrie shivered, reaching out for Kusac. He put his arm around her and drew her to his side.

The craft cut its speed and lowered its skids, slewing to a halt in a spray of swamp water. The hatch opened and a figure in a drab green one-piece leaned into view, holding a rope. He took a long look at them before speaking.

"Haul us in to the shore, will you? We've got to get this baby under cover as soon as possible."

Several hands caught the rope and hauled to with a will until they had the side of the craft near enough dry land for the first man to jump down.

"Well, if it isn't Davies," said Skai, grinning hugely as he stepped forward. "I told you it was a good excuse this time, didn't I?"

Davies grunted and turned back to the craft. Another figure was emerging.

"Just help me secure this rope onto the bow end," he said. "You've got plenty of time to crow. We've got work to do now."

While Skai and Davies jumped onto the nose of the groundcar to secure their rope, the rest of the Terran crew began to emerge. One figure stood poised in the hatch for a few moments before jumping down.

"Richard!" exclaimed Carrie, breaking free of Kusac and running forward to greet her brother.

He held her close for a moment before releasing her.

"You've really flown the nest and met some strange companions, haven't you?" he said, looking at Kusac.

"Richard," she began.

He shook his head and held her close again. "I know," he said quietly with one of his rare flashes of insight. "You don't have to tell me. I shall miss you." He let her go and went over to where Kusac stood.

"A bit different from our first meeting," he remarked with a wry smile. "I should have guessed. We had most of the pieces of the jigsaw at hand and just couldn't see the picture for looking."

"You were dealing with a family tragedy at the time," murmured Kusac. "Who else knows?"

"No one yet. Give it time. Word will travel, but by then you'll both be safe on the Mothership, won't you?"

"If not there, then with you."

Richard nodded. "You look as if you've been in the wars already." He indicated the bandage over Kusac's shoulder.

"Some trouble on the way here. Nothing serious," he said evasively.

Richard shrugged, accepting the other's reticence. He searched Kusac's face, looking for some human referent he couldn't find. "Do I need to tell you . . ."

". . . to look after her? No. I know it's not what you would like, but we didn't have a lot of say in it either," Kusac ended lamely.

Richard reached out and grasped his arm. "What I like doesn't matter, it's what she wants that counts. Tell me about it later," he said, smiling again. "I think they need our help to pull this groundcar under cover."

Eventually they had it hauled beneath the shelter of the tree and the overhanging blankets.

The need to conceal the vehicle had broken the ice, but with the immediate task out of the way, Carrie suddenly found herself flanked on one side by the Sholans and on the other by the guerrillas. Each side had its men grouped protectively around its Captain.

"Perhaps you'd like to introduce us to the Sholans, Carrie," said Captain Skinner.

It was nearly like culture shock again, so used was she to Sholan company now. Almost panicking, she took a couple of involuntary steps backward.

"This is Captain Garras, his First Officer Guynor, Mito from Communications, Vanna from Medical, and Kusac, their Telepath," she stammered, indicating them each in turn.

"I'm Captain Skinner. My people are Davies, Anders, Peterson, Hughes, Nelson, and Edwards. I know Kusac at least has met Richard Hamilton," he said, indicating Carrie's brother last.

"I do not like this," muttered Guynor, his tail flicking in slow, wide arcs. "We are outnumbered and carrying inadequate firepower. You should have let us use the rifles."

"I asked for heavily armed troops," said Garras quietly. "They have brought them. Having these advantages over us should make them feel less distrustful. Confirm, Kusac."

Carrie had been aware of Kusac monitoring the thoughts of the Terrans from the first and now, mentally, she joined him, adding to his interpretation her reading of their current emotions.

She felt his start of surprise, then his professionalism took over again as he collated both their data.

"He's picked well," said Kusac. "All are guarded, curious, and ready for trouble should it happen. They view us with varying degrees of skepticism, but there is no hatred and they wish to cooperate. The woman recognizes Carrie," he added, faintly surprised until he remembered the guerrilla Elise had been in contact with.

Garras nodded.

"If you back up any farther, cub, you will be in the swamp," said Vanna in amusement, briefly touching Carrie on the shoulder to alert her.

Carrie glanced round, panic on her face and in her mind. Colonial life was looming too large before her once again.

She felt Kusac reach out and take her by the arm, drawing her over to where he stood at the edge of their group. The familiar contact reassured her, banishing the fear.

Straightening her back, she took a step forward.

"Captain Garras wonders if you and your First Officer would like to look round our life pod," she said.

Garras looked as surprised as Skinner, though the Terrans couldn't tell.

"Yes, that would certainly be most interesting," Skinner said, glancing at Carrie.

"The pod is too small for all your men to go in at once," Carrie said apologetically, "but I'm sure they'll get the chance to see it later. Mito, I know, is dying to see inside the Valtegan groundcar."

"Um, yes. I expect she is. Anders, would you take the lady on a tour?" Captain Skinner asked.

Mito looked expectantly at Garras.

"Sure," said Anders, swinging his rifle over his shoulder out of the way. "No problem."

"Captain Skinner?" invited Garras, stepping away from his crew and waiting for the Terran.

The amenities over and the tableau broken by the departure of the two parties to the respective vehicles, everyone else began to relax.

Vanna was the first to move, ambling over to the Terrans to find out if there was a Medic among them.

Everyone was trying not to stare and yet still get a close look at the Aliens. Finding her opposite number in Hughes, Vanna encouraged him to be as frank as she was in their discussion. They, too, needed to trade information.

"Nicely done," grinned Kusac.

"Well, someone had to do something," she replied, equally pleased by the way the meeting had turned out.

"Your help in reading the Terrans was invaluable," he said. "That was also well done."

"Is that what you do when you're working as a Telepath?"

she asked, turning to walk with him to their sitting area outside the pod.

"That's one of the ways that you and I will work together," he agreed.

"Much more romantic than being a colonist," she said,
smiling up at him.

"Definitely," he purred, squatting down beside her as she
sat down.

They both looked up as the only woman with Skinner's
team came over to them.

She knew Elise, sent Carrie.

"Hi, I'm Jo, and you must be Carrie Hamilton," the
woman said, perching on the edge of an upright log.

Carrie took the proffered hand and shook it politely.

"I knew your sister," she continued. "We worked together
at Geshader." Her face clouded. "It was a blow to us all
when she was caught."

Carrie nodded, not wanting to reopen that wound again.
"Elise mentioned you. What brings you with Skinner?" she
asked.

"I'm here primarily as a language expert. When they got
the groundcar, they called me back from Geshader to monitor the Valtegan radio transmissions since I'd picked up a
fair bit of the language. I was glad to leave Geshader, I can
tell you."

"Was it that bad?" asked Carrie.

Jo shot her a hard look. "You don't want to know," she
said, her tone flat.

Carrie fell silent, at a loss to know what to say next.

"Say, we brought some coffee and food with us," said Jo.
"I expect you could do with a cup. I know I could."

"Definitely one of the better Terran things we will have to
import," said Kusac.

Jo gave him a look of stunned surprise, then stuck out her
hand. "Hello. I didn't know you could speak English so
well," she said as Kusac's furry hand enveloped hers. "I
mean, I knew you could, I heard your Captain, but it just
seems so strange to sit beside you and see you doing it," she
faltered as he let her hand go.

"I don't mean to be rude, but . . ."

"It's all right," said Kusac gently. "We all react to Aliens
in different ways. I'm Kusac, the Sholan Telepath. I assure
you I really do understand."

"I'm sure I'll get used to you, but it isn't easy to . . . relax . . . in nonhuman company after the Valtegans. We'll change, we have to. This is the turning point for us, after all." She looked at him sharply. "We can trust you, can't we?"

Kusac threw back his head and roared with laughter. "It's a little late for you to ask, but, yes," he chuckled.

"We're primarily Traders, and our home planet has become quite cosmopolitan, thanks to the various business interests of the three species with whom we trade. You have nothing to fear from us.

"Why don't you go and get your coffee. We'll wait for you in the pod and have our own discussion to rival theirs," he said, indicating the groundcar where Mito and the others—for several Terrans had joined her at the hatchway—were standing and talking.

Jo grinned, relieved. "I'll be back in a minute."

Carrie got up again as her brother came over.

"We're having coffee courtesy of Jo," she said. "Are you coming?"

"Try and stop me," he said. "You're the only way I'll get a look inside that pod of yours. I come way down on the priority list."

Vanna ambled over with Hughes.

"Did I hear the name of that drink you've been going on about?" she asked Kusac. "What are we waiting for?" She led the way.

Carrie hung back, letting the others enter first.

"You really have been involved with Aliens before, haven't you?"

"It was part of my training," he said. "Alien Relations is something I would have been involved with anyway at some point in the future."

He put an arm around her as they followed the rest. "Now you've experienced the difference between knowing up here," he tapped his head, "and understanding in the heart. Soon it will all fit together, don't worry."

"There's definitely more to you than meets the eye," she said, slipping her arm around his waist. "Did you notice Skai is back with his own people?"

Kusac snorted. "If that one values his skin, he had best stay at a distance from you."

"There's no need to antagonize him, Kusac."

"Me, antagonize him?" He raised an eye ridge at her.

"You know what I mean. He's terrified of you already after what Garras said to him. He won't bother me again."

"You shouldn't have been listening, Carrie. That was an invasion of his privacy," he said seriously, looking down at her and frowning.

"I take it you don't you want to know what he said, then?" she asked innocently as they stepped through the hatch.

"You imp! Yes, go on, tell me!" He grinned.

"Oh, nothing much. He just gave him a close look at his hands and explained that Senior Sholan Officers have the right to discipline their underlings if they break the Challenge code."

Kusac began to chuckle softly.

"He also said Skai could consider himself lucky if he, Garras, got to him before you did," she added, twisting out from under his arm and skipping over to the galley where Vanna stood.

"She'll drive you mad, you know," said Richard from behind him.

"Tell me about it," Kusac said ruefully. "She's a child and a woman rolled into one."

Richard laughed. "I can see you already know her well. It's very compact in here," he continued, looking round the interior of the pod as they joined the others.

"Cramped," corrected Kusac. "It's meant for six not seven, and was never intended to be a major electronics workshop as well as emergency living quarters."

Garras and his two guests squeezed past them on their way back out.

"Skinner said we would be bunking in the groundcar," said Richard. "Just as well if you're this overcrowded."

"I expect we'll end up in whichever vehicle the tech crew isn't working in," said Vanna. "It's a good way to get to know each other, though."

"I suppose it is," said Richard, sitting down on the bench seat that surrounded the column. "You know," he said, looking from one to the other, "you don't really resemble felines at all when you're upright."

Vanna sat beside him and grinned, Sholan fashion, making Richard draw back slightly.

"It's only their smile," reassured Carrie quickly, and her brother relaxed.

"We heard all about Kusac's masquerade," Vanna said. "We're an upright race like yours, but we've retained the ability to travel more quickly on four legs when the need arises. I expect that capability will disappear in time."

"You're so similar to us, yet so different," Richard said, "that it's unsettling. Being able to speak our language almost makes you more Alien." He looked sheepishly at his sister. "You've been through all this. I expect it sounds foolish to you."

"No, not at all. I just see things on a different level from you. With my mind, not my eyes."

"You always did," he replied. "I get the feeling these people are more your kind than we are."

"Can I come in?" asked Jo from the hatch.

"Of course," said Vanna. "Come and initiate me into the rites of making this strange beverage I've heard so much about."

Jo had brought the colony's equivalent of instant coffee and a large thermal jug with her as well as powdered milk and sweetener. She made up a large jugful which they carried outside. Mugs were collected and drinks poured for everyone, the tech personnel taking theirs with them to their work areas.

The small group that regrouped outside the pod to talk was comprised of Garras, Vanna, Carrie, Kusac, Captain Skinner, Jo, and Richard.

"This is good," said Vanna, sipping her drink.

"What brought you to Keiss?" asked Skinner, pulling out a pack of cigarettes and offering them around. The Sholans declined, but Carrie accepted gladly.

"I ran out days ago," she said, digging her lighter out of her trouser pocket.

"We've plenty in the groundcar," said Jo, throwing her a pack.

"Two of our colony worlds were attacked without warning some six months ago," said Garras, his ears almost flat against his skull with emotion. "Every living person on both planets was killed. Nothing was taken, just ruthlessly laid waste by massive air and ground attacks. Our people didn't even have the time to send out a distress signal. We still have no idea why it was done.

"On one planet two Aliens' bodies were found, bodies from a species unknown to any of the members of the Allied

Worlds. Because of our impromptu stay on Keiss," he said with a faint touch of humor, "I can now identify them as Valtegans."

Skinner nodded. "I can see we have a common enemy."

"We need to know where these Valtegans come from and what they are doing. We also need to know why they utterly destroyed two of our worlds yet left you alive. This species is a danger to everyone," said Garras.

"You mentioned the Allied Worlds," said Skinner. "How many of you are there?"

"Four core species, ourselves and three others with whom we have Trade treaties, but each colony is an independent member of the Alliance."

"I presume you are each searching and patrolling your own sectors of space."

Garras nodded. "Until now, we have drawn a blank on every world we've searched."

"How did you happen to get shot down?"

"The *Khalossa* dropped a score of eight-man scouters like ours, each on a three-month recon mission. We hit problems on the world before Keiss and told them we were running late. A new rendezvous was arranged and we proceeded here.

"We hit turbulence on the way down and failed to notice the Valtegan presence until we were attacked. The first two shots took out guidance, auto-distress, and communications, costing me my pilot and navigator," said Garras, his pain again very evident.

"The third hit breached the hull and injured Kusac," said Vanna. "Garras brought us down on manual and we crashed on the edge of the forest."

"I hit the auto-destruct and we took anything of use and left, only to walk straight into a Valtegan groundcar attack," said Garras. "Our engineer was the first man out." He stopped for a moment before continuing.

"We returned fire, but we were pinned down in a vehicle about to explode. As luck would have it, Guynor managed to lob an explosive device close enough to the groundcar to take it out and we escaped just in time.

"We headed for the cover of the forest, knowing that among the trees we could pass for the indigenous cats on this world, especially since we'd made sure our dead went up with the scouter.

"We knew the general location of this life pod, so we headed for it." Garras took a sip of the coffee. He wrinkled his nose with distaste and set it aside.

"Kusac was too badly injured to keep up with us, so we had to leave him hidden in some bushes to follow us when he could," said Vanna. "Getting the information about the Valtegans to the *Khalossa* was more important than one person's life, even if he was a Telepath." Vanna cast a look in Carrie's direction, but the girl said nothing.

"You aren't still mad at me?" she asked Carrie, lapsing into Sholan and putting her head on one side, ears flicking.

Carrie looked puzzled. "Why should I be mad at you, Vanna?" she asked in the same language.

"Back at the cave you were mad at me for leaving your lover behind."

Carrie flushed, looking away. "He isn't my lover, Vanna," she said quietly.

"Why not?" The Sholan sounded surprised.

Garras frowned. "Vanna," he warned.

Vanna turned to Garras. "I'm only asking why not," she said. "It's a reas . . ." she stumbled over the word, ". . . fair question."

Carrie began to panic. She couldn't cope with this sudden interest in her private life. Why was Vanna asking her, and in front of everyone else? It wasn't like her at all.

"Leave it, Vanna," said Kusac mildly.

Carrie felt her hair being touched and instantly turned around. Kusac had taken hold of a lock of it and was idly winding it between his fingers.

He grinned up at her from where he lay propped against a lump of wood. Carrie turned reluctantly back to the conversation.

"I want to know," insisted Vanna. "You love each other, so where is the problem?"

Why wasn't Kusac saying something? Why was he letting Vanna talk like this. She reached for him mentally but found him unconcerned, not seeing the questions as either a threat or an intrusion.

You're too far away, he complained, leaning forward to pick her up with both hands.

She gasped, taken by surprise not only at his action but at the strength required to do it.

He put her down beside the curve of his body, keeping his hands around her waist.

"Vanna," warned Garras again, "I won't have this interference."

"Solitude, Vanna," purred Kusac in reply, putting his chin on Carrie's shoulder. "She's too important to me for anything less."

Carrie was utterly bewildered. Why was he behaving like this? What she felt of him through the Link was strange and confused.

Are Carries tickly? came the thought as, with a flash of humor, his fingers began to tickle her ribs.

She squealed, knocking his mug over as she squirmed out of his grasp. She picked it up as she backed a short distance away from him.

"Kusac, what on earth is up with you?" she demanded, keeping a safe distance between them.

Garras leaned forward and took the mug from her, glancing over to where a burst of laughter came from the tech group.

"A mild euphoric?" he said, raising an eye ridge at both Kusac and Vanna. "I think this coffee has a stronger effect than that," he said in English.

"Oh, no," said Jo, trying hard not to laugh. "It doesn't make you drunk, does it?"

"I'm afraid coffee will have to be restricted to off duty periods only," he said. "Vanna, go and brew some strong c'shar for our lot, and take Kusac with you!" He handed her the mug.

"Yes, Captain," she said, getting unsteadily to her feet. She swayed gently on her way to the hatch, Kusac forgotten.

"I'm fine, sir," said Kusac, straightening up.

Garras shook his head. "On second thought, you'd probably be better out here since you're a Telepath. Did it have this effect on him before?" he asked Carrie.

"Not that I noticed, but then our coffee isn't as strong as Jo's."

There was another burst of laughter from the groundcar. "I'd better go and sort them out," Garras said, getting to his feet. "Excuse me, Captain Skinner, I'll be back in a minute."

Jo gave way to fits of laughter.

"I'm sorry, Carrie," she chuckled. "I know it's not really that funny. Maybe if they take their coffee very weak?"

"Maybe," said Carrie, standing up and turning to stare at the hatchway. The pod interior was always illuminated and in the galley she could see Vanna making up a jug of c'shar.

Mito and Guynor trooped past her and through the hatch followed by Garras. When he reached the galley, he spoke to Vanna briefly, then she went off to look in her medikit. When she returned, she added the contents of a sachet to the c'shar.

"Carrie," said Skinner, trying to draw her attention.

She turned—and found herself flying backward through the air to be caught by Kusac just before she hit the ground.

"Hello," he said, grinning down at her.

Stunned, she lay across his arms for a moment before struggling to sit up. He helped her.

With a theatrical sigh, she leaned back against him and shut her eyes for a second. "Ye Gods," she said. "What am I going to do with you? A six-foot drunken, playful feline!" She groaned.

"Don't you dare say that," she snapped at him as he opened his mouth.

He looked hurt and sent images of being misunderstood to her.

She pulled his ear. "Behave," she admonished him.

Vanna came out bearing a fresh mug, obviously making an effort to walk straight. She held it out to Kusac.

"Drink this," she said. "It'll work in about ten minutes."

"I'd rather not, thank you, Vanna," he said lazily.

"Orders," she said.

He took it. "But I feel good," he said. "I haven't felt so relaxed in days."

"So have some more tonight," she said before going back into the pod.

Carrie remained where she was for the moment, Kusac's mellow mood relaxing her, too. Then, abruptly, she sat up beside him so they were no longer touching. Once again, because they'd been in contact for too long, she'd felt their heightened sensitivity start to build.

Kusac looked and felt disappointed, but he accepted it and began to drink the c'shar. However, not to be totally beaten, his tail flipped onto her lap and lay there, the tip gently flicking.

Garras returned with his own mug of c'shar and sat down with them again. He grinned at Skinner.

"About that coffee of yours," he began.

Carrie began to laugh, getting a puzzled look from the other Terrans.

"You're a Trader through and through, Garras," she chuckled. "Captain Skinner, he's going to suggest that our coffee will sell as an exotic hot alcoholic beverage to the Sholans, a totally unique drink. Keiss will make a fortune out of that alone, never mind any other trade goods.

"May I suggest that you get Jo to draft a trade agreement with Captain Garras on behalf of his Clan as the major importers of coffee, citing you as the suppliers? If you don't, then Earth is likely to pick up this contract, and, quite honestly, why should they? Keiss needs the interplanetary trade."

Captain Skinner looked startled.

"She's right," said Kusac. "As a Telepath, I've done basic training with the Judiciary, so I can see the contract's phrased correctly, and my signature on it should carry some weight."

Carrie glanced sharply at Garras then at Kusac. This was the first time she'd picked up the Sholan Captain's curiosity over Kusac's background.

As Skinner thought the trade idea through, she began to check her inherited memories of Kusac. She soon gave up, finding only memories of a family that though loving had a strong sense of responsibility. She obviously didn't know what to look for and so was unlikely to find anything.

"Isn't it somewhat irregular to do that?" Skinner asked.

"Probably," said Kusac, "but I'll make sure the agreement will hold up in the Courts."

Skinner looked at Garras, who nodded.

"Telepaths work closely with the Judges as Truthsayers and Oathtakers because they can tell when a person is lying. Their signature gives the official seal of approval to any contracts."

"Jo?" Skinner asked.

"Go for it, Captain. It'll ensure that we have a voice of our own once official negotiations start among Earth, Keiss, and the Sholans."

"It seems like we have a deal, then," said Skinner, looking around the group of mixed Sholans and Terrans. He held his hand out to Garras, who hesitated briefly then took it.

Skinner's grasp was firm enough to trigger Garras' claws

and the Sholan quickly put his other hand on top of the Terran's to release himself.

"It takes very little pressure to extend our claws," he said, checking the other's hand to see no damage had been done.

Skinner looked at the five slight indentations. "We've a lot to learn about each other," he said. "What do you do when you seal a bargain?"

"I think this is my field," said Jo. "Carrie, you'll help me won't you? Language, behavior, and customs are so closely linked, after all."

"If I'm not needed for anything else," said Carrie, picking up the other woman's thought that once this episode was over, Carrie would find life very dull indeed if she had nothing challenging to occupy her.

Carrie leaned forward to help herself to more coffee. While appreciating the gesture, she hoped Jo was wrong. She was a Telepath like Kusac and she wanted to work with him as one. Among the Sholans her mental abilities were at least understood in part. Here on Keiss among the Terran community she was almost considered to have some kind of mental illness. Well, unless she was much mistaken, it was the Terrans who would have to change their attitude about people like her.

"You mentioned the *Erasmus*," she heard Skinner say.

"Yes," replied Garras. "Once the *Khalossa* is here, there is no need for your ship to turn back to Earth."

"What if all our attempts to reach your ship fail?"

"We're due to rendezvous with the *Khalossa* in ten days' time," said Garras. "If we fail to contact them within a day of that they will come looking for us. Obviously, they will be alert for trouble and the outcome will be the same, but it may take longer to subdue the Valtegans if our people are unprepared.

"We're working against time because the Valtegans were able to get hold of our ship's computer crystal. If they can manage to read it, they will have star charts for an immense area of our space as well as the location of the other planets our people were checking and the route for the *Khalossa*. We need to contact the Mothership as soon as possible and alert them to the potential danger we're all in." Garras stopped as Vanna came through the hatch.

"Everyone's fit for duty again, sir," she said.

Garras nodded. "Carry on."

He turned back to Skinner. "As for the *Erasmus,* once the trouble here is cleared up, we can send a couple of tugs to bring your ship directly here."

Skinner digested this in a stunned silence. "The next step will be to contact Earth and bring various leaders here for talks, I expect."

Garras nodded.

"Will we become part of your Allied Worlds?" asked Jo.

"It's not that simple," said Garras. "In the normal course of events, there would be negotiations taking several years, a trial membership period, then, if all went well and you had the capacity for interstellar flight—either developed by yourselves or gained through trade—you would be offered full membership.

"However, the Alliance is on a war footing at the moment, your sector of space—here at least—backs onto our colonized area and the Valtegans are known here. We need this sector adequately patrolled and we are stretched too thinly to protect another species."

Kusac retrieved his tail and moved closer.

"Given the fact that you are the only other Telepathic species we have met," he said, "for that reason alone our people will surely push for you achieving full membership as swiftly as possible. In fact, that may well prove to be the pivotal reason. With more Telepaths on our scout crafts, the better our chance at sensing the Valtegans' presence before their instruments pick us up."

"Then why didn't you sense them when you approached Keiss?" asked Jo.

"Like Captain Garras and Mito, I was off duty, asleep," said Kusac.

"Maran, our pilot, ignored my orders, deciding that there was no need to wake us as we approached Keiss," said Garras. "His overconfidence cost him his life."

"You keep mentioning Telepaths," said Skinner, lighting another cigarette. "What exactly do you mean? Reading minds and all that?"

As Kusac started to explain, Carrie's attention began to drift. Feeling restless, she got to her feet, moving out from the shelter of the trees. She looked out over the salt marshland to where the sun sat hidden behind a sea haze. Dusk was only a couple of hours away.

The sense of disquiet wouldn't leave her, in fact it was

growing stronger now that she was in the open. Mentally, she began to search, checking the people on their islet first. Nothing there, nor in the surrounding swamp. As her eyes were drawn upward, she sensed the Valtegans' presence. She could feel the high-pitched keening of the engines deep within her skull. Turning, she yelled to the others.

"Incoming cargo ship! Get under cover!"

They froze, looking at each other in bewilderment, Sholans and Terrans alike.

She ran back to where she'd been sitting.

"What're you waiting for?" she demanded. "There's a cargo ship about to land. Can't you hear it?"

She had felt Kusac's thought go out the instant she had called and she looked to him now for confirmation. As the noise grew to an unbearable pitch, she clapped her hands over her ears, trying to reduce it.

Kusac began to slowly shake his head in negation, then stopped.

"She's right," he said, scrambling to his feet and diving for the hatchway to kill the pod lights.

Garras shouted orders to the Sholans, who instantly left their work and began to double-check the camouflage.

"How long?" Garras demanded of her.

Carrie scanned the sky. There was still no visible sign of the craft.

"I don't know," she said. "You're the Captain, you gauge it from the noise."

Garras pulled her hand away from her ear. "There is no noise, Carrie."

"Don't be ridiculous," she said. "I can hear it clear . . . Oh, it's stopped."

Overhead, there was a faint boom followed by the almost inaudible whine of engines. The noise seemed to fill the air.

Blankets were thrown over the equipment and the Sholans headed back to the pod at a run.

"Captain Skinner," said Garras, turning back to the Terran, "I suggest you and your men return to your craft."

Even as he spoke, the Terrans had come to the same conclusion.

In the pod, Carrie headed for the external view screen.

"Can you change the angle of vision?" she asked Mito.

Mito looked at Garras, who nodded, coming closer.

"Use these controls," said Mito, showing her a set of keys on the keyboard.

Carrie looked at them in frustration. "I can't use them," she said. "They're made for you. If I had fingernails . . ." she spread her hands for Mito to see.

Mito looked at them, aghast. "I'll do it," she said. "What direction do you want?"

"Up for the moment. Track the cargo ship down."

They watched the dot on the screen get gradually larger, stubby wings extended to slow it down. It lined up to approach from the seaward side and as it lost altitude, it went beyond the range of their scanner.

"There's more," murmured Carrie, her eyes focused somewhere beyond the screen. "Turn the scanner 180°. There should be three groundcars on their way to the base now. Are we in contact with Captain Skinner?"

"Yes," said Garras. "He gave me one of their wrist communicators."

"Then warn him to keep under cover. The groundcars will pass within five hundred meters of here."

Suddenly, she felt light-headed and grabbed hold of the console for support. A hand reached out to support her and, gratefully, she let go and turned away from the screen.

"I'll leave it to you, Mito," she said tiredly, exhausted by the energy it had cost her to search for the danger.

"Well done," said Garras as she went past him with Kusac.

Kusac settled her on her bunk and went over to the galley where Vanna was already getting a protein drink ready.

"She's good," said Vanna, handing him the drink and a trail bar.

"Very," agreed Kusac. "I know of only one other person with that range. I wonder how rare her Talent is."

"I have a feeling Carrie's breadth of Talent is due to her upbringing rather than anything else," said Vanna.

Carrie opened her eyes and sat up when he returned, accepting the drink and bar from him.

He squatted down beside her. *Now will you believe you have a valid place among us?*

She could feel his pride in her work.

Yes, she sent, *but you have to admit that you're biased. I only need to exist to have a valid place as far as you're concerned.*

"Here are the groundcars," said Mito, "and there are three of them! How did you know they were coming?"

"I've always had a good sense of danger," Carrie said. "I didn't know what it was till I looked, and there they were."

"They've gone," said Mito with a sigh, "and they didn't notice anything."

"Is it safe now?" asked Garras.

"Yes," replied Kusac.

"Right. We've only got about an hour of daylight left, so let's get on with the job at hand and discuss the implications of that cargo ship and the groundcars later," said Garras, going to the hatch and opening it.

Carrie drained her mug and moved to get up.

"No, you stay here and rest," said Kusac. "If you prefer, I'll go outside with the others."

Carrie laughed. "You certainly know how to charm a woman," she said. "Those eyes of yours would melt stone! No, please stay," she said, serious for the moment. "What is it that you want to talk about?"

"Only that tomorrow I need to start showing you how we will work as a team. There's a way we can Link that will allow you to use me as a battery. You'll still be doing the work, but I'll help provide the energy so you need never overtire yourself as you did just now."

Outside, they heard Garras greet Captain Skinner.

"You were asking about Telepathy, Captain. You've just had a practical demonstration of one of its uses."

Chapter 10

As dusk approached, arrangements were made to exchange food and personnel between the two ships. Skinner, assuming correctly that the Sholans were already living on emergency rations and that they had similar tastes in food, had made sure the groundcar was well enough provisioned for both.

Since the techs were working on an interface using components from the Valtegan vehicle, he suggested that Mito and Guynor stay there overnight and continue their work with his crew. It was decided that Richard and Jo would remain in the pod to even up the numbers since space was at a premium for both parties. Garras elected to return to his own craft, bringing Skai with him.

Without the stress of Guynor's company, and with the addition of real food, their meal was more convivial than the night before.

"How are they getting on?" asked Kusac.

"The interface isn't a problem," Garras replied. "They've found a diagnostic port in the groundcar which looks like a standard item. We hope it will be duplicated on their base, but if not, they say that jump leads will work though they'll take longer."

"We're getting there," said Skai confidently, putting down his plate.

"What about Mito's software problem?" asked Carrie.

"Nothing new at the present," said Garras. "She's still working on it."

Kusac nodded.

"Skai," said Vanna, getting up and handing him her plate, "you're on dish washing duty tonight. You know where everything is."

She turned away, leaving him spluttering into his coffee as she collected her medikit.

"Kusac, I want to check your shoulder," she said in a tone that brooked no arguments. "You've put me off long enough."

Kusac got to his feet with a groan. "Very well," he said, moving over to her bunk.

Richard slid himself along the floor to where his sister sat.

"I forgot to give this to you earlier," he said, handing her a small drab green package. "It's one of our coveralls. I thought you'd be glad of a change of clothing by now."

Carrie gave him a swift hug. "You're wonderful!" she said.

"While we've got a few moments, tell me what's been happening," he continued quietly.

While they talked, Jo turned to Garras. "What's your planet like, Captain?" she asked.

Garras roused himself from his reverie. "Not dissimilar from here," he said. "Partially forested, with large areas of rolling farmlands and estates where our Families live."

"Don't you have cities and industry?"

"We have many large cities, but our heavy industry is now done in space."

"On Earth, our home planet, most people live and work in the cities," she said. "I'm afraid our heavy industry is still on the planet's surface."

Garras' eyes widened with surprise. "Your atmosphere must be heavily polluted, and what about the land? Your cities must sprawl over most of the surface."

"They do," she replied. "Unfortunately, it's proved difficult to persuade businessmen to move into space. We have our research stations there though, where they handle dangerous viruses and the like. At least it's a start."

"I hope you don't plan to do the same here," said Garras, wrinkling his nose in distaste at the thought.

"At first we'll have to. We need to get the raw materials to get into space before we can build there."

"Don't you mine the moons or asteroids on your home world?"

"Yes, but the costs are high, I'm told, and we certainly haven't got that kind of equipment on Keiss."

"Young lady, when our diplomats get started, make sure you tell them you need help to start mining those moons up there," said Garras, pointing to the roof of the pod. "Believe me, the number of craft you will need to defend this area of space, let alone your home world, will necessitate you mining off planet. To do it any other way would be to strip this beautiful world bare."

Jo was taken aback by the force of his words.

"My people would never allow this planet to be so wantonly used without offering to help you. Make sure you ask them."

"But it won't be without cost," she retorted. "How do you know we can pay, or will?"

"The cost will be little more than helping to keep this sector of space free from the Valtegans and, of course, Trade agreements between our planets," he said. "Do you think this too high a price?"

"No," she faltered. "Why should you be so altruistic?"

Garras sighed. "I've told you. Your space borders on ours, therefore it benefits us both. With you guarding our backs, we can concentrate on the areas of space where we have no near allies to help us."

"Garras!" called Vanna. "Come and see this."

Carrie scrambled over to see what was wrong with Kusac.

"What is it?" she demanded, trying to see past the Medic.

"Nothing, that's what it is," she said. "Only bare skin—slightly red I admit—but there should be a wound."

"Explain," said Garras, peering at Kusac's shoulder.

"We have a Healer in Carrie," Vanna said quietly, "and a damned good one at that."

"You're sure?"

"Look for yourself," she retorted. "There isn't a sign of that wound! What would you call it? I know I used Fastheal, but it doesn't work anywhere near this fast!"

Garras rubbed his jaw thoughtfully.

"That simplifies things," he said. He switched into Sholan briefly. "If she's a Healer, then any kind of disciplinary action against either of them would be minimal."

"Nor any question of anything but the minimum of tests once she proves she can Heal," said Vanna triumphantly, grinning at Kusac.

Garras touched Kusac's shoulder briefly.

"Leave everything to me," he said. "Your Leska and you are in no danger now. You realize you will both have to leave Keiss, don't you?"

Kusac nodded. "We know," he said briefly. "Are you finished with me now?" he asked Vanna, speaking in English again.

"Yes," she said. "There is nothing more for me to do with that wound now it's healed. I assume the fur will grow back normally."

"What's all the fuss about?" demanded Skai, coming over.

"Carrie healed Kusac's wound," said Vanna.

"Healed? How?"

"I'm not sure," replied the bemused Carrie as she gently fingered the new skin.

"Don't worry about it," said Kusac, reaching up to move her hand away. "When the need comes again, you'll be able to do it."

"What's so special about being a Healer?" she asked.

"We have very few Healers and our people believe they have been blessed by Vartra. They're treated with an almost religious awe."

Carrie frowned. "I don't want that," she said. "Do we have to tell anyone?"

"Yes, we do," said Vanna firmly. "It makes your relationship to Kusac more important and inviolable in the eyes of our authorities, and believe me, that does matter."

"Wherever we go, we're going to be different in one way or another, aren't we? Will we find anywhere to be just us?" Carrie asked, sitting down beside Kusac.

"I'm sure we will," he said quietly. He reached across to his locker and pulled her brush out.

Vanna drifted away on silent feet, leaving them alone.

Relax, he thought to her. *We are together. All is well for the moment.* He began to brush her hair slowly.

"That's something I need to do," said Garras, going over to his pack and digging out his brush. "My fur feels gritty and I'm shedding over everything. Vanna, could I possibly ask you to help? As a favor, if not by inclination," he added, seeing her hesitation.

Vanna grinned and her ears dipped in pleasure. "I accept the invitation," she murmured, taking the brush from him.

Richard and Jo watched the grooming session for a few minutes before Skai called their attention away.

"It's a ritual with them," he said. "As far as I can gather, it's only done by their partner or a close friend."

"There's some similarity, then, to the cat family on Earth," said Jo thoughtfully.

"Only superficially," Skai replied. "If you start thinking that way, you'll underestimate them. They are far more technically advanced than us, and somehow, I don't think another species gave them that technology. They worked it out themselves the hard way."

"What do you make of them?" Jo asked.

"So far, they've been aboveboard with everything, but they have to be at the moment, don't they?"

"Don't you trust them?" asked Richard.

"These ones, more or less, but keep an eye out for Guynor. He's a mean bastard and he doesn't like us."

"You surprise me," said Jo. "I found him pleasant this afternoon. Perhaps he only dislikes you."

"Lady, I've done nothing to him. It's Carrie he took a dislike to, not me," replied Skai, helping himself to more coffee.

"Why her? Because of Kusac?"

"You got it in one. They had a scrap over her and Kusac won. I know she's your sister," he said apologetically to Richard, "but he objected to him getting so friendly with her."

Richard glowered at him. "So did you, I expect."

"Me? It's had nothing to do with me since I saw which way the wind blew," he said sharply.

Richard sighed. "You've no idea what's happening, have you? You just assume what you consider the worst. What about you, Jo?"

"Uh?" she said, startled. "I've nothing on which to base an opinion."

"Kusac is a Telepath," explained Richard. "Whether you believe in it or not, that is his crew rating. So is Carrie. Jo, you knew Elise had a strong telepathic bond with Carrie, didn't you? Elise had an infinite pain tolerance because it was Carrie who felt her pain. That's why she gave nothing away to the Valtegans under torture. She couldn't feel anything, it was Carrie who suffered the torture—and us," he said bitterly, "we had to try to help her. That last time she not only suffered the pain, but also some of the injuries the Valtegans inflicted."

"Oh, my God," whispered Jo, her face ashen. "How awful for you all."

"There was nothing we or anyone could do for either of

them," said Richard harshly, reliving the scene again. He shook his head, trying to dispel the images.

"The shock of experiencing Elise's death nearly took Carrie, too, but then something happened. Or rather someone. Kusac. He'd been left by his people when their scouter crashed, and somehow, he picked up Carrie's mind at the crucial time when she was about to slip away from us. He saved her life, but at a cost to both of them." He fell silent.

"What was it?" asked Jo at length.

He looked up. "Apparently, among the Sholans there are rare pairings of Telepaths. Their minds bond irreversibly to each other in a way no one understands fully. That bond lasts for life."

"And that's what has happened to them?" asked Jo.

Richard nodded.

Skai shifted uncomfortably. "How do you know all this?"

"Carrie just told me, in a way I couldn't disbelieve," he responded wryly.

"I know what you mean," said Skai, a flash of humor briefly lighting his face.

"What is she going to do about it?"

"There's nothing she can do, Jo," he sighed. "Luckily, they seem to be the ones least concerned about it. I'm telling you two just to set the record straight," he said, staring pointedly at Skai. "There will be one hell of a row about them anyway, but I won't have anyone spreading malicious lies."

"Tell Skinner about it, then," Jo advised.

"No, that's for Captain Garras to do. He's already had a word with me about the matter. Just make sure that any idle chatter is put straight, that's all I ask."

The click of claws on the metal floor drew their attention and they turned round to see Vanna approaching.

"We're going to dim the lights now," she said. "Just pick a bunk and some bedding and make yourselves comfortable. I'm turning on the outside monitor so we'll know when it's light. If you need anything, Skai knows where it is."

"There aren't enough bunks to go round," said Skai, "and one still has electronics on it."

"Garras and I are bunking on the floor tonight," she replied, turning to switch on the monitor. "Good night."

Skai raised an eyebrow to the others. "Looks like Vanna got an invitation she couldn't refuse," he said.

"More likely didn't want to," countered Richard. "She strikes me as the sort of woman who knows her own mind." He got to his feet, yawning. "I'm turning in now. Good night."

"Tell me more about Carrie," said Jo, taking her cigarettes out and lighting one.

"What do you want to know?" asked Skai.

"Their Telepathy, what do they actually do when they work?"

"No idea. They go off on their own when they work together. As to what they achieve, Carrie found the cave where the Sholans were hiding and between them they found the exact location of this pod. They also telepathically taught the other Sholans English."

"Then there was the cargo ship and the three groundcars," added Jo thoughtfully. "Perhaps there's more than telepathy involved."

"You should know. Weren't you Elise's contact?"

"Not like that," Jo denied quickly. "She passed information to me at Geshader so that I could bring it out with me when I left."

Skai shrugged. "Then ask Vanna. She's their Medic and she's been collecting data from the three of us. From me, it's been some medical and cultural stuff. From the other two I've no idea, but I presume it's to do with their Link. Why are you asking all these questions anyway?"

"Skinner asked me to. You don't mind, do you?"

"Carry on. I don't feel like sleeping yet anyway."

"Tell me about Carrie and Kusac. What was the fight with Guynor actually about?"

Skai sighed. "Again, I don't really know since I don't speak their language, but it pretty definitely involved Kusac's friendliness with Carrie.

"Guynor went for her first, but Vanna stopped him, then he attacked Kusac."

"Is Guynor interested in Carrie?"

"Don't be daft," said Skai with a laugh. "He hates her and Kusac equally.

"After the fight, they went off for about half an hour. They were a lot friendlier when they came back," he added meaningfully. "She's just like her sister, a calculating bitch out for what she can get, no matter what it takes. In Carrie's case, from these Sholans."

Jo raised an eyebrow.

Skai had the grace to look away. "No, well I suppose not that friendly. Guynor did make a hell of a mess of his shoulder," he admitted reluctantly.

"I don't agree with your opinion of Carrie," said Jo, pulling a tin out of her pocket and stubbing her cigarette out in it. "I'd say she's beginning to find out who she is for the first time in her life. Elise's charisma tended to get her what she wanted irrespective of what it cost anyone else, including her twin.

"Carrie's not like that from what I've seen of her. I reckon she was actually the stronger of the two—she would have to be to put up with a sister like Elise."

Jo looked appraisingly at Skai. "You're pretty enough to look at, but Carrie wouldn't see that. As for Elise, yes, you'd appeal to her. She only ever used her eyes. Carrie doesn't, she looks deeper."

"What d'you mean by that?" he asked, bridling at the implied insult.

Jo shrugged. "Just that Carrie strikes me as someone who always thinks things through. Elise never did. She really thought she could do what she liked and get away with it. That's how they caught her."

"There's nothing to choose between them!" said Skai angrily. "They both seem incapable of having a relationship with their own people and have turned to Aliens instead. Look at Carrie earlier. She didn't stand with us, she was with the Sholans. She's always in their company!"

Jo shook her head. "It isn't that straight cut, Skai. Elise chose to go to Geshader to get the information we needed to fight the Valtegans. You hardly knew her. She really did hate them.

"Skinner wanted a couple of people on the inside and Elise volunteered. I got asked to go on an occasional basis because I'm a linguist and they hoped I could pick up their language.

"Carrie and Kusac—well, they have a Telepathic link and obviously Carrie trusts him. He's the only stable thing in her life at the moment. Look at all the changes she's gone through in the last two months, starting with Elise's capture and death. It's a wonder she's still alive and sane!

"It's also obvious they care a lot for each other, but what the nature of that caring is, I don't know."

"Well, I do. They're always in each other's company, they even sleep together. She won't let anyone else touch her!"

"Meaning you. Elise was the same. Perhaps it's part of being what they are, Telepaths. As for the Sholans, I've noticed how tactile a species they are among themselves, not just Carrie and Kusac." She turned to look at the bunks nearby. "And they're sleeping separately, Skai."

"Well, they would here, wouldn't they?"

"Vanna and Garras don't seem to have a problem," she replied, nodding to where the two Sholans were quietly enjoying each other's company. "In fact, they seem to have a much more relaxed attitude than we do."

"Have it your own way," he snapped, getting up. "You're as bad as they are. I'm going to bed."

Jo let him settle down before she took the remaining bunk. She had a lot to think about.

Time passed slowly the next day. After reporting in to Skinner, Jo resumed her task monitoring the radio output and Skai and Vanna were put to work fetching, carrying, and holding various items of equipment. Richard continued helping Anders.

Kusac pleaded the need for himself and Carrie to work on their "disguise" for the Valtegans and so they were able to retire to a quiet area some meters distant from the others. There he drilled her in the basics of shielding out unwanted contacts, lengthening her concentration span, and preventing energy leakages. Together they worked on building a more powerful illusion than she had previously done.

It was as grueling a task as that facing the rest of the crew, more so in fact because the results were less tangible.

The afternoon break came, and with it more delays. They had all gathered in the space between the two craft to drink coffee and c'shar. Vanna and Skai had provided a snack to see them through until dusk.

"Mito, what's the current status of the interface?" asked Garras.

"Guynor and Nelson are handling the final stages now. I've gone back to trying to work out a program to interrogate the Valtegan computer in the base," she said, munching one of the newly made trail bars.

"I'm still no further along. Without access to Valtegan software, the best program I can write would still take more than a couple of hours to run. Apart from the physical danger of discovery, our electronic presence is bound to be noticed by the Valtegan computer."

"Can our companions," Garras indicated where Skinner sat, "not suggest any way around your problem?"

"I've an idea that might work, if you're interested," Anders volunteered, glancing first at Garras, the accepted leader of the assorted crews, then at Skinner, his own superior officer.

"Go on," urged Skinner.

"It was something we used to do at college to keep one step ahead of our tutors," he explained. "All computers tend to leak radio frequency data, and we used to eavesdrop on our lecturer's reports as he was typing them out. We'd slow down the signal, then decode it."

He ground to a halt under Mito's intense stare. Her eyes had narrowed to vertical slits and she looked almost feral as her ears flicked repeatedly.

"Yes," she hissed. "It would work. We could monitor their transmissions at the Base, picking up the spare signals from the various computer terminals."

"We'd have to be close, though," said Guynor, leaning forward in his enthusiasm.

"How close?" demanded Garras.

"With our scanner, maybe as close as a hundred meters," he replied.

"How long would it take to get enough data?"

"A day, perhaps two," replied Mito, focusing her eyes again. "It depends on how often they communicate between the departments by computer. With the cargo ship in, it should be more frequently. We'd need to butcher the recording module on the pod, though."

Garras waved an arm expansively. "Do it. The pod is of no real long-term use to us. Take what you need. Who do you want to accompany you?"

"It will have to be one of your men," she replied, looking at Skinner. "We don't know our way to the Base, nor their patrol patterns."

"It had better be Anders, then," Skinner replied, "since it was his idea."

Anders nodded. "Any chance of a lift?" he asked. "I'd estimate we're over a day from the Base whether we head out straight from here or go back to our usual route."

A sigh went up from Terrans and Sholans alike. Skinner squinted up at the sky.

"Run a check on the radar, Peterson, see if there's any traffic about. Jo, see what you can pick up on the radio." He rose to his feet. "If it's quiet now, we'll take you out before dark."

Those named leapt their feet, speeding away to gather the equipment and information they needed. Vanna called Kusac over to help her put some provisions together for them.

As he followed her to the hatch, a hand grasped him roughly by the arm, swinging him round and slamming him against the outer hull.

Guynor stood in front of him, teeth bared.

"I haven't forgotten you, Kusac," he snarled. "I intend to see you brought to trial for your conduct. I may not be able to get you myself this time, but I'll see the law does! And if it doesn't, you'd better spend the rest of your life looking over your shoulder." With that, he thrust Kusac aside and strode through the hatch.

He'd barely had time to react when Carrie came flying over.

"What is it? What happened?" she demanded, helping him up.

"It's all right, it's nothing," he said, giving her hand a re-assuring squeeze.

"Guynor," she said. "His hate is driving him insane! Tell Garras."

"No, leave it, Carrie," he said as they went into the pod. "He can't harm me."

"Then I'll tell him," she said, stalking over to the Captain.

"Carrie!" he called after her but she ignored him.

When told, Garras shot a look first at Kusac, then at Guynor. He turned back to Carrie.

"I'll keep an eye on him and warn the others," he said.

For the next half hour everything was done at breakneck speed to get the equipment out of the pod, and the groundcar ready for takeoff.

"Get back as soon as you can," said Garras, watching Mito clamber safely into the vehicle. "Send your first report at midday, and your next at dusk, the same the next day. You're more likely to escape notice lying in low cover. Leave your jacket with me."

Mito unbuckled her belt and, taking the jacket off, handed them both to Garras.

"Don't take any risks: getting that information back to us is your main objective," he continued.

"Yes, Captain," she replied, then ducked into the interior of the groundcar.

"He fusses like a den mother," she said, belting into her seat beside Anders.

"If I've got my facts right, he's entitled to," he said, grinning back. "Unlike us, you have no military training at all and are purely civilians on a reconnaissance mission that went wrong."

Mito turned to look at the Terran communications officer. She was growing to like this man with the piercing blue eyes—a shade unknown on Shola—and the crop of curly fair hair atop a weather-beaten face. That face wrinkled again in good humor as he reacted to her scrutiny. She lowered her ears, looking away as her tail flicked with embarrassment.

"I don't mind," he said. "We must look as strange to you as you do to us."

"We are a military unit," she said, trying to cover her confusion with talk, "but not geared for combat on this mission."

"Ah, I got the wrong end of the stick. Sorry," he said. "Actually, I'm glad of this opportunity to work with you. There are many things I want to ask."

Mito's tail flicked again, this time with annoyance at herself. This was ridiculous! These men from another world were too compelling, too male. She found herself almost responding to him as if he were Sholan. It would not do.

Hard on that thought came another; was this the attraction that Kusac felt toward Carrie? She banished the notion, knowing it to be foolish. Leskas were bonded mentally first. Still, she had better be wary of herself.

"What do you want to know?" she asked, keeping her voice neutral.

"About your ships, your people, your planet. Anything that will help us understand each other better," he said. "We're going to be working closely with you Sholans for a long time to come and we need to explore those gray areas of cultural differences where misunderstandings could arise. Some of us have to pave the way for the diplomats. We aren't used to sitting down on friendly terms with an Alien culture."

She shrugged. It was obvious that he was more interested in facts than in her. "Ask away."

The next two days passed uneventfully for those in the swamp.

Jo, finding herself with some spare time, sought out Vanna, who was working on her medical notes on the computer.

"Mind if I join you?" she asked, sitting on the bench beside her.

"Not at all," said Vanna. "Give me a moment to finish this, then I'll be with you." She typed a few more sentences and closed her work down.

"How can I help?" the Sholan asked, turning away from the central column to face the other woman.

Jo hesitated. "You know I worked with Elise, Carrie's twin, don't you? Well, although I've only just met her, I feel I ought to look out for Carrie."

"I can understand that," said Vanna. "I feel the same about her myself."

Jo grinned. "That makes this a whole lot easier. Carrie's brother explained to me and Skai about her new Link, the one with Kusac, but I'd like you to tell me more about it if you can. After all, your people are the bona fide Telepaths."

"Tell me what you know," said Vanna slowly, "then I can fill in the sketchy areas."

"Only that the Link was established as Elise died and that by doing this Kusac saved Carrie's life. That the cost has been a more intense Link than he expected. A Leska Link?" She looked quizzically at Vanna, who nodded. "And that this Link is permanent."

"That's essentially it," agreed Vanna. "What do you want to know more about?"

Jo dug her cigarettes out of her pocket and offered one to Vanna, who refused.

"A strange habit," said the Sholan.

"It's the dried leaves of a plant," said Jo, lighting her cigarette. "It acts as a mixture of a relaxant and a stimulant. It isn't a healthy habit," she admitted. "I wouldn't bother acquiring it if I were you.

"Carrie and Elise were close, but how much of that was

because they were twins and how much was due to their Link no one knew. It seems to me, though, that Carrie is much closer to Kusac. Why? Wouldn't you expect there to be some inhibiting factor in the Link due to them being from different species?"

"You know how to get straight to the heart of the matter, don't you?" said Vanna dryly. "Telepathy isn't really my field. In fact, I've never really been that involved with any of them till this trip," she said. "I do know that they look at people on a different level than you and I would. They are less attracted to, or influenced by, the outer form because they can 'see' and 'know' them on a deeper level."

"What about the other species?"

"They are all very different from us. You Terrans are the nearest to us in physiology and outlook, and you have Telepaths. I know I have no difficulty in being at ease with your people, nor have most of our crew. Even Guynor seems to be able to be civil with anyone but Carrie!

"As for Carrie being closer to Kusac than she was to her sister, he is male, you know. Even loving sisters can see each other as rivals."

"It's more than that," said Jo. "Maybe you hit the nail on the head when you said he was male."

Vanna shifted uneasily. "I have to admit that even I've found myself looking speculatively at one or two of your male crew members. I've a feeling that a lot more of our people will find you attractive as a species, and the differences won't matter. In fact, that's what will attract them."

Jo digested this for a minute. "What do you find attractive about our men?" she asked abruptly.

"I'm not sure I can put it into words as I haven't really thought about it. I suppose they just seem more male than our men."

"And what do you think the men see in our women?"

Vanna shrugged. "Perhaps a fragility or a defenselessness that we lack because they have no fur or claws with which to protect and defend themselves. I have no idea. I haven't asked Garras or Guynor."

"Pheromones," said Jo succinctly. "If our people are attracted to each other, I'll bet that our pheromones are similar enough to trigger responses. Have you checked them?"

"No," said Vanna thoughtfully. "It never occurred to me. I only have the facilities for basic tests here, but once I'm back on board ship I can use the labs there. Garras wants me to become involved as a specialist on Terran physiology."

Jo nodded. "That makes sense. But pheromones still don't explain Carrie's relationship with Kusac."

"What relationship?" asked Vanna, turning innocent eyes to her.

"Come on, Vanna, don't be coy with me," said Jo sternly. "There's a look on Carrie's face every now and then that tells me the girl's besotted! And he's not much different, unless my reading of male Sholan behavior is totally wrong. He hardly ever leaves her side. Even you said they were in love with each other.

"My next question has to be, has he used his Telepathy to make her fall in love with him?"

"Don't be ridiculous!" said Vanna, ears flat, her tone one of absolute outrage. "How could you even think that? Even if Kusac were capable of wanting to do that, Carrie's mind is stronger than his! Mental manipulation is one of the greatest crimes a Telepath can commit. Kusac would never stoop so low." Vanna's tail was lashing from side to side in her anger and agitation.

"I had to ask," apologized Jo. "It's what her father, and others, will think. Personally, I couldn't believe him capable of that either."

"Guynor has already leveled that accusation against Kusac," the Sholan said, slightly mollified. "He will have to go before a Guild hearing when the Khalossa arrives. Have you any idea what the penalty would be for such a crime? They would destroy that area of his brain where his Talent is located. Do you think he—or any Telepath—would be foolish enough to risk that just to have a woman?"

Jo reached out to touch the other's arm. "Vanna, I'm sorry. I told you I didn't think him capable of it, but I'd rather it was me that asked than Skinner or her father, wouldn't you?"

Vanna's tail and ears began to still.

"What they feel for each other is theirs and real, not the product of their Link. Just leave them alone, don't interfere in something you don't understand. You could cause untold harm to both of them," she said, seriously concerned that the Terrans would try to force the pair apart.

"How, Vanna? If you don't tell me, how can I help them?"

"They don't need help, they need to be left alone to solve their own problems," said Vanna stubbornly.

"It's the Link," Jo said. "What does that Link entail? It's more than just Telepathic, isn't it?"

"It's not my business to tell you," said Vanna with finality, moving to get up.

"Wait, Vanna," insisted Jo, holding on to her. "Your people know, why shouldn't we? If we're to understand you, we need to trust you! Trust starts here, now, with each one of us."

Vanna hesitated, sitting back down. Common sense told her to keep quiet, but her instincts told her to trust this woman from the Terran world. Ignorance could cause more harm than the knowledge of what a Leska Link involved. She sighed.

"Very well. First, we don't know much about Leska Links because normally missions such as ours wouldn't carry Telepaths. Also, we've never met another Telepathic species before, so there has never been such a Link with a non-Sholan.

"Leska Links are rare to start with, even Kusac knows only a few bare facts. Back on the *Khalossa,* we have all the data and experts we need, which is absolutely no good to us at all at the present."

Vanna got to her feet and began to pace.

"The Link is permanent, and so complete that if one partner dies, so does the other. They feel each other's pain and joys, something like Carrie did with Elise only more positive."

"I didn't know that the Link was that strong. Still, it sounds pretty much like her Link with Elise so far," said Jo practically.

"Oh, there's more," said Vanna, stopping in front of her. "Telepaths don't like being touched unless they invite the contact because that carries messages, too."

"That explains why Carrie and Kusac touch each other so frequently."

"Yes, but with this Link goes a *compulsion* to touch, a sexual compulsion. They need each other, physically and mentally. They are life-mates, bound together by their Link."

"Ah," said Jo. "I think I see their problem."

Vanna sat down beside her again. "What I've described is a normal Sholan Leska Link. What Carrie and Kusac have is not necessarily the same. Now do you understand why we must leave them to sort it out for themselves?" she asked.

"Yes," Jo answered thoughtfully. "I'm also beginning to understand something more of Kusac's character."

Vanna raised a quizzical eye ridge.

"You obviously have less inhibitions about sex than we have, so Kusac must have had many opportunities to . . . er. . . become closer to Carrie, but he hasn't taken them. It shows a lot of forbearance on his part."

Vanna gave a low chuckle. "It has had the odd humorous moment," she said. "He's paying court to her, and, bless her, there are times when she makes it difficult for him!"

Jo grinned. "Now that tells me a lot more about them than almost anything else you've said!"

"You needn't worry about Kusac," said Vanna. "Unless I'm mistaken, he's well placed in the Telepath Clans. Carrie will be well looked after. She's good for him, and from what I keep hearing about Elise, he's repairing the years of damage Elise has done to her as well as being the first person to ever understand her Talent."

"How will Carrie fit into your society?" asked Jo. "It seems very male oriented."

Vanna looked surprised. "What makes you think we're male oriented?"

Jo gestured toward the hatch. "Most of your crew are men."

"I had this conversation with Carrie the other day," said Vanna, getting up and heading for the galley. "Let's have a drink while we talk."

Jo followed her over to the heater unit.

"Basically, we women mature earlier than the lads and while we get on with our training in the Guilds, they get conscripted into military service to keep them out of trouble.

"Pass me the mugs, please," she said, putting the jug of water into the heater and turning it on.

Jo took a couple of mugs from the shelf under the unit and passed them up to Vanna.

"What sort of trouble?" asked Jo, somewhat perplexed.

"The usual adolescent stuff, needing to prove their strength and virility," she said, spooning the dried powder into the mugs. "Carrie says your young men are the same but not for so long. You can forget our lads until they hit thirty, then something approaching common sense seems to appear."

"That's a long adolescence."

Vanna shrugged. The heater chimed and she took the jug out. "They don't waste their time here, they're learning Guild accredited trades. When they go back to Shola they do a year in their Guild and then they're fully qualified."

"Aren't they then disadvantaged in their careers because of their time in space?"

Vanna handed her a mug.

"Only for a year or two," she said, picking up her own mug and taking a drink. "Once you get to a certain level in your profession, all that matters is your talent and the dedication you're prepared to put into your work.

"Carrie and Kusac, working as a Leska pair, could have just about any profession they wish since Telepaths are employed in every level of our society. Here in space, at home in the Courts, Alien Relations, Telepaths' Guild, Medical . . . you name it.

"Now, I'm afraid if you want to find out any more about us you'd do better asking Kusac for a Telepathic cultural transfer," said Vanna. "It'll save me from covering the same ground so often! Also, I'm going to have to get on with my work."

"Thanks, Vanna," said Jo. "You've been a great help. I think I'll take your advice about the cultural transfer. Apart from saving us both a lot of time, it will be interesting to actually experience Telepathy at work."

As she began to move away, Vanna looked at her shrewdly.

"So what are you going to say to Captain Skinner?" she asked.

Jo laughed. "I can't hide anything from you people, can I? I'm going to tell him that I have no intention of interfering between Carrie and Kusac, and if he's got any sense, neither will he."

Work continued to go according to plan. The interface was finished, and they had even been able to manufacture a plug to fit the diagnostic port in the Valtegan computer. The Sholan computer had been stripped down to its bare essentials, leaving only the actual hardware necessary for what the Terrans had nicknamed the "burglar." All they needed now was the access codes.

Brief reports came in on schedule from Mito and Anders at the edge of the Base. Anders was always careful to head as far away from the Complex perimeter as he dared before using the wrist comm for fear of the Valtegans picking up his signal, but all remained quiet.

One piece of information they did pick up by direct observation was that the cargo ship was carrying not provisions, but unusually large numbers of Valtegan injured.

Traffic heading southeast across the margins of the swamp to Geshader and Tashkerra was heavy as the injured were ferried to the medical facilities, but as the Valtegans passed nowhere near them, this didn't concern them too much.

"I've never seen such heavy casualties," said Anders. "I reckon that this time they've come off worst."

"Give us the details when you get back," ordered Garras. "Close transmission now."

At dusk on the following day they called in and requested to be picked up. Once more the groundcar was hauled to the edge of the swamp.

Flying in the half light was no easy job. Eventually those waiting in the cramped interior of the pod heard the sound of the returning vehicle. Guynor turned the scanner to track it as it came in to land.

"Suit up," he ordered.

Skinner, Richard, Skai, Peterson, and Vanna hauled the emergency suits on, inflating them with the small auxiliary air supply before sealing the transparent head coverings.

"Davies," said Nelson into his comm unit, "Skinner and the others are coming across. The Sholans have emergency space suits which should protect them from the night life long enough to reach you. Stand by to open the hatch on my signal."

"Hold on a moment," came the reply. "I think I've figured out how to get this thing onto the land. If I can, it will cut the odds down even further in their favor."

"Standing by."

They watched as the noise from the groundcar rose to a roar before it lurched onto the islet, ploughing through the soil until it came to a stop a few meters from them.

"Good work, Davies," said Nelson wryly. "Apart from the

noise alerting everyone in the neighborhood, how do we cover those bloody great tracks that you've left before day-break?"

"You're never satisfied, are you?" came the reply. "When they're aboard, I'll borrow a suit myself to go out and throw some weeds over it till morning."

"See what the Captain says before you take any more risks," warned Nelson. "Get ready to open the hatch. We're sending them out . . . now!"

As the hatch in the pod opened, the suited figures ran awkwardly through in quick succession, Kusac standing guard at the door with a pistol ready to kill anything else that moved. As soon as the last person left, the hatch slid shut.

It took another quarter of an hour before Mito and Anders were safely aboard the pod.

As Mito pulled off her suit, she caught sight of Garras and Kusac wrinkling their noses.

"Don't," she snapped. "It's going to take weeks to get the stink of the swamp out of my fur! If you think it's bad for you, consider what it's like for me."

"Carrie and I will get damp cloths and wipe you down," said Kusac soothingly, taking the discarded suit from her unresisting hands. "What about you, Anders?"

"I could do with a wash and a change of clothes," he admitted, handing his suit to Kusac.

"Nelson, I don't suppose you have anything I could borrow?" he asked, looking across at the other man.

"Not much. I have a sweater here that you're welcome to, but no pants. What on Earth have you two been doing anyway? You're covered in filth."

"Valtegan patrol," said Mito briefly, trying unsuccessfully to brush the caked mud from the back of her shoulders.

"We had to hide in the swamp," explained Anders. "Luckily, it was during the day."

"The equipment?" asked Garras, eyeing the streaked satchels.

"No problem," he reassured, bending down to take the covers off the recorder. "Nelson, I'll take you up on that offer of the sweater, if I may."

Carrie took the brush from Mito. "Can I help?" she asked.

Mito's eyes widened in delight. "Thank you," she said. "If only this pod had a shower of some kind! I hate being dirty."

Carrie made sympathetic noises as she brushed the Sholan's fur vigorously, the two of them almost disappearing in a choking cloud of fine dust.

"I think that will do," coughed Mito, rubbing her streaming eyes with her hands.

"Turn the extractor on," ordered Garras, also beginning to cough.

Carrie stood back and let Kusac wipe Mito down.

"There," he said at length, "that's gotten rid of the worst of it."

"Thank you both," she said, raising her arms and beginning to sniff along them.

"I still smell," she complained, going back over to her personal pack and rummaging in it. With a small yelp of pleasure, she pulled out a vial of liquid and, unscrewing the top, began to sprinkle the perfume liberally over herself.

"I won't be able to smell anything now," she said happily.

Kusac sneezed violently, followed by Garras.

"Neither will anyone else," remarked Kusac dryly, putting the cloths away to be washed in the morning. "You're too concerned about your appearance, Mito. There's no need for it here, we're all in need of a shower and can probably only smell ourselves."

"In that case," she said, unstoppering the bottle and moving toward him.

Kusac's hand shot out and grasped hers firmly, making sure the bottle stayed upright. In Sholan, he said bitingly, "I'm no longer a boy to be trifled with, Mito. You had your fun on the Ship. Now it's over. Save it for Guynor, if that's what takes his fancy."

"Hey, what's with you two?" asked Anders, looking up from the work bunk where he had set the recorder.

"Nothing," said Kusac mildly, releasing Mito's arm.

She rubbed her wrist resentfully before closing the vial and putting it away.

"Just a practical joke," she said. "I don't suppose you left any food for us, did you? We could do with a decent meal before we start decoding our data."

"Plenty left," said Jo, getting a couple of plates and spooning some still warm stew onto them.

While they ate, Garras called Kusac over to him.

"What's your problem with Mito?" he asked.

Kusac squatted down on his haunches beside him.

"Nothing, Captain. Just a practical joke as she said."

"Weren't you two involved with each other before we crashed?"

Kusac looked distinctly uncomfortable, aware that Carrie was able to pick up the conversation.

"Not as such. She decided it would be fun to add an immature Telepath to her list of conquests, and being of a higher Grade, backed me into a series of situations I was unable to get out of at the time."

Garras nodded. "I noticed that she'd been trying to turn on the charm with you since your return."

Kusac grunted. "Well, she knows better now," he said.

"You've come a long way from the unsure lad who joined our team at Chagda Station," said Garras with approval.

"I want you and Carrie to take some of Vanna's sleeping tablets tonight. The strain of trying to sleep in such close confines without shielding is beginning to show on both your faces.

"Yes, I'm starting to master the Terran's facial expressions," he said in answer to Kusac's surprised glance, "and it's all too clear you are both suffering. We need you well rested for your part in this operation.

"I expect it's going to be another late night, so I suggest you get a pile of bedding and bunk down to one side of the hatch near the mainframe computer, then we can dim the lighting at that end for those of us who need to rest." He dismissed him with a wave of his hand.

Kusac went back to Carrie and while she searched for the tablets in Vanna's medikit, he collected their bedding and spread it on the floor where Garras had indicated.

Carrie made up a couple of mugs of the Sholan protein drink and joined Kusac on the blankets.

He took the drink from her. "You're jealous," he said quietly in Sholan, unable to keep the pleased tone out of his voice.

"No, I'm not," she said, trying hard to mentally squash it.

"Yes, you are," he said, letting her feel his pleasure. "I told you before, it's over and it meant nothing."

"Huh," she said, putting down her mug to untie her boots. "How do I know I can believe you? I'm probably no more important than she was."

"You're teasing me," he said delightedly. "No one's done that before."

He leaned forward and with his free arm swept her toward him. She found herself held close against his chest while he gently attacked her neck and ears, then she was sitting, breathless, on the floor again.

"Where are the tablets?" he asked, holding out his hand. "With those inside us we can sleep together tonight without any problems."

"Are you sure?" she asked, putting one of them into his palm.

"Positive. I want us to be close tonight," he said, his eyes never leaving her as he swallowed his pill with a mouthful of the drink.

Nelson watched curiously as Kusac unfastened his belt and took off his sleeveless jacket.

Carrie likewise took her tablet, then finished unlacing her boots. As she lay down, Kusac got up and switched off the light above them before joining her. When she had settled herself comfortably with her head in the curve of his shoulder, he pulled the blanket over them.

"Getting a mite cosy, aren't they?" Nelson remarked to Jo, who was sitting beside him on the bench seat.

"So what? They're both adults," said Jo.

Garras heard the comment as he passed them and stopped to answer Nelson.

"They're the ones who have to risk their lives by going into the base and transmitting our signal. I need them rested if they are to have any chance of success.

"If you've nothing better to do, follow their example and get some sleep," he ordered.

"Yes, Captain," Nelson replied.

"I expect they'll need you to translate for them, Jo," said Garras, moving away to join Mito and Anders.

"It's nice to know some things in the Universe are constant in this time of change," Nelson said wryly to Jo as he got to his feet.

"Pardon?"

"Superior officers," he explained. "Captain Garras is no different from Skinner."

"Ah," she said, enlightenment dawning as she, too, ambled off to do Garras' bidding.

Having finished their meal, Mito and Anders were now plugging the recorder into the VDU in the central column.

Mito settled herself onto the bench seat and switched the module on.

"Now, let's see what we've got," she said, loading the magnetic cube. The screen lit up with a series of cursive characters that Anders immediately recognized as Valtegan script.

"Yeah!" he whooped, "we got it!"

As they began to congratulate each other, Garras' quiet voice interrupted them.

"Well done. Now let's see if we can understand it."

Immediately sobered, Mito called for Jo.

"Coming," she replied, scrabbling among her belongings. "I'm just trying to find my notebook."

She joined Mito on the bench seat and opened her pad. "I'll have to check the word groupings against those in here. I've managed to compile a very small dictionary."

Mito leaned forward and unlatched the pull-out desktop for her. "That should make life a little easier," she said.

Jo scrutinized the screen, checking in her notepad every so often. She tore out a blank page and began scribbling.

"Scroll forward," she said.

After about half an hour, she stopped and ran her hands through her short dark hair, scrubbing at her eyes.

"Could I have a coffee or something to keep me awake?" she asked tiredly. "This is very heavy going."

Anders heaved himself to his feet and went round to the heater unit.

"Protein drinks all round," said Garras from his perch behind Jo. "What have you got so far?"

"I can only understand about one word in ten, but it looks like part of a draft for a new weekly roster for Base personnel," she said. "The lists appear to be names, one or two of which I can recognize.

"The next section seems to be an inventory of stores and provisions, but whether it's what has arrived on the vessel, or what they need, I can't tell at present."

"I reckon they'll only have a minimum delivery on that vessel," said Anders. "Most of the space would have been allocated to the injured."

Mito scrolled the page back until she came to a gap between the two separates areas of information.

"Make a note of these symbols," she said, tapping the

screen. "They look like they might be access codes for a central supply area."

Jo scribbled them down as Anders came back with a hot drink for her and Mito. Gratefully, the two women accepted the mugs, Jo leaning forward to recover her text position on the screen. Using her pencil, idly she scrolled forward several lines as she sipped her drink.

"Wait a minute!" said Mito, grabbing her hand away from the keys. "Look, isn't that the same pattern as before?"

Jo consulted her notes. "Yes," she said, looking up. "What do you think it is?"

"Could it be a code to log the reports in the central computer?" Mito hazarded.

"Looks like it," agreed Anders. "Ring it in your notes and we'll see if it keeps cropping up."

Jo did this, gulping down the remains of her drink as Mito ran the text forward again.

"Now this looks like a command," said Anders, pointing to a couple of isolated lines of script. "What could that be for? Can you identify any words?"

"Yes," said Jo. "That word says 'next,' I don't know that or that, but that one is 'due,' and the last is a time: 21:00 hours in our time."

"That could be the takeoff time for the ship, or the next transmission," said Garras thoughtfully. "Apart from the exchange of personnel, they must make regular status reports to somewhere off planet, if only for fresh supplies. That cargo ship came from somewhere."

"I don't know what you've been told about Geshader and Tashkerra," began Jo, turning away from the screen, "but they're virtually indoor cities. There are several different dormitories, bars, restaurants, gambling clubs, shops, even a holographic equivalent of entertainment videos, and, of course, the medical facility. All these areas are supplied mainly from off planet, via the Base."

"So they would need a regular system of ordering," said Anders. "How do you know all this? If you don't mind me asking, where did you fit in?"

"Exotic entertainment for the officer classes," Jo replied, her face taking on a hard look. "A well-favored Terran woman could get a limited amount of freedom around the city—freedom to pick up the sort of information both Elise and I got."

"It needed to be done," murmured Garras sympathetically, touching her gently on the shoulder.

Jo smiled gratefully at him, her face relaxing once more. She turned back to the screen.

"Tag that as being a possible takeoff or transmission time," said Mito, scrolling forward again. "Whatever it is, it should show up again on the screen later. I'd find a seat, Captain. It's going to be a very long night. We've got one hell of a lot of data to check before we can be sure of anything."

Chapter 11

The next morning, Kusac, Carrie, and Nelson woke to find the rest of the crew slumped deeply asleep in various uncomfortable positions. Jo had managed to stumble to her bed and lay there fully clothed, clutching her notebook. Mito had fallen asleep over her console, Garras was slumped against the wall on one of the bunks, and Anders had curled himself up in a pile of rugs on the floor.

"Looks as if they did work most of the night," observed Carrie, throwing her blanket over the sleeping woman.

Nelson wrapped his as best he could around Mito then went to give Kusac a hand easing Garras into a more comfortable position. He hardly stirred as they covered him up.

"How about we visit the groundcar for breakfast and leave them to sleep?" suggested Nelson, thumbing the hatch open.

"Sounds fine," said Carrie as she and Kusac followed him.

They caught the aroma of bacon and eggs cooking as they crossed over to the groundcar. Davies was already outside trying to landscape the skid marks leading from the vehicle to the water's edge.

Nelson stepped in through the open hatch.

"Good morning. Is there enough for three more hungry people?"

"Certainly," said Peterson, wielding a spatula. "Plenty for all," he said expansively. He peered past the three of them. "Where are the others?"

"They're still asleep," replied Kusac from the opening. "They worked through the night on the recordings so we're leaving them to wake up in their own time."

"Sensible," said Skinner. "There's no point in rushing things now, and tired people make mistakes."

Guynor rose to his feet, tail flicking spasmodically, ears

plastered flat and to the side. Pushing past them, he stalked outside.

Kusac exchanged a glance with Carrie, then they climbed into the interior. He looked round curiously as they settled themselves next to Richard and Captain Skinner. Basically, it was a standard planetary surface, people-moving vehicle. The control panels were in front of and at the side of the pilot's seat. In fact, that seat was the only one in the craft. Judging from the floor, the rest had been ripped out to provide extra space for the Terrans.

Peterson sat to one side of the hatch, his stove set on top of one of the several crates that lay in the vehicle. Some were being used as seats by those eating breakfast.

"Any idea if they got the access codes?" inquired Skinner, taking the plate that Peterson held out to him.

"The Captain ordered me to turn in," said Nelson apologetically, "but before I did, we knew that their recording had worked and that Jo was able to make some sense out of what they had."

Skinner sighed. "I suppose we can wait," he said, skewering a piece of bacon with his fork.

It was approaching midday before the sleepers stirred.

"Kusac! Guynor!" they heard Garras roar as he emerged from the pod. "Why the hell didn't you wake us sooner? We've work to do!"

Guynor and Kusac came at a run, skidding to a halt in front of their Captain. They were closely followed by Vanna.

"Guynor, fix some breakfast for us. Kusac, you and the girl finish working on your illusions, or whatever you call them. I want to move into the Base tonight."

Kusac nodded then headed off back to the other side of the islet where he and Carrie were working out of sight of the others.

"Where's Captain Skinner?" Garras asked Vanna. "We need to discuss backup tactics in case we have to get that pair out of there in a hurry."

Everyone apart from Mito and Anders was now in the clearing between the two craft.

"You've got what you needed?" asked Skinner, jumping down from the groundcar hatch and striding across to him.

Garras sat down on one of the pieces of log that served as a seat.

"We've got the codes and Mito has nearly finished the 'burglar' program," he said. "There was even a bonus. They picked up part of the new staff roster, including the night shifts. We've been able to plan an optimum time to go in."

"What about the access codes for the transmitter?" asked Skinner.

"That we do have. The night before last, they made a routine transmission requesting medical supplies. We have that code."

"Then we have everything we need."

Garras' ears twitched as he frowned.

"Not everything. We are having to extrapolate what we hope will be a valid command for the transmitter to start its Search pattern. Mito is working on it at the moment."

"We'll just have to trust it works," said Skinner. He hesitated before continuing.

"I'm afraid I'll have to insist Carrie doesn't go. This mission is far too dangerous to involve her," he said with finality.

Garras' ears went flat and his tail began to twitch like an independent entity. Even to Skinner it was obvious he was displeased.

"There are only two people who can go," he said. "To get into the base without arousing suspicion and send out that signal, we need the combined abilities of two Telepaths. It has to be Carrie, there is no one else."

"Impossible," stated Skinner flatly.

"We've been over this before. I've told you the nature of their Link. This task requires the extra power that they can only generate together. We need to send in two people. One of them has to look like a Valtegan guard, the other has to be a Terran female."

"Carrie's totally untrained in even the most basic self defense techniques. Jo would be better for this, and she has experience in dealing with the Valtegans. Surely Carrie could ... assist ... Kusac with his deception from outside the perimeter, in safety."

"You don't understand, my friend," said Garras. "Both of them are needed to deal with any Valtegans who get too curious. We can't go around shooting guards or knocking them out. When they failed to make routine reports or arrive at their destinations, it would only call attention to our presence. We need two hours, maybe three, of undisturbed time to make that transmission. There is no other way."

"Carrie is one of my people. I won't have her involved in this enterprise. The odds are too high against them getting out alive even if they manage to make that transmission," said Skinner angrily.

"She is a civilian and as such is not under your jurisdiction," said Garras less patiently, getting to his feet. "When the *Khalossa* arrives, Carrie will have to leave Keiss with us. She will be needed for questioning regarding Kusac's Telepathic Link with her. There is also a matter of a formal hearing and our authorities will not be denied her presence. The matter of her affiliations will soon be out of our hands and in that of the diplomats.

"You wouldn't jeopardize not only our plan to rid Keiss of the Valtegans, but future treaties—most advantageous to your people, believe me—for the sake of one girl? This is war, Skinner. You, as a military man, must be as aware as I am of the hard fact that one life is expendable when it is in the balance against so many."

"I know, dammit!" said Skinner angrily. "I also have to think of her father. When Earth gets here I'll be drafted back into the military, leaving him, Peter Hamilton, as the colony head on Keiss. Just having lost one daughter a matter of two months ago, what will it do to him to lose the other? He's going to have one hell of a lot to say about us risking his daughter on this mission. We can't afford to let her go."

"We can't afford not to," said Carrie quietly from behind the knot of conflict. "Unless I go, the message can't be sent. If it isn't sent, then we place not only the thousand Sholans on the *Khalossa* at risk, but also the Sholan worlds, Earth, and the rest of the Alliance. I think that this is too high a price for the safety of one person, don't you?

"Captain Garras, I'm going. If I'm a civilian, I can volunteer, can't I?"

With a sidelong look at Skinner, Garras nodded.

"Good. Then it's settled," she said. "Now will you two stop your bloody arguing and get down to discussing details?" With that, she stalked off back among the trees.

Garras and Skinner turned to Kusac, who spread his hands expressively.

"Don't blame me," he said, backing off hurriedly. "We couldn't help but overhear you."

A stunned silence remained after Kusac left.

Vanna began to laugh. "I told you that one was strong-minded," she said to no one in particular. "Manipulate a mind like that, Guynor? I'd like to see anyone try! Anyway, it's academic. In risking Kusac, we risk Carrie, too, whether or not she goes."

As she'd intended, it eased the tension and Garras resumed his seat.

Skinner looked across at him, a rueful expression on his face.

"Carrie's her father's daughter," he said. "I've had some rows with Peter in my time and doubtless will again," he sighed. "Well, it looks like she's taken the decision out of my hands, Garras. Carry on. This seems to be your show. You're the ones with all the answers."

"Not all of them, my friend," said Garras. "We're working together."

Guynor had been hovering at his elbow for several minutes. Finally, the smell of food drew his attention. He held out his hand and was given a plate of warmed up stew and a mug of c'shar.

Garras eyed the stew then his First Officer quizzically.

"It was all I could think of that was quick," said Guynor, retreating hurriedly back to the pod.

"We'll move out at the twenty-third hour, zero two hours your time," he said to Skinner between mouthfuls of food.

"We'll need all personnel aboard the groundcar so any nonessential items will be left in the pod. We can always retrieve them at a later date." He looked over at Skinner again.

"Can you go over our munitions with Guynor and work out a distribution of weapons? We have some explosives as well as longer range energy rifles. He'll fill you in on how they work. I want Carrie and Kusac both carrying our hand guns."

As he turned round to place the empty plate on the ground he saw Carrie beside the pod.

An exclamation from Mito drew Skinner's attention. Following her gaze, he noticed Carrie, too.

Mito reached out to touch the dress she was wearing.

"Where did you get that?" she asked. "It's lovely." She touched the robe only to have her hand pass right through it and come up against something solid. With a small yowl of fright, she leapt backward.

"It's all right, Mito," Carrie reassured her. "It's only our illusion. Do you think we'll get past the guards safely?"

Garras sat up slowly.

"Gods," breathed Vanna, walking round behind her, "I wouldn't have believed it possible!"

"We?" asked Garras.

Everyone experienced a slight blurring of their vision and then Carrie appeared clad in her usual shirt and trousers with Kusac standing slightly to one side behind her.

"We," she said.

"I thought it wiser not to suddenly appear as a Valtegan in the middle of our camp," said Kusac, grinning.

"A sensible precaution," said Garras, picking up his mug. "You two never cease to amaze me. If you can maintain that illusion for any length of time you should have no problem with the guards."

"We can maintain it long enough to get into the Base complex," said Kusac. "After that . . ." He shrugged. "We'll have to use stealth. At least we can tell Telepathically when anyone is coming."

"You'll be armed," said Garras.

As Kusac opened his mouth to object, Garras stilled him with a gesture.

"No arguments. You're taking firearms and you'll use them if you have to. That's an order. I want you out of there alive. I'll run both of you through a crash course in how to use the energy pistols when I'm finished here.

"Anders." He called the Terran over. "You'll be piloting the groundcar. This is what we plan to do."

Anders joined the semicircle round Garras, crouching down beside Carrie.

Garras leaned forward and began to draw in the dirt with a claw tip.

"We'll exit the vehicle near the edge of the swamp, under cover of the trees, leaving Kusac and Carrie to be flown to the Base. You'll then land as close to the gates as possible, leaving the hatch open and facing away from the guards. That way the rest of us have instant access if we need it.

"You two," he pointed at Carrie and Kusac, "will then proceed into the main building. The rest is up to you."

Skinner stirred, feeling he ought to make a contribution.

"I can see a couple of problems. Davies won't be able to watch for Carrie and Kusac returning, and keep an eye out for any Valtegans coming up on the opposite side of the craft. I can't see that there is any appreciable advantage to be gained by keeping the hatch open. We'll be in constant communication with the craft. We can warn them in the event of any threat.

"I also suggest that both Carrie and Kusac wear a wrist comm so they can contact us if they need help."

Garras nodded. "Fair enough. If the alarm is sounded, then you and Carrie," he pointed to Kusac, "make for the main gates and the groundcar. We'll come in after you.

"What kind of weapons have you got?" he asked Skinner, sitting up again.

"We have eleven projectile submachine pistols of our own and three captured Valtegan energy guns," he replied. "We've got plenty of ammunition for the pistols, but I don't know how much of a charge the energy guns have. No one could figure out what made them work in the first place."

"Show them to Guynor. He may be able to adapt something from our system. We each have a side arm, and Guynor mentioned rifles in the pod as well as explosives. If you've anyone good with explosives, perhaps they can work out some kind of small projectile bombs.

"Kusac, are you now planning to let Carrie appear to be entering alone?"

"No, that was just for our little demonstration," he said.

Garras nodded. "Right, let's get to it," he said, rising to his feet. "We've a lot to do between now and nightfall."

Once dusk fell, the time spent waiting until they could leave seemed like an eternity.

Carrie changed into the green one-piece her brother had brought, filling the pockets with extra charge packs for her gun, a torch, trail bars, a couple of drink sachets, and a hank of fine nylon rope from Davies.

"Where d'you get that?" she'd asked him.

"Skai and I can get most things given enough time," he'd replied with a wink.

Pockets organized to her satisfaction, she donned the hooded robe and fastened it with her belt, making sure the knife was easily reachable. At the other side, she hung the energy pistol and its holster.

"Have you briefed them fully on what to do, Mito?" asked Garras for the umpteenth time.

"Yes, Captain," she sighed.

"Go over it once more," he said.

"No," she said. "If I do it again, they are likely to forget due to saturation. They know what they're doing. Kusac does have some computer skills."

"What are you going to do if the computer doesn't accept the Search code?" asked Guynor suddenly.

Kusac looked up at him. "Read it from an operator and find a more suitable terminal if necessary," he replied.

"What happens if you're disturbed?" demanded Skinner.

"We won't be," replied Carrie. "One of us will always be on guard. We will sense if a Valtegan comes near us. You know all this," she said in exasperation.

"You might be taken on the way out," argued Skinner.

Carrie glanced at Kusac briefly. "We won't be taken alive," she replied harshly. "Now leave it, all of you."

"I've got a question for you," said Kusac suddenly, looking at Garras. "Where are we going when we leave here? If we're discovered, there could be a planet-wide search for us."

"We're heading for our base in the caves," said Garras. "It's more easily defended if they track us there. We should be able to hold out until help comes."

"How long do you anticipate that will be?" asked Nelson.

"At the most a week. When our ship arrives, it'll come in fighting."

"I hate to interrupt you, folks, but it's time to leave," said Davies.

There was a general shuffling of bodies as they prepared for takeoff.

Carrie felt herself going cold with fear. Her stomach began to churn and she felt light-headed. She groped for Kusac's hand, finding reassurance in its warmth.

Don't be afraid, Leska. Fear will weaken your will and concentration. Breathe deeply and remember all we have practiced. We will succeed, came his thoughts.

She took a shaky breath and forced herself to relax.

"Did you remember to get an imprint of what Valtegan Jo knows?" asked Richard urgently, leaning forward to touch his sister on the shoulder.

Carrie nodded. "Everything has been gone over dozens of times," she said tiredly. "Let me rest, please. I know you're concerned, but all you're doing is getting me worried."

The rest of the trip was in virtual silence. Flying so heavily laden in the dark without lights taxed Davies' ability to the full and there were several near misses as he skimmed low over the forest to touch down briefly near the edge of the swamp.

The radio burst into life, demanding their clearance code, destination, and the reason for their arrival.

Jo answered as best she could, claiming, "A Terran female from Geshader."

Carrie felt her blood run cold. This was suddenly too like what Elise had been doing. Pray God, they didn't meet the same fate.

"We'll be waiting opposite the gates, amid the trees at the edge of the perimeter," said Skinner, the last to leave.

"Davies, remember to lock the hatch and power down as if no one is aboard," he hissed, sticking his head back inside. "Good luck!"

As the craft hovered before landing, the guards at the gate trained a spotlight on them and moved forward to await their arrival.

Davies shut the engine down.

"Up and out you two before they decide to come over to us. Take care."

Carrie and Kusac scrambled to their feet, grabbed their packs containing the computer and the interface, and jumped out. The hatch slid shut behind them. It was a lonely sound.

Breathe deeply, Leska, came Kusac's thought. *Good. Now, create your illusion and we will go before they come to investigate.*

Quickly but carefully, Carrie drew the illusory robe around her, until she was almost aware of it herself. She looked at Kusac, nearly drawing back in shock from the Valtegan beside her.

She made a small noise of fright which she hastily stifled.

You look equally convincing, came the humorous rejoinder.

They moved out of the cover of the groundcar and into the spotlight's glare, blinking as they walked toward the guards. The guns trained on them lowered and one of the guards spoke briefly to Kusac before turning to his companion and making what sounded like a ribald comment.

Kusac replied equally briefly and they were waved on.

When we get inside, read them, he ordered.

Wanting to run every inch of the way, Carrie clutched her portion of the computer interface and schooled herself to follow Kusac at a sedate pace. They were heading for a large single-storied building with transparent doors where another two guards stood waiting.

Carrie felt a slight pull on her mind and quickly reinforced her illusion. She saw Kusac's image briefly waver then re-form. He approached the guards, motioning her to stop.

Again they were challenged, but this time Kusac replied fluently and some bantering followed. Hardly daring to breathe, she waited impatiently until Kusac ordered her to follow. One of the guards lowered his rifle and held the doors open for them.

Once inside the hallway, Kusac led the way off to a passage on the right. As soon as they were out of sight, he slumped against the wall, letting the computer rest on the floor.

"Are you all right?" whispered Carrie, grasping hold of his arm.

"I'm fine," he said, letting his disguise fade. "I'm just getting my nerve back."

He breathed deeply, shuddered, and stood up again.

"I had to 'read' the soldiers at the door or we wouldn't have got past them. Sorry, but I had to pull on you to do it. I think we can drop the illusions now."

"I wondered how you'd suddenly become so fluent," she murmured, relaxing briefly. "Let me access your knowledge then I can understand them, too. I didn't dare do it myself in case it affected my illusion."

"Haven't got time. They said they had no orders about a female being requested by one of the officers, but that is wasn't unusual. These are the living quarters here. I want to get out of the area before someone sees you and decides he really does want your company. Come on."

He picked up the computer and moved away from the wall, heading down the corridor.

"Where are we going?"

"To their refectory area. It's unlikely anyone will be there at this time of night."

As they hurried through the corridors, Carrie tried to sense any presences around them but she only picked up the sleeping rhythms of the Valtegans on the other sides of the doors they passed.

The lighting was dimmer now, with an orange-red tint, and Carrie began to sweat in the increased heat. She found it impossible to suppress her feelings of déja vu.

Kusac stopped to peer round a corner, then beckoned to her. Ahead of them was a darkened refectory, the serving area obviously closed for the night.

"Where now?" questioned Carrie.

"The office. They have to have one."

They picked their way between the tables until they came to the door leading to the kitchens. Slowly, Kusac opened it and they stepped inside. There was a heavy metallic odor in the air. He sniffed, recognizing it as blood. Carrie stirred restlessly at his side. She, too, had picked up the smell.

She pulled the flashlight from her pocket and turned it on. By the glare of the beam, they could see a desk in front of a wall mounted computer screen.

"Check the rest of the room," hissed Kusac. "They must have a diagnostic point in here."

Carrie quickly swept the beam around the room before flicking it off. Briefly, it had illuminated double doors leading to the kitchen area.

"Nothing," she whispered. "They probably don't have diagnostic ports at every console."

"What's through there?"

"Kitchens. You don't want to go in there," she said, reaching out to hold him back.

"Why?"

"The Valtegans like as much raw meat as they can get. Raw and still bleeding," she emphasized.

Kusac wrinkled his nose in disgust.

"We could wander around looking for a port until dawn at this rate," he muttered angrily. "Is there anyone nearby?"

"No," replied Carrie. "Wait! There *is* someone heading this way."

"Who?" demanded Kusac.

"A very hungry Valtegan who shouldn't be in this area," she chuckled.

"He'll do. How far away is he?"

"Far enough for us to get out of here and surprise him," replied Carrie, moving toward the door.

Silently, they crept out of the room and waited in the
shadows by the entrance.

Leave this to me, came Carrie's thought.

A nervous head poked through the door and looked about
quickly. It froze, eyes bulging in fear, then a Valtegan
walked stiff-leggedly into the room.

Kusac opened his mouth to protest but Carrie's answer
came first.

War, was all she said.

As the Valtegan halted, Kusac moved out of the shadows
and helped himself to the soldier's side arm. He placed the
muzzle under the other's chin.

"We need to find a diagnostic point for your computer.
You're going to take us to one. Do you understand?" he said
in perfect Valtegan.

Carrie relaxed her control and the soldier began to slump
until Kusac jabbed the gun harder against his jaw.

"One sound or one wrong move and you're dead," said
Carrie from his other side.

"Do you understand?" repeated Kusac.

The Valtegan blinked repeatedly, his eyes widening in
fear. He gestured toward a door at one side of the refectory.

Kusac removed the gun and signed for him to lead the
way.

You're learning, said Carrie.

Just keep monitoring him and our surroundings, Kusac
growled mentally.

The soldier led them through the door into a series of service corridors. The floors were uncarpeted concrete and the
walls bare except for occasional access ports for the various
utilities such as air ducts and power. At length he stopped in
front of a small alcove set to one side. He indicated the
VDU screen and computer terminal mounted into the wall
above a diagnostic port.

The soldier screwed his face up as if in pain.

"This is it," said Carrie, "and I don't read anyone in the
immediate area."

Kusac nodded and handed the gun to her as he turned
away to set down their computer. He heard a dull crack and
looked up sharply as the Valtegan fell bonelessly to the
floor.

"Why did you hit him?" he demanded.

"We need to restrain him if we're going to work," said

Carrie defensively, stuffing the gun back in its holster. "Unconscious, gagged, and tied up, he won't be a problem to us. We also don't want him alerting anyone else before we leave."

"You could have done it mentally," he said. "There was no need for violence."

"We'll untie him when we leave. When he's found, he has to have a physical reason for having passed out, unless you want his tales of mental control and strange Aliens being believed," she replied. "As it is, they should put it all down to concussion."

She reached inside her robe for the rope and began tying the Valtegan up.

Kusac eyed her askance. "You're making a thorough job of that," he said.

"I got Nelson to show me this, and how to use my knife," she said, tying the last knot and cutting off the slack.

Kusac grunted and returned to opening the computer case while Carrie started setting up the interface. She could still sense his disquiet over what she had done, but he was beginning to accept that the world they were now living in had harsher realities than his hitherto protected life as a Sholan Telepath.

Once their two units had been connected, Kusac sat back on his heels with a sigh.

"The moment of truth, eh, Carrie? Let's hope our people have got it right."

He leaned forward and plugged the lead from the interface into the Valtegan diagnostic port and switched on their equipment. There was a faint humming and then the VDU screen lit up. A series of symbols appeared as the Valtegan computer asked for verification of the access code. Their "burglar" clicked gently to life, beginning to run the program that Mito had set up.

A slight delay followed the printing of their reply. The same phrase was repeated and again their computer gave the same response. This time there was a longer delay while the computer whirred to itself. Finally another set of words appeared.

"It isn't accepting the first code," fretted Kusac. "Did you pick up anything of use from him?" he asked, indicating the prone figure of the soldier.

"Yes, but I don't know if this will override our program

without interrupting it," she said, reaching out and pressing several keys on the console. "It's a risk we'll have to take."

The screen cleared as if by magic.

"It needed an operator code as well," she explained. "I used his."

Now they were able to identify the phrases telling them their identity had been verified, and to continue with their instructions.

Carrie found she was able to breathe again. She squatted down beside Kusac, reaching out to touch him for reassurance.

"What now?" she asked. "Do we wait here till it sends the message?"

"Yes, I'm afraid so. We still have to monitor the screen and make sure no one approaches this area," he replied.

"And pray that the operator on duty, or the security system, didn't notice the delay over that damned operator code! Can you tell if we have got into the transmitter program yet?"

"Just about. There we go," he said, relaxing. "The worst should be over."

He shifted into a more comfortable position, back to the wall opposite the VDU.

"This is the long-winded part," he said. "It could take upward of an hour, depending on which quadrant the transmitter was facing before we started our Search test."

Carrie settled down beside him and tried to ease the tension in her neck muscles.

"Don't try," advised Kusac, putting an arm round her. "The extra adrenaline will keep you alert for now."

It was nearly three quarters of an hour later when Kusac shook her awake.

"There's someone coming!" he hissed, getting to his feet.

"Uh?" she muttered, trying desperately to get her brain working.

"Someone's coming, but they're too far for me to reach. I need you to Link with me," he said urgently.

"Ah, right," she said, finally managing to surface.

Taking his outheld hand, she was immediately aware of the presence of the Valtegan. Together they carefully entered the Alien's mind, ascertaining that his errand was a personal one which could easily wait. A small thought here and there and he quickly decided that he really had no desire to visit his friend via the service corridors. Without quite knowing why, he found himself blinking sleepily and returning to his own room.

"Let's hope there aren't any more insomniacs," sighed Carrie, letting the Link dissolve and returning her attention to the screen.

"Hey! Doesn't that mean we're actually transmitting?" she demanded, pointing at the display.

Kusac swiveled around.

"By Vartra, you're right! We've actually done it," he exclaimed.

The screen cleared, then their transmit code was repeated.

"Three times they said, didn't they?" asked Carrie. "Then it returns to the Search test mode and we dismantle our equipment."

Kusac nodded. "There goes the third signal."

The screen blanked suddenly, closing down their signal in mid-transmission.

"Oh, shit," said Carrie, jumping up.

A message appeared on the screen, flashing imperatively, emitting loud beeps.

"What's it say?" she demanded.

"It's asking who is using the terminal. Put that operator code in again," he said, scrambling to his feet.

Carrie typed in the digits but the message and the beeping tone remained the same.

"I don't think it's working this time," she said.

A second message flashed on the screen.

"Unauthorized use of transmitter. Security breached," he read as a klaxon began to sound.

Hurriedly, he switched off the machines, pulling the lead free of the port.

"Let's get the hell out of here," he said urgently.

They shoved the cables into the improvised cases, latching them shut.

"There's a quicker way out," said Carrie. "It avoids the main doorway. I picked it up from him." She indicated the still unconscious soldier.

"We'll still have to leave by the main gates, though. Let's go."

They headed down the corridor at a run, the klaxon wailing like a banshee all around them.

As she ran, Carrie was mentally searching ahead. Suddenly she slid to a stop, grabbing Kusac by the arm and pulling him back against the wall.

A door on their left began to open. She grabbed for her gun, pulling it free and firing just as a Valtegan stepped into the corridor.

The burst of energy clipped the soldier's upper arm, making him screech in pain.

"Damn," she muttered, taking aim and firing again. This time the Valtegan went flying backward without a sound. The smell of charred flesh filled the corridor.

"Oh, God," she moaned, slumping against the wall, the gun hanging limply from her hand. She felt sick to the pit of her stomach.

Kusac, mentally checking beyond the door, shook her firmly by the arm.

War, Carrie, he sent.

Carrie took a gulp of air through her mouth and straightened up, trying not to look at the Valtegan she had just killed.

They waited a moment but neither of them could sense anyone else.

Let's go, sent Kusac.

They checked visually at the doorway, closing it before continuing their mad dash. Carrie looked the other way as she passed the body. Finally the corridor curved to the left, ending at a metal door. They skidded to a halt. Hearts thumping and chests heaving, they gasped for breath. Over the sound of the klaxon, they could hear the pounding of many feet coming from behind.

Carrie nodded as Kusac glanced quizzically at her. He opened the door.

"Wait," she said, tugging at his half of the computer. "Leave it," she said.

He put it down and turned to look through the partial opening. Hearing the gun go off he jerked his head back round. The two cases were smouldering ruins.

Why?

They're useless now, to us and the Valtegans.

Cautiously, they stepped through the doorway, closing it behind them. A short blast of his gun and Kusac had sealed the mechanism shut.

They stood once more in a corridor of the main complex.

"Where is everyone?" whispered Carrie as she led the way down the right hand side.

"Probably guarding sensitive areas and all the exits," he replied.

Suddenly, she felt her arm seized by a clawed hand, and she was violently pulled to one side. She lost her footing and swung helplessly round to crash into the chest of a Valtegan soldier.

Nonretractable claws pierced her sleeve, penetrating through to her arm. Then she was released, only to be pulled round to face Kusac, the soldier's right arm pressed firmly across her throat. Automatically, she dropped the gun, her hands going up to clutch at his arm.

"Drop weapon," hissed the voice almost in her ear.

They both froze.

The arm across her throat tightened.

"Drop weapon!"

The orange light seemed to intensify as the noise of the klaxon began to fade. She saw Kusac drop his gun.

She could hear screams and smelled again the acrid tang of blood. Struggling, she tried to get away from her captors but there were too many. Too many, and they were holding her down, and, oh, God, but it hurt!

A Valtegan face swam into view, one she recognized. But he was dead, wasn't he? Hadn't Kusac killed him in the forest?

She blinked, managing to move her head a little and the visions faded. There was no one but Kusac in front of her and there was no blood—yet. This was the Base, not Geshader.

Again she blinked, her senses beginning to clear as she forced the memories back. The fear remained.

Kusac came up out of his crouch, ears laid flat back and tail lashing.

"What do you want?" he asked.

"I kill woman now, yes?" grinned the soldier.

"No," said Kusac with suppressed fury.

"Hands behind head," the Valtegan ordered, the grin fading.

Kusac raised his arms, overlapping his hands behind his head. "Let her go," he said. "You don't need her. You have me."

"Have both," snapped the soldier. "New Alien and woman." He lowered his gun and fired.

"No!" shrieked Carrie, lashing out with her left arm. Desperately, she twisted in his grip, half strangling herself before her right hand found the handle of her knife.

She heard Kusac's grunt of pain and the sound of him falling as she jerked her knife free, bringing it up to bury it in the Valtegan's chest.

He coughed, staggering backward, dragging Carrie with him. She pulled the knife free and stabbed him again, this time upward in the exposed throat.

He stiffened, the arm that held her tightening in a spasm before releasing her. The other hand, gun forgotten, clutched at the blade, pulling it free. Blood spurted out and he began to choke, drowning in his own gore.

Whimpering, Carrie backed off, watching as he crashed to his knees clutching his ruined throat. His mouth gasped for air he couldn't get as he slowly toppled forward and lay there.

A noise from behind made her whirl round.

"Get the weapons first," said Kusac, his voice taut with pain. "Then get me something to bind my leg."

"You're alive," she said, staring at him.

"He wasn't trying to kill me," he said, "just disable me." He looked down to where both his hands encircled his injured thigh in an attempt to stem the blood. "Which he's done. It would have been worse if you hadn't attacked him."

Still she didn't move.

"Carrie, we're sitting targets," he said patiently. "Get the weapons and let's get out of here."

"Yes," she said, finally moving to retrieve her gun. She stopped by the body and picked up her knife. Blood covered the handle and now her hands.

Carrie, sent Kusac, *I need to bind my wound.*

"Yes." She wiped her hands on a fold of her robe and bent down to check the soldier's uniform. The material was soft enough. Using the knife, she ripped off a strip from the lower edge of his tunic and hurried over to Kusac.

She knelt beside him, cutting part of the strip off to form a pad which she pressed over the gaping wound. The rest of the material she quickly used to bind her makeshift dressing in place. Concentrating on one job was helping her refocus her mind on the here and now.

"Don't make it too tight," he warned, wincing as he tried to flex the muscle while she knotted the binding.

She helped him stagger to his feet.

"This is becoming a habit I must break," he said wryly, leaning against her for support.

"Can you walk?" she asked, handing him his gun.

"I'll have to," he said, letting go of her. "Which way?"

"There should be a junction to the left about two hundred meters down there," she said, indicating the way they had been heading. "The side exit is about another hundred meters beyond."

"Let's go." He staggered a couple of steps then collapsed against the wall.

"Gods, give me a shoulder injury every time," he said, trying to joke about the pain as Carrie was instantly there to help support him.

"Why can't I feel your pain?"

"The filter I put in," he said, blinking his eyes in an effort to stop the inner lids closing.

"Let me take some of it."

"No. I can't use my Talent in this state. We need you to check for Valtegans." He pushed himself off the wall, keeping a hand against it for support. He began to limp down the corridor.

"Keep checking," he said.

They made it safely to the junction and as they turned the corner they saw the side exit ahead of them.

"I'm picking up large numbers of Valtegans outside," she said, "but we expected that. None around here at the moment. You wait here and guard the junction, I'll take a look at the exit."

He nodded, too exhausted by the pain to talk.

Carrie began to edge down the short corridor. On the right hand side she could see a door. She stopped, not sure whether there was anyone in the area behind it or not. There were so many Valtegan presences that it was getting hard for her to be specific.

The door swung wide and without even thinking, Carrie fired a continuous burst through it. She stopped only when Kusac, the skin around his nose and eyes gray with pain, touched her on the shoulder.

"There's no one alive in there," he said quietly. "There're

noises coming from farther up the corridor behind us. I'm afraid they may have gotten that door open."

Carrie lowered the gun and nodded, moving toward the exit.

As luck would have it, the door was transparent. Backs to the wall, they peered through. In the glow of the perimeter lamps, they could see the corner of a low bunker some five hundred meters distant.

"There's a group of Valtegans out there, round the far corner," she said, pointing. "Also some on the other side of the building. We'd be out in the open for most of that run."

Kusac looked at her. "There's no way I can do it, Carrie. I'm too slow with this injury. Can we reach Skinner from here?"

Carrie activated the wrist comm.

"Skinner, do you read me?" she said urgently into the tiny pickup. "Come in, Skinner." There was only a distorted hiss.

"Too much interference from the building," said Kusac. "Check behind us for Valtegans."

"They've found the body," she said after a moment. "If we get outside, we may be able to reach Skinner on the comm. At least we'll be better able to defend ourselves from the ones inside. It's our only chance," she said, looking up at him. "One way or another, we go together, Kusac. I'll not be taken alive."

He nodded slowly and pushed himself upright.

"I'll need to lean on you until we get out."

She moved closer so he could put his arm across her shoulders. Briefly, his hand touched her cheek.

She pushed open the door and they edged out into the night, keeping close to the wall. The bunker seemed so near now.

Kusac leaned against the wall and adjusted his grip on the gun.

"I'll watch the door, you keep an eye on that area," he gestured to the end of the building.

Carrie nodded, stepping carefully past him. The static from her wrist comm peaked loudly then faded.

"Come in, Skinner," she said, raising it to her mouth. Again the static peaked and fell. She looked at Kusac and shrugged.

"Leave it on," he said, turning back to watch the doorway. She inched forward, getting closer to the edge.

"Here they come," warned Kusac.

She swung round, dropping low to present less of a target.

The door opened and a Valtegan leapt out, ready to shoot. Kusac was faster and the soldier dropped to the ground.

Pressing his back to the wall for support, Kusac slid down till he was kneeling on his good leg.

A hand came out, pointing a gun in their direction. Carrie's shot hit it and the gun exploded in a flare of energy that made both of them blink for several seconds.

She moved up behind him.

"They're coming from the other side," she whispered before turning round again.

The gun shook in her grip. She brought her other hand up to steady it and took a deep breath.

"Kusac, is there a Sholan afterlife?"

"Huh? Yes. Yes, there is."

"Take me with you," she said.

A loud explosion split the night air, the glow visible from where they crouched.

"What in hell was that?" exclaimed Kusac.

Carrie's wrist comm burst into life.

"Skinner here. Come in, Kusac."

Carrie looked at her wrist in disbelief.

"Answer it," said Kusac.

"Carrie here."

"We know where you are. What's your status?"

"Kusac's got an injured leg, he can barely walk. We're pinned down, with Valtegans on both sides of us," she said, the relief in her voice audible.

"Stay put. We're on our way."

"Keep watching," Kusac reminded her. "We aren't safe yet."

In the distance, they could hear the sounds of fighting.

"The Valtegans at the front have scattered," said Carrie. "What about those in the building?"

"Still there."

They listened to the sound of gunfire and energy weapons getting gradually closer.

"Get down!" hissed Kusac, flinging himself down and away from the wall as the door burst open. Two Valtegans appeared, shooting indiscriminately down the side of the wall before disappearing back into cover.

Kusac raised his head and looked around. Carrie lay in a huddle beside the wall. She was much too still.

"Carrie!" There was no reply. He reached mentally for her and was instantly swamped by a blinding headache, but he couldn't sense her.

Pushing himself up onto his hands, he crawled toward her, heedless of the pain from his injured leg. Reaching out, he shook her by the shoulder. She sprawled limply on her back. Blood darkened the hair on one side of her head.

Touching her brought the confirmation he needed. She was still alive. Pulling himself closer he began to gently feel her scalp with his fingers. There didn't seem to be any depressions. He glanced at the wall. Several chunks were missing. She'd obviously been hit by some of the fragments.

A noise from the door drew his attention. He looked for his gun and discovered he'd left it behind. Where was Carrie's? Frantically, he glanced around till he saw it lying beyond her, out of reach. He froze, turning his head as a Valtegan emerged from the doorway, gun trained on them.

The soldier grinned.

Something whanged past his ears, hitting the soldier square in the chest. The Valtegan seemed to crumple in on himself before the force of the impact swept him off his feet, flinging him to the ground.

"Get your head down, Kusac," came Davies' voice from behind.

He leaned forward over Carrie's head, protecting her, too.

There was a muffled explosion followed by a blast of hot air.

"That should sort them out," said Davies, crawling up to them. "What happened to Carrie?" he asked, catching sight of her as Kusac sat up.

"She's been hit by pieces of masonry. She's unconscious, but I think she'll be fine."

"Shit. You're in a mess, too," the Terran said, looking at Kusac's leg. He thumbed his wrist comm.

"Davies to Skinner. We need that groundcar over here fast. We've got two casualties, neither serious, but they aren't walking anywhere. I'm at the main building, forward of the bunker on the northwest side."

"Copy."

Another figure emerged from the night to join them.

"Hear you need help," said Hughes, throwing a packet to

Davies. "Vanna gave me some field dressings. You see to Kusac. I'll check Carrie."

Quickly and efficiently, Davies removed the saturated wad that still miraculously covered Kusac's wound and replaced it with a sterile dressing.

They could hear a series of muffled explosions followed by one large one.

"Sounds like they got the groundcar pool," said Davies.

"What?" asked Kusac, twisting round to look at Carrie.

"We used your explosives to rig some rather nice little bombs. I used one on your friends in the doorway," he said.

"As well as taking out the main radar installation so that when the Sholans arrive the Valtegans will be blind, the others hoped to have enough left to destroy some of the groundcars. From the sound of it, they got enough of them to set up a chain reaction."

Kusac turned back to look at Davies.

"You took out their radar?"

"Yep. You heard the first explosion? That was it. Now they can't tell anyone what's happening, nor know when the Sholans arrive. And with some thirty groundcars destroyed, they're going to have a hell of a job moving troops about Keiss."

Kusac turned back to Hughes. "She's coming round," he said, seconds before Carrie began to stir.

Hughes gave him a startled glance.

"How is she?"

"She's fine. Just a couple of nasty cuts on the scalp and a lump or two. We'll check her out for concussion when we get her on board the groundcar."

They could clearly hear the whine of the groundcar's engines now, and within moments, it came into sight round the back of the bunker, settling down a few meters from them.

Carrie moaned and tried to sit up.

"Easy now," said Hughes. "You got a nasty bump on the head."

"Kusac?" she mumbled, looking owlishly around.

"Here," he said, taking her by the hand.

"Are we safe yet?"

"We're safe."

"Time to go," said Hughes, getting to his feet and picking her up in his arms. She let go of Kusac's hand.

Davies got up and helped Kusac to his feet, supporting

him as he limped the few meters to the vehicle where Vanna and Jo helped pull him inside.

Hughes brought Carrie down to the back of the vehicle to join them and Vanna began to do her own check on both their wounds.

"It's not that I don't trust you," she said apologetically, "but . . ."

"You just don't trust anyone but yourself," finished Hughes with a grin. "I understand."

"When we get to the cave, I'll seal your wounds and dress them properly," she said as the groundcar took off to rendezvous at the gate with the others.

Anders banked sharply to the right, sending them sliding toward the port side hull.

"Hey, watch it," Vanna complained.

"Sorry," he said.

As soon as they touched down, the others scrambled on board. Of the giant spotlights at the gate, only blind metal struts remained. The Base was now lit by the glow of many fires, the largest being the groundcar pool.

Anders managed to do a head count as they boarded and as the last man was hauled in, he sealed the hatch and took off, flying high over the fence and into the swamplands.

Remarkably, no one else had been injured.

"Did you send the signal?" demanded Garras, asking the question on all their minds.

Kusac nodded. "We sent it," he said.

Garras settled back, relieved. "Then it's only a matter of time."

"What now?" asked Richard. "What happens while we wait?"

"We lay the groundwork for a Sholan/Terran treaty," replied Garras.

"We get the basis laid for the diplomats so that they can't screw it up," added Skinner, with a rare smile. "Your father will already be on his way to join us, along with the leaders from the nearest towns."

"I'm not looking forward to that meeting," murmured Carrie uneasily.

Vanna leaned forward to pat her arm encouragingly.

"Don't worry," she said. "You're with us now, and you'll stay with us—more than that, you belong with us."

Kusac put his arm round her and hugged her close to his side.

"He daren't risk an incident by demanding you stay with him on Keiss," he said.

Besides, he continued mentally, *I have a feeling Skinner will convince him you are an ideal spy in our camp!*

"Do I truly belong with you, or will I be just another Alien to your people?" Carrie asked Kusac, turning a tired and bloodstained face to him.

"We belong together," he said gently, licking her ear.

Lisanne Norman

☐ **TURNING POINT**   UE2575—$5.99
When a human-colonized world falls under the sway of imperialistic
aliens, there is scant hope of salvation from far-distant Earth. Instead,
their hopes rest upon an underground rebellion and the intervention
of a team of catlike aliens.

☐ **FORTUNE'S WHEEL**   UE2675—$5.99
Carrie was the daughter of the human governor of the colony planet
Keiss. Kusac was the son and heir of the Sholan Clan Lord. Both were
telepaths and the bond they formed was compounded equally of love
and mind power. But now they were about to be thrust into the heart
of an interstellar conflict, as factions on both their worlds sought to
use their powers for their own ends . . .

☐ **FIRE MARGINS**   UE2718—$6.99
A new race is about to be born on the Sholan homeworld, and it may
cause the current unstable political climate to explode. Only through
exploring the Sholan's long-buried and purposely forgotten past can
Carrie and Kusac hope to find the path to survival, not only for their
own people, but for Sholans and humans as well.

☐ **RAZOR'S EDGE**   UE2766—$6.99
Still adjusting to the revelations about its past, the Sholan race must
now also face the increasing numbers and independence of the new
human-Sholan telepathic pairs. Meanwhile, Carrie, Kusac, Kaid, and
T'Chebbi are sent to the planet Jalna on a rescue mission that will
see them caught up in the midst of a local revolution . . . even as they
uncover a shocking truth that threatens both their species!

Kate Elliott

The Novels of the Jaran:

☐ **JARAN: Book 1**   UE2513—$5.99
Here is the poignant and powerful story of a young woman's
coming of age on an alien world, where she is both player and
pawn in an interstellar game of intrigue and politics.

☐ **AN EARTHLY CROWN: Book 2**   UE2546—$5.99
The jaran people, led by Ilya Bakhtiian and his Earth-born wife
Tess, are sweeping across the planet Rhui on a campaign of
conquest. But even more important is the battle between Ilya
and Duke Charles, Tess' brother, who is ruler of this sector of
space.

☐ **HIS CONQUERING SWORD: Book 3**   UE2551—$5.99
Even as Jaran warlord Ilya continues the conquest of his world,
he faces a far more dangerous power struggle with his wife's
brother, leader of an underground human rebellion against the
alien empire.

☐ **THE LAW OF BECOMING: Book 4**   UE2580—$5.99
On Rhui, Ilya's son inadvertently becomes the catalyst for what
could prove a major shift of power. And in the heart of the
empire, the most surprising move of all was about to occur as
the Emperor added an unexpected new player to the Game of
Princes . . .

A feline lovers' fantasy come true ...

CATFANTASTIC

More Top-Flight Science Fiction and Fantasy from
C.J. CHERRYH

FANTASY
☐ THE DREAMING TREE   UE2782—$6.99
Journey to a transitional time in the world, as the dawn of mortal man brings about the downfall of elven magic, in the complete *Ealdwood* novels, finally together in one volume with an all new ending.

SCIENCE FICTION

☐ FOREIGNER   UE2637—$5.99
☐ INVADER   UE2687—$5.99
☐ INHERITOR   UE2728—$6.99

THE MORGAINE CYCLE
☐ GATE OF IVREL (BOOK 1)   UE2321—$4.50
☐ WELL OF SHIUAN (BOOK 2)   UE2322—$4.50
☐ FIRES OF AZEROTH (BOOK 3)   UE2323—$4.50
☐ EXILE'S GATE (BOOK 4)   UE2254—$5.50